T0199118

A MURDER ON FIFTH AND DICE AND THE RUIN OF FIFEVILLE

William A. James, Sr.

iUniverse®

A MURDER ON FIFTH AND DICE AND THE RUIN OF FIFEVILLE

iUniverse books may be ordered through booksellers or by contacting:

iUniverse
1663 Liberty Drive
Bloomington, IN 47403
www.iuniverse.com
1-800-Authors (1-800-288-4677)

ISBN: 978-1-5320-6012-0 (sc)
ISBN: 978-1-5320-6014-4 (hc)
ISBN: 978-1-5320-6013-7 (e)

Library of Congress Control Number: 2018912270

Print information available on the last page.

iUniverse rev. date: 11/07/2018

To Those Who Lost Everything When Fifeville Was Ruined

Contents

Chapter One

"Roy," a huge Baby Hughie who resembled the cartoon character-only in size-but not in color, whined in a voice that sounded like Fat Albert, another cartoon character, "I hope you're strapped man." His big eyes were like boiled eggs with a miniature eight ball iris that seemed like a dot in each one. They showed that he was scared. "I got my Thirty Eight, man."

Sweat ran down his deep-chocolate face. His fat nose trembled, a trembling that went all the way down into his Denim Outfit, and on into his red Air Jordan's. He had his gun tucked into his waistband. He clutched it with his right hand. His oversized T-Shirt stuck to his back from his sweat. He did a little quarterback rookie dance in an attempt to come to grips with his fears. His left hand brushed the blue-and red New York Yankees' baseball cap that he had perched on top of his head with the brim turned around backward.

A tall, lean man, wearing the same T-Shirt and Denim Outfit and Air Jordan's, sporting a red-and-black Baseball Cap perched on top of his head, pranced back and forth on one side of the comer of Fifth-and Dice Streets looking anxiously up one Street and then down the other. Although he was built and was very muscular like a football player, he was shorter than the other guy. He was too shaking a little.

"Blue, I got strapped with a 'Glock-Nine.' I was lucky enough to get my hands on one just yesterday. The Crew bust-a-cap in a couple-a Jamie Charles's Crew and they jacked them pieces. I got one of 'em. 'Master D.' done fixed that Posse with Glock-Nines, Tech-Tens and automatic Twelve-Gauge Guns, dog. "When Jamie 'nem roll up in here, that's what we will have to fade. But we're soldiers like 'Malcolm X and The Fruit of Islam,' yo. We gotta go down like them and your Brother Ivy did. We got to represent. That's how it is, dog. Yo, we're Gangsters, aw-ight! We can't back down and can't give up; you with that?"

"Roy, man, I wish this gang war was over, G. I'm tired of seeing people getting capped, dog. It'sa dog eat-dog! That's all it is, G., 'n-it don't make no sense. We be deep in this beef for going on three years. When is it go stop? Jamie 'nem done kilt so many of our O'G's man. We done kilt a few of them, too!" Blue walks to the side of their two-story, white, stucco house, with the little brick deck with four steps. He is on the Fifth Street Southwest side of the corner.

Roy eased over to the other corner to stare down Dice Street. He gestures with one finger pointing at Blue and another to just off the comer of Fifth to Dice. "Yeah, Blue, I feel you, Dog. Cousin Ivy, your Big Brother, the illest O'G out there got popped just a couple of years ago. He's our Main Yard Dog, yo. Jamie 'nem rolled up on 'im and just bust-a-cap in 'im. I ain't, nor any of our Crew, ever got a bead on Jamie or his Low-Riders, Blue. But that day's coming. Maybe, it's go be today, Dog. You feel me?"

What Roy said got Blue even sweatier. Bead after bead ran down his face. His eyes danced with great emotions, his hand shook violently as the thought of what Roy was suggesting dug into his psyche.

Roy sensed that his cousin was not really feeling the moment like a Big Dog should. Jamie and 'the Posse' gunned Ivy down right down there, Blue. Right here near the Crib, yo." He points down Dice Street "Now, Jamie done put the word out there that he's coming back over here to take you and me out You know we can't run and hide nowhere. I'm the Man-In-Charge after Ivy. Then it'll be you, Blue. That's why Jamie wants to kill two birds with one stone. Aw-ight?"

Blue got a little sick to his stomach. He fought against the compulsion to vomit. He felt like he had to put up a front like he had been doing all of his life growing up following behind Ivy and then Roy. "Well I 'ma get ready then. Them Junk Yard Dogs, Jamie, and that Posse, man, thinking they go roll up in here on our Turf and just cap us without a damn fight Nosiree, Bob! That shit ain't happening in this Gangster's life. I know they got the fire-power, but we got the balls. That's for-real, dog. I ain't never capped nobody, but I been with you and Ivy when y'all did the deed. I seen how it's done then. I can do it to Jamie 'nem, yo." Blue struts up Fifth in front of their home. He's full of fake courage.

Roy steps to Blue and slaps hands with him. They Gangster-point at each other and then made a peace sign with the trigger fingers on both their hands to cross those to form an X before their faces. That was their Crew Sign. They both yelled: "We Be Ready To Go!" (fhey meant: Fight to the Death!)

Screeching car wheels brought the fears that Blue felt back to the surface. He got his gun out as quick as he could. "Roy, man, sounds like that 'chine getting closer-and-closer. It's one-a them gangster rides too. I can hear that growl a mile away. Dog, we gotta get ready.We've gotta catch Jamie 'nem in a crossfire, yo. That's the only chance we got. Then we'll have the Posse off our backs. It's enough action out there for all of us. Why they gotta be so damn greedy? It's that Cat, Master D. That's who be behind all of this shit, Dog!"

Roy yanks his Glock-Nine out of his waistband. Blue draws his Thirty Eight Revolver. They are both on the Fifth Street side of the comer back-to-back with Blue looking down Fifth Street and Roy looking up Fifth.

A beige Ford Trooper Two SUV jets up Dice Street It has a red racing stripe from its front bumper to its back. All four doors of the vehicle are suddenly flung open. A tall, lanky, man jumps out of the back of the Trooper Two. Two like him jump out behind him, and two Twelve-Gauge Automatic Shotguns are pointed out of the Vehicle aimed at Blue and Roy.

All three of the first characters wore large multicolored Tam Caps over long Dreadlocks. They all had mustaches, and long matching beards. They sported Tan Khaki Safari Suits and black Combat boots. The three outside of the Vehicle were carrying Uzis. The first one out had a sinister smile across his face. The other two were chuckling, like a couple of clowns.

The tallest one of the Jamaican denizens stepped forward and swaggered a few arrogant steps toward Roy. He raised his Uzi. His voice was a rich baritone. "I done tol' ya! You Westside Crew, Bloodclots, Bandulu, stay ofn the Streets bangin'! The Streets be mine. But like Ivy, y'ere hard of hearin'. Ain't ya? But Jamie gon' teach ya. Lemme give ya a good lesson, mon. Ivy, him six feet under, now! Tain't nobody goin' ta jail neither. The lawman don' be messin' with The Posse's business. We rule!

"We be takin' over all the action in the 'Ville. Nobody can be dealin' wit' out ya dealin' for me! Dis be me Town now! I don' wanna see ya

Westside Crew out afta. dark dealin' on any of me blocks till you're working for Jamie and the Posse. Gotta give ya Bangers over here another example, like Ivy."

Roy raised his Glock-Nine. "Ivy was my cousin, Mo' forker. Let me show you what he would've done had he got a chance, yo!" He squeezed the trigger of his Glock. A bullet whizzed past Jamie's head.

Blue dropped his gun. It was like he had disappeared. He ran to behind the house as fast as a rat running for its life from a big old cat. He heard the gunfire. Sounded like :firecrackers at McIntire Park on the Fourth of July. Blue covered his ears. He was scared to death. He didn't want to die.

An old lady with gray hair came out on the deck. She walked slowly. She wore a long white dress that flowed around her like a gown. She had a pair of white house-slippers on her feet. She was hard of hearing but she could hear enough to know that some kind of commotion was going on right in front of her house. She thought she had better get out there to see who was acting up today. Since this year, 1983, had come in, Fifeville had changed, and a lot of the change was happening right on the comer of Fifth and Dice.

The old lady was called Grandma Slokum by everyone who knew her. She was an old retiree from the University of Virginia. She had worked up there for forty years as a Maid and then a step up, as a Nurse's Aide. She was on the Missionary Board at First Baptist Church on the Northeast edge of Fifeville on the comer of Seventh Street Southwest and West Main Street. Everyone on Fifth Street knew her to be very kind and charitable especially to the children.

When Bruce Hall's fourteen year old daughter, Letitia, came to Sister Slokum's house one evening after school and complained: "Grandma Slokum, please help me. My Dad He won't let me go out of the house no more. He makes me stay in and after Mom goes to work-he makes me do dirty things with him. I hate doing the nasty with my own daddy. Please help me." She sobbed in painful bursts.

Grandma Slokum replied, "Hush child. Come on in the house so nobody will hear what we're talking about. You can tell me all about it. I think I can help you." Her voice was angelically soothing.

Bruce Hall, a forty-five year old Orderly at the University of Virginia was arrested that evening after he got off work. He was later sentenced to five years for Statutory Rape, and was registered as a Child Molesting Sexual Offender for the rest of his life. Letitia was put in foster care. He had an older daughter, twenty-year old, Margo. She had been abused up until she was eighteen. She had gotten married to a young man she had fallen in love with from the Washington Park area, who knew that she had been abused but had been sworn to secrecy by Margo. But, after Letitia, the scandal was out. His wife Lulu divorced him. She claimed she didn't know that he was molesting their daughters. Their oldest child, a son, Raleigh, was twenty-five, but claimed he did not know that his father was raping his sisters. That family broke up became estranged from within and became a whispered by-word on the lips of gossipers forever after.

When Grandma Slokum ambled out on her deck, a bullet from Jamie's Uzi ricocheted off the steps. It struck the old Saintly lady between the eyes. She dropped to the deck immediately. A crimson tide spurted out of her left ear. She had fallen to the deck and was balled up with her head cocked to the side.

Even though Jamie and his Posse Gunmen hadn't finished the job they set out to do, they lowered their guns. Jamie screamed: "Let's go mon! We gon' bring JuJu down on us! We don' kilt an Elder!"

All of the Jamaicans scrambled into the Ford Trooper Two. Blue heard doors slamming. His heart beat like a snare drum on a rock 'n'. roll set. The revving of their ride meant that they were getting on up out of there. That puzzled him because they should be coming around the house after him. But . . . he was willing to let that sleeping dog lie.

Guilt started to rise from Blue's gut up into his chest. He was afraid that Roy didn't make it. All the guns going off meant that Roy must've gotten hit big time. He had run! He had left his main Dog on the set alone to fade their main enemy. That was not something the Crew could get with. That was next to snitching. All of the Crew probably would be out to bust-a-cap in him. For that reason he thought it may have been better for him to be gunned down by Jamie 'nem. Blue did something else "a Gangster ain't never s'pose-ta do: he slid down into the grass and just let out his tears. He uttered: "What kinda Damn Gangster am I s'pose-ta be?"

Blue bounced up and ran back to the sidewalk. His glance darted up and down Fifth Street that ran from North to South, from West Main Street to Cherry Avenue, to Dice, that ran from East to West from Ridge Street to the comer of Seventh Street Southwest. Looking around, he did not see any trance of Jamie 'nem. He did see a few onlookers on their porches. A couple of old women were wagging their heads and whimpering softly. A couple of young people were standing on the other side of Fifth Street with their arms folded like people at a funeral. Then Blue saw what they were reacting to.

Blue first spotted Roy lying on his side so that his head was a little around the comer of Dice Street. The rest of him was on Fifth. A flood of blood ran from Roy into the drain near the comer. His body was a patch work of bullet holes. Half of the back of his head was just like hamburger. His Glock was still in his hand. His other hand had been blown off.

Blue cried out: "Roy, what done happen Dog? Oh shit, it's all my fault. I left you alone, man. I'm so damn sorry, word! I wish Ivy was here, man. This shit don't make no sense. We gotta stop doing this really bad shit, man. We just killin' one-nother off and shit!"

When Blue looked toward the steps of the house, he saw Grandma Slokum with blood oozing out of her ear and running down the steps to the Street. He at first dropped to the sidewalk. He couldn't believe what he was beholding. He jumped up and ran in a frenzy to the steps. He cradled Gradma Slokum's head in his hands.

"Granny! Granny! Grandma. Don't . . . Don't leave. Why you gotta go? Ivy, Roy, now you, I'm all by myself.

"I'm go get that Jamie Charles, and that goddamned Posse if'n it's the last thing I live to do. I'm go blow them forkers 'way! I swear to you, Granny! If I don't kill nobody else!" He yelled into his dead Grandma's good ear, hoping that his words would travel to the other world to her somehow. "Jamie don' kilt a Saint. You ain't never hurt Jamie'nem or nobody. Why they had to cap you? Don't make no sense to me?"

The cops' sirens would usually make Blue flee the scene. But now, he stayed on his knees holding his grandmothers head rocking to and fro, crying like a little child that had just lost its mother. A black-and white Cruiser jetted down Dice Street with its red lights flashing and its siren on full blast. Blue could not turn Grandma Slokum loose. He felt like all that he had in this world was gone. His reason for living had bled way. He was holding her for as long as he could, just rocking, rocking, rocking ... trembling.

The doors of the cruiser swung open. Two cops got out of the cruiser and trained shotguns on Blue.

One heavyset cop with sergeant bars on his sleeves walked slowly over to Blue with his shotgun aimed at Blue's head. He kicked Blue's Thirty Eight away from him that he had dropped when the gunfire started. It hit against the sidewalk's edging and came to rest in front of the other cop. This cop was shaking like he was facing "King Kong," as he picked up Blue's gun and tucked it into his belt

The Sergeant yelled: "Get your black hands in the air and your black ass on the sidewalk right now!"

Blue was thinking these blue boys must think ... they think I did this! He yelled: "Hey, Five-O y'all got the wrong one. I could never do that to Roy-or my Granny. What y'all figuring?"

Cop number two stepped closer to Blue until his shotgun barrel was inches away from Blue's head. "Look, asshole, shut the fuck up! Get down on the sidewalk! Roll over and fold your hands behind your head- do it now! Or I'm gonna pull the trigger on this gun an' your brains gonna be all over the place like you done to that one over there. You got that?" He pointed toward Roy's corpse.

Blue knew that these white boys were scared. He knew they were anxious to put an end to his Crew and the Gang Banging that had come to the "Ville." He didn 't want to be a dying example of their frustration with not being able to stop "The Gang Thing." He obeyed their orders. The first cop hurried up and laid his shotgun on the sidewalk. He pulled Blue's hands down and cuffed them. He helped Blue to his knees. He ordered him, "Now get the hell in the back of that paddy wagon. You're gonna be charged with the murder of this little Granny, and her Son. You may have a lawyer present before questioning. If you say anything, it may be used against you in a court of law. Do you understand your rights, you Black Ape?"

Blue nodded his head to mean he understood his "Miranda Rights." The Sergeant shoved Blue along toward the paddy wagon. He gave Blue a final shove as he got to the back doors of the vehicle. "Watch your step, boy," he yelled. Then he tripped Blue so that he fell into the Van to land on the floor with a loud thud. A crowd was gathering across the Street but no one uttered a word.

The cop driver of the Van got a chuckle out of that bit of police brutality. Blue heard the cop calling in his arrest: "This is Sarge Patrick White. We got a 187-Double Homicide on the Comer of Fifth and Dice Streets. We have a suspect in custody. We have him on record already. He is Benjamin Luther Slokum known on the Streets as 'Big Blue.' He is the Brother of Ivan Ramon Slokum-known as 'Ivy.' He's deceased, killed by a rival gang some time ago. Blue is the Cousin of Leroy Shelby Slokum-who was killed in what seems like a domestic dispute over here. Leroy is in our data base as 'Roy the Enforcer.' He did his jobs for The Westside Crew over here. We think Blue here must've gone bunkers. Looks like he offed his Grandmother an' Cousin. He may have been getting ready to do himself when we rolled up. He was holding his Granny's head and the gun was near his big foot. He was sorry he had done the deed. He was holding her head and crying like a Big O' Black Baby when we spotted him on the scene. Dispatch, just 'tween you and me, I wish he had gone for that gun so we could save the State a lot of money. I would've liked to have ended this the easy way-you got me? We're be at the station directly. Ten-Four Good Buddy."

Blue was lying on the floor of the Van sobbing. He had never killed anyone. He had never beat-down anyone. He had just been along with his Brother Ivy, and his Cousin Roy, when they did all of that. He felt like he couldn't help who he was kin to. That was God's judgment. All Blue felt was his fault was that he was fronting-acting like a "Gangster." He wondered how Ivy and Roy had gotten away with all of the violence and killings they had done? Nobody ever arrested them. He wondered what was up with all that He knew that two black cops were bringing drugs they stole out of the crime-scene warehouse and had given them to Ivy and Roy to sell in the 'Hood. Blood was on their hands too. Why didn't someone arrest them? They arrived at the police station in minutes. Blue trembled as they unloaded him out of the Van.

Chapter Two

With shackles and chains on his legs, cuffs on his wrists, and with three hate-filled white-cops prodding him with their nightsticks, Blue was ushered into a backside door of the Charlottesville Police Department, located in the downtown area off East Jefferson Street. Once he was inside of the narrow darkened hallway that led to a holding cell, horrible blows seemed to be coming out of the air down onto his young head.

He complained: "Why y'all beating me down? I ain't done nothin'. You cops must be deaf, or somethin'. I done tol' ya-you got the wrong one. I didn't even get off a shot today! Check my gun ... it ain't been fired, yo. It was Jamie 'nem . . . Ow! Shit! Fuck! ..."

A fat black cop yelled, "Shut the fuck up! We didn't ask you yet what part you played in those killings today. You'll get your chance to explain what the hell went down on that Corner today-you can bet on that! It's you so-called gangsters who're giving all of us Blacks a bad name. I hope they get rid of all of you all-an' it'll be good-riddance *too;* you got that? Fuck all of you! Now get the hell in that chair over there and don't open your mouth unless somebody asks you to." He pointed his finger in Blue's face.

Blue heard the door slam shut. He was in an iron-chair that was bolted to the floor. He was in a six-by eight foot room that had a metal table in the middle and the chair he was chained to, and a large wooden chair across from the other side of the table. The walls were blood-red in color. The ceiling was white with a very bright light shining down on his head. On the table was a portable Royal Typewriter with a piece of paper already in it The floor had black tiles on it. There were no windows. Brue could not hear a sound in that room other than his own breathing. An overwhelming odor of Pine Sol permeated the air. That stench nearly made him vomit Then the wide door that he had been ushered through to get into this little bit of the "Pit of Hell!" slammed open. In walked two cops. One was a fat very dark-skinned Black man, and one looked to Blue to be mixed with black and white, or maybe he was a "Spic."

The mixed-looking man wore a black suit, a red-and-black striped tie over a blue shirt, and a highly polished pair of brown wingtips. He was short but very muscular with a noticeable scar on his left cheek. His red hair-as was his compatriot's-cut short in an oval design like cops everywhere sported those days. His black eyes seemed fixed in an evil gaze and it looked to Blue that he never even blinked his eyes. He walked like a Bull in a Cow pasture. He carried a clipboard. It had some kind of document attached to it.

The very dark-skinned cop wore a blue-and-white uniform. He was half-smiling and half-grimacing at Blue as he and his sidekick moseyed into the room.

The mixed-dude slammed the clipboard on the table and it slid over to in front of Blue. "Ben, you can save yourself and us a lot of trouble here. All you have to do is sign this confession and this can all be over in a couple of hours. You understand me?" He leaned down and placed both his rough-looking hands on the table. The other cop came over and stood beside Blue. He got an ink pen out of his shirt pocket and slapped it on the table in front of Blue and snarled: "Sign the damn document, oaky; let us get home and do other things. I'm sick of looking at your ugly ass already."

Blue knew that he had confessed to nothing to anyone, so he said, "I ain't go sign a damn thing! Y 'all." The mixed-looking dude got very agitated. "Look, nigga, I'm the Chief Interrogator for the Homicide Division. I'm Captain, Victor Splendera. Standing next to you is Marcus Thom, my interrogations officer.

We're trying to help your dumb ass! Don't get smart with us. We can make things a lot harder for you.

"If you want our help, you gotta come clean with us. Tell us what you did to your Granny and your Cousin. Maybe we can get a deal for you with the District Attorney. But you ain't acting right, right now; you got that? So, are you gonna do this the hard way, or the easy way?"

Thom pushed Blue's head so that his face almost hit the table's edge. "Just sign the last page on the bottom, Negro-that's all you got to do!"

"No ... I didn't do nothin'. I ain't got nothin' to confess to. I didn't kill nobody-especially not Granny or Roy. You cops must Be OUTTA -ya-minds, man. What 'cha trying to do to me?" Blue's voice was low and whining like Miles Davis's horn on a slow Jazz run.

Splendera's demeanor became very fierce. "Look, you King Kong look-alike. They got a new place for your kind over in 'Angola, WVa'. It's a private place-not like 500 Spring Street down in Richmond, where you'd be a 'fat bitch' to some bloody convict. It'll be a lot better than what you're facing for a double homicide. You're looking at Life without parole. I may can get you set to get only twenty years, and you'd be eligible for parole in about seven-who knows, with good behavior, you might get out then. But if you don't sign that confession right there, all bets are off, 'Big Blue.' The cons love fat boys like you. They can't wait to get their hands on your ass. Sign asshole! Or I'm gonna feed you to them shit-pushers like you were hog feed."

Blue screamed: "I ain't signin' nothin'! Cause, I didn't do nothin'!"

Thom kicked Blue's left side and Splendera kicked him from his right side. When they kicked him they screamed: "Sign the damn Confession-Sign it! Sign it! ..."

Blue was suddenly free of the chains and cuffs. He ran to the arms of a beautiful, light-brown, woman with long, black, straight hair. "Come here to Mama, Benny. Don't you stay out in that sun too long, you're get blacker than Sambo. I don't want you to get no darker than your daddy." Blue was a little boy again at about four years old with his mom, Velma, and his Dad, Herbert, and he was so happy living out at Ridge Street Extended. Eight year old Ivan called out to Blue: "What you did with my football, Blue? You had it last?"

"I'on kno? I left it out in the yard. Why? What's so important about that old football?" Blue whined. "Years ago, Burley beat Dunbar, ten-nothing. Them Crimson Crows didn't even get a score against the mighty Burley Bears in 1956. Burley was undefeated and unscored upon that year. Daddy got a game ball.

Coach Smith gave it to daddy 'cause he was once one-a Burley's main supporters. If I lose that ball, Dad will never forgive me," said Ivy, darting about in the spacious yard looking here and there for his ball.

A tall man, who had the physique of Joe Louis, came into the yard prancing like Prizefighter. He wore a gray business suit, black wing-tipped shoes, and a white shirt, red tie and a gray dress hat He was an Insurance man for Universal Insurance a company from out of Atlanta, Georgia He had been working in an office on Third Street Northwest since his discharge from the Army in 1961 where he had been a Tank Mechanic. He picked up the old pigskin and yelled at Ivy, "Run a slant, Ivy." It was 1971.

He flung a left hand pass up in the air toward Ivy. He ran up under it and it slipped through his opened hands. "Ah, shoot," Ivy moaned.

"You'll get better. We Slokurns all get down with some balling. It's in our blood. We were Burley Bears from way back. until Burley closed in 1967. Go on in the house and wash up. Get ready for supper." Herbert Siok.um smiled at the pride of his life, his two strapping sons, bounding up the cement steps of his two-story Jeffersonian-styled home. He'd gotten it built with a loan through the GI Bill.

A shapely nut-brown woman came to the fancy front door with it's windowpanes featuring Swans in silhouette. When the direct sunlight shone on them they sparkled so that it seemed like they were spreading their wings to fly, especially when you opened the door.

Velma wore her Betty Crocker red-and-white plaid dress under a white apron with small yellow ducks patterned all over it She always wore pink. bunny slippers in the home and low-heeled black. shoes when she went out She stood in the doorway akimbo. "You all come on in to the table. Supper's ready. I don't want my food to get cold. Nothing is worse than cold fried chicken. Come on now. Blue, stand up straight."

Blue grimaced but replied, "Yes 'sum." He knew she hated how he slumped his shoulders sometimes. Ivy bumped against Blue. "Ivy, behave, or it's going to be no dessert for you!" Velma scolded.

Herbert laughed. "Ah, Vel, boys will be boys. Gotta let 'em get out there and experience life in the rough. It ain't gonna be easy for them. I know things are a lot better than back in the 1940s. But we got a terrible fight on our hands, still. They got to get ready to play on the 'Football Field,' of the man. Sometimes, they're going to have to push and shove a little."

Velma laughed a little humorless chuckle. "Yeah, Herb, but not in my house. I just waxed them floors.

Been at it all day long. No tussling on my floors. Take that outside, after supper."

Herb laughed back. "Boys y'all heard the boss. Cool it. Hustle them rolls, chicken, greens, and mashed potatoes on down the hatch. Then we can play pass the pigskin after that. I'm go show Ivy a little about wrestling. I heard that he was interested. When he get over at Lane, Coach Dean Rayburn will be glad to have a husky dude like Ivy. Wrestling is hard work. man. It takes a lot of practice. Well let's eat."

They were in a dining room that had an Antique Table and six chairs that had a section so that it could seat eight It was Tudor styled. It had been handed down from the Tinsley side of the family, Velma's people. Herbert had had the whole set refurbished and varnished. It had a matching cupboard, and a china cabinet After they all were seated, Herb waved his hand, and they all bowed their heads.

"Lord, we thank you for the food we're about to receive. Bless the preparer; and in your Grace sanctify it for the nourishment of our bodies in Jesus name, Amen." Herb graced the meal on the table.

Four years later, Blue was eight and Ivy was twelve. It was 1975. Gerald Ford was President He came into office after President Richard M. Nixon's "Watergate Debacle." But Nixon's greatest debacle was that under his administration, a "War on Drugs," had been initiated, covered in a mantel of antidrug legalism, that was more a "War on Blacks, Poor Whites, and Minorities." He resigned.

Herb came home one evening and took off his suit coat. He passed out on the living room floor right away. He gripped his stomach and cried out, "Vel ... I'm not feeling too good. I ... I'm hurting."

Vel called the Rescue Squad. They came to the Slokumes' Residence with the emergency lights of their transport vehicle flashing and its siren blasting. Two men in white jumpsuits got out of the vehicle with a portable stretcher between them. Blue could see that his father was unconscious.

They rolled his dad away in that white van with the red writing on its sides. His mother got in the cab of the vehicle with tears easing down her cheeks. Blue pleaded: "Is Dad gonna be alright? Is Dad okay? What's wrong wit 'im? ..." His father had seemingly never had a sick day as far as Blue could remember.

Vel tried to reassure Blue, "Your Daddy's going to be okay. God will take care of it all as always. Y'all just wait by the phone. Ivy, call Grandma Mildred, tell her Herb is up at the hospital. We don't know what is wrong with him, yet." Ivy made the call then:

Ivy ran into his room and grabbed his dad old football and started tossing it up a little and catching it like he always did when he was distressed. He was scared as hell. His aunt Catlin Alisa had died suddenly from a ruptured appendix just a year ago. She was Grandma Slokum's only other child. Her son, Leroy Shelby was living with Grandma Siok. um, over in Fifeville, because he had no one else to take care of him. His father was unknown. Aunt Catlin was a Single Parent. She and Roy had been living in the West Haven Government Project over on Hardy Drive, after Vinegar Hill had been demolished, 1958-1964.

Blue went into his room and got on the bed. He balled up into a feudal position and put his thumb in his mouth. He tried to rock himself to sleep. That's what he'd do to deal with anything threatening or uncomfortable, or anything that frighten him. He wanted to hear that his father was going to be okay.

It was early the next morning when Velma came back home. She walked like she was carrying the weight of the world on her shoulders. Blue got off his bed and came into the front room to hear what she had to say. Ivy nearly ran into her. She was reluctant to speak.

"Boys . . . brace yourselves. Remember your Daddy always told you 'God works in mysterious ways.' But, I can't . . . see. I can't." She burst out crying. "Can't see how a merciful God could take a man like Herb away from me and his beautiful boys, but he's gone! We all need Herb so badly for so many reasons. "Oh . . . God, I can't stand this-no not this, now! My Mom Susan lost your Grandfather Sawyer rather suddenly. I never got over losing Daddy. Mom survived but for a short time before she died. I don't know how I got through it all. After I graduated from the seventh grade, I met your Daddy. We courted for eight years. We were in love, so we got married, and y'all came along just right. My life's been so complete. I never dreamed that I would be going through that pain again. Oh God, Help Us!" She dropped to her knees. "Herb had Colon Cancer. It's a common killer amongst us Blacks."

Ivy and Blue dropped down beside her to hug her. Blue said: "Mom, I'm here for you always. Don't wony about that. I love you."

Ivy said: "Mom, you gotta stay with us. Don't you leave us. I'll take care of us all if I have to. Daddy would want me to do that. I love you. We all go miss Daddy. I don't know how I'm go get along without him. It will only be possible if you're here with us."

Velma hugged her sons tight to her. "Momma will never leave her babies. You're all I've got now. I'll take care of both of you. I'll get a job up at the University. You'll see.

When the 761.st Tank Battalion was deactivated on June 1, 1946, Herb could have been discharged from the Anny then. Most of his fellow soldiers at Fort Hood were mustered out of the Anny. He was transferred to Fort Bragg North Carolina. He had been promoted to Tech Sergeant in the 761.st". Under President Eisenhower, his desegregation efforts made it possible for Herb Slokum to be assigned to the Tank Maintenance Division as a Sergeant Major at Bragg.

Herb had put up his age to join the Army in 1941. He was actually fifteen then. He was stationed at Fort Benning Georgia for Basic Training. He got his GED while working in the motor pool there. He got promoted to Team Leader, to Corporal, then to Sergeant. He got assigned to Fort Hood and became a Mechanic for the 761.st"- newly formed Tank Battalion under the Command of General George Patton. He only served with the 761" one year before it was deactivated. He achieved the rank of Tech Sergeant.

He met a little woman while he was on leave in 1946. He assumed she was a little older than she actually was. He was twenty years old. She was fourteen. Though they did a lot of heavy petting, nothing else got done until eight years later. He was twenty-eight and she was twenty-two. He saw her as more beautiful than all of the women he had seen in Paris, or Italy, and certainly more than any from Germany. Though he had sampled them all, he tied the knot with Velma in *1955*.

She lived with her family on Starr Hill next to Vinegar Hill, off the West side of Fourth Street Northwest. She was kin to families in Charlottesville and Albemarle with the last names: "Belle, Tinsley, Brown, Ragland, Jackson, and Walker."

Sawyer Tinsley ran a little Barbershop on Commerce Street on Vinegar

Hill in the 1940s. Susan had a Salon Chair in the back of her husband's Shop. She dressed hair back there. Velma helped out even after her Soldier boyfriend had asked for her hand in marriage.

It was not long after the announcement that Sawyer collapsed on the floor of his shop was rushed to the UVA hospital and died rather suddenly. Susan pined away after that. She became a piece of dried fruit, a dead vegetable. She soon joined her husband in the Oakwood Cemetery located between Digg and Oak Streets Southeast. Velma was a basket case for months after the untimely loss of her parents. She was their only child. Her business holdings evaporated. Business claims leveled against her took away her home and all of her belongings.

In *1955,* Herb married Velma in the office of Reverend Benjamin F. Bunn at First Baptist Church on the Comer of Seventh Street Southwest and West Main Streets. Herb pledged to take care of her till the day he died. She was moved in with Grandma Mildred Slokum who had a big house on the comer of Fifth and Dice Streets Southwest in Fifeville.

In 1961, Herb was discharged from the Army. Two years later, Ivan Ramon was born. Four years after that, Benjamin Luther was born. He got a GI loan and built a house out on Ridge Street that resembled the homes he's seen up at the University of Virginia on Rugby Road where many professors lived. He felt like he was an Insurance Agent and could afford to live like that; and, his little wife didn't have to work. She was content to stay at home with the kids.

In 1975, Vel's world was seemingly to her coming to a close. She had only a seventh grade education. She did get hired at the University of Virginia's Housekeeping Department as an entry-level Maid. That did not pay her enough money to keep a decent meal on the table; nor could she pay the taxes on their home. The house started to take on a rundown appearance. Her neighbors complained to her by letter: "We have a Tenant Agreement over here that you have to keep your property up to our standards or we will buy it and you'll have to move. Repairs are overdue on your house and lawn. This is our final notice."

On this day, Velma came home wearing her gray and black "UVA Maid's Uniform." She got completely undressed in the living room of her spacious home. She knelt down to the floor in her panties and brassiere. She bobbed her head to and fro. She screamed: "Herb. You gota. come up from wherever you're at. I can't do this all by myself! Herb, why'd you have to leave me like this? I can't do this all by myself. You gotta come back to us-we need you-you gotta come back! ..."

Blue and Ivy burst through the door that evening to find their mother trying to call through the floor to the ground, through the earth all the way to Heaven to her dead husband. She sobbed rocking her head back and forth. Her hair had turned white as snow. It stood all over her head. She had neglected to comb it again. She had lost touch with good grooming since Herb's untimely death. Her body gave off a musty odor like those winos on skid row over on Short Fourth Street Southwest.

Blue cried when he witnessed his mother's eyes opened wide matching the appearance of hens' eggs. She was gone-gone crazy-nuts. "Mom, don't do that We got-you. We'll take care of you; me and Ivy will. Dad left you a little pension. You got a job. We can do alright if you stay with us. Mom . . . Get off the floor. Get up ... put some clothes on ... Please!"

Ivy dropped down on the floor beside his stricken mother. He wept "Mom, you gotta stay with us. We love you too much to lose you like this. Mom ... Dad can't come back. He's gone-dead! We gotta let'im rest in peace! Think about it Mom! How sad Dad would be if he could see you now! He wouldn't be at peace. Mom. Mom! Please Mom. Get off the floor and get some clothes on. Let us see that you're still with us. Please Mom"

Vehna was taken to the University of Virginia that night by the Rescue Squad. Grandma Slokum came back to Ridge Street with the grim news. "Boys, Vel's gonna be up at the UVA Davis Ward for a little while till she can get her bearing. She's been talking out of her head. Seems as though she thinks Herb done come back to take her away with him. She sounded like a little gal laughing and giggling like she did when Herbert courted her years ago.

"Y'all's go have to come stay with Grandma for a while. Well at least 'til Vel gets back on her feet I'll take care of my favorite grand boys. All y'all's my favorite. Y'all can be with Roy more. Maybe he'll have you Ivy to look up to so he won't hang-out with some of the crowd that's been moving into Fifeville lately. You're near 'bout his age Blue. Maybe you can help him get his head on straight. I heard from Vel that you're doing fine in school. I hope you'll be able to get Roy's head back into his school books. He's hanging around the Pool Hall down on South First Street He and Bobby

Blueblood's trying to be pool sharks or something. 'That Boy's too young to be hanging around that hoodlum trash he's attracted to.

"Y'all get ya' things in your suitcases. We'll come back for the rest later. Hurry up, I gotta go back up to the Hospital to see 'bout Vel. She had a bad episode today. Threw up all her food. 'They couldn't find no reason. Said she ain't physically sick or nothing. They can't find a natural thing wrong with her, 'cepting what's in her head. Poor child.

"When I lost your Grandpa Lincoln Willis, I nearly lost it too. He was stationed in Centreville, Texas in 1918 in-a Army Cleaning Detail. Wasn't no combat soldier. But they ruled him missing in action. He wasn't never sent overseas or nothing. But he was killed in some kind of action. I been getting a little check since his death. I got a big one right after the chaplain came and told me that World War I had taken my handsome Link. I had to raise Herbert and Catlin Alisa alone. I did the best I could. I'm go do the same with y'all. You'll see. So come on with Grandma. We got a long way to travel through life children."

The next day, Grandma Slokum came back from the UVA Hospital with the distressing news: "Boys, ya Mama, Vel, died this morning from Cardiac Arrest God help us all," she sobbed.

Ivy fell to the floor. He was out cold for almost an hour. He came to whimpering: "I ain't go trust no God that done that to my family. I hate . . . everything! I'll get even I'll get it on now!"

Blue sat in a leather sofa. He rocked to and fro. He looked like a little kid that was told to go take timeout Tears eased out of the comers of both of his eyes. He trembled all over. He didn't utter a word.

Roy walked back and forth around the room. He growled out of the side of his face that was in a fox snarl: "We gotta get to the vein of this shit, man. We gotta draw blood. That's how Buscake, James, and Bubbles used to get-down. They did it to the death. Fuck! The Old Homeys 'round here, they'll tell you: 'Ain't no way to go but to they asses, man.' It's time to forkin' throw-down, right now! We're damned if we do, and fucked if we don't! It's them bad-asses who got they hand on the trigger. They got the 'Fear of God!' in these mo' forkers here in the ''Ville.' We gotta elevate that mo' forker. Them sonsabitches killed our babies in Alabama. They killed Medgar Evers! They killed Dr. King! They killed Malcolm X! They might've killed Aunt Velma up at that O' Racist Hospital, shit! That's all U-V-A is anyway. I 'ma little man and even I know that, Grandma!"

Grandma Slokum interjected, "Roy, that ain't no way to talk right after we lost your Auntie. Ivy, Blue, it'll be better if you boys go to school over yonder and get a free education. I could only get seven years of schooling. Law wouldn't allow me no more. You can go all the way. You can become like Walter White, Luther P. Jackson, Carter G. Woodson, Elijah Muhammad, or Dr. Martin Luther King, Jr. Do that. That's the best way for y'all to go. Don't listen to them hoodlums who're like stray dogs in the alleys. You go end up in an early grave, or in prison for life if you don't listen to Grandma-y'all better hear me now!

"Ivy, you're going on over yonder to Buford Hill Middle-School. Get all you can over there. Then go on to High School and graduate. Do good and you could end up in college. If yo' grades be good 'nough, you might get a scholarship to go to any school you want to. Do that You're turning thirteen. You're old enough to know better.

"Blue, you're just eight, but you're big for your age. You're go get some plaque over how dark-skinned you are. But Dr. George Washington Carver was dark-skinned. Look what that scientist did with just a Peanut Do that, Blue. You're smart Blue. I can see the good in you. Let that come to the surface.

"Roy, you've always been so full of hate. You're always skipping school. You do that to hang out with the worst elements 'round here. They go lead you right to Hell through an early grave. You got to let go of the pain, son. Seek God. Let Jesus Lead you to Peace. That's the only real peace you ever gonna truly have anyway. You'll be a Seventh Grader. That's all the schooling I was able to get All of y'all gotta chance to be good boys. All of y'all go on over yonder to Forest Hill Elementary and become 'A Credit to your Race.' Yall hear what I'm saying?"

Blue is lying on a bunk in the jail. He tries to rub the side of his face that was very swollen. It hurts him too much. He was so sore all over his body that he could barely move. He was only conscious for a moment. Then:

Chapter Three

Blue's consciousness was fleeting. He was drifting between twilight and daylight, from the world of dreams to actual reality. He mumbled: "Them . . . racist cops and Black wannabes, they go try to get me ... to confess. I ain't goin' down for offing my Granny, or my Cousin. I didn't do that! ...

"They didn't have to beat the Hell outta me. Ow-w-w, I'm hurtin' all over my body. I feel like road kill looks, yo. They ain't got no business beatin' nobody like this ... no for damn sure"

Blue passed out After a while of drifting through walls of red, blue, and green, and hearing the groans and moans people made when they were about to face eternity, Blue heard a familiar voice:

"Blue-e-e-e! Blue-e-e-e-e! Blue-e-e-e-e-e!"

Blue was suddenly back in his jail bunk. He exclaimed, "Ivy. Is that you? How come? Am I dead, or something? Or, are you a ghost? What's up with you, Ivy?"

There was silence for a moment Then again, **"Blue-e-e-e-e-e!"**

Blue recognized the voice as belonging to his dead Brother, Ivy. "Ivy, I know that's you, Dog. What's Up? Man, lemme see you. Can you do that? We need you G. Jamie 'nem's all up in the 'Hood, man, big-time. They be gunning the Crew down on every comer since you been gone, yo. Ivy, them Posse Bangers 'bout to take control. They done capped Roy, man. Granny caught a stray bullet. I'm all by myself, now, Dog. Since you calling my name, can you just lemme see you?"

Ivy's still invisible but answers Blue: "Yes, Blue, I can let you see an image of me. But brace yourself. In this life-your world, Blue-I can only appear to you like you last saw me. Concentrate, and I will come into view." Ivy's voice is similar to the wind lowly howling.

Blue turned himself in his bunk away from the jail-bars to face the left side of the wall. He saw a little Circle of Light growing in the middle of the wall. "Ivy, is that you, Bro?" Blue's voice echoed.

The orb of light grew larger until it resembled a bright car-light The image of Ivy was molded out of the middle of the light It grew larger and larger until it seemed to be eight-feet tall.

Blue was a little startled. "Man, Ivy, you too tall, yo. You're still wearing your Thug Threads, like I last saw you on the Set, but ... but they make you look-well-Dead! It's the same outfit you's wearin' when Jamie 'nem capped you, man. G. that's too weird.

"What's wrong with your eyes, G? They ain't movin'. They all bloodshot, and shit. What's up with that, Bro? Man ... Ivy, now you're scaring the Hell outta me lookin' like you're lookin'. I ain't used to seein' no ghost.es, yo!"

Ivy's lips did not move, nor did his facial expression change as a voice echoed all around his image. It still sounded like a low-howl of the wind.

"Blue, my beloved little Brother. You don't know the truth behind what I've done in life. How I've wasted all of the time God gave me on this earth. I let hate consume me. I became a purveyor of it I was a cold-bloodied killer, Blue. Hate tuned my emotions to ice. It became all I could feel; all I could express.

"It ain't cool to have all of the homeys in the 'Hood scared of you, Dog. The girlies and the cats secretly hated me. They were just too scared to say it to my face. Our mothers and fathers couldn't walk the streets at night Too scared. I created an atmosphere of fear all around me. Fear becomes hate when it is allowed to fester in the heart, Blue. The people had every right to fear me, yo.

"Blue, I took Roy with me one night on the Set You, we could not trust to be cool with what we were about, Dog. Master D's people told us about a cat who was ripping off our stash we had over on Grove Street in the garage of that old two-story abandoned house. Buddy Doherty and his homey, Sid Rankin were slipping in the basement door and copping our weed, and heroin. Nobody was s'spose ta know we had a stash over there. So, my Crew was called upon to put a stop to the punks who dared rip Master D off.

"We scooped Buddy up one night after a pick-up basketball game at

Tonsler's Park. Roy beat ′im down with a rubber hose. Nobody would dare interfere. We put him in our Jeep Cherokee. We rode the dude out to Pantops Mountain to a place off Thomas Jefferson Highway on *250* East He never regained consciousness. We snashed him out of the backseat of the ride. I shot ′im in the back of his head one time. Roy shot 'im in the back three times. We left him lying on the side of the road.

"We capped Sid in West Haven. He lived with Joy Jamison. Had a son with her. Sid saw us coming, and tried to run down an alley. Before he could climb up a fence in back of the alley, Roy shot 'im in the back. I emptied my thirty-eight in him. The dude turned over and died right in that alley. I'm so sorry for those killings, Blue."

Blue interjected: "Ivy, I didn't know for sure that you and Roy had put the hit on Sid and Buddy. I heard only that one of the Crew had done them in. Man, that was a brutal hit., yo. But when you're on the set you gotta have 'Ice Cubes' in your Blood, like I'm gonna have when I get even with Jamie 'nem ..."

"BLUE-E-E-E! No-o-o-o-o! That's not the way to go." Ivy's voice rose like a sudden gust of wind before a coming storm.

"Before we were terrorizing our 'Hoods, with our guns and drugs, man, Mr. Benjamin Tonsler lived over here. Booker T. Washington used to pay that great educator visits right over here in Fifeville. Mrs. Rebecca McGinness grew up down on the corner of Sevenths and Six-and-a-Half Streets. She was Becky Shelton Then. Sonny Sampson, the great Music Teacher and Band Leader grew up down there. He was the Grandson of Mr. Tonsler, who had been a Principal at Jefferson Elementary School.

"**Many** of the prominent people coming to Charlottesville, ended up visiting Mr. Tonsler who was the most outspoken of Civil Rights and **NAACP** Advocates in The ′Ville.

"Vinegar Hill was once the center of Black Cultural Life in Charlottesville. It got tore to the ground in 1964. Most of the rich Blacks moved their businesses over to Fifeville. We had Denver's and Belle's Convenience Stores; Mrs. Safornia's Beauty Salon; Isaac's Grocery Store on the Comer of Seventh and Dice Streets, it is now A Church of God In Christ. We got Este's Supermarket on Cherry Avenue; and, a number of Hustle Houses on Dice, Sixth and Sixth-and-a-Half Streets. Rich Blacks bought homes over here and Fifeville became the center of Black Cultural Life from 1964 on. We lost Zion Union Baptist Church on Vinegar Hill. But we have First Baptist and Mount Zion over here.

"Reverend Bunn of First Baptist, and Reverend Hamilton of Mount Zion were not just Pastors, they were active Civil Rights Advocates. They helped to change the City of Charlottesville, man.

"But Master D came out of nowhere in 1965. Dope addiction followed wherever this vicious dude showed up. He set his sights on Fifeville. Dope houses opened their doors on Grove and King Streets; Prospect Avenue; Tenth and Page Streets, and Garrett Street. The drugs started to flow like water, so did the guns and quick money. Gangs formed all over the City, man, calling themselves 'Crews.' When we moved in with Grandma, we had to join The Westside Crew. But you also had The Washington Park, West Haven, Tenth and Page, and Garrett Square Crews. The most notorious was The Prospect Avenue Crew. It got the Westside Crew going. We were part of that group of Bangers.

"I know now, Blue, Master D was supplying us all with guns, dope, and quick money. The Northwest Crew that rolls on Tenth and Page, Rose Hill Drive, Gordon and Grady Avenues, had a bad ass dude we all called 'Coach.' He was the Leader, CO, over there. He was kin to the basketball coach that was once at Burley High. Roy and I was contracted to take that huge dude out, Blue. Master D said that 'Coach' was getting too big, mouthing off, and whatnot. Roy and I got Skeeter Gardener, and Pops Richards together from over here, and we rolled on 'Coach' an' his Crew. After the shootout, Sketter an' Pops lay dead, but so did 'Coach.' I got grazed by a bullet, but Roy didn't get touched. He fired the shots that killed 'Coach,' who crawled into a 'Tornado Tube,' in the play area of Washington Park. That's where he bled to death, and the cops found him the next day. The rest of Coach's Crew ran like scared dogs.

"Blue, that's why Fifeville is now becoming a Slum. The rich moved away. They left behind boarded up houses and businesses. Belle's and Denver's no longer exist. Nothing is still standing. Este's is nothing but a 'Ghetto-Store' now. Good people just want to get away from all the bad noise, man, and the killings, dope, and us Bangers making their little Girls pregnant. We Are The Problem!

"Homey, Bro. Get outta gun-trafficking and dope-dealing, Blue. Don't let nobody like Master D talk you into putting a hit on anybody. It'll just make you a cold-bloodied killer. See: Roy and I went over to Forest Hill like we were going to school. We skipped school most days. We hung out with Tullie Joe. He was the CO of the Prospect Crew. At Twelve I was 'jumped-in' to that Crew. For Roy it was when he was just ten. Grandma thought we were going to school. We were bangin' everyday, Blue. I never went to Lane, man. Nor did Roy. Ah, we left the house, but never arrived at school. Grandma never attended any of the **PTA** meetings. So, we just pretended, you know. Then I pretended I had just dropped out when I turned sixteen. We were frontin' for days. You're in school, Blue, stay in school.

"Listen up, Dog: It don't matter if you're the baddest, illest, gangster on the Block when a bullet finds your heart. You're still gonna die. As I drew my last breath I realized that. I wished I had lived another way as my Life Hashed Before My face.

"Those guns and ammunition we used came from outside of our 'Hood. Think about it, Blue.

"The money we thought we were making from selling drugs, pimping the girlies, selling guns and ammunition, and murder for hire, we spent at high-priced clothing stores, car dealerships, 'Bling Stores,' and overpriced sportswear stores. We rented rooms in so-called fancy hotel and motel chains, and whatever, G. We bought expensive booze and champagne, beer and exotic liquors. In other words, it was a lose-lose situation, Blue. The money that came in went right back out from us.

"Every gun and ammunition we bought and used against a Brother the whole 'Hood loses. Every girl or woman that we pimped, the whole 'Hood loses. All the money we used to buy expensive nothings, like gaudy clothes, overpriced alcohol, and Jewelry ('Bling'), we all lose, Blue. We're just helping to do our own people to death, G. We're taking what little we have in our 'Hood and spewing it out like a flush of the toilet We're the poorer for it. It ain't 'bout nothin', Blue! All of our Gangbanging money goes right out of the 'Hood back to the top-dogs. We end up creating 'another Ghetto.' I hope you follow this, Homes ..." Blue was sarcastically shaking his head at what the Ghost of Ivy was saying. He could not belie-re that his tough-talking Brother was "Bitching-Out!" like that. Could another

Ghost be impersonating Ivy? He had to wonder. While he was pondering what Ivy had just said, another Orb of Light came into view.

Grandma Slokum's Ghost appeared to stand beside the Ghost of Ivy. Blue saw that she had on a sparkling white gown that went from her neck to the floor. The hemline of it seemed to be stained with a red substance that resembled Blood.

Her hair was brightly shining like the sunlight that gave off a glistening sheen that radiated all around her. All around her head were star-like sparkles like at a fireworks display. Her eyes were beautiful, but were more like blazing fire.

She was clutching in her right hand a Gold Chain. In her left hand she held a Silver Chain. A Miniature Silver Zodiac Sign of The Twins was attached to it A Golden Crucifix was attached to the Golden Chain. Unlike Ivy, her image was not fixated and dead-looking, but made humanlike movements like a live human. She sighed long and hard as her blazing eyes seemed to burn into Blue's psyche. Her eyes became so sad that Blue could feel her real sorrow all the way down in his Soul. He observed what could be only coming from a Ghost: Grandma Slokum's eyes moistened and red droplets eased out the corners of them that resembled Blood that spilled down her golden cheeks. Her voice was something like Ivy's, but was a lot more mournful. It sounded like the lonely moans that a Dove made when calling to it's mate.

"Blue . . . Blue, you're going to be just as guilty as Jamie 'nem . . . if you do what I see that you have in your heart. If you go out and you and your Homeys hunt Jamie down and kill him and all of those who helped him Murder Roy, Ivy, and Me, you'll just be setting the stage for more of the thousands of senseless murders that are taking place in Charlottesville, and the rest of the cities all over America. I can see the Souls of innocent people over here screaming to 'The Lord of Justice.' They can't cross over into the 'Arms of The Ancestors,' because their 'Souls are caught in Limbo,' 'til their killers come to a just end. The murdered victims' wails continue. A lot of Souls are waiting on a just end of Jamie 'nem. So you see, your murder of them will not be a Just End. There's more to it than that.

"Blue ... the mothers what born you all and the Grandma's what raised you all must bear some responsibility too. That's why my gown is stained in Human Blood. It represents the innocent shed-blood that I must wear throughout Eternity. I didn't do enough to train you all differently. I confess: I gave you all a roof over your heads, and I figured that was enough. Least, that was all that I thought should be required of me. That was the 'Great Lie that was buried in my heart throughout my Sojourn in Life.' I let the Streets of Charlottesville raise you all. Those Streets are filled with every bit of grit and grime possible.

"I went to my Missionary meetings. I attended all of the Prayer Breakfasts. I helped cook all of the Convocational Meals each year. I was very active at First Baptist. But . . . I neglected you boys, my Grandsons. I couldn't see it then. I had my head in the clouds looking for 'Heaven-On-Earth.' I'm so sorry I let 'The Devil' get to you all. It's all my fault"

Blue had to interrupt her there: "Granny! Grandma-I know I know ya' done your best raisin' us!

The mess we got into was our own fault. We all knew right from wrong. But we chose to do bad all by ourselves. It ain't none-a your fault, Granny. You can't blame none-a that on yourself.,.

More 'Blood Tears' eased out of the corners of Grandma Mildred's Eyes. Her ghostly voice got a little tremolo as she poured out her heart: "Blue. Hush, Lil' Blue. You don't understand. You never took a gun or knife to anyone. But, you still got a lotta Blood on your hands, Son"

That statement upset Blue. He protested, "Granny, I ain't never disagreed with you to your face like Roy or Ivy. But you's so wrong 'bout the 'Blood Guilt!' I never kilt nobody! I saw 'em kilt and all. I earned the guns away from the scene after the murders, but I never pulled no triggers, though. That was all Roy and Ivy 'nem. You be a Ghost, yeah, but even a Ghost can be wrong sometimes."

Grandma Slokum's voice got a little louder like the opening peal of a thunderstorm. "Blue. Blue, Son!

Listen to me. And make no mistake about this that I'm saying to you.

"Son, when you sold drugs to an Addict," her voice grew softer, more sorrowful and deeply sad. "And that man got high, jumped into his car and drove it at top speed on Route Twenty-nine and ended up ramming his car into the side of a Mother driving her two boys from a boy scouts' meeting, and all four died in that crash, that blood is on your hands.

"When a disgruntled husband bought dope from you one evening and took an Uzi he'd bought from Big Blue-Jesus and Don-Don Twister from over in 'West Haven Projects,' and went up to Washington Park and killed his wife and a man he thought she was seeing on the side-but was just a Blood Brother she had just met for the first time, some of that Blood is on your hands, Son.

"A man bought PCP from you and Ivy, went home got high on it and killed his two boys ages two and four because he thought they were 'full of demons,' that blood is on you all's hands. Blue that little girl that got killed over on Prospect Avenue when she wandered into the room where two opposing Gangbangers were getting ready to shoot at each other, and they shot this child in a cross-fire and it died, the guns came from you and Ivy. A member of your Crew was one of the gunners. He was just 'putting in time on the Set'-as you all call it-but you all got Blood on your hands.

"If you took any of the money made from gun-running or dope-dealing, you got blood on your hands, Blue. Your Soul is Sanguine-Red right now with innocent Blood, God Help you!

"My Gown is pure like my Good intentions were when I thought I was raising y'all right in my own self centered, self-righteous way. My Noble Intentions aside, I succeeded in raising three young men who became cold-blooded Killers, that's why the Helm of my Gown is edged in Innocent Blood!"

Blue was sobbing as the truth cut deep into his heart. He thought he was innocent because he never fired a gun at a victim. It never occurred to him that what he was doing was just as deadly. He yelped like a little puppy, still trying to justify his actions. "Grandma . . . Granny . . . I've tried ta' give ya' a little money. All I knew how to do was hustle. I didn't mean to kill nobody. I was just on the Set and had to Kick.-Back. like the Homeys said I had to do. I'm so sorry now for all that . . . I wish I had a chance to do it all over again. I'd rock the whole scene differently! I'd do it right. I was just tryin' to make a little money to help you out, though, Granny,.

Grandma Slokum's voice grew loud like thunder again: "The road to ruin is filled with good intentions.

Son ... you gave me Blood Money! That's why I'm wearing the stains on my Spiritual Character. It is the Blood of your innocent victims. I am guilty! I'm guilty because . . . I knew deep in my heart-even though I tried to deny it to myself-where that money was coming from. I lied to myself. I used the lie: 'No, my boys are good boys. They wouldn't do horrible things to people. I raised them better'n that. They wouldn't. They just wouldn't.'

"But, over on this side of things. Over here in Limbo. I have to constantly face the truth. I see the Souls of those people who have been killed. Bloody murder scene after murder scene that's the environment-the only thing-I get to see. I can hear the screams of you all's victims. I can see their blood running red on the ground like a river. I've got to be tortured like this throughout Eternity. It's too horrible!

"I did not speak out when I should have. I just prayed to God. I just 'left it all up in Jesus' hands,' and let bygones be bygones. I didn't do what I knew to do to help you all-and to help Our People. That's the worst kind of hypocrite. And, me, A So-called Godly Missionary Woman."

Blue's sobs grew stronger and more frequent He croaked out "Granny. Granny. Granny! Oh, how can that be? How can all that be true? You's always in the Church. You seemed to care for everyone. I ain't never seen you turn away a hungry person, or one who asked you for help. You've been a good Mother, Grandmother, and Church Lady ..."

Grandmother Mildred Slokum's Ghost declared in a loud thunderous voice: "Blue. I saw you sporting Diamond Rings, Silver Chains with Gold and Silver Crosses, and I knew that you didn't have a Job. I saw Ivy and Roy standing on the Comer of Fifth and Dice mostly every day, all-day-long.

"There was no way you all could carry around the kind of money I knew you had in your pockets legitimately-I tried to explain that away inside of myself every time the thought plagued my mind. But I saw the same thing happening all around us, so I held my peace. No one spoke out and so I didn't either!

"Even when the Blood started to flow as the Gangs grew around over here and more victims paid with their lives, I held my peace. Like so many parents over here, I didn't stop y'all. I didn't do nothing really to pull you all away from the Grit and Grime in the Streets. I should've tried . . . I let you all go to the gutter right before my own eyes-and while you were living in my own house.

'Worst of all, I appreciated the money you all slipped into my hands from time-to-time. I excused the fact away that I knew that it was Blood

Money. Blue . . . I should've refused every dime of it. I didn't. God Help Me, I didn't! I can't take that back. Oh, God, I wish I had!

"Blue . . . Ivy can't find any peace over here. His Soul can't get away from the Screams of the Dying Victims he murdered in senseless Drug Turf-Wars. His Soul is condemned to wander in the Afterlife, fleeing from the horrors he caused to the Souls he dispatched into an Untimely Death. Some of the young men he killed were in the Prime of their youth. They may have grown up to become great men in Our Race who might have cured Cancer or something. But Ivy introduced them to their eternal end too soon. So he will never be At Rest, nor will his Soul be Free! He may never escape his Eternal Fate!"

Blue is so afraid of what he hears from the Ghost of his Grandmother that he does what he normally does when overwhelmed by some hysterical tragedy. He reverts to a state of denial. "Granny. I try to not believe in them 'Eternal Things' you used to talk about so much. I don't wanna ..."

A horrible scene appeared back behind Grandma Slokum. Blue heard eerie, lonesome, wails that penetrated to his very Soul. Then he saw gunshot victims with bullet holes all over their bodies with blood oozing out of their wounds. He heard earsplitting screams and groans. He smelled a sulfuric odor. He allowed: "I'm getting sick to my stomach. I can't stand this. Turn this off." Blue vomited up salty puke.

With his stomach still convulsing, Blue saw that the ghastly images were absorbed into the Ghost of Ivy. Ivy's voice bellowed: "Blue ... Blue ... Blue, I wish I could turn it off! I'd be so glad to be able to do that. I can't! I can't! I can't Blue!

"1nat is the terrible reality you're headed for, Lil' Bro. Lest you change your way of thinking. Lest you replace that Hatred inside with Love. Blue, You Can't Hate Your Way To Love! Just like: You Can't Kill Your Way To Peace! It is impossible. That was my Error!

"Already, Blue, you may not think so, but you got a lot of Amends to make. I'm trying to do that now, by coming to you as a Ghost. I'm in Limbo between two Worlds: One is 'Dante's Inferno,' and the other is The Bosom of The Ancestors.' The stain on my Soul of the blood of the innocents may keep me in Limbo for the rest of This Dispensation. Then, I'll be Judged by the Righteous to see if I've done enough as a Ghost to be forgiven for my Evil Misdeeds done in my Fleshly Body. I'll have to Haunt

Fifeville for as long as this 'Hood exists, to try to prevent the Homeys from following the Wicked Example I set for them while I was alive. As a Ghost my task is most difficult. No one wants to listen to a Spook!

"Blue ... Blue ... Blue ... Listen to me," Ivy's voice thundered like during a huge thunderstorm. "Baby Brother, don't kill nobody, man. Don't do it for any reason, not for revenge, nor for so-called Justice, nor for any reason you can think of. No matter what anyone may do to you. It is always better to forgive anyone who may trespass against you. Let that one pay for his sins. You keep your Soul Free! For let me tell you what awaits you if you kill unjustly, Blue:

"My whole body feels like it's on fire. I can't cool off. I'm dying of thirst, but I can't drink. I feel so hungry, like near starvation, but I can't eat! I have lusts for women, that must go unsatisfied. I feel like I'm tired as a Rabbit Dog after a long hunt, but I can't rest There Is No Rest For My Soul! I must wander the Earth and Suffer for all Eternity! I must watch all of Humanity living their Lives enjoying all that I can no longer participate in. I'm doomed, Blue! Nothing on this Earth is worth coming to this Horrible Existence.

"BLUE-E-E-E! Change While You Can!"

Ivy's and Grandma Slokum's Ghosts disappeared in a Streak of Lightning and a loud lingering peal of thunder. Blue trembled all over at what the Ghosts had said. But his hatred for Jamie 'nem still prevailed in his heart. Then-

Another bright-red Orb of Light shone on the jail-house wall. It grew suddenly like the turning on of a *very* Flashlight. It became a likeness of Roy. He was like the little lye-bottle Devil, without horns, or a pitchfork, or tail. But Roy's Ghost was red all over. It was fixated like Ivy's had been. Its big-red eyes had black holes instead of irises. The voice that emanated from it was like rushing water at a dam.

"Blue, Blue, Blue, My-man! Yo, G, You're a Big Dog. Yo-yo-yo, I'm two-years older than you, yo. Know what I'm sayin'? But I never matured like you Brother-man. My mind stayed at the five or six year level when it came to how to live, yo.

"My Moms lived on Vinegar Hill 'til they tore it to the ground. She moved to West Haven and had me. I ain't never got to meet my real father. Bill Banks was serving life in prison I now know for killing his wife. My

Moms was from the bad side of the family. I grew up on Hardy Drive watching the homeys deal drugs. I saw them pimping the girlies. My Moms was one of them. I even witnessed Dennis Mayes offing one of his women he called a 'stubborn Bitch' for not taking on a john she thought was too large for her. He beat Ennie Woodford to death right over there on Tenth and Page. Man, Dennis was the Only Father I ever had. I tried to be just like him. He taught me how to kill without any conscience. It was a little hard at first, but after that second one, I got to do it like some-a them crooked cops. Like Big Daddy Dennis, I got my first Girlie when I was twelve. I got my first baby shortly after that, yo. I was dealing Crack big-time.

"I got two Crack-Babies over at West Haven, even after I moved in with Grandma. She didn't know nothing 'bout that, yo. The one I got pregnant was named Millie Lee Johnston. That was in 1977. That same year I got a baby with Cadence Pete who lives over on Prospect Avenue. I had both she and her Mother on Crack. Millie had Twins, Sean and Cecilia. Cadence had my Son, Mallory . They're all round about five goin' on six right now.

"The way I got so many women at so young an age was I got them strung-out on Crack. And sometimes I got they Mommas strung-out too. I was they 'Candy Man.' They saw me as a 'Great Big O' Yard Dog!' I just thought treatin' women that way was how it ought 'ta be. That's what Big Daddy Dennis taught me. It was why I didn't stay in the World too long, I was just too wicked, Blue.

"Home-Slice, I wish I had at least taken care of my children, yo. Like me, they never got to know they Daddy. I'd see them often, but I tried to ignore them all, man. They Mommas was so strung-out it didn't matter, as long as I gave them a Hit of Crack now and then. Blue, that was too pitiful. They'd sleep with any Cat that came along with a 'Rock of Crack.' My babies with those women were born strung-out on Dope, yo. I'm so sorry now about that, Blue. Those kids ain't go never be right, man.

"Blue, Mattie Pace over on Prospect lost my Twin Daughters. They came here so strung-out on Dope that the UVA Hospital couldn't save them. I never knew they names. I didn't care. That happened just before . . .

you know . . . Jamie happened to me. Mattie took an overdose of Heroin. She choked to death.

"The women I messed with were all on Welfare, G. I got most-a they welfare money every month. They didn't take care-a they babies cause-a me! The dope that killed my Twins came from me. The Dope that killed they Momma came from me. That makes me a Killer of my Own Children, and a lotta other children in the 'Hood. It ain't Hip! It ain't Cool! And it ain't 'bout nothin' but self-annihilation. That's why my image is so sanguine-red like Blood. I was-a 'Bloody Mo' Forker!' That's all I was.

"Blue, wherever dope is sold, it kills people, families, and they 'Hoods. Just take a look at Church Hill in Richmond. Look at Northwest Washington, DC. Southside Chicago, Harlem, New York, Detroit, and North Philadelphia. These Cities are dying from Gangsters and Dope-Trafficking. The People are destroying themselves from within, just like we're doing here in Fifeville.

"I sold Dope in Fifeville to the Old, and the Young, to school kids . . . didn't matter. I thought I was a Big Shot doing that, yo. Now, when I think about how I abandoned my People, an' my Children, to the Crack-Pipe and Welfare-Pimping, I wished I had 've been killed a lot sooner, that would've been better for everybody, Blue. There are a lotta women and young mens who's *HIV* Positive cause-a the Crack and Heroin I sold them. It led to the spread of AIDS. Blue, I was the worst kind of Monster.

"THE GREAT CREATOR done showed me how my living Children will grow up to be Gangsters and a Prostitute. They're already using Marijuana at Six, man. They won't make it as long as I did. I can't see eighteen years for either of them without them going to jail, or being gunned down. I'd give anything to be able to come back and warn them, Blue. They go become Killers just like they dead Father was.

"Blue, seems like my short life went for nothin', yo. You got a chance to not go out like that, G. Take it My Cousin. Take it and live! Find my kids, and Ivy's, and help them change, Blue. They're Slokmn Blood, man. You got a chance to make a difference. Do your best to make Amends for us all. It's too late for Ivy and me, we're going to have to face Eternity the way we entered it But you don't have to go down that Path. You can speak to the Homeys and they'll listen to you just because of Ivy's and my reputations. But you can deliver a different message then we did. THE GREAT CREATOR is counting on you, Benjamin Luther Slokum! . . ."

Grandma Mildred's and Ivy's Ghostes appeared beside Roy's. Grandma Slokum spoke: "Blue son, we can only stay in the material world a short while. Then we must return to the Ethereal World, where we will be alone to wander endlessly to nowhere.

"Roy sees only himself. He may look up at intervals and see the Angels of God. But they will be looking scornfully at him.

"Ivy will likewise travel through the Ethereal World. He is at a Higher Level than Roy, but still alone with his thoughts until the End of the Age. That is all that is on this side of Creation for Ivy and Roy. ·

"I am trapped at the top of The Purgatorial Order. I can see other Souls who are in the same position that I am in. Like Ivy and Roy, I am without the comforts of a Human Body. We can only present a Spectral Image of ourselves. But I can feel the Cold. Like Ivy and Roy I cannot change my situation. It is fixed by the Life I Lived while I walked the Earth. Therefore there is no Human Association on this side of things. We must remain Alone, Silent, and Contrite until The End of This Age.

"When I make myself appear, I seem to be wearing a Halo. I have that because I stayed there with my Grand Babies when I didn't have to. So, I have a Halo like all Grandparents do who raised their grandchildren. All of the Unrequited Love that you show while you walk the Earth will earn you some recognition from THE GREAT CREATOR!

"Blue, go find your Nieces and Nephews and steer them away from the Thug-Life. Be there for them.

That Love if shown, may Cover the Multitude of Your Sins.

"Blue, Listen! This is most important! Meditate on what I am about to tell you and keep this very close to your heart from this moment on. You will tum away from the World Ivy and Roy exposed you to if you understand what I'm going to say to you.

"Grandson, The Guns and Ammunition that y'all bought and sold came from factories from over in White-Man's Land. The Dope is grown in the Lands of People of Color in Asia, Africa, and Latin America. But it is imported to America by many and several White Men. When you sell Dope to your fellowman you're just helping to kill-Off Black People. But you are helping white people grow richer by the Genocide you perpetuate against your own people. Some Whites in-charge in America want to kill us all slowly, Blue. They are making Millions doing so. Can't you see that, Blue, Honey?

"Think about it. The Dope and Guns are causing you all to form Gangs to kill one-another. Fathers abandoned their children to the violence. Mothers take food out of their children's mouths so that they can give that money to Crack-Dealers. If this continues, it will put an end to Poor Blacks in America-that's the most of us, Blue, Darling.

"I'm g-going to ask you to do somethin' that's extremely hard to do It may hurt you all over to actually do it, but it is what you must first do. I want you to completely forgive Jamie 'nem. That is the only way that you will be totally free-and that tis the only way that our People will fight fire with water instead of more fire! Blue . . . It is the only way that many of us, if not most-will survive! We don't want no more of us to end up like Ivy, Roy, and Me,

The Ghosts of Grandma Slokum, Ivy and Roy, suddenly became a Dusty Mist, that became a Hazy Cloud, and then that dissolved into nothingness.

Blue mumbled: "I must be dreamin' or somethin'. Can't no ghosts be talkin' ta' me like they was human. Man-I got's 'ta be buggin' out or somethin'. It Must be cause-a the beatin' them Law Dogs put on me, yo. They done near 'bout kilt me. Man"

As Blue tried to turn over on his jail bunk he was startled by a suave-dude, who spoke in a shrill, croaking voice. The dude could've passed for white or black. He was probably mulatto or something.

Blue was between being awake and in a dream-like state. The dude standing in the jail cell was like a character out of a movie, like the 'Super Fly,' but was more real than that He had on a light-blue, two-piece suit that seemed to be of silk or some other very shiny threads. His pink big-cuffed ruffled shirt was graced by diamond-studded gold cufflinks, and had ample edging on its ruffles. He wore a broad blue tie featuring nude girls of different races seemingly in dance poses on the front of it. It was graced with a diamond studded gold tie-pin. His Alligator kicks were so highly polished that they were like bright lights around his feet. He primped around in the cell only looking at Blue out of the side of his face as he started to Rap:

"Yo, Blue, Baby. I'm Master D, The Grand Mack Daddy, yo. Can't let you go without dropping this heavy shit on you, Dog. Hey, yo, check this shit out:

"I'm the Pimp of the time. Yo, I'm rocking the rhymes. Hey! I'm calling the shots, cause I run the shops. Gold Rings, Diamond Things, Crack-and all of that! Cause I'm the man with a million-dollar Plan. My Mo-Joe's working all over the world; on every street corner-and all over America! The Dope-Dealer is just another one-a my squirrels. Unless I say so, you can't get down with none-a my girls.

"I'm the Man, I got the Ruler in my hand; to measure the worth of all the Players; and the Gangsters, the bunnies and the honeys; the bitch-who'es and mother lodes who rock the block. Check this out: I can get you a hold on every Sweet-Honey on the street that you ever wanted to meet.

"I got quick dough to give you, yo! Dog, I'm Money-bound, I got Bankroll all over Town. That's how I get down! Get on my route and you'll never do without! I don't care what Grandma Mildred, Ivy, and Roy say, you stick with me, Dog, or Jamie 'nem gonna do you in one day! G. are you feeling me? ..."

Blue had to interrupt there: "Look, yo, I know who you be. Man-my Grandma would call you, 'THE DEVIL!' Hey, I done seen too many movies 'bout you dog. So you can't ..."

The Mack Daddy got a little bit agitated. "Blue-Blue, yo-yo-yo, Dog! They don't call me by that name no more. I'm now 'MASTER D, THE GRAND MACK DADDY!'

"I rule the streets, all the rackets, and I'm in all the businesses in America and the World. They're all in my tree. They all owe me. Or they got to deal with my people. They all got to be afraid of me, yo. They better confide not do anything to get on my bad side! I may not be Heaven sent, but I can kill a President! Nobody fucks with me, Dog, for-real. They all know I got the power down here! Blue, it ought to be a bet: Why would you wanna get away from all of that?

"Check this out, yo: I can get that Honey, Doisha, who is all the Rave. I can turn her into your sex slave, dog! Jamie gets her any time he wants her. Yo . . . think about it, it's time you made her purr!

"I got ten-thousand dollars in fine threads you can have from over there to, right here. Home-slice, I own the guns and ammunition factories all over the World. I make all the bullets. I direct the battles in every war-even in gang wars, cause for sure, I run the damn Show, G!

"Look up my-man, I'm ready to give you some Dap in Charlottesville. All you'll have to do is kill Jamie, an' you can rock the map. And you've gotta say to me that you will never speak another word about what Grandma Mildred's Ghost dropped on you, today! Then all you got to do is Hit the Streets and make Jamie Pay. He's your sworn enemy anyway, yo. Like old school, I'll make the good times roll for you, Dog!"

Blue had heard enough: "Yo, Mr. Grand Daddy, or whatever; you check this out: Your costly suit an' shiny shoes be damned. You can take your gold watches, diamond rings and whatnot, and go fuck yourself You ain't 'bout nothin'! Grandma, Ivy, and Roy 'nem's all dead cause-a you! I can't get with that. I 'ma go back to the streets and make that change that Grandma wants me to make. Fuck that Thug-Life you're rapping about. See ya 'round Sucker, you lose; you got that?"

The Mack Daddy stomped the floor for a minute like a Flamingo Dancer. His eyes grew blood-red. His twisted mouth got even more turned up around the edges. His beady-little black eyes grew even narrower. He yelled as loud as he could in his croaking voice, as he shook his red-Afro and it bounced around on his flat head: "We'll see about you, Blue, okay. I'll make you pay! You gonna have to 'Pay The Cost To Be The Boss!'"

The GRAND MACK DADDY faded away as Blue's consciousness completely revived. He thought

"Ain't it funny how The Daylight Just Caused 'Master D.' to be blotted out?"

Chapter Four

A rotund jail guard that resembled the "Pillsbury Dough Boy," in a brown uniform, with a black mustache that resembled "Bruto's," in the "Popeye," cartoon series, spoke to Blue, who was curled up in a jail-bunk. "Mr. Blue Siok.um. How're you doing this morning?"

Blue mumbled: "I'on kno' ... I'm hurtin' all over. Feel like I hit my head, or somethin'. What happen ta' me?"

The fat guard got a twisted smile on his huge face. "Well ... Let's just say, you had me worried there for a little while. I was gonna run you up to the UVA if you didn't come out of it by this morning. I reckon, well . . . you must've fell and hit your head on that iron bed, or something like that You don't remember nothing about what went on, Mr. Blue?"

"I remember two cops askin' me questions an' all. One of them kicked me up beside my head. That's what I remember ..." Blue said rubbing the left side of his sore face. "Owl Man that's hurts like Hell!"

The jail guard chuckled sarcastically. "Well. Mr. Blue, you were mumbling the names of your departed relatives all through the night At times, it was like you were having a great-big-o'-nightmare. That was why I didn't send you to the Hospital. I could see that you weren't dead or dying. You seemed very much alive. One time, it seemed like you were tying to rise up out of your bunk. You were crying, and you vomited all over that sheet on your bunk. That let me know you were still in the 'Land of the Living' ..."

Blue spoke excitedly, "You mean I ain't been awake? Now, I get it ... I was knocked the hell out! You say I fell and hit my head, but I got to wonder. Did those cops beat me down like that? I got a big headache, and too many bruises all over my head and arms to done just fell out of bed and hit my head on this bunk in here. I can feel that I took a hell-uva beatin'! That's what really went down, ain't it?"

The jail guard shook his head but tried to ignore Blue's questions. He frowned before he answered.

"Well ... Mr. Blue. It's just good to see that you're fine. But . . ."

Blue shook his head a little and cocked it to the side. "Well, yeah. Y'all done beat up on a Minor. I ain't nothin' but sixteen. I know y'all can't do that to somebody underage. Now what 'cha got to say 'bout that?"

The jail guard stepped back from the bars a little. He put his left hand up to his top lip and twirled the end of his mustache a little. "Well you don't have to worry too much. We won't charge you with resisting arrest or assaulting an officer; and, certainly not with killing anybody. That gun we found along beside you is illegal though. We could charge you with that-but, no we won't. See, you're one-a those in the Young, Loud, Fast, and Stupid Generation. Y'all don't think before you do nothing. You just follow some shitty leader who may be as wrong as Hell-like some-a your Civil Rights Leaders."

One of the things the guard ranted and raved about hit home for Blue. "Did you say . . . I ain't go be charged with killin' nobody?" His voice filled with excitement.

"Yep. They ain't got no reason to hold you. The gun beside you had never been fired. Only your sidekick's gun had been fired. The bullets from it didn't hit your Granny. We're gonna have ta' let you go Mr. Blue.

"A Miss Misty Burgher Meister, a volunteer up at The Salvation Army on Ridge Street, ran down the alley between Fourth and Fifth Streets Southwest. She saw the whole thing. We can't use her name on anything legal, but she says, you ran around the house and hid. Roy and the Posse got into a gun battle. They shot Roy and your Granny. They fled like scared crows when your Granny got shot.

"We ain't gonna file no gun charges on you. You can go home and see about burying your kin-folk. We've called your Legal Guardian, 'Franklin Frye Tinsley.' We're gonna release you into his custody as soon as he arrives down to the jail. Now, how does that sound?"

Blue was glad to be getting out of jail, but, not so glad to be released to Uncle Frank. He hated the fact that Daddy Herb had "stolen" Velma out of the Tinsley family. Even though Herb was not that dark skinned, he was thought to be too dark to marry into the muckety-muck Tinsley Family. Uncle Frank didn't want anything to do with the "lowly Slokum Family." Now, Blue would have to be under the care of someone who hated him worse than "White Racists," for two years.

Blue wanted to know: "Did Miss Burger Meister see who did the killin's?"

The jail guard got a little twisted smile on his fat face. "Yep! We've on that right now. One-a the Posse boys pulled the trigger. We got to figure out which one did that."

Blue wondered what the Hell? "Man, I told-ya' who did that, the whole time y'all was beatin' my ass down near 'bout to death! It was-read-my-lips-Jamie Charles, I know the Dude's name. Go get him, he did this shit to my family. Why y'all pussy-footin' round like that?"

The guard chuckled humorlessly. "We can't just take the word of a Suspect. We have-ta verify what you're saying through some other witness. Miss Burger Meister's only one witness. There were fifteen or twenty people standing around on their porches and some in the streets that day. We're questioning them. Then, we can make some arrests based on our investigation. That's how the Law works, Mr. Blue."

Blue shook his head. "Man, my Granny was scared. Everybody in the 'Hood is too scared to talk to any of y'all. They all know if they 'Snitch' the Crew will take 'em out, or one-a they family. So ain't nobody gonna say or do nothin' ta help y'all in your investigation. If Granny had pulled one-a us off the Set, the Crew would've got to her, or would've taken us out in revenge, yo. That's how it be, man. That's why someone outside of the 'Hood had to be the one to rap to y'all."

The jail guard shook his head too. "Mr. Blue, that's a damn shame, now ain't it?"

"What'cha mean?" Blue asked.

"Well, you Negroes, ah, Blacks, you all're living in a climate of fear. That's not living at all. I think that is the worst way to live. President Reagan is making a lotta changes in the government so that you people can get out of the ghetto and do better things. But you can't do nothing if you don't get out of the drugs, fear, and the stupidity of killing one-another. That's all to it."

Blue agreed with the "half-truths," the guard spoke. "Yeah, dude, I got that. I heard the word: 'Reaganomics,' before, but ain't nothin' but more guns, more drugs, and no jobs trickled down to us in the 'Hood so far. Grandma Sloknm b'lieved in President Jimmy Carter, though. She was a Democrat.

"I b'lieve we gotta make things better for ourselves. There ain't gonna be no Magician in the White House, or anywhere else, who's go move us up equal to y'all. We go have-ta do that.

"And as for the stupidity of us killing each other, you people have been doing that from Day-One. That's led to World War One and Two. In America y'all fought a War for Independence; a French and Indian War; A War with Spanish America; The Indian Wars; The Civil War; The Vietnam Conflict; A Conflict with North Korea; and now, a Cold War with Russia and the Communist Countries. A lotta Whites are killin' each other and have been every day. But y'all always manage to get back together to protect yourself aft.er y'all's small and Great Wars.

"I grew up in Fifeville it's true, but I ain't ignorant. I read books. I made good grades at Buford, Forest Hill, and now, at Lane. I got a B Average. I got some knowledge. But I choose to be with my 'Peeps'-in case you're wonderin'-that means 'People,' in the 'Hood. We hate 'Nerds,' and 'Snitches,' more'n death. So I don't t:ry-ta represent none-a that, yo. I been t:ryin' ta be a Down-Thug. But, I don't have the stomach for a lotta that. Too much killin'. Too much jazzin' the girlies. Too many single-moms. Too many dope addicts. It's all going down to the 'Cross-Roads,' already, yo. Too many of my Peeps are ending up like Granny, Roy and Ivy; kno' ah' I mean?"

The jail guard answered: "Yep, I do. I hope a lot more people like you come to think like you seem to be doing. I sense that a dramatic change is happening inside of your head, if not in your heart. What I don't understand is, how? Thugs don't usually come around like that after someone put a hit on their love ones. What'll make you stay in school and learn? What makes you feel the way you say you do now?"

Tears came to Blue's eyes. "Man, it's like 'Scrooge, in The Christmas

Carol.' Three Ghosts visited me while I was out, Ivy's, Roy's and Grandma Mildred Slokum's. They spoke to me plain as you're doin' right now.

"'What I got from them all was: I know now what Granny'd been talkin' 'bout all the time she tried to talk to us. I know there is a 'Life After Death. There is a Promised Land.' You will go there to answer for the 'Deeds done in your Natural Body.' There is a higher place than this present life where 'Truth and Justice,' actually exist. That thought alone 'Gives Me Happy Feelin's,' and 'I wanna Share It all over The 'Hood,' an' with everybody.

"When I get out of here, I'm goin' ta go back to Fifeville and I'm gonna t:ry to save the Homeys from the wrong path I was helping to lead them down. I share the guilt for being responsible for some-a the deaths of so many people-including my love-ones. The Ghosts changed me. I know a lotta people don't b'lieve in Ghosts. I didn't either 'til now. But I 'ma changed man now. I don't wanna be a Thug no more. That's all over for me."

The jail guard had allowed the corners of his eyes to get a little bit moistened. "Mr. Blue, that's good to hear. Very seldom does that happen in here. Most people like you get harder after coming in here and going through the process. But I can see that you're that one-in-a-million who is going to be different."

Blue stood at the jail bars in his briefs and sport socks. The jail guard handed him a red jumpsuit. He had soiled the clothes he had been arrested in to the point that he could no longer wear them. The jail did not have any inmate laundry services, so his clothes went out with the last batch of garbage. Blue got in his jumpsuit as quickly as he could. He figured it was certainly getting closer to the time for him to "get on up outta there." He got dressed and took a long look at the jail guard.

"What?" the guard asked. "What's the matter? What 'cha you looking at me like that for?"

Blue locked-in directly eye-to-eye with the guard. "Man, I take issue with one point you made, yo. Why you think I'd wanna, so-call, 'Leave The Ghetto?' Why can't I go back to it and help change my 'Hood? Wouldn't it be better for us all if my Peeps got our own act together?

"That's what I wanna do. I wanna go back and try to fix what's broke, especially the things I helped to break-you feelin' that? I don't wanna see y'all tearin' down no more of our 'Hoods, like you done ta' Vinegar Hill, yo. You kno' ah mean?"

The guard turned away from Blue's direct stare. **"Mr.** Blue, it may be too late for a lot of your neighborhoods. It's way too little too late! All you can do is the best you can. Trust in God! And let the System Work-and hope for the best! Can you understand that?"

Blue grimaced. "Look, man ... The System did its work to 'Gospel Hill,' it's now part of a piece of land that the new UVA hospital is going to be built on. Twenty-five or thirty families lost they homes to 'Eminent Domain.' Vinegar Hill now features 'Micky Dee's, and Wendy's-where's-the-beef,' and a big ol' Hotel what done replaced a lotta homes, and what used ta' be Black-owned businesses. Zion Union Church was raped by the Caterpillars, and building wrecking Crews. Where it once stood is now just a blank space on the Hill. Down there, it looks like some-a the pictures I seen in books about World War Two of what Germany looked like after America, Russia, France, and Britain got through bombin' it. Is that what ya' mean when ya' say, 'Let the System work?'"

The guard looked perplexed. He didn't know what to say, so he conveniently changed the subject. "Mr. Blue, your name is Benjamin Luther Slokum. But on the street you got the handle: 'Blue.' Why?

"Now, I understand why they call 'Big Blue Jesus'-who is actually Brock Thomason-Blue. He's very dark complexioned. He's 'Blue-Black.' But you're just nut-brown. How did you get the handle: 'Blue?'"

Blue shook his head. He was thinking: Why that Mo' Forker's think.in 'bout my Street Name for? What's up with that? But he decided to answer him. "Well, yo-it's like this: My Pops had great respect for Luther P. Jackson and Benjamin Quarles, two very respected Historians. So he named me Benjamin Luther after them. For my Moms and Grandma Mildred, my name was such a mouthful. So they took to callin' me, Bee-Lu. The 'Hood got ta' teasin' me an' 'Bee-Lu' got messed up an' became just 'Blue.' That's all to it. It ain't got nothin' ta' do with my skin-color."

A loud buzzing noise shocked Blue. He jumped back from the jail bars as they slid to one side and the door was opened. The guard allowed: "Your Uncle must be at the front desk. I reckon it's time for you to be getting out of here. You go on down the hallway to the front desk and they'll process you on out of the System-and Good Luck, Mr. Benjamin Luther 'Blue' Slokum. It's been real good talking with you-you take care now."

Uncle Franklin was waiting for Blue at the front desk. He had a twisted frown on his almost white face, with his dark-brown hair. He resembled "a tawdry-looking twin of Johnny Carson." He like the rest of that part of the Tinsley Family could pass for white. They disassociated with anyone darker than a paper bag even their close-kin family members. Blue's family-members were just too dark for them.

"You don't have to stand before the Chief. I'm your 'Legal Guardian' as of right now. I got the Power of Attorney over Mildred's Estate. You can't claim that until you're of age. That won't be for another two years yet. You're just sixteen," Uncle Frank said. "I have 'Custody' of you now!"

Blue was all frowns. "Uncle Frank, what does that all mean? Where will I live? Will I still be going to High School? How we gonna do all that, seeing as you live out in White Hall up in Crozet in a 'White Only,' neighborhood?"

Uncle Frank didn't want to answer a lot of questions. "Look, Ben, Blue, whatever-I can't take you up to White Hall. Nobody up there can ever know that I'm your Uncle; not even the West, Jackson, or the Jones families. We've all crossed over. Nobody wants to be a 'Damn Stupid Nigger! That's all to it!'

"I can't be seen coming and going down there in Fifeville. So, we will have to contact each other by phone. No one has to know that I don't live in Fifeville unless you tell somebody."

Blue was more than perplexed. "But how're we gonna settle things? Grandma had a Policy with Universal Life. I think she said it was for round 'bout (2) three-thousand dollars. I know she had 'bout two thousand in a Savings Account up at Virginia National Bank. She said that 'When I die, I want y'all to get a equal cut of what's left after expenses.' I'm the only one left now? How're we gonna do that?-I'm just a Minor? "W'ho owns the house now?"

Uncle Frank's face reddened. "If you think I want any of it, let me tell you, boy, I got a Farm up in Crozet, and I got an Apple Orchard on it. I grow Apples for the Byrd Apple Cider Brewing Company. I don't need any of your little penny-ante inheritance. So, 'Gangster,' Blue, don't worry about what Mildred left you all, hear boy!

"What my Accountants and Lawyers have discovered is that Mildred owed fifteen-hundred in Back Taxes on the House. That left three-thousand-five-hundred. The funeral is going to be handled by Belle's Funeral Home on Commerce Street. He's going to charge eight-hundred for both Mildred and Roy. That leaves twenty-four hundred, after three-hundred for taxes and fees.

"You can live in the House 'til you're eighteen. Then I'll have the Deed put in your name. Right now, I hold the Deed of Trust. You can stay in School I'll have a Carrier deliver one-hundred dollars every month until it amounts to twenty-four hundred. Then you will be on your own. You can get on the ICU Program at School You'll be able to work part-time up at the UVA. I hear that they're hiring a lot of you boys up there. So much the better for us all. That's it Blue, boy. Do you understand how this is all going to go down?

"One thing, though, you must never show up at my Place in Crozet. I will not acknowledge you. My wife is white, and so are my children. They don't want to have nothing to do with you, boy-is that clear?"

Blue got a nasty snarl on his face. "Unc' Frank, if you call me a 'Boy!' again, I'm go take you out, yo! Is that clear?" he yelled.

Blue and Uncle Franklin Frye Tinsley went on out of the front doors of the jail to East Jefferson Street.

Blue went one way and Uncle Frank went another.

Grandma and Roy were *buried beside her husband and Ivy on the left side of Oakwood Cemetery. It was an area of Oakwood that was overgrown with weeds, shrubbery, trees, and some discarded trash. It was Unhallowed Ground It received no maintenance, mowing, or decorations.*

Chapter Five

It was late in the evening before Blue got back to his home on Fifth and Dice. The streets were almost deserted, except for a couple of the Crew walking around like sentinels on guard duty. Blue got the key that was hidden in a metal box under the steps. He opened the front door and walked into the house.

The memory of Grandma Mildred was so strong that he could almost hear her asking, "Blue . . . is that you?" Or hear Roy dashing into the front room to verify that no enemy had invaded the place. Or hearing Ivy call out, "Blue, what ′sup Dog? How's the Set going down? Everything alright, yo?"

Blue would answer, "Hey, yo, everythin's kickin' it like it ought-ta. Y'all can chill" He'd go on up to his room upstairs beside Grandma Slokum's. Ivy and Roy always slept downstairs. But now there was nothing but, "The Sound of Silence," in the place. That was pretty scary to him.

He was thinking: *What am I go do now? I'm all alone. I ain1" go tnobody I can really turn to. I gotta do this all by myself. I guess I gotta stay in school. I can't roll with the Crew no more! I got to get on up outta there. I gotta get my Homeys to give-it-up. I gotta get em to turn away from the Dope, Murder, Bling, and Grangbangin'. That G-Thing ain't cool at all, its suicide. I don't want no more parts of it!*

Blue went into Ivy's room and moved a tall bookshelf back a little. There was a little door behind it that was once an opening to a little closet. The closet was about six-by-four feet. In that space Ivy, and Roy *kept, "hot-money," stacks of tens, twenties, fifties, and hundred dollar bills.* Blue never knew how much was there, only that it must have been thousands of dollars. He knew that the money was "Blood Money." But he decided he'd have to use it He knew that what Unc' Frank was going to send him, and what he'd make as an ICU participant was not enough to eat off of, pay the utilities, and school fees. He could work twenty-five hours-per-week, at two-dollars-per-hour. He knew that the UVA paid semimonthly. He could expect to make about one-hundred dollars each payday. His take-home pay would be about eighty-five.

Early in the morning the very next day after Blue had gotten out of jail, a loud knock on the front door woke him up. He got into his Levi Jeans, and a pair of Air Jordan's. He pulled on a Red Skins Sweat Shirt. He scooted down the steps to the hallway to the front door. He snatched it open.

"Yo, Blue, I gotta drop some news on you, Dog!" Harry Anderson, Ivy's main "Yard Dog," was standing on the deck wearing Levi Jean pants and Jack.et, tan Timberland Boots, and a black Sailor's Cap. Those were "Crew Soldier's Battle Attire." "You gotta get strapped, man. Brutus Hanson, over on Sixth and-a-Half Street, our New Crew Officer (CO), done got tipped, yo. Jamie's got word that you were getting out today. He's getting a couple of his Low-Riders together right now. Me an' my Main-Dog, we been sent over here to represent!

"Blue, they gonna roll up in here and take-out whomever gets in their way. Word! I sent for Poochie Burton, who took over for Roy. Poochie go be wearing a Camouflage Ranger Outfit. He'll have an Uzi tucked away in the folds of his jacket. I got a fully-automatic Glock, Thirty-Magazine, Pistol. We want you to come stand with us against Jamie 'nem. We'll make sure things go be different this time, yo. You feel me?"

Just then Poochie arrived from down Fifth Street. He was wearing a green, Ranger's Camouflage Outfit with tan Timberland Boots, and a black Sailor's Cap. He wore a pair of dark glasses. Both men had full black beards, and heavy mustaches. Both were about six-one tall, and looked to weigh two-hundred pounds. Both showed no signs of fear. They were ready to throw-down to the very end.

Poochie was out of breath. He warned: "Blue, man, yo, word-up, all the Homeys up on Grove, Ninth Southwest, Nelle, Seventh Southwest, Sixth, and Upper Fifth, done threw-in with Jamie 'nem. Sixth-and-a Half is still behind you, Blue. I was too close to Ivy to let his Baby Brother get taken-out like that, yo. So, I'm with you to the bitter end, Dog. What you want me to do, yo?"

With a sad voice, Harry said, "They saw what happen to you and your Peeps, Blue. They's scared that Master D will have them taken-out just like that along with they family. So, they're trying to play it safe by joining the Rats and going along with the Plan.

"I'm with you and Poochie. I go way back to before Ivy came in. I helped to 'Jump Ivy an' Roy in!' I loved y'all's Grandma Mildred like a Mother. I'm fired-on-up against Jamie 'nem. I wanna do Jamie-to the-death! Yo-Word! You feel me?"

The screeching wheels of a vehicle meant that someone was recklessly driving towards Fifth by coming around the corner from Seventh to up Dice. All had to know that Jamie 'nem were on their way to the Comer of Fifth and Dice.

A new, black Cadillac Escalade rounded the corner. The front door swung open before it came to a complete stop. Out jumped Jamie Charles, attired as always in a tan Safari Suit, black Combat Boots, a red blue-and-green, multicolored tam-cap, on top of long Dreadlocks. He was holding an AK-47 Machine Gun in his left hand. It had a Thirty-Shot Magazine stuffed in it. Jamie was snarling and frowning like an enraged Doberman Pincher.

"I see ya' still standin' on me corners over y'ere, mon. Tain't no bloodcloth Thugs goin-ta be pon me corners less I say so. Roy be dead! Ivy be dead! Where-ya goin' Lll' Blue Boy? Ya-go run 'way, piss ya' pants like ya-did a-fore? Ar-ya go join me Crew or die? Tain't no ot'er way!" Jamie yelled in a Jamaican scream. He walked back and forth waving his AK-47.

Harry drew his gun and so did Poochie-but nobody fired.

There were guns pointed out of the Escalade's windows. They did not fire either.

Blue got tears in the corner of his eyes. He stood still. He trembled all over, but not from fear.

Jamie continued to rant and rave: "Blue . . . ya' ain't got no pistol in ya' hand. Why ya' bitchin' ot' like a r'assclot Bandulu ar', Battymon? Get-up on-ya feet like a real mon, an' face the wrath of a Rastamon 'Haile Selassie-n-Jah-be-praised!'

"Them tears in ya' eyes be for naught-ya' d'ink Jah go come sav-ya? Y'ere-a Thug, now! I'ma send-ya below to the damned. Ya' hear me, Bloodclaat?"

Those holding deadly weapons pointed at their enemies were so shocked they lowered the weapons. To them what they were witnessing was "Fucking Amazing!"

With big tears running down his cheeks, Blue blurted out: "Jamie, you don't know what-ya doin'. You be ready to help our people's haters, yo. While I was knocked out in the jail cell, I got in touch with my Dead Peoples. They came ta-me like Ghosts, an' they dropped a mighty message on me.

"They 'splained that we's killin' one-nother wit' guns, dope, single-parentin', and whatnot! Man, we gotta stop all that shit!

"Jamie . . . I hate what-ya did ta-my family, yo. Just a coupla' days ago I might've been able to pull a trigger on-a gun an' take-ya out. But right now, I swear 'fore God, I ain't go never kill a Human Being, or do nothin' ta-cause the death of my fellowmen. Bad as ya-are, you's one of those.

"Let my homeys go. Go-head-on kill me. I don't care. But let the killin' stop wit' me. In the name of 'Jah,' or My God, I'm go forgive-ya ahead of time. I'ma do that 'cause I know ya-don't know what-ya doin'"

Jamie's face twisted up like the features on an African Death Mask. He yelled: "What! What-ya be sayin'? I 'ma get . . . I don' heard 'nough! I gotta shut this bumboclot mouth, dirty r'ass bud up! Master D wants-'im dead!"

Everyone raised his gun and got ready to use it. Blue closed his eyes and let the tears run down. He was expecting the worst. He was thinking that at worse he'd get to go to "The *Bosom of the Ancestors*", A Blinding Light appeared in the cloudless sky. It was like an extended streak of Lightning that lasted for about five minutes. Blue observed that Jamie, and his Crew, and his Sidekicks were standing up like in a daze, like they were asleep. The Ghost of Grandma Slokum appeared to Blue. Her clothes were brilliantly bright like the Sun. There was no stain on the Hem of her Gown. Her voice was musically smooth like someone singing in a choir.

Grandma Slokum spoke to Blue and he could feel every word she said deep inside: "Benjamin Luther, you will be able to carry on your work now. Ivy will no longer be in pain. Roy will be able to move around freer, but they will not be let out of Purgatory. They must remain until the End of this Dispensation.

"I have been let out of Purgatory! My Garment has been cleansed. I have been forgiven! We helped to turn you around and THE GREAT CREATOR has granted us a reprieve of our former condemnations. You can now go forward, but Beware! The Road Will Get Rougher after this moment, Grandson. Remember We Love You! THE GREAT CREATOR loves you and our Great Ancestors Love you. We will wait for you in Paradise. You will come to be with us forever if you continue in 'The Path of Righteousness!' I will not be able to appear to you again. THE GREAT CREATOR will guide you "

Grandma Slokum's Ghost seemed to rise up from the sidewalk towards Heaven. She disappeared like a streetlight being turned off. Blue blinked his eyes. He felt emboldened and courageous inside.

It seemed like Jamie and his Crew came back to life. So did Harry and Poochie. All of them had dropped their guns on the sidewalk.

Poochie moaned: **"Man,** what just happened?"

Harry asked: "Blue, did you see that Blinding Light, Man? What was that!"

Blue blinked his big eyes. His face had a certain shine on it like a newly polished tile floor. It was something about the way that the comers of his mouth seemed to have changed. It made his natural frown become a genteel smile.

"I think I done had another one-a those experiences that Grandma Slokum used to say, 'Was the Lord speakin' ta-me.' I'm go pay attention to it this time," Blue said.

Harry asked: "What'cha mean Dog?"

Poochie asked: "Ya' mean you getting outta the Crew, Blue? Y 'know, we get 'Jumped-In,' but the only way out is Death, yo!"

Jamie dropped his expensive gun on the sidewalk when the Blinding Light appeared. He saw the clear outlines of The Ghost of Grandma Mildred. She was pointing her right trigger-finger at him. Jamie yelled: "Mon . . . Bredren . . . Jah done cursed us! JuJu is 'pon Me. Babylon is comin' down now. We gotta move 'way from over here from this Bumboclot, Bandulu, place, lest we be damned!"

He forgot to pick up his gun-left it on the sidewalk. He slammed the door of the Escalade shut. The vehicle sped away scratching its wheels as it went along.

Blue, Harry, and Poochie went into the House on the Comer of Fifth and Dice. They all forgot to pick up their guns too.

Once in the front room Blue said, "Listen, y'all. I can hear sirens blastin' an' whatnot. Ain't that funny?

"I know ain't nobody over here called Five-0. What 'sup with that, yo?"

Harry frowned, "Man we gotta go get them pieces off the sidewalk, yo. That might put you back in the Slammer, Blue. We left them out yonder ..."

Poochie said, "I'ma come help-ya, Dog. Blue you lay low. If the cops pick us up ya-won't go-down for gun possession. I'll swear the pieces were all ours."

Blue looked out of the front room windows and saw a Black-and-White Police Cruiser and a Paddy Wagon arriving on the scene on the Fifth Street side of the Comer. Several heavily armed policemen jumped out of the Paddy Wagon. Another Cruiser arrived and more heavily armed policemen jumped out of it.

Harry and Poochie had just gotten to the front door, but had not gone out of it. They came back to the front room windows to observe what was happening, so they could "Cop a Plea!" with the cops that the guns belonged to them and not "Big Blue!" but only if they had to.

The cops walked slowly up and down Fifth Street, and a little ways up and down Dice Street, with shotguns mounted on their shoulders at-the-ready to shoot at any "Suspect." But they saw none. Two of them gathered up the guns on the sidewalk. They scooped them up and put tags on each one. Those doing so wore helmets and thick-dark-glasses. They all looked carefully at the house on Fifth and Dice but none approached it. Blue thought that was mighty strange. Just like that-they got back into their vehicles and sped away.

One wearing sergeants stripes on his uniform had the audacity to wave at Blue, Harry, and Poochie before he got into his vehicle. His wave was a dismissive wave like a, "Good Riddance" gesture.

"Somethin' ain't right 'bout all this, man. What, vas them cops over here for? Who called them? Why did they look so disappointed at findin' out nothin' happened?" Blue asked. "Why didn't they even ask us at least one question?"

Poochie shook his big head. "Man, let's go 'round to Brute's house on Six-and-a-Half an' see if that Cat knows what 'sup with that shit. Blue, ya-gonna have some 'Juice' with Brute, yo. Ya-stood Jamie 'nem down just wit' ya stare. Them Posse Dudes just ran like rabbits, Dog! Check that shit out, yo!"

"Yeah Dude, but that's not what it's all about. I'm feelin' a new direction, yo. Let's go on over ta Brute's pad. I'll run it all by y'all over there," Blue said.

It is in the afternoon when Blue, Poochie, and Harry bopped to the five-room bungalow in the middle of Six-and-a-Half Street. The house is situated so that it is not too far from the corner of Cherry Avenue. Two similar houses are located before it on the left going South. Two houses are situated after it. Four similar houses are situated on the right side of the narrow street across from where Brutus lives. Six-and-a Half Street starts off the Comer of Seventh Southwest and Dice. It extends for about a-half mile straight to Cherry Avenue. It is difficult for two cars to be driven past each other on that Street. There was no sidewalk, only curve and gutter.

A five-foot hulk of a man came to the wide front room windows as Blue, Harry, and Poochie walked to the front of the white and green stucco house. It had a porch and green and white metal porch furniture. He was wearing Black Culottes, Red Air Jordans, a White-Bulky T-Shirt, and a Blue-and-Red New York Yankee's Baseball Cap. He was called "Brute" because of his musculature. He was built like a giant, like "Goliath." His voice was very bass, and sounded almost like he was hoarse when he talked.

He came out on his porch carrying a Glock Nine in his waistband. "What!" he exclaimed. "How you snitchin' Bitches be still walkin' round. Jamie was s'sposed-ta end all-of-that shit!"

Poochie and Harry both had Glocks in their waistbands-it was standard equipment for them. They reached for those instinctively.

"What 'sup with you, Brute?" Harry asked, excited and surprised at what he was hearing.

Poochie let his hand relax because Brute was pointing his Glock in their general direction with it laying to the side. Brute's big horse's eyes were glaring at them, and he could see what could happen. "Brute, my man, what-ya talkin 'bout. I'm one-a the Crew's Main-Yard Dogs. I wou'da never snitched on nobody. Wha'cha mean, yo?"

Nervously, Blue said, "Me neither. What 'cha mean, G?"

"All three-a y'all been pegged by Master D as Snitchin' Bitches. Blue, he says that's why the cops let-ya go. Ya-rapped! That's the only way they let-ya go without chargin'-ya wit' nothin'! I know how the System works, yo.

"Harry, and O' Poochie here, they's too close to the Slokum family. All y'all gotta go! I'm in charge now. Either y'all gotta go or me. I ain't goin' nowhere," Brute bellowed.

Blue scratched his head. "First of all, Brute, I gotta ask-ya somethin' man. I've always wondered who this 'Master D Guy,' is. I ain't never seen 'im.

"You ever seen 'im, Poochie? You ever seen 'im, Harry? Or have you, Brute?" Brute said: "No, I ain't never seen the Dude."

Harry said: "Come to think of it, I ain't never seen 'im either."

Poochie said: "Some little Light-Skinned Dude would come by my Crib with a note tellin' me who'd have-ta go next. Another tall dark Dude would show up with a brown envelope with the payment after the job was done. But I ain't never seen Master D. Wouldn't know 'im from Adam, yo."

"See, that's what's been botherin' me, yo. Who we be workin' for? Who we be killin' for; sellin' Dope for; Pimpin' for? It be some Dopey Dude we ain't never seen. We be nothin' but stooges, yo. None-a the O'G's be retirin' rich. They all're in jail, dead or on skid row. But this Master D who we all been workin' for just keeps rollin' on. What' sup with that shit, yo?" Blue asked.

Brute was holding the Glock in his right hand. He lowered it to his side. He was in wonderment.

"Come-ta think-a it, when I had-ta cap-a dude's knees, or break some-a they fingers, some guy fittin' the description y'all just gave came with a note too. And that same Dark Dude stopped by with the payment after the job. We be Master D's Flunkies, yo. That's where it's at!

"That same Light-Skinned Dude was by here yesstiddy. He gave me a note that said Blue had Snitched. Ya-know Snitchin's worse than killin'! A

Snitcher gonna have-ta be eliminated. So, Blue, your name came up, and the note said that I needed-ta send Poochie an' Hany ta go down with you.

"I's told that I was gonna be the 'CO,' Lead-Dog, 'stead-a Jamie Charles.' But that I couldn't get 'Made,' ′til all traces of the Slokum Family had been done-in. I knew that Jamie ′nem were the 'Great Eliminators.' I′ma fool, yo.

"Poochie, you ain't been nothin' but good-ta me. Ya-done everything I asked ya-to do. All the cold bloodied shit, you took that on like a Big Dog. You got that money from the streets, yo. I should've never let nobody turn me ′gainst -ya!

"Harry, man I was wit' y'all when Ivy got 'Jumped-In.' I was wit' y'all when Roy got 'Jumped-In' too. I 'ma O'G. I go way back. I'm gettin' where I'm gonna have-ta give that shit up. So, I was gonna throw-in wit' Jamie 'nem cause it seemed like they's gonna be the wave of the future. I needed a little insurance!

"Blue, I be sorry, Dog. I deserve a bullet ′tween the eyes, man. Since I came up here from Carolina, I've known-ya Peeps, yo. I done ate ya-Grandma's Cookin'! Master D. done made a fool outta me!"

Poochie pulled out his Glock. So did Harry. Brute stood with his Glock by his side. He let it drop to the floor. He got down on his knees. He wouldn't look up at the men he had betrayed.

"Go-head-on, shoot! I deserve it!" Brute shouted loudly.

Blue ran over and got between Brute and his would be assassins. "No! Don't do this! That's what that Sucker, Master D wants us ta-do. He's puttin' one-a us against the other, ′til all of us kill one-nother! That Mo' Forker's tryin' ta-do 'way with our whole 'Hood, yo. Can't y'all see: We're just a bunch of stupid Patsies. We ain't even a decent Gang. We're just mindless Thugs, Young, Loud, Fast, Violent, and Stupid! "That shit caused me my Older Brother, My Grandma, an' my Cousin Roy. All my Peeps closest-ta me. "Brute, I don't want nothin' ta-happen-ta you. I want, you, Harry, and Poochie ta-come-in with me on this deal: We'll go find as many Homeys as we can, an' turn 'em against the Crew. We'll create a 'Crew for Peace!' We won't deal drugs! We won't kill nobody! We won't sell guns, an' we won't pimp none-a the women in our 'Hood.

"I 'ma go to School an' finish. I 'ma go-ta college if I can get in one. Y'all ought-ta do the same if ya' can. We need-ta get married an' give the

'Hood (2) an example of how they ought-ta live 'stead-a being hired guns for Mast.er D. Don't leave the 'Hood, like so many good people be doin'. Let's stay an' fix what we done broke."

Brute stood up, ran over to Blue and bear-hugged him. Tears ran down his muscle-bound face. He turned Blue loose and just stood there crying not embarrassed at all. "I'm with you, Lil' Blue. I'm with you, yo!" Brute said.

Strange enough, Hany and Poochie laid their guns on a metal chair on the porch. They came over and gave Blue a Crew Salute. They slapped hands and hugged him from side-to-side in that special way. Then two of the hardcore Thugs in the Crew joined Blue and Brute in a heartfelt cry; because inside, the "Hardest-core Thug" is still just a "Little Boy" in need of "Familial Love." He got lost in the shuffle when growing up, and became like a "Cornered Animal," like the difference between a Housecat and a Feral Feline. But even feral cats can be tamed.

Red-and-Blue Police Emergency lights started blinking. They punctuated that evening's arrival.

Chapter Six

Blue sat in the Courtroom different days and saw Brute get twenty years, without the possibility of parole, for the guns found in his house. Brute took all the blame for those. Forensics showed that one had been used in the murder of Buddy Doherty.

Harry had a Half.Ounce of Marijuana in his coat pocket on the day of his arrest. He got fifteen years for possession of Narcotics. He could get paroled in five.

Poochie got ten-to-twenty years for Brute turned State's evidence against him. He pleaded guilty to Aggravated Manslaughter and Drug Trafficking Charges. He could get paroled in seven years.

Blue was surprised that he did not get arrested or charged with any crime even though he was there when Brute, Poochie and Hany were snatched out of Brute's house, laid out on the sidewalk, handcuffed, and slung in the back of a Paddy Wagon like sides of slaughtered beef. The cops had ignored him. One pointed a finger at him and gestured, "Pow!" "He wants to put The Fear of God in me," thought Blue.

Jamie Charles was picked up the same day as Brute, Poochie, and Hany. Blue heard that he was charged with racketeering, murder for hire, and tax evasion. He was given two-life terms without the possibility of parole. The Posse seemed to have disappeared after Jamie Charles's arrest.

Blue went to Charlottesville High that fall. He shed his Thug outer-garments. He took to wearing two piece suits that he bought at Ed. Michtom's on West Main Street. He had three: a blue, brown, and a green one. For variety he mixed and matched the pants and coats to those. He sported a tie and white shirt every day. He exchanged his Air Jordans for Three pairs of penny loafers: a black, brown, and blue pair.

Blue applied for the Interscholastic and Corporations Utilization (ICU) program and got accepted. He was hired to wash dishes at Newcomb Hall in the UVA's main kitchen five-to-ten p.m. five days-per-week.

Blue missed seeing Roy, Ivy, and most especially, Grandma Slokum. He was not afraid to stay in the house because he had seen "Granny," in a dream and in "Spirit Form." He'd seen Ivy and Roy as "Ghosts." So, he thought, "I don't have any reason to be afraid of seeing them again." He took comfort in the fact that "Granny might be Looking Down on me to protect me. I think she is."

He knew how to pay the utility bills: gas, electricity, and sewage payments. What he did not know was how to pay the Real Estate and Private Property Taxes. There was no one to confide in. The Slokum family had turned against Mildred Slokum because, "She seems to be raising Criminals," Blue's aunties and uncles said. They wagged their heads when they saw Mildred at Church, and looked scornfully as she sang "Precious Lord Take My Hand "that brought tears to the eyes of the Pastor and many listeners in the Congregation at First Baptist Church. But all of her close relatives whispered behind her back and stayed their distance from her, and or her, "Wayward Boys," after Church. So, now that Grandma Slokum was gone, Blue was on his own. He had to figure out everything by himself.

Dressing the way he did was his first way of putting some distance between him and the Thug Life. The Crew stayed away from Blue because the cops were always watching Blue's house looking for some reason to swoop down on him and remove the last O'G from the Crew. They didn't want to get caught up in that.

Members of the Crew took to wearing odd-looking styles that Blue didn't recognize and couldn't get with. They wore baggy jeans, that they let hang off their buttocks. Some looked like a bean stalk in a feedbag sack. They had on bulky T-Shirts that made them seem clownish. Instead of wearing Timberland Boots, they wore Tennis loosely stringed, and unknotted. Many were Jeri-curling their hair and sporting braids that resembled Dreadlocks. They were copying the "Convict Persona," and wearing clothing that projected that. They still sold dope, pimped, and misused the young girls and women, and were just as violent as ever.

Many mornings Blue did not have to have his alarm clock wake him up. Some of the Homeys had large Portable battery-operated Radios and Cassette Players they called "Boom Boxes," that they played at top volume on the streets. They were pumping up sounds from Groups like NW A (Niggers With Attitude), Run DMC, and Public Enemy Number One. What Blue heard was not Music like he'd heard from James Brown, Sam Cooke, Major Lance, Jackie Wilson, Garry U.S. Bonds, Marvin Gaye, Joe Tex, Otis Redding, The Temptations, The Impressions, Four Tops, and Smokey Robinson; Dianna Ross and The Supremes, Dion Warrick, Patty Labelle, Tina Turner, Gladys Knight and the Pips, and Martha and The Vandellas: sounds out of MOTOWN. The groups he was used to listening to sang and played Love Songs.

But what the young Homeys were listening to was poems being chanted to sycophant beats with rhythms that resonated with the African-Talking Drums, and Congo Aesthetics. The Music seemed to coincide with Blue's reckoning of the Folk Proverb: "They Are Young, Loud, Fast, Violent, and Militant!" The music also seemed to be advocating a move away from peaceful protests to "Violent Revolution."

Blue was facing his last two years of School slaving in the UVA's kitchen wondering what his 'Hood was becoming. After all of the murders, arrests and convictions, the deaths of all of his closest loved-ones, literally nothing had changed, despite Reagan's so-called "get-tough on crime, and just say no to drugs," policies.

The Posse had disappeared or had become invisible. The Crew had split up into sub-crews that were divided against each other. There was the Westside Crew, the Tenth and Page Crew, the Rougemont and Sixth Street Southeast Crews, and the Washington Park Crew. When members of these various Crews bumped into one another at Tokyo Rose's Cafe, or Hardy's Restaurant, on Ivy Road, or The C&O Dance and Dine, on West Main, late at night, fights would break out and sometimes gunfire.

The Banging Life Blue wanted to leave behind. It was not who he wanted to be anymore. He took some of the money purged from the Blood of Crew Victims, and bought a forty-eight inch screen Color TV. He took to watching its screen whenever he wasn't hitting the books, or sloughing around in the grease and garbage in the kitchen in Newcomb Hall, washing dishes.

The ICU program was set up to acquaint students with the possibility of pursuing a career after high school graduation. An Association between the State, Federal, and local governments, and local businesses offered low-income students after-school jobs. These jobs were supposed to orient the students to pursue careers in the company they worked for after school. In the Newcomb Hall Kitchen, all Blue saw was Black Students stacking bus pans of dishes onto a conveyor belt so that they could go through a huge dishwashing machine. Then they had to unload the cleaned dishes onto racks and push those out into a hallway so the serving staff could haul them up on elevators to the main dining room to serve the students. Blue didn't see anything in doing that job as directing him to a clear career path. He stuck with it because he needed the hundred-seventy bucks it paid him. But he had no intentions of becoming a Career Dishwasher.

On the Dick Clarke Show, Blue saw Black performing Artist like James Brown, Major Lance, and Diana Ross and the Supremes singing their latest hits to an all-white audience. Before that, he had seen only artists like Pat Boone, Ricky Nelson, and Elvis Presley being featured on such shows, when he watched TV over at Brute's house. The Ed Sullivan Show featured Sammy Davis, Jr., Nat King Cole, Johnny Mathias, Eartha Kitt, and a new sensation: The Jackson Five, featuring Michael Jackson. Blue saw white chicks screaming and falling out all over the audiences at the performances of those Black Artists.

On the radio, Blue heard some new black artist "Rapping." They had names like "Dr. DRE. Easy E., Iced Cube, Ice Tea, Snoop Dogg, and Ja-Rule." The lyrics they spat out were filled with the pejorative, vulgar, terms: "Bitch, Who'e, Nigger, Mother Fucker, Honkies, and Cop Killers!" The DJ announced that this new Music Genre was "Hip Hop's, Gangsta Rap!" It was restricted to very late-night airing.

At School, Blue's face had been in the Daily Progress after he had been arrested as a suspect in the murder of his Grandma, and Cousin Roy. He wore a suit and tie every day to distinguish himself from the "Gangster Persona." But the new musical genre was red-hot to white kids at Charlottesville High.

He came to school this morning and walked onto the front lawn at School lined with neatly-trimmed Cedar Trees, around the Jeffersonian styled building. A couple of blondes with their hair worn frizzy to approximate an Afro, had on Jean Hot Pants so tight until way too much cleavage was exposed in strategic places. They had on tight halter-tops that also revealed too much of their private areas.

One came over to stand on either side of Blue on the broad long sidewalks gracing the School's front entrance. One flicked her bouncy hair. "Hi there," she said. "I know who you are. You're Big Blue the 'Gangsta' from over at Fifeville, aren't you?" She giggled.

The other said: "I dig where the Rappers are coming from. I love their Vibes, man. Those guys tum me on big-time! You're a real 'Gangsta,' right?

"I'm going to have a little party over at my house on Fifteenth Street Northwest this Friday. We live next to the Fraternity and Sorority Houses. A lot of Sorority Girls come to my parties. We all love 'Gangsta Rappers.' Do you Rap? Will you be able to come to my party-I'd love to have you, please."

He felt very uncomfortable. He said: "Look . . . I'm . . . I don't like to be called 'Big Blue.' My name is Benjamin. You can call me Ben or Benny. I'm not a Gangster. I used to hang with them one time, though. Now I'm a straight-up kinda guy. I'd probably be way too boring to you all at your party."

The girls winked at each other. One said: "Can you come wearing your 'Thug Threads,' though?"

Blue was not used to being popular at school. He didn't want to come as a "Thug," but he wanted to go to the party as the "New Me."

"What's y'all's names anyway?-and how old are you? Are y'all twins? You look so much alike."

One of the blondes was a few inches shorter than the other. She stepped in front of Blue. "My name is Carolyn Eileen Crossman. I turned eighteen this May. I'm a senior. I will graduate next May. I'm not her twin." She pointed to the other girl.

"No, we're no kin, Ben. I'm Cynthia Van Whitten. I'm seventeen. I'll be eighteen in December. Maybe our people came from the same part of Europe, or something-I don't know. Who cares?" the other blonde said. "Our parents don't know it yet, but we're going to bring them into the Twentieth Century in a very big way. We're of the age of consent, and, whatever! Even though we're just seniors in High School. Are you down with that?" she spoke very excitedly.

"I'll come to your party if I can come as just a Dude without Thug Fare. I don't want to be classed like that anymore. I just lost most of my family behind that Gangster scene. I want to be part of a new scene: Hope, not Dope. Love not Hate. Doing Good not Shedding Blood! That's where I'm at now. If I Rap about anything, that's what it's gonna be 'bout. Can y'all dig that?

"But, yo, I'm only a lowly underclassman. I'm just a junior this year. Are y'all sure you wanna invite me to your get-down? What 'cha homeys gonna say about that?"

Carolyn said: **"Hey,** that's age discrimination, Dude. We're trying to get that cut-down too. You're just *two* years or so under me. That's okay by me. Everybody will dig that over on my side.

"I knew Roy, and Ivy. They never came to my Sister's, Yolanda's parties, but believe me what Ivy and Roy supplied made the life of the party-if you get my drift. Blue . . . ah, Ben, I'm no Prima Donna, okay?"

Cynthia said: "I date a Black guy. His name is Briscoe Manley. He's going out for Linebacker this year. He's a junior like you. My Dad doesn't approve, but my Mom, Paulina says, 'God works these things out to suit Him. I hope He'll lead you to do what His Will Is. The Times They Are A-Changing!'

"Dad turns up his nose at him but, I know once he gets to really know Briscoe, he won't be able to not love him like I do. I've been on his side since I got out of Saint Anne Bellfield's Prep in the eighth grade. I came over here to public school and found Briscoe's charms. I'm with him and he's with me." She hugged herself and shook from side-to-side for a minute.

Ben was feeling these White Chicks in a big way. "I had no idea that you guys knew my Peeps, Ivy and Roy. For Ivy, y'all must've been just little girls. Roy, maybe y'all might've known him a little better. I'm sorry they sold your people drugs and shit, though. But that's what Thugs be about. That's why I'm outta the game and whatnot. A lotta young people got to be messed up from what we were doing ..."

Carolyn said: "Ben, we live in a Free Country. I say let people do what people want to do: drugs, sex, and whatever. The government's too strict about all of that. I think they ought to legalize Pot. I been smoking it since

I was a so-called, 'little girl,' and it has not done me any harm. I was glad when white girls could freely date black guys. I've been doing that too since I've been a little girl. We're get there slowly. I'm talking about Freedom. Real Freedom to do what the Hell We want to!"

Cynthia said: "You got that right, Carolyn. You with us, Ben?"

Both hugged Blue one on each side of him. He pulled slightly away from them. "I want some of the same things that you do but for different reasons, I reckon. I don't want to see any kinda Dope legalized. It'll do more harm than good. People are better sober, off alcohol, dope, and tobacco. I've put all of that shit behind me. I want a clean slate. That's why I say, I'd be boring at your party. Still want me to come?"

Carolyn and Cynthia looked at each other and winked again. Carolyn smiled broadly at Ben, showing even dentist-regulated teeth. "Man, I remember how you used to be dressed around here. You got that 'Thug"-Thing inside. We just have to help bring it back to the surface, man," Carolyn said.

Cynthia bumped Ben with her well-developed hips. She let her mid-body rest against his for a few seconds. She stood directly in front of him as she said: "Think of what you'd be missing if you don't come find out what's going on, Mr. Blue, Ben, yo," she whispered through puckered lips.

Ben got a little bit nervous. He'd never gotten too close to white girls before. He always feared that something might go wrong and the system would lynch him in the name of law Enforcement Gerald Scott Stints, a Black Knights' Star Running-Back, had a white girlfriend named Virginia that he saw at school mostly. They were juniors. When a teacher caught them wrapped-up in each other's arms in an unused room near the cafeteria, she called the Principal.

Stints had a Five-Cent (Five-Dollar) Bag of Pot in his back pocket The girl had four rolled-up Reefers in her jean pockets. She was expelled from school for the rest of the year. Stints was tried as an Adult and got forty years for "Possession of Narcotics in a School Zone with the Intent to Distribute." Statutory Rape Charges were thrown out, because Virginia and Gerald were of the same age. Ben knew that Gerald's real crime was "Having Sex with a White Girl." Now he was imprisoned without the possibility of parole. Ben wanted none of that He moved away from

Cynthia and she moved closer toward him. "Don't be scared of us, Ben. That's the way they want us to be. We got to pull together, you and me. If you're not Free to be together with me, than, I'm not Free either. My Dad, Milton, and my Mom Paulina, were hippies. They both had dated Black people before, but they're t:rying to keep me away from black guys. No way, man! I can do Pot right in front of them, but I've got to sneak around to be with Briscoe. The whole system of American Racism stinks like Skunk Shit if you ask me, Ben."

Bashfully, Ben smiled and said: "Will there be any Black Girls at your party? I'll be sure to come if there is."

Carolyn patted Ben on his back. "Yep, Big Ben, there will be. I know a girl you'd probably dig a whole lot She's a junior here from Harlem New York. Her father is an Assistant Coach for the Cavalier Football Team up at the UVA. I bet you'd groove on her, she's a real beauty. She likes tall, dark, and handsome guys like you. I got a feeling she'd get-down with you, you being a 'Thug' and all. She likes 'Bad Ass Boys.' So, yes, we have some Black-Hotties at our Parties. I can see by the glint in your eyes that you're very interested now, right? Yeah-you're into that, huh?"

Ben smiled. "Don't get me wrong, now. I'm not a racist or nothing. I like white-girls too but a Brother still gotta be careful in the South, yo, and that's For-real. Kno' ar' mean?" Ben said. "Yep, Ben. I guess I gotta let you get away with that one. But I'm down," Carolyn said.

"Me too; okay, gotta get to class, the bell's ringing. Ifl don't see you before, see you Friday, Ben, okay," Cynthia said.

Ben went up the steps to his homeroom behind the Principal's Office. His homeroom teacher, Mrs. Greta Pollstein, was a tall, thirtyish, bosomy Blonde with darting deep-blue eyes. She had a Marilyn Monroe Body, and long, silky blond hair, and she was very pretty even though she wore no makeup. She wore a fashionably-tight blue dress. She had on flat-black slippers. She wore no socks, or nylons. Her voice had a cigarette rasp to it as she said: "Class, now come to order. I'm sending around a roll-sheet Sign your initials beside your name so that you will not be marked absent for today."

Ben signed the roll. The bell rung and Ben went on to his first class: "American Political Systems."

The Government Class was just down the hall in room 151 from Ben's homeroom. It was taught by Dr. Wilk.es Straighter. He was an old gray-haired, bespectacled, professor that talked often of having parents that survived the "Nazi Holocaust." His thick white mustache was fluffy as were his eyebrows, and his neatly trimmed Van Dyke beard. He wore blue Seersucker suits during the warm months and gray Tweed's during the winter months. He had seemingly two pairs of wing-tips that he wore every day. One pair was brown, and the other black. He was like a copy of Colonel Sanders of the Kentucky Fried Chicken Franchise. His skin was swarthy and his nose prominent. He was a little on the fat side.

Dr. Straighter was a graduate of Duke University, where he had earned his BA, and MA degrees. He received his PhD from the UVA and remained in Charlottesville in the 1960s·. He married into the McMillan family from the Farmington Country Club region that exists on Old Ivy Road in Western Albemarle County. It is an "Old-Money-area." Dr. Straighter was "a big-fish in a little pond."

On this first day of school Dr. Straighter asked the Class, "How was your Summer Vacation Class? I hope you all had a historically relevant experience as I suppose that some of you did. For your first assignment for this Class, write a short five-page paper about what you did during the summer. I want to know how that relates to our current political situation. How have Reaganomics affected you, your family, and this area? I want well thought-through analysis. I hope you all have already read chapters one-through three of your textbook. ff you have not, you may be excused to go to the Library and do that at this time. The paper is due at the end of this week. Anyone failing to meet that deadline will be assigned an F-grade. Is that clear Class? All papers must be typed and double-spaced. Let's begin ..."

Several people including Ben made their way up to Dr. Straighter's desk to get a paper-pass to go to the Library for that class-period. Ben had just picked up his books that morning. He had not opened any one of them, yet. He had taken History classes the year before. He was used to writing papers like the one Dr. Straighter required, but not so soon as all that.

The first three chapters were about the Federalist's Papers. They were short and to the point about the debate on whether America should have a Strong Central Government, or should State's Rights Prevail. Ben did not see much wiggle-room to relate his particular summer experiences to what was written in that Government History Book.

After Government Class, he went to Advanced Creative Writing, then to Algebra II and Advance Mathematics, then to lunch. After lunch, it was to Biology, Physics, and PE Classes; but Dr. Straighter's assignment had fixed itself in the forefront of Ben's mind. The rest of the school day was like a dream. He wanted to write something that would get right down to the heart of what he had gone through that summer. He got home, threw his backpack full of books onto the sofa and got out his Government Book. He had been in a Creative Writing Class the year before. He had "Aced it" His Teacher, a beautiful, young Black Lady, named, Miss Vivian Lass, "is too pretty to be a Teacher," Ben thought. She was five-five, had a full Angela Davis Afro, and resembled Irene Gardner of the Black Panthers. Her figure was like the movie star, Pam Greer's. She always wore tight-fitting but proper dresses, blouses, and short skirts.

She had encouraged Ben, "Benjamin, you have great writing skills, young man. You write very impressively, and I recommend that you take your writing more seriously. You could become another James Baldwin, Richard Wright, or Langston Hughes. Next year you will be a junior. I hope you will take the other part of my class so that I can help you develop your writing skills even further. Have a good summer, Mr. Ben Slokum."

Here he was on day-one with a chance to make good on Miss Vivian's good faith. Ben skipped eating supper. He got out his Royal typewriter, stuck in some paper, and the words flowed like rain.

Ben typed like a madman for an hour each evening before going up to the Newcomb Dining Hall. He pulled his five hours, then came back home to type for another hour before he went to bed. He typed at about sixty words-per-minute. By Friday he had finished a six-page paper. He titled it: "The Ruining of Fifeville."

His main points were that "Reaganomics" were based on a theory of so-called, "Trickle-down Economics." The fact that no money had trickled-down to Fifeville, and that "Affirmative Action programs like WINN, Head Start, and EEOC," that had helped low-income people get "a leg up," in life, had been disallowed or unfunded by the Reagan

Administration, meant that affected people had to find other ways to Survive.

Ben went on to say that, "the State of *Virginia,"* under the "deregulations and tax-cutting mandates of the Reagan Administration," forced "the State to find ways to replace the federal dollars that 'Block Grants negated,'" and meant that the UVA had to do a lot of "budgetary belt-tightening." The Main Source of Employment for the people living in the Fifeville Neighborhood, The UVA, had to trim down its staff to the bare-bones. 'Whole Departments like "The Dietary, Housekeeping, and Building and Grounds Maintenance Departments," were phased out. These labor areas were replaced by private companies that rehired none of the loyal Fifeville workers-who were mostly Blacks-and unemployment skyrocketed.

The immediate affect was that a number of people who had been born and raised in Fifeville sold their homes for whatever they could get for them. "A lot of homes that were thriving are now just boarded-up Hovels no one wants to buy. The tax-base is gone." For some, it seems that all hope is gone.

"The young people are rebelling against the system by using 'Hustling,' as a way to 'Get-Over,' meaning as a 'Survival Tool.' So Gangs, that call themselves 'Crews,' have sprung up all over Charlottesville, and Fifeville, like the one we all call, The Westside Crew.' I used to hang with them because I was raised over in Fifeville. But I've decided that they were not the way to go because, a rival Jamaican Gangster, Jamie Charles, killed my Brother, Ivy, my Cousin, Roy, and my Grandmother, Mildred. I now hate gangs and will fight against them for what they have done to my family, but more importantly, for what they are doing to my 'Hood."

That morning at class-end Ben reluctantly turned in his paper. He shyly ambled up to Dr. Straigher's desk. He put his paper on top of all of the others and quickly turned around and slipped away like someone might be running after him.

The old professor smiled. "Have a good weekend, Mr. Ben Slokum," he said. He picked up Ben's paper with a look of amazement on his stoic face. "On the surface, this paper looks promising," he added. "True that," Ben answered. "Thank you, Dr, Straighter, I think," Ben said.

He was out the door to his next class, thinking about how to swing working at the UVA dining hall, one of the programs Reaganomics had left in place, and going on to Carolyn's and Cynthia's party some kinda way. Maybe, he could get a pass for this one night, he hoped.

He was able to get a pass for that Friday night by promising to work that Saturday night instead. The week had put some pressure on Ben and he felt like he needed some kind of release. Now that he did not drink, smoke, or do drugs, what was left, he wondered. Roy and Ivy didn't know it, but "Blue" had never been around the way with a girl. He had almost a couple of times. But a feel and some very heavy petting were as close as he had come. He'd always spied on Ivy and Roy. He saw how much they eqjoyed being with girls.

What Cynthia and Carolyn said about that Girl from Harlem made Ben think.about what meeting a girl like that might mean. Could she be the one to end the Drought? "Anticipation, Anticipation, Yeah!"

Ben got on the city street bus at the comer of Melbourne Road and Concord Drive. He had a bus pass for High School Students. So, he did not have to ride the Yellow School Bus. He took a seat in the middle of the bus near the side exit door. The bus had come up Melbourne off Grove Road from *250* West After Ben boarded the jammed-pack city transit, he was glad that a passenger had just exited at Grove and Concord Drive. He hated standing on the bus all the way down Grove Road to Park Street to East High, up to Fourth Street Northwest to West Main to the comer of Fifth Southwest Man that could be really tiring after a nine-to-three school day.

On the way to his 'Hood, Ben thought about how he had wanted to go to Lane High off of Preston Avenue before he graduated from Buford Middle School. But Lane closed in 1974. In 1958-59, Governor J. Lindsay Almond had ordered all public schools closed to keep Lane from complying with the US Supreme Court's May 17, 1954 Ruling: in *Brown v. Board of Eructation of Topeka, Kansas,* that "public schools in Virginia must desegregate." By 1969, all public schools in Charlottesville had complied with the Mandate, after being closed for a little over one year (1958-59), and after a three-judge panel in the Virginia Supreme Court had ruled that "there will be no more equivocation. The State must comply with the Supreme Court's ruling immediately, with all deliberate speed," then Governor Almond relented.

The unexpected consequences of the above rulings were: 1) When all of the African-American Students arrived at Lane High in 1967-69, there was not enough room to fit them all in that present building and its limited facilities. A new school had to be built No land was available within the Charlottesville City limits. So land was purchased out in Albemarle County. 2) Most of the Black teachers at Jackson P. Burley High on Rose Hill Drive, and Jefferson Elementary on Commerce Street were fired, forced into early retirement, or told they would have to go back to College to update their qualification to be certified to teach in public schools in Charlottesville. 3) Where most Black students in Charlottesville once lived near the schools they attended, after 1974, most of them were bused to the newly built Charlottesville High School to a predominantly-white hostile community. 4) Most of the teachers were white at Charlottesville High, and some reflected the communal hostility held by their neighbors. For two years Ben-called Big Blue Slokum then-hung out with gangster-wannabes and those who were "Gang-Banger Groupies." Although Blue was only "Fronting as a Gangster," he had a bad reputation from associating with his Brother Ivy and his Cousin Roy and other members of the Westside Crew. Now, Blue wanted his nick.name, and the life associated with it to disappear, "like Jackson P. Burley High School had in 1967."

Ben started at Charlottesville High in 1981. He still flirted with the idea of being a "Gangsta." He found himself in a strange place in that huge School. The other black students his age were few and far between. Only a couple of his Homeys had survived the transition from Buford to high school. Most had dropped out except Twins, Tyler and Hubert Hawthorn. As soon as they came over to Charlottesville, they disassociated with "Blue." The Hawthorn family moved out of Fifeville. The former "Gangsters," started taking on "White Airs," and ignored "Blue," making it known to him that they wanted nothing to do with him or the Crew. So "Blue," had to find new friends among the "white groupies." Thus, Carolyn and Cynthia wanted him to be their new "Gangster," friend. He had fronted as a Gangster before, well, he thought he may as well play along with that idea to see what he could glean out of it. And . . . he would try to make something out of the nothing his life had been up to then.

He got home that evening took. a shower and had to think. about what to wear to the Party. Thug-fare was out. But he wanted to be "laid-back," and "down." So he decided he'd wear a pair of black Gucci Jeans, and a Gold-and-Black Phat Farm Sweat Shirt, and Beige Nikki Kicks with black strings; and, no socks.

Ben walked up Fifth Southwest to West Main. The evening was nice. The sun was sinking slowly into the western sky. Evening shadows started to emerge reminding Ben of the Ghosts of Ivy and Roy. At the same time that he wanted to forget them, they were his Brother and Cousin. He couldn't just forget who they had been1 yet that was what his Conscience demanded that he do.

He walked up West Main toward the UVA Hospital. He got to the Comer of Seventh Street Southwest and West **Main. A** contingent of the Crew always hung out on that Corner in front of the C&O Depot Hardware Storage Facility. They were just kicking it and shooting the Bull. As Ben walked by one named Burns, called "Bull," Fortune, a Herculean type who stood at over six foot tall confronted Ben. He wore the Culottes and Baggy T-Shirt of the Crew. He got in front of Ben on the sidewalk.

With his finger up in the air pointing at Ben's face, Bull spat out his displeasures. "Blue Slokum. You trying-ta get out, yo? I ain't tryin' ta-hear that shit. How ya--gonna stay in the 'Hood, then? You gotta be in it 'til ya-die, yo. You gotta be true ta-what Ivy an' Roy represent, G. Your Granny's blood calls for ya-ta-be on the Set gettin' even, yo. Why ya-tryin' ta-bitch out, G?"

The other nine or so Crew Members stood with their arms folded watching Bull and Ben to see what would come of that Beef. They expected to see a violent confrontation right there on West Main. If a Dude step to you; you had to represent. You supposed to throw-down. Your reputation depended on it. One of them, Bull or Blue, had to come out on top. The winner would take all. Bull patted his waistband. He had a Glock tucked in it. Blue saw this.

Ben was a little bit nervous, but he stood his ground. "Bull, man, I done seen enough blood on the ground, the sidewalks, and my life. I swore to the Ghost of my Dead Grandma that I'd change my life by giving up the Banging, and help to convince Cats like you, that life has better things to offer, if you go about living another way. I'm hustling them school books now, yo. That's all I'm gonna be about. I'm preparing to help you and anyone like you get on up in life, Bull. Do you really wanna kill me, stop me, cut me off?" Ben spoke in a mournful voice.

"Bull, Marvin, your little Brother got shot to death by Jamie 'nem. How many more of us do you wanna see in early graves, man? I'm trying to get to the bottom of all this shit that's been going down lately, Bull. It's a shit-load of trouble all over our 'Hood, our bodies, and our lives. I'm starting to think we're all gonna go out like that, Bull. I don't wanna see that happen, man. You got a baby with Sheila Mea Johannes. The little Dude looks just like you, too. Give 'im a better chance by setting a better example for 'im, Bull. Yo man, I got a party to go to. Let me go on, Brother-you feelin' me, G?"

As hard a Thug as Bull was, he could feel what Blue was rapping to him. He grimaced, but moved aside so that Ben could go on through life. He quickly wiped away the moisture in the comers of his big eyes.

Ben arrived to the Corner of Tenth and West Main near the front of the largest grocery store in Charlottesville, The Safeway Store. The parking lot was full of cars and people were hustling groceries out of shopping carts into nice cars. They were getting their weekend shopping done. Some Crew Members were in the parking lot selling dope to many shoppers exiting the store. Ben wondered how The Crew could get away with that, with "The War On Drugs," being on, and all.

When Ben walked down Tenth to the Corner of Hardy Drive, a group of Crew Members were selling dope to drivers in cars driving past and stopping briefly to "cop the drugs." Then he made it to the Corner of Tenth and Page Street, and he saw more dope being peddled. He went up Tenth-and-a-Half Street to Gordon Avenue. He saw the same thing, even all the way to Fourteenth and Fifteenth Streets Northwest.

The Crew Members were the roving Drugstores, but the so-called, "Upstanding White Citizens" were their principal customers. A deep sadness pervaded Ben's psyche. He felt like crying inside.

The thought that he, Ivy, and Roy were integral in such a destructive way to impact so many people's lives made Ben feel queasy in his stomach. It caused a little pain in his guts. He wondered: *what can I do to undo the damage I have helped to inflict on so many young people?*

Carolyn told Ben that she lived at 1007 Fifteenth Street Northwest. It was off the Comer of Grady Avenue, one block over from Gordon Avenue. It was near Rugby Road. Her house was surrounded by Sorority and Fraternity Houses. Sigma Nu Sorority was only two doors away from the Whitten's residence. The girls chanted: "Sig-Nu, We Love the Gold and Blue."

As Ben approached the residential area of "The Better Half," he heard sounds being played by a Reggae Band blasting: "I Shot The Sheriff, But I Didn't Shot The Deputy ..." that came from a brick building that was like a miniature version of the buildings of the Rotunda on the Campus of the UVA, with large capitals and broad steps and a wide deck in front with those Greek styled windows, as were many of the Frat's and Soror's on Rugby, upper Gordon and Grady Avenues, and on Fourteenth and Fifteenth Streets Northwest.

The music was coming from the Sigma Nu's place. There were wall-to-wall people all bearing red plastic cups of some liquid they were dipping out of what appeared to Ben to be a big, green, plastic, trashcan. Some were dancing, and others were screaming "Sigma Nu, We Love the Gold and Blue!" What they were shouting sounded something like, "Louie, Louie, Ah, Baby We Gotta Go Now ..."

Ben saw a couple girls who wore very short gold miniskirts, blue blouses, white fishnet stockings, and very high-heeled, black-pumps. A vignette on the bosom of their blouses was like a white flame surrounding the fancy-Greek letters, *"Sigma Nu."* It seemed like to Ben that the whole crowd was drunk out of their minds that early in the evening.

Ben walked over to 1007 Fifteenth Street wondering what he would find there. He came to a two-story house of bricks painted white, with a green-gabled roof, and a full balcony on the second floor. Carolyn saw Ben coming up the spacious cement walkway that was edged in red bricks. Nearly-trimmed boxwood hedges bordered each side of that. She ran out to meet her "special guest."

"Ben, Blue . . . oh, whatever . . . It's so good of you to come. Come on out to the backyard. I want you to meet my Mom and Dad. Since I told them all about you, they're dying to meet you, okay!" Carolyn said in a sing-song way. "They're on the grill. I hope you're hungry. We got everything back there, Ben. Everything you could want to eat, drink, or smoke." She giggled after she said that.

Carolyn wore a red and blue, Tie-Dyed T-Shirt that came down onto her thighs. Ben could see that she had on no Bra. And under that, she had on a black pair of thin bikini panties. She had on a pair of red flip-flops that revealed her bright-red toenail polish. She smiled seductively at Ben. She grabbed his hand and led him around the large building big enough for fifty people to reside in.

Ben heard loud-party laughter as he came into the backyard area. He saw Cynthia with a tall, very light skinned guy that had a big head full of reddish-very-nappy hair, and large greenish eyes. His skin was so pinkish-brown that it was not very far from White. Ben wondered what her father could've been objecting to when it came to Briscoe dating his daughter. Briscoe was nearly white like Cynthia. He would not stand out in a crowd of whites.

Two people grilling hotdogs, hamburgers, stakes, and smoked-sausages, smiled broadly. They wore their hair frizzy like Carolyn's and Cynthia's. The man wore US Flag-striped Bellbottoms. But he had on a black and green, tie-dyed T-Shirt. The woman who Carolyn mostly resembled had on a green and black tied-dyed midi-dress. The woman had to be Carolyn's Mom, Ben thought. She was a look alike. "Mom, I want you to meet, Ben-'Blue'-Slokum," Carolyn said, adoringly. Then she winked.

"Hello .. I'm Sylvia-Sylvia Manuel Crossman and this is my Husband, Lucas Mann Crossman,"

said a slimmer version of Carolyn. She wore the same frizzy hair, but it came down onto her shoulders. Ben thought her face kinda resembled a grown-up, Shirley Temple's, except she did not have the ringlets. What she did have, "was body for days."

Ben could see where Carolyn got her good looks from. Carolyn's Mom "had it going on!" Ben noticed that Mrs. Crossman was wearing a pair of silver-colored Clogs. Her curvaceous body made the clothing she had on look like "Red Carpet" attire. Her lips were like Marilyn Monroe's, like a miniature "Cupid's Bow." Her blue eyes were like the sparkling waters off the shores of Virginia Beach. Her voice was husky like Bette Davis's. She blinked often as she talked. "I'm pleased to meet you Mr. Blue, ah, Ben. Caro's told me so much about you. Sorry to hear about what happened to your family. Tragedy stalks us all. I've lost both my parents to Cancer. But you hang in there."

Ben loved this lady right away. "Thank you for caring, Mrs. Crossman. I can see where Carolyn's good nature comes from. I"

Mrs. Crossman reached out and hugged Ben all at once. She pulled herself tight to him for a couple of minutes. Ben felt the delicious pressure of her breasts pressed tight against his chest Then "that old fear," came between his and her embrace. Without meaning to, he quickly pulled away from Carolyn's Mom.

She chuckled and said: "I can see that you're a little shy. That's a good thing, I guess. What I'm wondering is, how you're not all 'Thugged Out!' like I heard-well, that you were like that. But I can see that is not an adequate description of you at all. You're much more handsomer than that!"

Carolyn interjected, "Mom, you're embarrassing me!"

Lucas thought it better to speak at this point., "Well, hi there, Mr. Blue. We're both Teachers over at Walker Middle School. We like to think that we are good judges of character-that's what Sylvia probably meant I know she didn't mean to make fun of you or anything. Chunk it all up to the 'Generational Gap: that is so prevalent these days among so many of our young people, who are questioning everything we parents thought we believed. But . . . that's a good thing. I can go along with a lot of that It's nice to meet you Mr. Blue." He followed his wife back over to the huge bricked-in grill. He hadn't shook Ben's hand nor had he come within two-feet of him.

Ben thought Lucas resembled the Actor, John Wayne. He spoke in that same tone of voice. But he was unlike Wayne, who was a notorious Cowboy. Mr. Crossman was an Elementary School Teacher, Ben thought that was no job for "A True He-man."

Carolyn grabbed Ben's hand and led him away to meet Cynthia's parents. "Don't mind my old folk, Ben. They're struggling with the 'Terrible Changes' we young people are forcing upon them. Their cute little-petite world is coming to an end-and there's really nothing they can do to stop the flow, Ben. That's what's wrong with them. They just have to get over it!"

Carolyn took Ben over to two adults sitting on a green lawn chair. "Hello, Mr. and Mrs. Milton and Paulina Van Whitten, this is Benjamin

Slokum. I don't see Cynthia. I guess she's mingling with the kids especially those from Sigma Nu. I believe one day she'll pledge for that Sorority. Well ... Ben is one of our popular classmates." The old-gray bearded man wearing a collarless clergy-shirt grimaced.

Ben came over to the older-looking parents of Cynthia's. Mrs. Van Whitten had on what looked like a laid-back Nun's Habit, but her dress was unbuttoned from her knees down. She was graying around the edges, and she wore her hair like the Mona Lisa. She had on no makeup, and wore black beads around her neck. Ben didn't know what to make of her. She had a very stem look on her wrinkling face that was more a frown. She wasn't enjoying herself at all, and that was obvious. Her fat husband wore all black.

Carolyn stood very next to Ben. She whispered, "The Whittenes are not having any fun, huh?"

Ben answered: "I wonder why they're even here? This is a party for young folk. She and her husband's way past that time in they lives." Milton and Paulina were St. Anne's administrators. They ignored Ben.

Carolyn turned closer to Ben and put her left hand on his right shoulder. "Listen Ben . . . it's like this: My Mom an' Cynthia's Mom's very good friends. They've been watching over us like Ducks do their Ducklings. My older Sister, Yolanda, was always one who opted for something different than the run of things. If everyone else had on blue clothing she'd wear red just to be wearing something different.

"When Lane was integrated, right away Big Sis saw a chance to choose something, or someone, different. She started flirting with the darkest-skinned 'Dude' she could find at school. His name was Pomeroy Slaughter, from up on Charleston Avenue. He was a short muscular Dude with the biggest, prettiest, brown eyes you ever seen. His hair was very wavy and he parted it in the middle of his head. He looked a little like a darkened 'Alfalfa' on 'The Lil' Rascals,' He was a very sweet guy, Ben. All the girls loved him.

"He took a very great liking to Yolanda. They were seniors. They could leave school on Fridays early with permission from their parents. Yolanda told Mom she was going to join the Glee Club. Pomeroy worked in the typing room of the School's Newsletter. He helped **Big Sis** forge the official looking papers that my parents innocently signed.

"Pomeroy's Mom, Mini, is an LPN at the UVA. His father, Radiant, is a Chef out at Boar's Head Inn on 250-West. Neither one of them wanted their son to date an 'O'fay girl.' That's what they called us 'White Girls.' Ben, Yolanda fell madly in love with Pomeroy, and he was crazy about her.

"So, Ben, Yolanda's and Pomeroy's Love was one that their parents thought should never be. Yolanda used to joke: 'Lil' Sis, Pomeroy and I, we're a modem day Romeo and Juliet; right?'

"Ben, they found more and more ways to be with each other. It was not long until Pomeroy got her to give-in to their basic natural urges. Look, they made love, or what the hell, Ben. They started fucking like the world was gonna come to an end. That was unofficially announced to the public by a noticeable swelling in her stomach. She was so proud of that. But Dad nearly fainted when he found out from the hospital that 'my little girl is no longer a virgin.' He demanded that she have an abortion.

"My Mom agreed with him when Yolanda told her who the father of her baby was. Yolanda told me that she and Pomeroy had no other choice but to run away and get married. They now live in Washington, D.C. in an exclusive neighborhood. She has no contact with Mom or Dad, and they have declared her dead to our family. I know that Pomeroy went to law school and Yolanda studied cosmetology at Howard.

"So Cynthia's parents are here to make sure they give her enough rope to sate her youthful urges, but not to end up pregnant and or married to what my Dad calls, 'A Juicy Buck.'"

There were tears in the comers of Ben's eyes. "Damn, that's a very tragic story, Carolyn. Racism is keeping your family divided against each other. Skin color is doing that to mine. Half of us are passing for white. The two halves don't associate with one-another. My own Uncle hates me worse than a K.K.K. Member. I can't even go visit him, and he's s'spose-ta be in charge of my inheritance over in Fifeville-but that's a long story. We can talk about that later.

"Carolyn, who's that pretty brown-sugar girl over there? Is she high school or college? Man, she's got it goin' on, yo. Do you know who she is?"

"Yes, Ben, her name is Moisha Andrea Melrose. We call her 'M'n'M,' Oh, you think she's hot, huh? Her father is Philip Munford Melrose. He was once an Assistant Coach at Howard University. They come from

Harlem, New York. He's now a Linebacker's Coach for the Cavaliers. You wanna meet her, Ben?"

With a shy grin on his face, Ben said, "yes, but first I got a couple of quick questions: Why does Cynthia's Mom dress like a wannabe Nun? I thought you said that they were once hippies."

Carolyn cleared her throat for a little bit. "Well those are not 'quick questions,' but here goes:

"My Mom says both Cynthia's parents were orphans who were left at The Notre Dame Cathedral Seminary and Convent in Washington State when they were mere infants. She was oriented by the Nuns there to become a Nun. He was oriented toward becoming a Priest.

"When they were students later at The University of Notre Dame, they found that their curiosity about Sex, Love, and Life were stronger than their vows to celibacy. So they became friends, then lovers, and then were confused about their vows to God, the Virgin Mary, and the Catholic Church.

"They left the Faith and the University of Norte Dame, and wallowed in their newfound freedoms of day-in and day-out, drugging, hot-lust and impiousness. They moved to California and went out into the desert and joined a Hippie Commune and got lost in that culture for a few years. Then, Paulina came up pregnant. All shit broke loose then.

"Their Catholic Faith precluded any thought of them having an abortion. So, Paulina suffered through what Mom says was a horrible ordeal of pains, swelling of her hands and feet, and eventually she had to be confined to bed, 'til Cynthia could be delivered by C-Section.

"Paulina blamed their estrangement from the Church for 'God's punishment of her.' She demanded that she and Milton get married right away. They did. Then she found out that she would never be able to have another child. She considered that further punishment. She temporarily left Milton and dated Black Guys for a short while. But she realized that she was not mentally balanced.

"Her psychiatrist encouraged Paulina to seek to restore her relationship with Milton as a start toward mental healing. They got back together and left California. They ended up back in school, here in Charlottesville, Virginia. After schooling, they remained here because here turned out to be a great place to raise their daughter, Cynthia. They were both hired to teach at St. Anne's Bellfield Private Catholic School. "Mrs. Paulina Van Whitten wears a semblance of a Nun's Habit and some Rosary Beads around her neck as a reminder of what she left behind in a Faith she couldn't really ascnbe to keep. Mr. Milton, cut loose at first when he got to Charlottesville. Cynthia says that he slipped around with their 'Colored' Maid at least a few times. Paulina may have suspected that but never mentioned it. She just fired the Maid. She decided that a Maid was too much extravagance for a 'Humble Catholic Family,' even though they were far estranged from the Church. So, they have remained as you see them now. Got it?"

Ben had somewhat of a puzzled look on his face, but he had heard enough about that, so he said, "Yeah, got it-now, lets' go meet Miss Beau-ti-fid, yo"

Carolyn raised her hand high in the air and beckoned to a caramel-colored girl that stood at five-five. She wore a blue Calvin Klein's Walking Pants and Vest outfit with beige pantyhose, and a pair of tan, Stacked heeled Lady Timberland Boots.

Ben was thinking: "Man, this Chick fills those threads well. She's the Bomb! I think I'm in love at first sight.

He checked out her Angela Davis Afro, It was reddish-brown. Her eyes were like those of Coretta Scott King, majestic but very dignified. Her face was naturally pretty without any makeup. She smiled showing even pearly-white teeth. She walked along confidently, with gold bracelets on each of her wrists. She made her way through the crowd to Carolyn. Ben was as nervous as he could be. He was trying to control himself, but was having a time doing so. No girl had affected him like that before.

Carolyn grabbed Ben's hand in her left hand, and Moisha's hand in her right hand, smiled and said: "Moisha, meet Benjamin Luther Slokum-'Big Ben.' Ben, meet Moisha Andrea Melrose-'M'n'M.'"

Ben's eyes were spread open wide. All he could think to say was the old cliché: "It'll melt in your mouth not in your hand." Moisha didn't smile at that remark. Ben followed with: "I'm sorry, Moisha . . . I kid around a lot. Didn't mean to disrespect you, though." He extended his right hand.

Moisha laughed. "You Brothers down here in the 'Ville,' you're so way out there. I'm not offended. I can take a joke; alright? Nice to meet you, Big Ben." She squeezed his hand gently at first and tighter as Ben shook her pretty, soft, hand for three minutes.

"M'n'M, I'm real-down with meeting you, yo. I'm not lying when I say you're the prettiest girl at this party, from your head to your toe. I really would like to get to know you better. You think that might be possible?" Ben said. He noticed that she just faintly smiled without answering him.

Carolyn loudly cleared her throat. She pointed her finger at Ben and shook her head a little. Moisha laughed, "You're jealous, Caro, I bet," she chortled.

"No-no-no, **M'n'M,** I was just letting Big Ben here know, my boyfriend is coming over here right now, and I'm gonna be out of here. That's all," Carolyn said. "You guys have fun."

Ben recognized the Black Dude bopping over to the center of the backyard area where a crowd of young people had gathered. He was the second-string Running-Back for the Cavaliers. He'd been a star from his Junior Varsity days at Lane to his senior year at Charlottesville High. He was Callahan McMeans. He was tall and lanky, with long-powerfully-built legs. His arms were not as powerful looking as his legs, but he was quite an athletic specimen. He was wearing a blue-and-white Cavalier Jersey sporting the number: 34. His name was printed on the back of it under the Cavalier's Logo: consisting of a depiction of the head of a blue-three-musketeer wearing a French hat with a long-feather. He had on tan Khaki Slacks and brown penny loafers. He came over and locked lips with Carolyn for about five or six minutes. Ben figured that he had to be two, three, or four years older than Carolyn. He realized that was what she meant when she said that, "Age Discrimination, we're trying to cut that down too." McMeans was a senior at the UVA.

Carolyn with a broad happy smile on her face turned towards, Ben and said: "I think you already know Cal, right? He was tight with Ivy at one time until, well, you know."

Ben responded, "Yep, I've seen him shooting hoops down at Tonsler's Park with the Crew. But, I never seen you all together before. Hey, I'm down with it, yo." Blue thought, "That's what her Dad meant by a 'juicy Buck!'" **He** waved as Carolyn and her man ran through the crowd and disappeared. He wondered where Cynthia and Briscoe had gone-well, he almost knew- "to Love-Ville, yo!"

Ben realized that Moisha had not been drinking and was of a sober state of mind. So she was not high on any dope. He thought that was amazing. He looked around and noticed that it was getting very dark, and almost everyone at the party was sipping some "Green Punch" out of red-plastic cups. Then, he saw one girl then another, getting out of their lady's bags what seemed like compacts.

It dawn on Ben, that they were not going to "powder their noses" in the traditional sense, because the powder in those compacts was Cocaine. A number of straws were produced. The compacts were being passed around and a number of people were snorting up the powder with the straws. Ben saw a couple-a packets of "Horse (Heroin)," being passed around. Some pinched them open and snorted them up as well. A group of kids had a Boom Box and were playing Marley's Reggae Hits: "I Shot The Sheriff/But I Didn't Shot The Deputy. IT The Cap Fits Then Let Him Wear It. Love, Love, Love" These were openly smoking joint-after-ioint of Marijuana. He saw kids dropping Acid; popping pills; and realized from the smell of the punch, it was laced with Grain Alcohol. The party had become a true "Dope Thing!"

M'n'M looked up into Ben's eyes and searched them for a few moments. "You don't drink or drug do you, Brother-man?" she asked.

"No . . . I lost my most important people to that crap," Ben said. "I can't have any fun at a get-down like this one. at I'm seeing just remind me of the reason all my Peeps got mowed down too soon. I'm bored like a lone boulder out in the desert wishing a bird or something would come light on it. You feel me?"

Moisha smiled, "Brother Ben, let me answer your earlier question: Yes, I'm gonna get to know you better. You can start by walking me home. I live just over on Fourteenth Street Northwest, at 1114. My Pops is renting that house. He's a Linebacker Coach up at the UVA. They got all of those rough Black guys coming up to the UVA now. I reckon the administration figured that the team needed a hard-down Black man to keep all of that in perspective." She chuckled. "Dad grew-up in Harlem."

Ben took her hand and they left the party hand and hand.

Ben felt inside that he was partially responsible for what he had witnessed at that party. That Dope! Judging from what he's seen on his way up to that party, a lot of that Dope had been sold to those kids by the Crew. It made Ben gag a little. He had to fight back the tears. He was glad when they arrived at the huge white front door of Moisha's house. It was a two-story redbrick edifice, with green-shuttered windows with yellow and green awning on the bottom windows. Tall steps led up to the front door that suddenly came opened.

A heavyset, very light-skinned, red-headed, rotund man appeared on the steps. He had on a Sweatshirt with the UVA Logo in front of it, a pair of dark-blue shorts, and a pair of black-leather moccasins and no socks. **His** voice was deeply bass. at stray you're dragging home this time, **Mo?"** he bellowed, looking directly at Ben.

"No Pops, this one's not-a stray. He's the real deal-I'm betting." Moisha crooned. "He doesn't smoke, drink, dope, or do any of that jive, like that Jamaican freak Jamie Charles used to do! The one that you liked so well. He's in prison now."

Her father looked Ben up and down. Where do you live?" he asked sharply.

"Sir, I live in Fifeville at 222 Fifth Street Southwest. I 'ma junior at Charlottesville High," Ben said nervously. He wondered how Moisha had known who Jamie Charles was?

"Oh, you're one-a those 'Brownie-Townies,' aren't you?" Mosiha's old man said. Ben was puzzled. "I don't know what that is, sir," he said.

The old man got a very sinister expression on his face. "Well what it means is, Mo doesn't need the likes of you distracting her. Fifeville, isn't that where all of the drug and gang activity is taking place? "Moisha gave Ben a quick kiss. "See you at school. You better run along now." She ran up the steps and on into the house. Her father followed behind her.

Ben walked up Fourteenth Street to East Main. He went down the Street thinking: at did Mr. Melrose mean: "Fifeville . . . where all of the dope and gang activity's taking place ..." I've seen just as much dope in the very heart of the middleclass up at the UVA as I've seen in Fifeville. Something is really wrong about this shit, and I'm gonna get to the bottom of it all.

Chapter Seven

Ben and Moisha became an item at Charlottesville High. Their romance, though Platonic, was heating up as the year came to an end. It had started with an argument. Shortly after the confrontation with her Father Philip, Ben couldn't get out of his mind what "Mo" had said about Jamie Charles. So he brought that up one day after some kissing and heavy petting at recess.

"Mo, what kind of a thing did you and Jamie Charles have. I can't get that off my mind. Don't get me wrong, I love you, Baby. But I gotta know ..."

Mo pulled away from him and stood face-to-face with him. "Ben, Pops introduced me to Jamie just before he was indicted for all kinds of criminal shit See, Pops' people are originally from Madagascar, and some are from Mauritius. Pops came to America with a group of people who were followers of a 'Prophet' called 'Daddy Grace,' who established a group of Churches in the South in the Carolinas, and in New York to rival 'Father Divine's' multiple-temple organization.

"I don't know much about Pops' people. They all up and left after the death of Daddy Grace in 1960. I was not even born yet and don't know much about that But Pops grew up in Harlem, New York, an Orphan of Bishop Lithu Mutilala. This follower of Daddy Grace ran a home for boys. Pops had been left behind by his people. I heard that he was 'an illegitimate son of Daddy Grace.' Many women claimed they had children by Daddy Grace, over a hundred. He denied all of their claims except for a couple.

"My Moms, Maya Oro, came to America from Kingston, Jamaica. She followed the teachings of Haile Selassie, a Descendant of the son of The Queen of Sheba and King Solomon, called the 'Loin of Judah,' and was thought by some to be the Messiah for Africans. She and Pops met at

Bishop LM's Temple in Harlem, and were finally allowed to marry after some four years of heavily supervised courtship, and a sizeable fee to the Bishop. After that, Pops left the Chinch and that Faith.

"My Pops says that my Moms considered herself to be of the 'Rastafarian Mansion of Joseph'-there were allegedly 'Twelve' of these corresponding to the Twelve Tribes of Israel; that also corresponded with the month they were born in. She was born in February and was in the same 'Mansion' as Robert (Bob) Nesta Marley, the Reggae Performer, who died in 1981. 'Smoking Ganja,' is what Pops says that Moms called 'Marijuana,' was part of the ritual of 'Mental Purification' that Rasta people engaged in constantly, using it as 'a Sacrament and an aid to Meditation.' Smoking Pot was to them like Americans taking a glass or two of wine with their dinner, or at Communion. Pot was believed by them to be put here by 'Jah,' (God), 'to help Mankind seek and achieve enlightenment'

"Though Moms would visit other Churches, Temples, and Religious Organizations, she privately maintained the practices she had grown up observing in Jamaica. Her name, 'Maya Oro,' means 'Gold Daisy.' It best describes a type of Hashish, now typically grown in Mexico, called, 'Gold Leaf Hash,' that was originally grown all over the Caribbean that gives the user a very potent high.

"My Pops grew up surrounded by Jamaican and Haitian Immigrants. Those who followed a form of Christianity-Catholicism, Daddy Grace-ism, Father Divine-ism, Pentecostalism, and just plain-old Baptism-deplored what they called the 'Primitive Practices' of the Immigrants that they had brought to America in the 1960s, 1970s and 1980s.

"Pops says he and Moms had a number of knock-down, drag-out yelling matches, and then Pops violently assaulted Moms. He broke her arm. She left right after that attack. She left with a bag of her 'Ganja' and the clothes on her back, but she left me behind. I don't remember her. I feel like she abandoned me, but I ache for her. I just wish I could get to know who she was, and to hear her side of things. But it seems that was so far not meant to be.

"Pops couldn't so-call, 'get Moms to give up her 'pagan habit' of smoking pot religiously,' now ain't that some shit? Look around you! Everybody's doing that shit nowadays. Pops says Moms went back to

Jamaica to her hometown in Kingston. One day I wanna visit there and search for her or her remains, and or her ashes.

"One bad thing though, is that Pops and Moms and the people I grew up around in New York never considered themselves to be 'Negroes.' They believed that 'Jah' created them. But, 'The White Man Created The Negro (Nigger)!' So they don't relate to us in our struggles against racial discrimination in the same way. My Pops actually discriminates against 'Blacks' too. He doesn't want me to associate with what he says is 'The Niggers!' He wants me to find a nice Jamaican, Haitian, or White man in America. That's how I ended up meeting Jamie Charles. First though, Ben, on my Driver's License in the Race Box, it is marked: 'Caucasian.' It is the same on my Pops' License. Secondly, some Jamaicans don't see you or your family members as I see you-as descendent from 'Mother Africa.' They see you as part of the enemy.

"There is a very Bloody Civil War going on in Jamaica. There are two factions: 'The Peoples National Party (PNP) and the Jamaican Labor Party (JLP).' The PNP is Communist backed. The JLP is backed by America. Jamie Charles was exiled to over here because his people supported the **PNP.** They were run out of town. They hate Americans. Black people are to them just more Americans. They hate all Americans so much that they will kill one at the drop of a hat. They have no conscience problem when it comes to that.

"When I discovered what Jamie Charles was up to, I told him to get lost. Pops had met him at a dinner party at the UVA Pavilion I for Contributors to the Athletic Fund. Pops brought him home to meet me and I went out with him on a couple of dates. He seemed charming at first. But I soon discovered that he was full of hatred, and wanted to help foment a communist revolution in America. That was our last date.

"Jamie and I never got it going on. I still got my Hymen-Maidenhead intact, in case you're wondering.

Hey, I'm not ashamed to be completely honest with you. I'm saving that for the man I love."

Ben had heard a lot to digest. One thing puzzled him, though: "Mo, Jamie Charles was not a naturalized citizen? I thought he was. I knew that he was up to no good, but I thought he had become an American. "\Why did he hate America so bad? Did your Pops know about what Jamie was up to?" Ben asked.

Mo, stammered a little. "Ben ... l-l-l . . . I'm not sure whether Pops knew or not. Once I no longer dated Jamie, Pops wouldn't let me talk about him any longer. I just had to wonder about that one.

"When the Socialists made inroads to power in Jamaica, hundreds of JLP people were rounded up and assassinated. For humanitarian reasons, American diplomacy made it possible for hundreds of those to migrate to America and seek political asylum. The PNP simply infiltrated those being allowed to come to America as refugees with their spies. Their mission I think was that they were to undermine American society in every way possible. Selling dope was one way. Selling guns to Gangs was another. They created a notorious gang to carry out murders and to regulate clandestine criminal activities-that we now call the Posse-was those spies' major success.

"Jamie did not want to become a True American. He always wanted to return to Jamaica. He hated America for backing the JLP and for supplying them with the support of arms and humanitarian aid so they could hold out against the PNP for as long as they did. He felt that America was so afraid of the spread of Socialism in South America that this paranoia kept the Civil War going on in Jamaica way too long, and many of Jamie's relatives had been brutally murdered in that conflict his Moms, Pops, and little Brother. His two Sisters were gang-raped in the streets and then gutted like sheep or slaughtered swine and left in the alleys for the wild dogs to feed upon. This was not our fault., but Jamie blamed all of that on all Americans. He hated and wanted to destroy us all.

"Ben, I love America. I don't want anything to happen to our democracy. There are a lot of things going on over here I don't like: like the way America discriminates against Women in the workplace; or the way Blacks and Minorities are excluded from many professions for no other reason other than race; or, that Gays and Lesbians are hated, oppressed, and sometimes murdered in the streets of America for just being different But we can fix what is wrong over here without fomenting a bloody revolution. We can change the laws. We can vote. We have a chance to evoke change. That is not the case over in Jamaica, or Cuba, or Columbia, or the Philippines, where Communism is making inroads over Democracy. Ben, Darling, that's what we are all up against.

"By the way . . . no matter what the authorities have written on my Driver's License, I see myself as a 'Black Soul Sister.' I'm one-a y'all, Dog. You feelin' me?"

Ben laughed. "True that I'm feelin' ya, Baby, an' I love-ya too. Come here. Lemme taste your beautiful lips." He kissed her long and hard and sought her tongue with his. Once he found it, he caressed it for ten-minutes. A huge lump developed in the crotch of his pants. That had been happening a lot lately. "Ben, I've never felt like this about a boy before. I want to ..." She pressed herself tightly against the bulge in his pants. "It feels so good when you're standing so close to me like this," she chimed.

Ben whispered: "Baby, like Marvin Gaye said: 'Let's Get It On!'"

That May, Ben had saved enough money to buy a second-hand Blue Tuxedo from The Young Men's Shop located downtown on the Mall. It threw-in a pink ruffled shirt with blue etching on the ruffles, and a blue bowtie. He bought a pair of black patent leather shoes. He looked in the mirror in his hallway.

He whispered: "I look good if I do say so myself. I'm gonna be with my Honey tonight, For-Real!" He leapt up and tapped his feet like "Bojangles Robinson, or Fred Astaire." He was out the door, up Fifth to Main to the old Memorial Gym at the UV A "to where the junior-senior prom was going down."

The UVA had built a new forty-million dollar Gym up on the hill back of Copley Road. It had amble parking spaces, nearly two-thousand, wherein parking was a major problem at the Memorial Gym, just down the hill from the Clemons and Alderman Libraries. Fans had to park wherever they could. Super Giant, Ralf Sampson, had made Basketball a Thing at The UV A. The Team was rated Number-One in the ACC for most of that Season-where that had never happened in UVA's recent sport's history. It included Twins Ronnie and Bobby Stokes, Craig Littlepage, and Othello Wilson. Since The Cavaliers had been forced to desegregate, Black Players like the above were upping the quality of the Cavaliers' standings so that they were Nationally Rated as never before. So fans needed more parking-spaces to come cheer the Cavaliers on. To solve the problem the UVA built a multifaceted Gym with the most modem indoor swimming facilities, Saunas, a modem weight-room, and a forty-two thousand seating capacity around the most modem basket-ball goals, and signal and lighting capabilities. It was named, "The Field House."

Ben felt as though his feet never touched the ground as he whisked himself up West Main to University Avenue to be with the "Girl of my Dreams-the one I love and completely adore," he crooned.

Coach Philip M. Melrose had forbidden Moisha to date Benjamin L Slokum ever as long as she lived under his roof. M'n'M had answered her father's mandate with, "Yes, Pops, if you say so," followed by a sly grin on her beautiful adolescent face. But she was with Ben at school during every recess, at sporting games, and during prep rallies. It's a wonder that Phil never found out what M'n'M was doing, because so many people knew that she and Ben were "an item." They were always standing around hugged-up so tight no one could get a straight pin between them. Sometimes it seemed like they were necking for the whole lunch period instead of eating lunch. IT Philip knew he never brought it up to Mo.

But to go to the prom, Mo improvised a clever plan. She had Winifred Stacy, a well-off White Boy to escort her to the junior-senior prom. Stacey agreed to front for Mo. He too had to cover up the fact that he was going to meet a Black girl, Raquel Moon, that evening. His parents were Jewish and would never have agreed to such a meeting. Both Winifred and Mo agreed that they would arrive at the Gym, separate and be with the one they loved for the rest of the night. They would hook back up late that night and return home as if nothing out of the ordinary had happened; then, Mo found out that Winifred had other plans.

When Ben got up to where West Main became University Avenue, he saw cars parked everywhere. UVA Cops were writing tickets all over the place. Nobody cared. Well-dressed couples were emerging out of the cars wearing gowns and tuxes of every galore. A black Eldorado Cadillac Limousine pulled up and Mo got out of it wearing a light-blue gown by "Versace." She looked like a Fairytale Princess to Ben.

Ben stepped from behind a small boxwood bush smiling like a Cheshire Cat. "Hi, Beautiful," he said. The Cadillac pulled away and stopped. A tall, smooth-black-skinned girl with long-black locks and the figure of

Cleopatra was wearing a beige gown that resembled what a bride would be wearing, got into Stacey's Limo. A Black man drove the Limo away.

"Winifred's eighteen and Raquel's seventeen now, Ben. They're going to elope. They're going to Las Vegas and get married. Guess who'll be coming to dinner next, Boo?" Mo said with a chuckle. They both laughed out loud. She took Ben's arm and asked, "Where to, Love?"

Ben stopped, turned to face her, kissed her long and hard and whispered, "Baby, I never told you this before, but I got my own place-least it'll be my place next year. I'll be eighteen then, and my Uncle Frank will have to sign it over to me. I've been on my own since my Grandma was killed. Let's go there; okay?"

"I love you, Ben. I feel like I will always love you. I'm not naive though, 'Big Blue,' and I know you don't like that handle, but I've talked to you and told you things I've told no one else about my family. It comes naturally when I'm with you. You may not continue to love me, but I will be there for you.

"Darling, there was some kind of spark that got ignited the day I first met you at the party. It is now a full-grown explosion. I want you to be my first Lover-my first man-my One and only." She kissed Ben and clung to him out of breath for the moment.

Ben put his right arm around her waist. "Let's walk down to the comer and flag a Cab. The Chaperones will miss us, but they're going to miss a lot of kids tonight. If nobody gets raped, who'll care? They got too many other things to worry about."

They strolled up University Avenue to West Main, past Rugby Road, then, Madison Lane, then Chancellor Street, and on past Elliwood Avenue; then onto the Comer near The Comer Market, beside John's Pool Hall and McAdoo's Cafe, then they ambled over to a stand of Taxis in front of the UVA's Ground Floor East Main Entrance. Ben hailed a Yellow Cab from the Cab Stand over there.

Ben opened the backdoor of the Cab, helped Mo get in by lifting the trail of her dress as she did so. He ran around to the other side of the Cab. He was all smiles. "To 222 Fifth Street Southwest," he said to the Cabdriver. The fat nut-brown man, wearing a uniform that resembled one worn by bellhops at motels, frowned. He looked back at Mo and chuckled.

"Yessir," the brown doughboy said. "Right away, Sir."

Ben got in the Cab and sat as close to Mo as he could. He was quiet as the Cab went the short distance down East Main and turned right onto Fifth Street. He noticed that Mo had a little frown on her pretty face the closer they got to his house.

"This place over here is getting down a little," Ben offered as an explanation to Mo an uptown girl. He knew that she was expecting to see a better neighborhood than what was in front of them. "I'ma have to work to better the 'Hood soon's I can," Ben said.

Mo gave him a sweet-little smile. "Baby, I'd go to wherever to be with you, Boo. No matter how it looked it'd still be Heaven to me, if I'm with you. I love you that much," she crooned.

The Cabby had to intervene. "Hey, yo, man, that's how it starts out but wait a couple of years, man.

You'll be out driving a Cab after hours just to get outta the house-trust me!" he offered.

Ben and Mo thought that was awfully funny. They laughed out loud, but the Cabby did not laugh. They arrived to the Corner of Fifth and Dice. Ben paid the Cab fare, got out and ran around to Mo's side and helped her get out of the backseat. The Cab drove off leaving them in the dark except for a streetlight across from the Corner. Ben picked up Mo and took her to his front door. He put her down and unlocked the door. He picked her up again and took her over the threshold. When he put her down this time she locked lips with him with a searching hunger that only young lovers have.

"Let's go upstairs, my bed is up there, Beautiful," Ben whispered.

Mo sighed. "Ben, it's so beautiful in here. For a bachelor, you've kept this house spotlessly clean. That furniture in the front room looks expensive. Those sofas and end chairs had to cost a lot. Pops makes a lotta money up at the UVA, but we wouldn't be able to afford these"

"Mo, Baby, Granny knew how to go to rummage sales and auctions when rich white folk were getting rid of stuff they no longer wanted so that they could get newer stuff. So over the years Granny got all of this furniture that way. That's all it was," Ben said.

Ben had a petite red and blue comforter on his bed with pink roses all around its edges. He pulled it back exposing silk sheets, his Granny used to use for guests, and two large, ornate, fluffy pillows.

Ben stood still waiting to watch Mo undress. She beckoned to Ben, "Come unzip my gown, Love," she crooned.

He stood behind her and eased the zipper on her light-blue gown from the top to her waist The gown fell away ending up around her ankles. She stepped out of that She eased down her fluffy-white half-slip, and that fell to her ankles next She was down to her "Victoria's Secret" red V-Shaped Panty-Bra, with black Nylons Combo. She had on a thin-black garter belt She paused.

"Ben ... aren't you gonna get undressed? That Tux is unnecessary right now, Love," Mo said. She giggled.

Ben started pulling off his shirt, pants, shoes, socks, down to his black Hanes' Briefs and white Gaul shirt. He had peeped at Roy and Ivy going through the motions with the girls, but he had never been alone with a near-naked one himself. He didn't know what to do, so he stood there like a kid caught with his hand in the cookie jar.

Mo sensing his premature jitters, whispered: "Come here, Ben. Touch me. Hold me close like we do at school behind the curtains on stage back of the auditorium; like we do in the back-rooms in the school press area. I'm here for you now. We don't have to hide. What do you want me to do? I want you to make love to me."

Ben pulled her tight to him and kissed her until all of his fears subsided. He picked her up and gently placed her on his bed. She helped him remove her garter belt and Nylons, then her Bra and Panties. She giggled again. He thought she was the most beautiful sight he had ever seen, from her head to her voluptuous excellent breasts, to her smooth stomach, her narrow waist to her full hips and her dark-brown, full-bush, love mound in the middle-she had it going on. She was a little nervous, but smiling and reaching out to him. "Come on, Boo, I'm ready," she said.

Ben got out of his underwear. His manhood stood at attention. Mo looked intently at it. She reached out and gently fingered the rigid head of his huge six-seven-inch male-mallet that more resembled a large serving spoon. She pulled Ben to her, positioning herself so that she was guiding him into her Feminine-V. The lips parted as Ben gently humped and thrust forward.

Mo groaned. When Ben started to pull back, she whispered: "No, don't stop-I know a little pain has to come before the pleasure-I've been told. I want the pain and the pleasure-I love you-I want you ... ow-oh, ump!-um"

Ben had never experienced anything that felt so fiercely and deliriously good in his life. He felt thrills all over his entire body. It was hot, wild, splendid, sensual, delicious and loving. Mo had tears in the corners of her eyes, but she was repeating: "Oh, Baby, Oh God, Ah Hell, Oh-oh-oh-oh-oh ... Stop! Don't Stop!"

She kissed his neck. She sucked his bottom lip into her mouth. She sank her fingernails into his back at one moment and ground her body to him seemingly with all of her might. Her eyes rolled back into her head and she made unintelligible noises, letting out spurts of air through her lovely lips. "It's so good!" she yelled. "Ben, I love you, I love you. I-I-I love you so much, Baby!"

All of that passion was all that Ben could stand. Roy had told him to "hold on for as long as you can when on top of a girlie so she'll love to love you!" But now, Ben could not hold on any longer. He had a volcanic eruption, spurting multiple gushes of lava. His whole body was in one huge orgasm. He kissed Mo all over her face, neck, breasts, and stomach, and would have gone down farther when he saw it. He hadn't bothered to tum out the lights.

There were bloodstains on the sheets. "Mo, what have I done to you, Baby?" Ben yelled excitedly.

Mo was feeling a little soreness inside herself, but what Ben said tickled her so much she had to laugh. "Ben, Baby, I can see that you've never been with a virgin before. We always bleed the first time. I'm not bleeding as much as Carolyn or Cynthia said they did.

"You've taken something away from me that no one but God can give back. It's tore a big part of my virtue away forever. It's only natural that a virgin would bleed, right. Otherwise, I'm not really hurt. I'm sore . . . but not hurt." She was still lying on the bed under a sheet.

Ben quickly got up and put on a pair of tan cargo shorts and a white t-shirt. "Baby, shouldn't I take you to the Hospital? All of the women I've seen Ivy and Roy doing-it with, I never saw one of them bleed. The only time I saw that was when they came on they periods. But never from having sex," gushed up out of Ben.

Mo chuckled. "You've never seen one of them deflowering a virgin then-that's all. I guess that's another good thing about you, Love. You're not some used-damaged-goods who don't know anything else except shitting on women. Just between you and me, that's how I see my own Father. He sees all women even me-as dangerous and untrustworthy. He'll probably be waiting up for me when I get back home. Then maybe I'll let the truth come on out then. He can't get you for Statutory Rape because I'm of age, and we're around the same age. I probably got you by a month. I'll never admit that we did anything.

"Pops has had several women since he and my Moms separated, hut he has never had anything good to say about any of them, especially after he got them to fuck. Then he equated them to being, 'another stupid Bitch-like Maya!' I hate hearing him say that about women in general, hut more so about his hateful feelings toward my Moms," Mo said, with tears easing down her lovely cheeks.

Ben picked her up and sat her in his Jap. "Baby, I love you and I will always love you. I love you more now since you gave me your most precious gift-your Virginity. I believe that you're my wife now." He put Mo down on the bed again. He got down on his knees and took her trembling right hand in his.

"Mo, will you marry me as soon as we graduate High School? We will elope right after the graduating ceremony. I wanna be with you for the rest of my life. You're the only girl I've ever felt anything for. But I'm so glad that I met you and now you're my Lover and Friend. I believe we could go through anything together. I can trust you with my life, my love, and my deepest secrets."

Mo pulled him to her and laid his head on her breasts. She whispered: "Ben, yes, Darling. I will let no one or nothing come between us. We will stay as we are until we graduate. We will leave right after that. I know my Pops will never accept you as my husband, but that's alright. I will not let him take the best thing I've ever had away from me. I won't go through life wishing I had followed my heart instead of my head. Yes, Darling, I will many you anytime, anywhere Yes!"

She put one of her supple nipples into Ben's mouth. She delighted in the joy that seemed to have given him. When he got ready to go again, she pulled away. "Ben, Darling, give that a couple of days to a week; okay?" Mo said. She giggled. "Ah-h-h, Ben ... Ah, that feels so good!"

Ben laughed. He rubbed the bulge in his pants and laughed again. Then it dawned on him: "Mo, how're we gonna get you back home without your Father finding out what?"

Mo put her clothes hack on and stood in the middle of the bedroom thinking. "You call me a Cab.

When I get home, I will have thought up a likely story to throw my Pops off the right track. He doesn't trust me anyway. Sometimes he acts like he did not believe that I was actually a virgin. He'd say things like, 'Mo, if you get pregnant., I'm going to make sure that you get a job and support your own child. Mo hear me?' I'd just ignore that shit. But I knew that he meant what he said. But the only way around that is, I'll go home and face whatever. Trust me Love, it'll be alright," Mo said.

Ben went downstairs to a little area near the kitchen to the Bell Telephone on a lamp table that had a little built-in bookshelf around it, and dialed the number for Yellow Cab. He came back upstairs.

"Mo, the Cab's on its way. I loved being with you tonight. I'll never forget what we meant to each other, Baby Girl. You're my Girl from now on-don't ever forget that okay."

Mo walked much slower than before she had been so active with Ben. She grimaced a little then got herself together. "Don't worry, Ben, I'll be alright. We'll be alright. We'll be together. I won't let anything come between us, no matter what; okay, Boo?" All of a sudden she said: "Baby, I know that Jamie was the killer of your Family. I wasn't gonna bring that up 'til you were ready. But I know all about that. You got me on that?" She saw tears come to Ben's eyes. He trembled all over.

"Ben, this old house with these Cedar-Paneled walls has great potential. I could do wonders with it It's good that you're gonna inherit it I look forward to working with you on that-okay then," Mo said.

"I got you on all-a that, Mo," Ben said. He hugged her and they kissed long and hard, then the horn of the Cab honked two, then, three times. Mo scurried down the steps with Ben in tow. He kept his left hand on her back to the front door. "See you at school. Remember, Mo, I'm crazy 'bout you, Baby Girl!"

Tears came to Mo's eyes. Before getting in the back of the Cab, Mo turned and waved and threw a kiss at Ben. She whispered: "Everything's gonna be fine." It was in the wee hours of the morning.

The Cab came to a stop in front of Mo's house on Fourteenth Street Northwest She got out very quickly and while holding the hemline of her dress so that she could run faster, she was in the door, breathing hard from anticipating facing the music. Her Pops was not waiting up for her as she had assumed he would be. In a way, that disappointed her a little. She wondered why he was being so obvious. She figured that he must've believed that because she had supposedly gone to the Junior-Senior Prom with a rich-white-guy that she would give-it-up to him. "Oh, Men!" Mo said. She ran upstairs to her bedroom.

The good thing was she didn't have to lie about where she had gone and what she had done. She got undressed, wrapped a towel around her middle, and went to the bathroom over to the bathtub. She ran it full of sudsy water. She sank down into that. She thought.: "Tomorrow will be another day. I'm no longer a little-innocent girl. Ben introduced me to the 'plains of womanhood.' I feel so warm and fuzzy inside because I have made a real man out of him, as well. I may be a little sore, but I know that will pass."

After her soaking bath, Mo felt a slight bit of cramping in her pelvic region. But she had expected that She'd been schooled by Carolyn. She took a couple of aspirins and got into bed wearing a fluffy nightgown. Bright and early the next morning, Mo was awakened by loud banging on her bedroom door. She jumped right up. She got ready to face the "Fifth Degree," from her Pops. She got out of bed and put on a thick flannel bathrobe. "I'm up now, Pops. Come on in."

He walked in wearing a blue Nikki Jogging Jump-Suit with matching tennis. "I believe you got home very late last night. How'd it go? Hope you had a goodtime. Maybe, you got a good prospect for the future. You're a very pretty girl, Mo. That Stacey guy could do a lot worse than you. You all would make a beautiful couple. Just think how pretty your children would be. I'm gonna go for a Jog. You can 1alk to me when I get back.

"I've got a little surprise for you after breakfast Fix pancakes and scrambles. Use that smoke sausage I got yesterday from Foods of All Nations, it's supposed to be Kosher, or something. I'll see you back in about an hour,. Pops Phil said. He scurried on down the steps and on out the door. Mo fell back to sleep. After breakfast, Pops led Mo to the back of the house. She saw a new Yellow and Black Volkswagen Beatle parked in the driveway.

"Pops, thank. you . . . but, why?" Mo asked. She was excited about Pops finally giving in to her request for her own vehicle, like Carolyn and Cynthia already had, as soon as they had finished driver's Ed. But why was this "Thing," happening all at once without her being allowed to voice her opinion about what kind of car she wanted?

"Mo, Honey, since your Moms left us, I've always tried to look out for you to do what was best for you, and to steer you away from what I know to be bad for you. Some of the choices that I see that you wanna make will be terrible for you down the road.

"Like, I know that you are spending a lotta time at school with that 'Brownie-Townie' you dragged home some time ago. He's not one of us. He's a 'Negro,' we're not one-a them. Our people came from Mauritius, Mauritania, Madagascar, and Jamaica, Guyana and Haiti, in South America. I don't know why you're trying to lower yourself. Why do you wanna class yourself with those people, them Negroes?"

Tears came to Mo's eyes. "Pops, what do you think Mr. Bob Marley meant when he sung: 'Africa Unite?' Who do you think he's speaking to?" she asked. Tears came down her cheeks.

Philip put his hands on his hips. "Mo, I think he's talking about those people in 'Darkest Africa' suffering from Apartheid, like in South Africa, Mol.alllhique, and Rhodesia. But I don't think he meant for us to unite with those backward people. Why ... he couldn't"

Mo stomped her feet a little as she uttered: "No Pops! He's talking about all of us who have some African Blood coursing through our veins. He's talking about Pan-African Unity. Bob Marley had a white father, but he was very proud of his African Blood. He spoke out against Apartheid. He spoke out against Tribal Factionalism. He spoke out against Ethnic Cleansing, and Religious Massacres. He wanted all people of African Descent to connect with each other and relate to each other as Brothers and Sisters.

"Pops, Black people are not Negroes! They are not 'Niggers!' Negro is just another way to say 'Nigger!'

Black people are now calling themselves: 'African-Americans!' We're proud of the African-Blood that we have coursing through our veins. I see myself as a 'Black Soul Sister!' I see that 'Brownie-Townie' as my equal, or your equal; and, I will not discriminate any more than Carolyn or Cynthia would, Pops!"

Philip shook his head in disgust. "You young people are confused, misguided, and led astray by 'demagogues' calling themselves 'Civil Rights Advocates.' I'm leading the boys on my team away from that kind of ridiculousness. I tell them to be proud of the fact that they are not in Africa. I tell them to be 'patriotic Americans.' This is the greatest Country on Earth. The 'Negroes' have it better here than anywhere in this World. Why would they wanna change what they already have?"

Mo's tears grew larger. "Pops, some of what you're saying is correct. But, Black people want Racial Equality. We don't want anyone dictating to us where and how far we can go in life based upon our skin color. Sometimes, I'm discriminated against in stores, restaurants, and theaters, because of the color of my skin. Whit.es look at Carolyn and Cynthia like, 'What are you palling around with that Nigger for!' I want that idea to change so that Black-Skinned-or people of color-can be seen in the same equalitarian way as anyone who is white-by the way-a lot of them have 'Black Blood' coursing through their veins too, like we do Pops.

"So, Pops, if you think that car is going to make me easier to control, you're wrong. I'm not your pet. I will not allow you to lead me around with anything like I was a dog on a leash. I'm you daughter. All of the expensive things like Bolivia and Swiss watches; Louis Vuitton shoes; Grisogono jewels; J-Crew body suits; Lady Timberland boots; Emilo Pucci gowns; and whatever, Pops, will not make me more amendable to your absolute control. That's why I think Moms left you in the first place."

"Enough! That's all I'm going to take from you, Moisha Melrose. Go to your room!" Philip screamed.

Mo screamed: "I hate it when you treat me like a little child. I'm a grown woman, Pops. You're not going to be able to run my life. You're not going to be able to dictate to me who I can see and who I cannot Car or no car, I'm not one-a your little-Black-Cavaliers, waiting to find out how you want them to go out and entertain the whites in the stands. I'm going to be Free soon-no matter what you think, Pops."

She ran up the steps in tears. Philip wrote a note and taped the car keys to it. He taped all of that to Mo's bedroom door. He went on out his front door.

When Mo opened her bedroom door she saw the note. It said: "Mo, you can drive this car registered in my name and on my insurance as long as you stay away from that black trash you want to fraternize with. I'll take that car away the minute I hear that he's been in it."

Ben and Mo got Invitations from both Cynthia and Carolyn to come to their graduation ceremony, but both declined. They both had great. er things on their minds, like how to be together and do that so that it wouldn't get back to Mo's Father. The car helped, but was an obstacle also. Mo knew that someone at school was undoubtedly looking out for her Father. So they felt they had to lay-low at school.

"Pops, I want to become a Registered Nurse. I see that the UVA has a Program that I can get into that could lead to me getting some help with tuition and make it easier for me to transition into a four-year degree in Nursing Science after I graduate from Charlottesville High. I want to sign up now. In the meantime, I'd like to work this summer as a Nurse's Aide to get familiar with dealing with patients and Nursing Services. Would you agree to that?" Mo asked her Father at Boars Head Inn in the main dining hall.

He spilled some brown sauce over his thick-cut of Prime Rib, smiled at Mo, took a cut of the succulent steak, chewed it up and swallowed it down. He gulped down some Rose, wiped his mouth on a cloth napkin and sighed. "Yes, Mo, I believe that will be wonderful. I was wondering when you would make a choice that could lead to a bright future for you. With your propensity to take care of stray cats, stray dogs, and stray people, I feel that you would make a fine Nurse. An RN at the UVA-or anywhere-will be a great career path for you-it may even lead you to go on and become a Medical Doctor. I say, go for it, Mo!"

Mo smiled and dug into her thin slice of Prime Rib. She was thinking: "That was the hard part. I'm glad that is over with."

"Pops, I'm going over to visit with Carolyn for a little while. Winifred

Stacey is in town," Mo lied, "and I'm hoping we can hook-up. I haven't seen him since the Prom. Don't wait up." It was late in the evening.

"Good Girl!" Philip said. "I think I'll watch 'Roots' on HBO. Go-on, ha\C some fun. You deserve it. I got your transcripts in the mail today. Mo, Baby, you got all 'A's,' I'm so proud of you."

"Thanks, Pops." Mo dashed out the front door got into her VW Bug and sped away to Ben's house.

Once she arrived there they were in each other's arms for a couple of hours making hot love!

"Ben, you can get a job this summer in Subsidiary Nursing as an Orderly. I'll be a Nurse's Aide. We will be together all summer, unless my Father finds out that we're working that close together. I don't think he will. Besides, I'll soon be on my own. We'll both be graduating in a year. You already got a house. I'll many you so fast it'll make your head spin. We'll be together forever, Darling," Mo said.

Mo got home the next morning at about seven in the morning. Her Father hadn't long gotten up and was still going through his morning exercises. He lifted up his head as he was coming out of his push-ups. "Morning, Mo. Is everything alright?" He asked.

"Everything's gonna be just fine, Pops," Mo said, with a giggle bubbling up out of her Soul. "Gotta go for my five-miler. See you when I get back," said Philip.

Chapter Eight

Ben got a job with the UVA on Barringer Five, "The Davis Ward," where mostly white mentally disturbed patients convalesced, those with mild mental maladjustments, on the four-to-twelve p.m. shift.

Mo was hired part-time. She worked on North One, where new mothers and their babies stayed until they could be safely discharged. Mo worked from five-to-ten p.m. each evening.

It was in late August, 1984, and their final year of high school was about to begin. Ben was dog-tired each night after work. So was Mo. They were able, however, to spend a lunch-break together each night Mo worked only twenty-five hours per-week: Monday-Friday. Ben worked forty-hours-per-week. He was only off every other weekend. Sometimes he was off during the week on a Wednesday and or Thursday. Mo would slip away from work. and drop by Ben's place for a "Love-In," on those middle-of-the week days.

That year Mo was allowed to leave school early on Fridays because of her high grade-point average, and she had enough credits pending to graduate without taking a full load her last year. Ben needed all of his credits to graduate on time. He had academically fooled-around during his freshman and sophomore years, and he needed to make up for those "D" and "F' grades he had gotten in a couple of core-courses so that his grade-point average would be in the passing category for graduation in 1985. In his junior year all of his grades had been "A's."

Ben fell asleep in his classes at times. He was able to maintain a "B" average in all of his classes except in Advanced Communication Skills, an elective. He fell down to a "C," in that class and it distressed him somewhat because he loved to write, and he imagined going on to college to sb.ldy for an MFA in Communication Skills after high school at Howard University in D.C. or James Madison University in Harrisonburg, Virginia. In both cases Miss Vivian Lass had written very strong letters of recommendation supporting Ben to both schools. So, Ben worked harder on getting his grades up in that class.

Ben started a daily journal wherein he noted many situations and horrible things he saw happening at the UVA. Mo gave him much information about what she saw on her floor. Their working at the UVA on the floors they worked brought them face to face with the after effects of drug addiction.

On this evening, Ben had just gotten let-in through the locked metal doors that separated Davis Ward from the rest of the "civilized" world. After coming through the doors, whitened walls and black and white tiled floors, like always, made him depressed. He entered the large foyer that had soft-fluffy green-leather sofas and end chairs all around the walls of it, that was usually empty until visiting hours from nine a.m. until nine p.m. The ceiling was high and grey-looking with very soft lighting. The only portraits on the walls were of Thomas Jefferson, George Washington, James Madison, James Monroe, and Robert E. Lee.

Ben was one of four Black Orderlies whose job consisted of helping to restrain recalcitrant and or disorderly patients during their mental crises, or when they totally broke with reality. With some that happened every other day. With others, they were like well-groomed, mild-mannered, seemingly very intelligent people until they lapsed into a psychotic episode. Then they became like growling wild animals with no grip on reality or common sense. They may defecate and eat it; suddenly take off all of their clothes and parade around like that was normal; or rip a sink. off the wall in the restroom. After the brief episode was over, they would become their "genteel" selves again. Ben never knew what to expect from day to day. Most of the patients were white women. There were twenty of them and five men. The Ward could only accommodate thirty patients at a time in rooms around the outer edges of the foyer and a large Nurses' Station in the middle of the Ward. The Head Nurse was a heavy-built German woman named Hilde Dutch Heine. She had muscles like a man. She looked to Ben to be a man with large breasts, and no hair on her face. Her hair was black and worn short with a little white nurse's hat on top that had a blue, red, and black stripe on its brim. The other ten or so nurses had just a red or a blue stripe on their hats. Ben knew those stripes meant something, but what, he never got to know that The orderlies brought in a young Black women that seemed to be in her early twenties or younger. She was mumbling something: "What y'all done with my baby? What'cha done to me? I'ain crazy! Why-ya got me in this straightjacket for? I wanna go home! Lemme outta here! ..."

The woman was hysterically strong even though she was restrained in a straightjacket and was being held by three nurses and two orderlies. Nurse Hilde came out of the Nurses' Station with a long hypodermic needle. She approached the mumbling woman and literally stabbed her in the upper arm with the needle. She injected a syringe full of tranquilizer into the maddened patient. In a couple of minutes she had calmed down and fell into a dead-sleep, and she let go of her piss and shit right at that moment.

That's where Ben came in. He had to help clean up the wheel chair, remove the soil linen, and help the nurses dress the patient that was like a wet dishrag.

On her chart, Ben read that her name was "Maxine Locklear Mandrake." She was from Charlottesville, lived on Sixth Street Southeast, and was just nineteen years old. She had just miscarried at five months pregnant. She was a "Crack Addict."

An LPN told Ben in strictest confidence: "Brother Ben, they found her out in the field off Rockland, between Lankford and Rougemont Avenues wandering around in very bloody clothes. She was high out of her mind on 'Crack' man. It'sa damn shame what that shit's doing to our people, man. She doesn't know that she's lost her baby. They found it in the field. They say it was still struggling for its life when the rescue squad came. 1be baby died. I used to do 'Crack,' Ben. I'm so glad God freed me." She cried.

Ben went to a side-room. Tears streamed down his face. He knelt down on the floor and prayed: "God, forgive me for my part in what's happening to my people. I'm so sorry. Help them Lord, Amen!"

That night, Ben and Mo got together, jumped into her 'Bug' and slipped away to his place for a little 'Quickie,' rendezvous. Ben couldn't get in the mood, nor could Mo.

"Baby, what's wrong?" Mo asked. "Don't worry, when we get together,

I tell Pops I had to work late." "It's not you, Baby Girl. It's me," Ben moaned.

"What's on your mind?" Mo asked, sitting up in bed and leaning on her elbow. She got out of bed and put on a pink bathrobe. She had taken several pieces of her clothing to Ben's place, especially underwear, robes, and extra pants and dresses. She sat in a little flowery-print French night chair that was next to a smaller twenty-eight inch TV setting on a little stand near the bed that was much smaller than the huge forty eight inch one in the living room. Ben had gotten America-On-Line Cable now that it was cheap enough. Both TV's were connected to it.

"Mo, I can't get what I saw at work today out of my mind. It's one thing when what you see is happening over there, or something. But when it's so close to my 'Hood, it's another thing altogether," Ben said with a sad whine to his bass voice.

"What's that, Baby? It must be bothering you a lot. You've never just laid there when we were in bed together. You've always been so ready to go-even before I was. So, drop the bomb-get it off your chest," Mo said. She raised the edge of her robe and scratched her left thigh. That diverted Ben's attention for but a couple of minutes. She knew then that what he was feeling had to be pretty heavy.

He got out of bed and put on a pair of black Levi Jean Shorts. He sat next to Mo in a shellac-pine-knot chair that Grandma Mildred had bought at a flea market. "Mo, a young girl in her teens came up to Davis this evening. She's from down on the Southeast Bottoms: You know in that area around lower Lankford Avenue, at the end of Hartman Mills Road, and the south side of Rockland Avenue. She was in bad shape, and was still high on 'Crack.' The Nurses say that she had just had a miscarriage of her little baby. They found her Baby Girl dead in a field near Rockland Avenue down around there.

"It made me cry real tears, Mo. We used to sell 'Crack' to anybody that had ten bucks, me Roy and Ivy. I feel so guilty. I wish I could take it all back now. They claimed that they didn't have room enough for that girl, Mo. They're sending her up to Staunton to 'Western State Hospital,' for further evaluation. She won't admit that she miscarried and left her baby girl, she had carried for about five months, in that field near Rockland Avenue. She was screaming hysterically that the Hospital Staff had her

Baby hidden somewhere and she wanted them to go get it and bring it to her! They couldn't locate any of her folk, yet.

"So, they're sending her up to that psychiatric nightmare, because she's black and poor and they don't want to treat her on Barringer. So much for desegregation at the UVA, huh, Mo?"

Tears came to Mo's eyes. "I know where you're coming from, Ben. I was with the Nursing Staff when that girl came in. Her name is Maxine. They were short-staffed up on North One on the OB/GYN Ward. I had to help out.

"After they controlled the bleeding, Maxine wouldn't calm down. Even though they gave her a mild tranquilizer, she got even more hysterical.

"We knew from the emergency Room Staff that she was high and had tested positive for Cocaine. We eventually had to tie her down on a gurney and send her up to Davis Ward. That's what you're describing, Ben. I agree with you that it's real sad. I'm glad that you got outta the game, 'Big Blue.' You're no longer responsible for the Dope Sickness in the 'Hood. You're no longer 'Big Blue' anymore.

"We can become Activists against Doping and especially against Cocaine/Crack Addiction. That's the way to go now, Sugar."

Ben shook his head in agreement with Mo. "Gonna do that, if no more, Mo," he said, teary-eyed.

He turned towards Mo suddenly. "Mo, how does your Father believe you when you tell 'im that you're working overtime? ICU doesn't allow Students to work. overtime," Ben asked.

Mo got her blue-and-white Nurse's Aide Uniform, put it on over her head and shook herself until it fell to cover the length of her body. "Well . . . Let's see how to answer that "Ben when I asked my Guidance Counselor at school about the ICU Program, he laughed. He made no bones about the fact that I qualified for a better program. He said that I needed to get into a program that would lead to a professional level that ICU couldn't prepare me for. So, he gave me an application to take home and have my Pops and I fill out. It was for a Program called 'DECA: ar' . . . Distributors' Educational Coq>oration Association.' It pays three-fifty an hour for twenty-five hours per-week, no taxes gets taken out It's salaried, so no matter how long I hang around the Hospital, I get paid the same one hundred-seventy-five dollars every two weeks. I'm supposed to save it for college tuition.

"So, Pops believes me when I tell 'im that I worked a little late, or something-though, I'm starting to feel a little ashamed and guilty for lying to my Dear Pops so much-but it's the only way I can manage to get to be with the one I love, right now."

Ben jumped up out of his chair. "What? . . . I only got paid two dollars per-hour. I got taxes taken out of that This year, I was encouraged to apply for a State job as an Orderly. They said that they had no more money in the budget for ICU. I'm only being paid two-fifty an hour now as a State employee. What's up with that, yo?" Ben said, with his temper revving up a little.

Mo smiled. She walked slowly over to her Lover, embraced him, pulling him closely to her. She whispered: "Ben . . . here's what's up with that." She stepped away from him then, she raised her voice:

"See, Honey, I'm classed as a 'Caucasian.' You're classed as a 'Negro, Black, African-American.' They can't discriminate against you like back in the day. So they have all of these subtle ways to promote white supremacy and color-based racism. They want us 'people of color' to hate and discriminate against you all. So they tell us that we're white *too;* or that we're whiter than you all. They treat us a smidgen better so that we will get the idea that our color makes us more deserving of better treatment But the truth is they hate us equally as much. They want us to help them eliminate you all. Then they will tum their racist guns on us next. That's really what is up, Ben, Darling. I'm not going for that shit, Love. But some people are.

"That's why people like Jamie Charles were brought over to America in the first place. They became 'armed camps,' they called 'Posses' to help the Whiteys kill off the 'Niggers!' Can't you see that now?

"From Vietnam, we have the Viet Cong; from Mexico we have the Mexican Mafia; from Korea we have the 'Mong.' From Puerto Rico we have the Latin Kings and Queens. From Haiti we have the Creoles; and, they all have been propagandized into believing that they're better because they have lighter-skin than so called 'Blacks' in America. They're all encouraged to discriminate against African-Americans. On a lotta Identification Cards, they have Caucasian marked in 'their Race Boxes!'

"I have some Ethiopian Friends who are 'Blacker' than you or I. But they have the ludicrous classification for Race on their ID's as 'White!' So are Cubans, Columbians, Mexicans, and people like from the Continent of India; also people from Arabic Countries. Those people who parented my Pops put that shit in his head that he was better than you all. See what I'm saying?"

Ben kissed Mo. He whispered: "Mo, you are so smart That's one-a the reasons I love you so much. We can't get it on tonight cause it's getting to be too late, and I know you'd better make the scene at your crib before your father comes looking for you, or he calls the Cops-that's a whole-other story. We don't want that to come between us. I'll see you at school and at work tomorrow. I love you so much, Baby."

Ben watched through his windows as Mo scurried out to her Bug got in it and drove away.

That following Monday at school in the Cafeteria, Ben had two hotdogs on his tray, a bag of Lays Potato Chips, and a can of Pepsi Cola. Mo had a Taco Salad and a cup of unsweetened tea. They sat in the middle of the spacious, noisy, lunchroom where they had to talk loud just to hear each other.

"Mo, I don't know if you've heard, but Maxine died, that Girl that miscarried the other night" Ben said in a groan.

Mo set her salad on the orange-colored tabletop, with the Black Silhouettes of the heads of 'The Three Musketeers,' Charlottesville High's Mascots. She spoke as though she might choke on each word. "Oh No . . . How? What happened? I thought she was in stable condition before they transported her up there to Western State Mental Hospital ... Oh God, what did they do to that Girl? I've lost my appetite!"

"Mo, calm down, Baby Girl, it wasn't nothing you did, or anyone at the UVA did. Head Nurse Heine said that Maxine died from 'Septicemia,' or some such thing. I think it's 'Blood Poisoning.' I've heard of 'Toxic Shock Syndrome,' where bacteria get into the blood somehow-through a cut or open wound.

"I've looked up that because my Cousin Arlie got that. She had to go to the UVA and was up there for a whole week before the infection got controlled. The doctors said that it was caused by 'Staphylococcus Aureus

Bacterium.' That those Germs are all around us but don't hurt us unless they get into an open wound, and you don't get treated quickly enough."

Mo scratched her cornrows. She asked: "But Maxine didn't have any open wounds. She had just miscarried. How did the bacteria get up in there, Ben? Maxine got antibiotics at the UVA; right?"

"Well, Mo," Ben replied, "She was found out in that field off Rougemont, near Rockland Avenue. Ain't nothing but old wine bottles, trash, and whatnot around there. Junkies go there to shoot up, smoke Crack, and to snort Heroin, or sometimes, Cocaine. She probably got high and fell down in a daze in all of that nasty shit around there. When she got into her miscarriage, she probably put her grimy hands right down between her legs full of all the dirt and germs around there, Mo. That's how bacteria must've got into her. The antibiotics used at the UVA didn't kill all of that It continued to grow. Up at Western State, she got sick real fast, and all they probably did was give her some more 'Dope' to keep her sedated. On a bed check they found her dead; and, she might've been using dirty needles for a long time, too."

Mo frowned, "That Staph Germ just did her end. That Girl was dead before she completely came back to herself. It's a damn shame to go out of this world not in your right mind. Well maybe Baby and Mother are together in Heaven, I hope. God help her," she allowed, "Ben, a lotta young women are coming through OB/GYN having babies they don't want They don't even know who the fathers of their children are. Too many of them are Black, Single, and Very Poor. Some of their kids come here addicted to Cocaine, Ben. Their mothers were and still are Cocaine Addicts. We know that they're on welfare and whatnot. Social Services take care of them, I guess. I know they're on Food Stamps, Aid to dependent Children, and Rent Subsidies. Some of that get traded for Dope.

"I wish I could put all of those sick, drug-dealing, Bastards who call themselves 'Players,' or 'Hustlers,' into the hottest part of Hell's Fire. They're destroying the Black Community from within. Isn't that what is wrong with Fifeville, too?" Mo shouted.

With moist eyes, Ben answered: "True that, Baby Girl. When I get on up outta here at Charlottesville, I'm gonna do everything I can to put a stop to this shit, yo. I helped to set it up, and I'm gonna help to tear it down."

Tears came to Mo's eyes as she said: "Baby, I'm with you all the way. Just let me know what you think I should do. There's the bell. See you up at the Hospital tonight"

"I don't like them Law-Dogs, but I'll even work with them to get this shit off the streets and outta the 'Hood! I'm gonna research and find out where all of this bullshit came from, and attack it right where it all began. I'm gonna get to the bottom of that barrel of Dope, I hope you feel me!" Ben said.

In May, 1985, the junior-senior Prom came and went without much notice to Ben and Mo. It was just another night for them to concoct some cover story and get together for a "Loving Goodtime."

After the third time, on the Friday night of the Prom, Ben was out of breath. Mo was in Ben's arms, with her body sweaty, sex-scented, and still pressed close to him. She was savoring her last long orgasm. She pulled away briefly from Ben. He was so satisfied that he wanted to go to sleep as usual. But "Benny-Boo, I gotta tell you something very important," she let issue out of the side of her lovely mouth in a sultry way.

"What ... I know it was good. It's always good, Baby Girl, cause I 'ma Black Don Juan!" Ben bragged teasingly.

"No Ben. It's way more serious than that I'm ... I'm ... Well, Ben, you're gonna be a Daddy. I had my last period in March. I'm two months late. I'm never late. I'm glad school is almost over.

"Ben, I'm gonna apologize to Pops. He's been too good to me-though I don't agree with a lotta things he says-I know he's taken very good care of me. He's been there for me. I don't even know my Moms. I don't know if she's alive or dead. I've been lying to Pops for over a year now. It's time for both of us to level with Pops about everything, especially now that he's going to be a Grandpapa. I want to tell him about us. I want to tell him about how much I love you and I cannot bear the thought of not being with you. He was once in love with my Moms. He ought to understand."

Ben got up and put on a black PUMA Jumpsuit He did that so abruptly that it alarmed Mo. She said: "I thought my news would make you happy. What did you expect from all of the fucking we've been doing?

I never used any contraceptives. You didn't use any condoms; so, what the fuck, Ben?"

After walking around to the foot of the bed, Ben cleared his throat "No, it's not that. I never expected to be a father so soon . . . I don't know-well . . . It's a little sooner than I may have wanted it to happen, but it's alright with me Baby Girl. Let's get It On.

"Yeah, we can go tell your Father. I already gotta house. Things are gonna be great We can get married next month right after the graduation ceremony. We'll come on back to this place over here for good. We can start our new life together. That'll be great, Mo Baby. I love you, and I'm gonna love our Baby like no Father has ever loved a child before. If it's a girl, you can name her. If it's a boy, I hope you will let me name him, like 'Kunta Kinte' did his daughter, in 'ROOTS.' Yeah, I read it, Baby Girl. It's dope, yo. How's that sound, Mo, the only woman I'm ever gonna love?

"By the way, I've been accepted at James Madison University and Howard University. But that don't matter. I'd rather be with you and our child-on-the way than anywhere else in the world, Love. Us together is all that matters to me. I will never leave you, and I hope you feel the same way."

Mo jumped out of bed and ran to Ben to bear-hug him. Pressing her beautiful, sexy, body to him got him ready again. But he pulled back. "Mo, we gotta take it easy now. You got a 'little Bun in your oven,' and I don't want nothing to happen to it on my account Kno'ar' mean?"

"Yeah, Boo, but if you be gentle we can still get it on anytime, I already looked that up," Mo said with a little giggle. "I'm going to cook a special supper and invite you, only Pops won't know 'who is coming to dinner' 'til you **get** there. We will tell him what's going on with us then. If he gets outrageous, I'll leave that evening. Is that alright with you? I'm determined, we're going to be together no matter what-I love you!"

Mo spent her whole day, starting at breakfast to late in the evening, in the kitchen cooking up something special. Philip could not figure out what had gotten into his Daughter. She hated cooking and hanging around the kitchen. That morning, however, he went quietly on about his business. He had to get the Cavaliers' Defense ready for Clemson's power-offense that coming Saturday.

When he got home that evening, he was pleasantly surprised to find that the dining room table was set with their Silk Tablecloth and Napkins, polished Silverware, and Crystal drinking glasses. A noble floral display was in the center of the brown mahogany table with eight chairs around it that resembled an English King's table. Red, Pink, and Yellow Roses were arranged in a large Crystal Vase in such a way that they resembled the face of a woman, Mo had set in the middle of the table.

Philip set his brown-leather carryall bag down with the Cavaliers' Logo on its side in the hallway because he *w.as* so astonished at what he was witnessing. He realized: *Mo is finally growing up and turning into a pretty little lady.*

Mo stood near the entrance of the door to the dining room, at the end of the hallway that led from the front door to the backdoor to the screened-in back porch. She was dressed in a white gown, but had a black apron that also had the Cavaliers' Logo enlarged on its front. It had been a gift from her Pops for one Christmas or another. She had never worn it until this evening.

"Pops, go on into the showers, I'll get supper on the table, we have a very special guest coming for dinner this evening. And remember Pops, I love you, but I got my own life to live, too"

Philip thought that statement was a little strange, but a lot of things teenagers did were strange. So he ran on up to the shower got undressed and got in. He didn't stay in it as long as he usually did. Mo's strange behavior was pressing him forward. He wanted to know what she was really up to. Maybe, she wanted a bigger, newer car or something like that. He got dressed in tan slacks, a white Van Heusen shirt, blue-silk socks, and Oxford Penny Loafer-typical Virginia-Gentlemen's attire. The odors coming from the kitchen were oh-so-magnificent.

"Pops, you come on and sit at the head of the table in the King's Seat." Philip was so proud of his only Progeny. "Who's coming to dinner, Honey?" Philip asked. "He must be somebody very special."

"Pops, he should be here any moment now. Let me pour you a little pink champagne. I got a bottle in the cooler, on ice, chilling in the pantry. Let me go pour you a glass, okay?"

"Yeah, sure," Philip said.

Mo came back with a tall glass of fizzing champagne. She gave it to her Father. He took a sip and smiled. He heard the doorbell rang.

Philip got up to go answer the door. Mo raised her hand, "No Pops, I'll get the door this time. You enjoy your drink." She took off her apron, and laid it on one of the chairs in the middle of the table. She skipped to the front door like a little girl because she was so excited.

"Oh, I'm glad you made it Come on in. I want you to meet my Pops the right way this time. He's at the dinner table relaxed and waiting to see what's up with me and whatnot." She put her arm in the fold of Ben's arm and they slowly walked down the hallway toward her Father.

"When Ben and Mo got to the dining room, Philip jumped up from the chair he had been seated in. "What in the name of San Miguel are you doing now, Mo?" he asked in a voice that sounded like some monster out of a Star Trek mystery.

Mo smiled nervously. Her words came out like Dorothy's in the Wizard of Oz: "Pops, this is the man I love. No matter what you think about him, I love him, and I have since I first met him. We' re going to get married right after our graduation ceremony ends. We want your blessing. We need that"

Philip spoke pointedly, shaking his trigger finger at Ben as he yelled: "You . . . you . . . I will never give my blessing, Mo. Not so that you can many this . . . this poor excuse for Humanity!"

Ben walked over to Philip wearing his most fierce 'Gangster' façade. "Why are you so dead against me, Sir. I'm poor it's true, but I got potential. I love your Daughter. I'll be good to her. That ought to be enough for a start, Sir," Ben said. He spoke forcefully but in a respectful way.

Philip ran to a cabinet in the back of the dining room. He got out a silver box, opened it, and pulled out a fistful of Hundred-Dollar Bills. He yelled: "Take that and get-the-hell-out! That's what you Brownie Townies really want anyway, ain't it? You don't love my Daughter-you don't know how to do that It's not in you to do that. You just don't have it in you, Sambo!" He threw the money on the floor in front of Ben.

Mo got between Ben and her Father. "Pops, I'm prepared for that kinda reaction outta you. I figured you would not understand. So, I packed my suitcases ahead of time. I'm eighteen now. I'm leaving with Ben tonight. You can give us your blessing, or you don't have to.

"You can't stop me from being with the man I love. I'm going to have his Baby. We're going to be a family. It's gonna happen whether you want it to or not. Now, it's up to you, Pops," Mo nearly screamed.

Ben growled from down in his stomach. "Sir, I don't want your money unless it's to help us get married.

Otherwise, I have all that I need in this world as long as I'm with Mo." He hugged Mo tightly to him.

Philip got a dazed look on his face. He stumbled back to the King's Seat at the table and hung his head and cried. He moaned: "I should've put you in an exclusive Private School, but I wanted you to be freer than that. I never thought you would tum to the 'ghetto' after experiencing a life of having everything you ever wanted. I gave you all my love. I was your Mother and Father.

"Now, what thanks do I get? You've gone out and sullied yourself with the lowest part of Humanity and for what, lusts, a goodtime in bed, or just to experience a little slutty tryst like that Newspaper Heir? We ought to be trying to move up to a better life, not the reverse. Look what it's got your Mother?"

Mo broke down in tears. "Pops, you drove her away just like you're driving me away. You never remarried because you drive every decent woman you ever dated away. You're too demanding. You're too domineering. You're too self-centered, and much too damn arrogant! Pops, you're a 'Racist!' You're just like a 'White-Racist,' only you're not White! You're a main part of what is wrong with us who are all descendants of Africans. How can you coach Black Players if you hate their race so badly? Do they know how you really feel about them? Don't you know that white people laugh at you behind your back? I've seen them doing it. I don't ever want to be like that, Pops. I will never raise my child to think like that, like you tried to do with me.

"I'm going upstairs and get my bags. I'll put them in the Bug and Ben and I will drive out of your life forever if you don't change. Or, we will get a Cab if you want the keys to your German-Made Jalopy!" Mo screamed at her Father.

Mo struggled at the top of the steps with her two heavy suitcases. Ben ran up the steps to help her carry them down. She stood waiting for her Father to say something-something repentant. But he just buried his face in his hands and sobbed. Mo walked past her Father sobbing, big tears fell from her eyes.

"By the way Pops, there's Cherry-Glazed Cornish Hen in the oven, stuffed with Rice Pilaf, with a sautéed Beets, Squash, and New Peas Medley. Enjoy!" Mo yelled as she rushed on past her Father who seemed so locked in his own selfishness so that he couldn't break. free not even to say goodbye to his only child leaving home possibly for good. "Goodbye, Pops," Mo groaned.

"Goodbye, Sir. I'll take good care of your Daughter, you'll see," Ben said. Ben had on his Prom Tux that he had first met Mo in. Once they got to the car, Ben said: "Mo, something powerful is going down."

Chapter Nine

A couple weeks after Mo had left home and moved in with Ben, she was still grieving over how she and her Father had separated. The Graduation Ceremony was held in the auditorium of the Basketball Arena at the UVA in the Field House Gymnasium in the second week of June.

Mo sat through the whole ceremony nearly in tears because her Father did not attend. He always stressed that she should do well in school, and that she should graduate and go on to college. She had done well in school and she was already accepted into the UVA's School of Nursing Science with a full scholarship for four years. No matter what had happened recently between her and her Father she wanted him to be at her graduation. She had only been away for a little over two weeks, but she thought: "Oh, I miss my Pops so much We have never been apart from each other since I can remember. I love Pops! He is the First Man in My life!."

Ben noted that Mo was sad, moping, and teary-eyed since she had moved out of her home with her Father to come live with him. He knew that he had to remedy that problem before it took root and became an "unmanageable traumatic tree."

"Moisha Melrose. Maisha Melrose ..." her name was called twice by Assistant Principal, "Merlyn Baugh." Mo was so deep in thought about how to fix things with her Father that she didn't hear her name at first But then she rose and strolled up the aisle in her dark-blue gown, with her square-hat perched on top of her head with the orange tassel dangling. Instead of feeling joy, she felt a deep sorrow. 'When she reached the tall, blonde, Miss Baugh, at the podium, a "Marilyn Monroe" with a little less makeup, dressed in her PhD gown with its multiple-colored hood, Mo burst into tears for a couple of seconds. She took the diploma and hurried across the stage past, Dr. E. G. Holloway, a City Councilman.

She stumbled past Vice Mayor, Celine Mayberry to the edge of the stage, down the steps and back to her seat.

Ben's eyes were on his beloved all the way up to the steps to the podium to get his diploma. Look to him like it took forever for his name to be called, because there were too many "R's" graduating that year. He hoped the rest of the alphabet was not so popular. He wanted this thing to be over so that he could get with Mo and comfort her.

He could see even through Mo's gown a noticeable hump. She was going on four months long. She was still experiencing a little bit of morning sickness. But other than for her sadness, her skin had taken on a beautiful glow. It was typical of pregnant girls.

Dr. E.G. Holloway was the Minster who had said the opening prayer to initiate the Ceremony. Vice Mayor Mayberry had delivered the speech. Ben was glad when she stopped speaking and the Assistant Principal came to the podium to call out the names for the graduates to come get their diplomas. Ben's mind stayed on Mo, the woman he wanted to go marry right away-even though he had no idea how to get all of that done, so soon. He felt like love would lead the way.

After Ben got his diploma in hand, he signaled to Mo to head on out of the auditorium, like a few graduates had, out the doors yelping and screaming with joy, that "It's all over-High School is a thing of the past! ... Yahoo!"

They left the ranks of the packed auditorium to one of the exit doors and Ben picked Mo up, heavy as she had become, and kissed her. They had already gotten a Blood Test at the UVA, and a Marriage License. He knew that these essential things had to be done before the rest could happen. Luckily the benediction was not long in being executed by Reverend Holloway.

Ben saw the horde of graduates and their parents and guardians swarming the huge parking area around The Field House. The Gymnasium emptied out like water pouring over a dam. People were hugging and crying out in joy. Then the City Officials came out of the massive front doors of the Gym to the steps leading to them. They shook hands with various people. Ben spotted Rev. Holloway on the steps. He ran to him all at once. He was the Pastor of Zion Union Baptist up on Preston Avenue, a Church that was "thrown out" when Vinegar Hill was demolished in 1964.

"Rev, sorry to bother you-but I gotta ask you something very important," Ben blurted out

"No, young man, you can never be a bother to me," the fat, light-skinned man, that seemed to be in his late forties, in his gray suit under a Purple Robe with Gold Lapels, said graciously. "Just tell me how I can help you."

Ben was very nervous. "Sir, my girlfriend and I need to get married right away. That's her over there under that Weeping Willow Tree. You can see the need, Sir." Ben said.

The Reverend smiled. He rubbed his dean-shaven face, except for a very-thick, brown mustache. He was bald-headed, except for a little lock of straight-brown hair dangling off his forehead. "Come by my office next week and my secretary will schedule a quick-date for us to get to the bottom of what you are suggesting. We're located across from Washington Park. You can't miss it-it's got a huge Cross built right in front of it that goes from the roof to the foundation. The front of the Church resembles a triangle. See you then. I love you and God Loves you more!"

Ben shook the Pastor's hand. He felt an overwhelming burst of joy inside, but Mo's sadness put a damper on that as soon as he went back to her at the Willow Tree.

"Mo, Darling, I got it all set up. We can go meet with the Reverend next week. He's the Preacher at our Graduation Ceremony, now he'll be the one who will marry us. Mo, that's great, right?" Ben said.

Mo groaned, "Ben . . . I hope my Pops will get involved with all of this. I want him to be there when we get married. It would mean so much to me, for us, and this Baby soon to come in five months."

Ben shook his head in agreement with her. "Be it ever so humble, there's no place like home; and be they ever so crummy, there's no family like yow- own," Ben allowed. "Mo, I get you on that. I know what you mean when it comes to family ties. I feel you.

"Maybe your Father is not as hard as he seems on the surface. No Dad thinks the guy stealing his 'little girl's heart' is good enough for her. That's how we men be. It's probably that way with women too.

"Let's get in the car and drive on home. Maybe things will get better in time. Least that's what I'm hoping for."

Mo had on a loose-fitting white dress under her robe. She took off the bulky robe and cap and handed those to Ben. "I'll feel more comfortable without all these clothes on. I feel so hot. like, I'm burning up. I wish I had me some vanilla ice cream. Oh ... please take me over to the A&P at Barracks Roads Shopping Center and get me a brick of vanilla ice cream-please! I gotta have some right now!"

Ben knew that Mo was craving. So he did not argue with her. He ran over to the middle of the parking lot got in the Bug and came back to the Weeping Willow to pick Mo up. She got in the car and they sped three blocks over to Copley Road to Emmet Street, turned left on Emmet and made the two blocks to The A&P on the south end of Barracks Roads in five minutes.

Ben got out of the car and ran into the Supermarket, the largest one in Barracks Roads, and came back really soon with a brick of Pet Vanilla Ice Cream. He bought a table spoon also. He snipped the tear-open sealing on the side of the brick of ice cream. He lifted the top up.

Mo dug the spoon into the ice cream, got out a big chunk and devoured it. She handed the brick back to Ben. She became very tired and sleepy right away. "Let's go home, Baby, I'm dog-tired," Mo said. "Aren't you gonna eat more of the ice cream? You told me to get a brick. Now, you've only taken a spoonful. I could've gotten that down the street at Baskin & Robbins" Ben complained.

Mo burst into tears. "Ben, you're always fussing at me. Let's go home. I'm real tired. Don't fuss, Ben!" Mo yelled.

Ben knew that what he was hearing were her hormones talking. So he kept quiet. He was thinking: "Man, is that what Mo's being pregnant gonna mean? Oh Man!"

Mo complained as Ben drove south on Emmet to University Avenue. He turned left and drove to West Main. He was sorry he had chosen to go that way. Mo started to whine.

"Ben, Pops won't even take my calls. He got one-a them new answering machines. It shows the callers' numbers and ID's. What am I gonna do? What are we gonna do to bring Pops around? We gotta think of something before too long. What?"

Ben was glad to get to the front of his house at last, though it was not really that far away from the Gym. Mo got quiet when they pulled into the little driveway behind the house. He helped Mo out of the car and hugged his arm around her waist as they went up the Dice Street side to Fifth. Both Ben and Mo were surprised at what they saw.

On the deck was a large bouquet of yellow Roses. They were arranged in the likeness of a Swan. There was a large white envelope on top of it. Mo got new strength from the sight in her view, ran forward and grabbed the envelope.

She opened it and pulled out a typed letter with a certificate inside. She read what was written within aloud with tears streaming down her cheeks:

"Dear Moisha. I'm sorry for how I've been acting lately. I'm going to need some time to get used to Benjamin Luther Slokum. But I'm going to try with all of my heart for your sake and for the sake of the child you are bringing into this world.

"You will find enclosed a certificate entitling you to a four-hundred-dollar-a-month Stipend contingent upon your successful work at the UVA. A check will be mailed out to you each month that your grade point average stays above passing, and you remain registered as a full-time student, for each semester. Show this Certificate to the financial aid office at the time of your registration. I'm paying for this Scholarship.

"In about a month I want you and Ben to come to dinner again. This time we will sit and talk like adults about what the future holds for us all. In the meantime I hope you all will consider moving away from where you are living to a better neighborhood. I will be glad to help you with that if you want me to.

"Mo, call me. Let's talk. Come by to see me at any time. But don't bring Ben until the dinner. I hope you will understand that I need a little time. I love you and I will surely love the child you are having with Benjamin. He's named after one the 'Twelve Tribes,' you know. His name means: 'Son of the right hand-thus the favorite Son.'

"Moisha, your name is Hindi and it means: 'Very Intelligent Woman.' Maybe, it's meant by God that you two join. I will throw caution to the winds. I will pay for the wedding wherever you all want to have it. Get back with me on that. Okay?

"Mo, this man is your choice for a husband. I will not *try* anymore to come between you and him. I ask your forgiveness, and the forgiveness of Benjamin. Tell him what I'm saying in this letter. "Love you, little Mo. Call me soon, Your Pops."

Mo dropped the letter to the floor and grabbed Ben hugging him tightly. "Pops seems to be having a great change of heart, Ben. Oh, that's why I love him so. He may not start out right but he will end up doing what is best for me. I don't know how he got such a terrible attitude toward my Moms. But he has always been there for me. Ben, maybe, things are starting to look up for us."

Ben pulled away from her for a moment. "Mo, there's only one thing that's not down with me.

"Baby, I don't want to leave the 'Hood. It's where I am. I mean, I want to stay and make things better over here. I believe that this is possible no matter how bad things seem to be going right now. I have the hope that if two of us will put forth the effort, God will step in and do the rest, that's what Granny always used to say. I'ma take her up on that.

"If we all kill one-nother off, or move away, or just disappear, what will become of the 'Hood? Too many houses are getting boarded-up already. The Desegregation Laws shouldn't mean that our place in this life ought to be deteriorated. Black 'Hoods ought to be able to remain Black. How is it gonna help us if we all get flushed down the toilet of progress? Can you feel me?"

Mo gave Ben a little nervous smile. "I'm with you, Love," she said. "I've always said that. I meant it when I first said it, and I mean it even more now. Wherever you are, that's where I wanna be.

"Ben go get the ice cream. It's gotta be getting real soft now, but I still want it. I still need it, please."

Ben ran around to the VW Bug, snatched the door open got the ice cream and it was almost runny. He ran with it back to Mo. He gave it to her after spilling some on his shoes.

As neat as Mo usually were in everything she did, she sat down on the deck of the steps and took the spoon out of the bag and dug into what was left of the brick of ice cream. It ran down her chin, down onto her gown. She gulped it down in a hurry, getting it all over her mouth like a little girl.

"I'm glad that I took those Graduation Gowns on back right after you gave me yours. We would have to pay fifty-seven dollars for each of them if we had gotten ice cream stands on them. They would not have taken them back. So go ahead, Baby. I can see nothing in the world means more to you right now than eating that brick of ice cream," Ben said. He laughed.

Mo looked up at him and smiled and then burped. A full-moon lit-up the night sky.

A month went by. Ben had turned eighteen in mid:June. He noticed that the hundred-dollars he'd been getting each month from his Grandma's death-benefits had not arrived. It was mid:July and he had found out that neither JMU nor Howard would extend enough scholarship money for him to attend either of those Universities. He would have to come up with a sizable amount of money to be able to pay tuition and fees. Attending either of those schools was now impossible.

Besides, Mo had a full-scholarship to attend the UVA So Ben knew he had to find some other way to get a "foot in the door," so to speak.

Repeated phone calls to his Uncle Franklin went unanswered. Ben thought about going up to Whitehall to pay Unc' Frank a visit, but thought better of it. He knew he might get shot as a prowler or something if he showed up in that racist neighborhood where his Uncle lived and "passed for white." So a visit was out of the question.

A loud knock on the front door this morning woke Ben up, even though Mo, whose stomach was protruding out and up making her look like a human balloon, slept right on. Ben jumped out of bed and darted down the steps to the hallway, then to the front door. He opened the door and a well-dressed looking white man wearing a two-piece black suit handed him a brown envelope. "You've been served, Sir. Have a nice day," the wearer of the black suit chirped.

Ben opened the brown manila envelope and pulled out an official-looking document bearing the Seal of the Clerk of Court for the City of Charlottesville. It read:

"Mr. Benjamin L. Slokum, This is to notify you that the property at 222 Fifth Street Southwest has been confiscated and presented for resale for Taxes Owed to the City of Charlottesville, Virginia. A Private Party has paid the Real Estate and Personal Property Taxes on the home at 222 Fifth Street Southwest. Real Estate IV is in charge of the Real Estate Negotiations. You must 'yield up the property.'

"You have forty days from today's date to 'File a Rebuttal.' You must be represented by Counsel. The Property at 222 Fifth Street Southwest that was once in the Trusteeship of one Mr. Franklin F. Tinsley did pass into the hands of Mr. Benjamin L. Slokum as of July, 1985. The Property is in the arrears of $3000.00 tax owed to the City of Charlottesville, Virginia, with penalties and fees. The full tax burden is now upon the shoulders of the Inheritor, Mr. Benjamin L. Slokum.

"Real Estate IV will cause the Property to pass legally and permanently into the hands of a Private Citizen if said Inheritor does not dear all debts owed to the Guarantors of Tax and fees Owed to the City, and Real Estate IV. You may reply to this summons and notice in Person or by Counsel."

It was signed by the Clerk of Court.

Ben went outside dressed in his pajamas and sat on the steps of the deck. He was wondering: "What the fuck am I gonna do now? I got a girlfriend who is pregnant and fat as an Elephant, with both feet swollen, and her legs are swelling too. I'm working as an Orderly on the UVA Nut-Ward. I thought I was going to be the owner of Grandma's House. Now I know that will never happen. What will I tell Mo? We can't afford no Lawyers. I don't know what in the Hell I'm gonna do!"

Ben jetted back into the house, got showered, got dressed and was gone without waking Mo. He knew where one of The Real Estate IV's offices was. He decided he'd jog down to the bottom of Fourth Street Northeast where part of Vinegar Hill once stood. Real Estate IV was on the Fourth Floor in a huge brick Building on top of Guarantors Savings and wans at the front entrance of the building. The Unemployment Office was in the same building, overlooking the Omni Hotel right next to it, between McDonald's and Wendy's Restaurants. Ben hated what Vinegar Hill had become. He didn't want that to happen to Fifeville. But it looked like it was headed that way anyway.

When Ben got back home that morning, he felt a disgusting grinding pain in the pit of his stomach. What he was hoping to build a new life on, the foundation was being ripped away just like that, and there was nothing he could seemingly do about it

Mo was up and was in the bathroom throwing up. She should've gotten over that already, but it seemed to be coming back on her again.

After being only five months pregnant, she was as big as a woman would be in nine months. She still had four months to go. Her cravings had shifted from ice cream to Molasses and Butter. She had half a-pound of butter whipped into a bowl that she ate with a tablespoon. Then one day she gulped down a whole pint-jar of creamy peanut butter.

"Where you been Ben? I got up and I couldn't find you anywhere. My ankles ache so bad. My feet hurt me so bad when I try to walk," Mo screamed. It seemed like she might break down and cry any moment.

"Feel like a whole troop of soldiers is moving around in my guts," Mo whined.

Ben had a lot on his mind. He wondered what to tell Mo. She was starting to have a very difficult time carrying her "Little Bundle of Joy," to term. The news he had to drop on her would only make her feel more miserable. Grandma Mildred had always told Ben though, that, "Telling the truth is always the best. Every lie will require another one to cover the first one. That can go on forever. So don't start. The truth will set you free!" So Ben decided he would throw caution to the winds. He'd tell Mo what was really going on.

"Mo, come on down to the front room. I want you to sit down in the softest end chair over near the sofa. I've got some bad news to drop on you," Ben spoke in a very low groan.

"What is it, Baby, what's going on with you, now?" Mo asked. She rubbed her stomach through her bulky housecoat. "This child's got to be a girl. It's so rambunctious. It can't wait to get out here into the world," she said, as she ambled on down the steps and into the front room.

"Mo, Darling, we might have to move out of this place. Unc' Franklin, my guardian, has let the taxes go unpaid on this house. It will probably cost us nearly ten-to-twenty thousand dollars to keep this old house.

"We're gonna have to hire a highfalutin Lawyer. We'll have to pay off the three-to-four thousand dollars in back taxes to some unknown person, first. That keeps growing every day that it remains unpaid. Then we will have to pay the person that paid off our back taxes whatever he wants to charge us-that could go way up into the thousands of dollars. I don't know what to do.

"Mo, this house is where I mostly grew up in. I moved &om up on Ridge Street when I was a little boy.

You see, that's why I keep Granny's and Roy's and Ivy's rooms exactly like they left them before they were killed. It's in memory of them. It's all I got from them. Ivy and Roy left a few thousand dollars, up in a crawl space in the wall, but I've spent most of that now. So all I have of them is in this house. It's like this house is my life, and my life is this house. You feel me?"

Mo stopped complaining about her tough pregnancy for the moment. "Boo, I do. I feel where you're coming from. I don't have any place like this in my life. Pops have been renting since I can remember. I don't know if I would be able to leave a place like this if one existed in my life.

"Who is in charge of the negotiations for this house?"

Tears eased down Ben's cheeks. "It's that big, O' Real Estate Company that's been buying up all the houses you see boarded-up 'round here. It's Real Estate IV. They won't even tell me the name of the person they're representing. I would go talk to him." Ben was up pacing around in the room.

Mo stumbled up off her chair. A little piss circle remained on the pillow of the chair. She said: "Go set-up a meeting with Real Estate IV and see what you can work out with them. Okay, Ben?"

Ben shook his head in agreement "I'll get dressed and jet right on back down to Real Estate IV," he said.

He was at the Omni in a jiffy because he drove the VW Bug. He found a space in the spacious parking lot in back of the Omni. He trudged on over to the front of (what was then) referred to as, "The Savings and Loans Building." He wore a blue blazer, tan slacks, and penny-loafers. He sported a red-white-and blue-striped tie and a light-blue shirt He wanted to impress the people at Real Estate IV.

When he walked into the front entrance of the building, with the wide plate glass window with the Logo of the bank broadly painted on it in red-white-and-blue decorative lettering, a Black Security Guard wearing an S&C Security uniform that resembled a black police uniform with different red insignia on its sleeves approach Ben.

"Hold it right there! Where are you going?" the tall, Atlas-built Guard called out to Ben. 1bis guy had a bald head, but a full beard and mustache. He was like a "Black Co'jac," with a beard. He was carrying a Billy Club and a Gunn, so Ben stopped before reaching the elevator. He wondered: "Where was this guy earlier this morning?"

Ben raised his hands like when he was confronted by the police. "I'm Ben Slokum, here to see Miss Elle Louise Dubois, up on the Fourth Floor at Real Estate IV. I saw her this morning. I'm here to do a follow-up meeting."

The Guard looked Ben over. He asked: "Do you have some **ID?"** He was grimacing at Ben.

Ben lowered his hands slowly. He saw the Guard put his hand on the white handle of his Thirty-Eight Smith & Wesson Revolver that was in a side-holster. He got out his wallet, took out his driver's license, and handed that to the Guard.

The Guard looked it over and shoved it right back to Ben. "Now, let me call up to see if you can go up to see Miss Dubois right now," he growled.

Ben noticed that there was no one else Black in the place except for the Guard. Several White Customers were coming and going into the customer-lines of S&L that were not open that morning when Ben had first arrived at the S&L Building. The Bank's counter area was sealed off by a glass-petition that went from one side of the building to the other. It had been raised half-way up into the ceiling.

The Guard went over to a little comer office that had a black phone setting on a small round table. He dialed a number and spoke into the phone. He promptly put the phone down and came back over to Ben. "Sorry for the inconvenience, Man. But we have been robbed several times. That's why they got me here. I have to make sure ... You unner'stan' me?" the Guard said. "Take the elevator on up to Four."

Ben rolled his eyes. "Dude, I'd expect more'n that from a Brother, yo. Look at how I'm dressed. Do I look like a Bank Robber to you? Not all Black men are crooks! Not all Black people who come down here, do that, so that they can get into some kinda trouble. What the Hell is up with that, yo?"

The Guard stepped defiantly close to Ben. "Nigga, look! I've been here now for a couple of years. I know what the fuck is going on in the 'Hood, and out of it-you got that! When the bad shit goes down, my job, my wife, and my children gon' be on the line. Fuck that-and you too, if you can't get with that Now you carry your black ass on up to the Fourth Floor before I throw you on out that big-O' Front Door!"

Ben turned and headed to the elevators just to the right of the front door. Like it or not, he understood where the Guard was coming from. He pushed the Up-Button to summon the elevator. It came promptly. A tall, blonde wearing a tight-fitting red-mini-dress, and black thigh boots, came out of the elevator. When she saw Ben, she grabbed her black carryall lady's bag and clasped it to her side. She shot past Ben like he might be in pursuit of her. She didn't stop until she was outside of the building. She looked very afraid.

Ben stepped off the elevator into a spacious waiting room area that had several plush white-leather covered sofas and end chairs, and a mahogany coffee table that sat in the middle of the area that was filled with the latest fashion magazines. There were three desks, one in each comer of the area. The walls had dark-green tiles, and the ceiling had light-green tiles. A line of florescent lights went across the middle of the ceiling.

"Hello. May I help you?" a high-pitched female voice asked Ben. She was sitting at the desk closest to the elevators. No one sat at the other desks. She was fat and buck-tooth. She had beady-little blue eyes that were set in a large-tan brow. Her hair was beige and was worn in a page-boy style. She had on a purple dress that came all the way down to her ankles. Her face was overly made up making her look like she had on a costume mask. She stood up as she spoke. "May I help you find somebody?" she asked Ben again.

"I'm here to see Miss Dubois," Ben said in a loud and clear voice. "The Security Guard said ..."

One of three doors around the walls of the area was flung open. In walked Miss Dubois. She was wearing a tight black mini-dress and matching pumps. Her brown nylons were shiny and had a yellowish sheen about them with beige sparkles all over them. She was very shapely and very bosomy. She was very well made up to resemble a movie star or someone like that She actually resembled Lucy Carmichael of "I Love Lucy," Ben thought.

But her voice was like Joan Collin's. "Hello Mr. Slokum. Come into my office. Good to see you this morning. Would you like a cup of coffee?

We have some set up in back if you would like some," eased out of Miss Dubois's full but sensual lips that were made up to look like the surface of strawberries.

"No Ma'am, I'm anxious to talk with you about what's happening to me. I'd like to get on with that if you don't mind," Ben groaned.

Ben had met with her before at one of the desks out front He followed her into a large meeting room this time that had a conference table with about twelve chairs around it Up front in that office was a large desk and a fluffy white-leather end chair next to it. Beside those there stood a portable blackboard with several pieces of chalk on its chalk-rest.

"Have a seat Mr. Siok.um," Miss Dubois pointed to the end chair. She sat in a fancy-grey swivel chair behind the desk that was like the sofas and end chairs. "What can I do for you this morning?" she asked.

"Miss Dubois you've told me that you cannot divulge the name of the person who paid the taxes on my property. But I really would like to get to talk with him. I don't want to move out of that house. It means the world to me. It's where I grew up. All of my fondest memories in life have happened in that house. I'd like to find a way to stay in there until I can buy it back from you all," Ben said.

Miss Dubois turned to a large gray line of file cabinets back behind her desk. She got up out of her chair, opened one of the draws of the cabinets and got out a manila folder. "Our client will allow you to rent the house for the time being, if you simply do not want to move at this time.

"You will have to do that through this office. Would you be interested in doing that Mr. Siok.um?"

Ben rubbed the right side of his face. "I guess I would. My girlfriend and I are getting married. We have a child on the way. I would like her and my child to live with me in 'our home.' I don't want to move. Hopefully, I'll soon be able to buy the house back. from whoever's got it now. See what I'm saying?" Ben said. His voice was full of remorse.

"Yes. Yes, I see what you're saying, but I don't think the house is going to be on the mark.et for some time. Right now the rental fee will be a-hundred-dollars per-month, and a one-time hundred-dollar deposit. You will need to fill out an application with us, pay the first month's rent and the deposit and you will be able to remain on the property. Is that amendable to you, Mr. Siok.um?" Miss Dubois said.

Ben gave no other answer than to snatch the application out of Miss Dubois's hand, got up from the chair and headed to the elevators. He thought better of his actions. He returned to the chair. He filled out the application. He wrote a check for two-hundred dollars from his Virginia National Bank Checking and Savings Account. He dropped that on Miss Dubois's desk.

She gave him a property survey report. "Mr. Slokum go back to 'the property' and do a survey of the infrastructure and report back to me any flaws, repair needs, and or, substandard conditions pertaining to 'the property.' All of those will come out of your deposit when you leave the property. Understand?" she said.

"Damn," Ben snapped. "What'll you gonna want next? Lemme get the Hell on up outta here!" He took the three-page survey and headed to the elevators. He was very pissed. He felt like he'd been treated like a stray dog that came out of the woods into someone's yard that hated dogs. The Security Guard was in his little Guard Room now taking it easy. He wasn't scrutinizing anyone like he had Ben when he came in. When Ben had first come in there was no Guard. He went up to Miss Dubois's office without being made to feel like a crook about to rob the place. The Bank wasn't open yet-maybe that was why no Guard.

Ben felt like he'd better get on out of that building before his bad side came bursting out like the "Incredible HULK!" He made it to the parking lot and got into the VW Bug and sped home like a "Bat Flying Out Of Hell!"

The only good thing Ben could glean from what had just occurred was that he would get to live in the House that was much more than "the Property," as Miss Dubois like to call it, but was his "Home!" That was what Ben was very afraid of losing.

Mo was up and had finally gotten herself together. She heard what seemed like a firecracker exploding. The sound came from the direction of Tonsler's Park. Then she heard three more "Pop! Pop! Pow!" noises, that came from the Fifth Street area near the Park. She heard "Damn-Man-Motherfucker!" followed by what she knew were gunshots. She trembled all over.

She wondered what kind of neighborhood had Ben moved her into?

Several buildings were boarded up and no one was trying to rent them. Teenagers were wearing their Jeans hanging off their hips-even the girls. There were groups of guys wearing red or black bandanas around their necks or tied around their heads. When school was open these kids stayed out on the Streets in the same places every day. Mo wondered was Ben wrong about this place being worth saving? How could that happen?

Mo heard Ben coming in the front door. She made it down the steps to meet her husband to be. "How did it go, Baby, down at Real Estate IV?" she asked.

Chapter Ten

"Mo, I got the papers all filled out and signed. What I don't understand is: why is it that no one from Real Estate *N* came over here to inspect this House for the Company? Why are they just letting me fill out a Building Report on my own? That doesn't make any sense. What's up with that?" Ben said.

Mo was thinking: "It may have been better if Real Estate *N* had refused Ben the right to rent this house. I don't really want to live over here; but, I will never go against Ben's wishes. I know how he cherishes the memory of his Grandmother, Cousin and Big Brother. But I hope we can move from over here at some time in the near future. This neighborhood is way too scary of a place for me!"

Mo hugged Ben with a little smile on her puckered lips. She kissed Ben a brushing kiss on his full lips. "Baby, we got four months to go and we'll be parents. We're living in a House already-as renters-and we might buy a House lat.er-I mean this House. But . . . Ben, we gotta go ahead with getting married. I don't wanna have our child while we're not married, yet You feel me?" She wanted to change the subject a little for the moment

"Mo you can't go out anywhere. Your condition is not good. But, I tell you what: I'll try to get Reverend Holloway to come over here and perform the marriage. We can have a Church Wedding lat.er, if you want to. I know that is what your Father has in mind. I'll bet that the Rev. will go along with our plans. What do you think?" Ben looked at her hoping she would get with him on that proposal.

Mo looked up into his eyes and smiled. "I'm with you, Baby, whatever you wanna do, it's alright by me," she crooned. "Oh Ben, sometimes, I feel like this baby is going to bust-my-gut The OB/GYN people say my pregnancy is normal. That the baby's heart sounds healthy and all. I guess that is all good."

Ben shook his head. "Mo, time is moving on. In two months, the UVA will be starting classes. You won't be able to attend Orientation, and all that Will you be able to start school on time?"

"I'm one ahead of you on that, Boo. I've already talked to the Dean of the School of Nursing Science.

She's agreed to let me start during the Spring Semester in January instead of September," Mo answered Ben's worry about that.

"Baby, I won't be able to go off to college like I once thought about doing," Ben said. "I'm gonna have to work and help you take care of our little child. I've already applied at Piedmont Virginia Community College. It's that new College up on the hill across from Blue Ridge Sanitarium on Route Twenty that used to be Old Scottsville Road.

"I've enrolled in day classes at PVCC. I like the looks of the Small Businessmen's Administration Curriculum. I'd like to be able to understand what Real Estate IV is doing to us. So I'll be taking classes that will be over by five each evening.

"I've got a job lined-up at Kentucky Fried Chicken on Cherry Avenue as a Second Assistant Manager. I'll be working from about five p.m. 'til one a.m. Saturdays through to Wednesdays. I'll be off Thursdays and Fridays. That'll give me time to study. I'll be mostly the clean-up supervisor. I'll have to do the closing paperwork when the Manager and Assistant Manager are off. One of them is off on Mondays, and the other on Saturdays. They only get one day off per-week. I'm gonna be working forty hours per-week salaried at six-fifty an-hour. That's around two-hundred-sixty per-week. We get paid every two weeks.

"The restaurant closes at nine every week night, and at eleven on Fridays and Saturdays. All I have to do is make sure that the workers clean the place per-specification. I'll get some time to go into the office and hit the books, though the managers gave me a thick manual to study too. In a year, I'll take a test to see if I can move up to management. The problem is, if I pass, I'll have to go to wherever the Company needs an assistant manager or manager trainee. I'm really not that interested in becoming a full-manager. I just want to be working bringing in something to help take care of you and the Baby. How do you feel about all that, Mo Baby?" Ben said a little more cheerfully than lately.

Mo was happy to hear that Ben was thinking about moving forward. "Ben, Darling, that sounds like my Boo has got his head on straight.

"Pops wants us to come to dinner as soon as it's convenient for us to do that. What do you want me to tell him?" Mo said.

Ben smiled. "Oh-by the way-Rev. Holloway says any time we want to, he will come perform the ceremony right here in our Home. When do you want to do that? Let's get on with that right now if that is alright with you, yo," Ben said with a playful little chortle. "I'll go to dinner with your Dad any time."

Mo was six months pregnant in August 1985. She seemed to be carrying an elephant as big as she had grown. Ben thought it may have been because of the food she had been craving and gulping down. Her blood pressure was way up. She had tested positive for a slight bit of Sugar Diabetes. She was overweight and she felt miserable. But early on this Monday, Rev. Holloway and his Church Secretary, Mrs. Darlene Plains, were standing on the deck at *222* Fifth Street Southwest. The Rev. Dr. Holloway gently knocked on the door.

"Hold on I'm coming," Ben called out. He pulled the front door open and ushered in Rev. Holloway and his beautiful Secretary-who resembled Lena Home-into the front room area of the house.

Rev. Holloway wore a Blue Robe decorated with red crosses on its lapel. His Secretary wore a red dress that completely covered her shapely body from her neck to her ankles. She carried a black-covered Bible and a manila folder with some other papers in it. They strolled pontifically into the living room.

Mo was seated on a soft sofa dressed in a "White" dress, and no shoes, her feet were too swollen.

The Rev. walked over to her took her right hand and Ben's left hand and said: "This union that you are about to enter is not to be taken likely. It is a most sacred oath that you are about to swear to God and before man. So that, Whomsoever the Lord Joins Together in Holy Matrimony, Let No Man Put Asunder." The Rev. turned their hands loose. He stood in front of them and read from a little black book. "Benjamin Luther Slokum do you promise to take this woman, Moisha Melrose, as your Lawfully

Wedded Wife, to have and to hold, in sickness and in health, for richer or poorer, forsaking all others, and unto death you do depart, answer by saying yes or no?"

Ben was very emotional. Tears eased out the comers of his eyes. He was dressed in his Prom Tux. He looked deeply into Mo's eyes. He bellowed, "Yes, yes, with all my heart."

The Rev. smiled at Mo next "Moisha Melrose, do you promise to take Benjamin Luther Slokum as your Lawfully-Wedded Husband, to love and obey, in sickness and in health, for richer or poorer, forsaking all others, unto death you do depart? Answer by saying yes or no," he asked Mo.

Mo burst into tears. She wiped her eyes on a fold of her gown. "Yes, yes, yes forever and ever!" gushed up out of her.

"Where are the rings?" the Rev asked.

Ben got a little box out of his right pants pock.et. He gave Mo one ring and he kept the other.

The Rev. said: "Now place the ring on each other's ring finger of the left hand and repeat after me: 'With this ring I do wed.'"

Mo got up for that part of the wedding vows. She slipped the ring onto Ben's finger and he did likewise.

Both were standing looking into each other's eyes. Both were shedding tears, as they vowed.

The Rev. uttered: "Now Benjamin you may salute your Bride."

Ben kissed Mo long and hard, until the Rev. cleared his throat **"Mr.** Slokum. Ah ... ump, Mr. Slokum. Mrs. Plains will take possession of your marriage license for a week. She will have to file that with the State Bureau of Statistics, and with the Magistrate of Charlottesville. Your Marriage Certificate will arrive very shortly in the mail. It will be signed by me.

"My fee for all of that is Fifty Dollars. I hope you will consider Zion Union as your Church Home in the future, and when you get ready to 'renew' your Vows, you might do it at Zion Union. ff I'm still the Pastor, I would be so glad to officiate at that momentous occasion. By the way, I will issue you a temporary certificate showing that you were married today at about ten a.m. by me with Mrs. Plains as a witness.

"I will have to be on my way. I will have to officiate at a wake this very afternoon. I wish you all the best In Jesus Name, I pray that you will prosper and be in health and that your children will be healthy and wise. God Bless you all." The Rev. and Mrs. Plains headed on through the hallway to the front door.

Ben paid the Rev. Usually, he would walk whoever was visiting him and Mo to the front door, but not on this day. He kissed Mo over and over again passionately. He really wanted to do more but was afraid because of Mo's condition. She brought him to a climax by hand. She washed her hands in the john.

"Baby, bring me back some bananas tonight when you get off from work, please, Honey." Mo said.

Ben got dressed into dark-blue pants and light-blue shirt with a little white-blue-striped cap that was the uniform he had to endure at Kentucky Fried. He also had to endure a little black bowtie as well. He had a big name tag that had a picture of Colonel Sanders' head, and written in red: "Finger Licking Good!" on top of Ben's name in black: "BENNY." He put on a pair of black steel-toe boots that were required by KFC. He was ready to go to work. He was scheduled to work that day from three to eleven p.m. the Assistant's shift, she was off that evening. Hard as he had to work, filling chicken orders, watching the cashiers at four posts on the counter and a drive-through window, he felt like not going to work that evening.

Mo was glad that she had finally formally become "Mrs. Moisha Slokum." That felt so good to her, so right, so divinely correct Since her Pops had given his consent to her marrying Ben, nothing would stand in her way of being "The Happiest Woman in Charlottesville!"

She got a shiny coffee pot out of the cupboard. She filled it with water to make hot water so that she could make a cup or two of hot chocolate. It was getting late, nearing midnight Ben was still at work at KFC, and had been in school all that day. She made herself a tall cup of hot chocolate.

Maybe it was her imagination, or the wind blowing in a low howl, or something, but Mo thought she heard a mournful sound coming from the front door area. It had rained a slow drizzle for most of that evening. The air was moist and thick, and had that feel to it, that even though it was not yet cold, that was on its way. The trees had started to tum to brown. Some leaves were red, some yellow, and some slightly green. The Fall wardrobe that it wore was beautiful, but bespoke that the harshness of Winter, with its cold, sterile, white frosty, attire would soon have to be endured. The hoarfrost sparkled like diamonds, but long unprotected exposure to it can be deadly. The word, "Deadly," stuck in the psyche of Mo.

Halloween would be coming soon. The little costumed ghosts and goblins will come and collect little bags of candy Mo had prepared to give in answer to their question: "Trick or Treat?" It was all make believe. Ghosts were not real to Mo, even though she had heard Ben talk about being visited by his dead relatives; and that Grandma Slokum's Ghost had actually scared Jamie Charles away, saving Ben and his sidekicks, Harry and Poochie. But, Mo thought that was mostly Ben's sublime imagination, and not anything actually connected to true reality.

The howl that Mo heard that night was like a woman crying in very hush-hush tones. It seemed like the woman was out on the deck. Mo moseyed over to the front door, unhooked the safety chain and pulled the door open to see who was out there. Not a soul was out there, but Mo saw something that made her tremble all over. On the deck, the rain had breaded up in places that seemed like it had become "Fresh Blood!" The low wind was blowing through the trees in the back of the house and the screams were coming from the wind blowing through the limbs of the trees. But Mo wondered: "Blood out here?"

Mo knew that Grandma Slokum had been killed on the deck. Ben had washed off all the blood and had painted the deck with two coats of paint. She could not see how any blood could be left over from that Mo slammed the door quickly. She found amazing strength to climb up the steps to the bedroom she and Ben were using. Like a little girl she got under the covers. Strangely she went to sleep into what seemed like a trance.

A tall, heavyset woman came up out of the deck. Her skin was like polished brass. He hair was bright white and glistening. She wore a sparkling-white gown. She resembled the description of Grandma Mildred that Ben had given to her of his "Granny." The Woman spoke in a husky, but relined tone: "Moisha, I love you Dear Heart. Ben has done us Royally by marrying you. And you shall bring forth much good fruit that will walk upright before 'THE DIVINE CREATER.' Be of good cheer . . ."

Loud knocks on the front door woke Mo up. Mo had fastened the chained night-lash. She had to undo that so Ben could completely open the door.

At the door, Ben was tired but tolerate. "Baby, why do you have the lash on the door like that? Has someone threatened you? What's the matter? Did somebody say something to you today?" he asked.

Mo cried: "Ben, I heard some noises on the deck. I went to the door and I could've sworn, I saw real blood out on the deck. I came back into the house and laid down because I didn't feel well. I had a dream or nightmare about 'Grandma Slokum.' Her 'Ghost' said that I will bring forth much good fruit-whatever that means. We don't need a lotta kids. One will be plenty, right?"

Ben had to just shake his head. "Baby, it's probably your Hormones kicking in again. You know what happened here some time ago. I didn't see any bloodstains on the deck," Ben said. "Your heightened sense of the realization of what transpired here conjured up what you say you saw, that's all. I've heard other girls seeing worse things while carrying their babies. You're okay, alright, Mo? You're just my beautiful little pregnant wife."

Mo's frown turned into a small smile. Then she laughed. "I am acting a little paranoid. I got to admit, I am thinking about what happened to your family. I heard 'The Good Rev. Dr.' say that he had to go to a wake right after our wedding. Earlier I had heard what I believe were gunshots, Ben. They sounded like they were coming from down on Fifth Street near the Park.

"The news said that some kinda dispute had resulted in a shootout by combatants in the Park. Why are people shooting at each other down there? What's going on there that is important enough for sane people to go to war over?" Mo said. "Baby, that's enough for all of us to be paranoid about."

"Mo, come here and sit down on the sofa beside me." Ben seated himself on a sofa in the front room.

Mo came in as best she could and sat beside him. She looked up into Ben's big handsome face.

"Mo, Darling, that's some of the insane shit that we sane people over here gotta fix. Today, at the Park, at around six, I heard a commotion going on over in the Este's Supermarket parking lot, you know, right across from

KFC. Some guys wearing dark-blue, or black, bandanas tied around their heads, also had on black, or blue, walking shorts, and black Nikki Sneakers, and Los Angeles Raiders' football Jerseys and other paraphernalia. They were beating an old-looking man that had stumbled drunkenly onto the parking lot. Look like these guys came running after him from Six-and-a-Half Street across the Exxon Station driveway. Two of them had sawed-off baseball bats and were hitting the old guy a couple licks a-piece with the baseball bat. Then about four or five of them started kicking and stomping the old guy, who looked to be unconscious lying on the asphalt.

"I got to the phone in the office and called 9-1-1. I told them what I saw and they said they would send someone right away.

"Mo, I saw another group of guys sitting over on the hill behind Tonsler's Park's basketball court. They were all wearing Saint Louis Cardinals' Jerseys, white culottes, and black Air Jordan tennis, and had red bandanas tied around their heads. A couple of them had sawed-off baseball bats in their hands.

"They all stood up and watched the other group of guys beat-up the old guy, who was wearing a bright red shirt. These were all 'Bangers on the Set guarding their Turfs.'

"It took the cops two-hours to show up. A group of them came on the scene wearing black paramilitary garb, carrying automatic twelve-gauge shotguns, and long electric Tasers. But by then, all of the assailants had left the scene, leaving behind an old guy bleeding on the asphalt. It was like they had been tipped off that the cops were coming. Even the other guys on the hill had left. No one would help the old guy.

"A Sergeant among the cops came over to the restaurant to talk to me. I was the one who had called them. He asked me if I knew the names of any of the men who had taken part in the assault. He said that 'the old guy, a local wino, was probably not gonna survive the beating because he had too many broken ribs.' He said, that 'This is a Felony-Murder Investigation, and if anyone in the restaurant has any information to call the number on this business card,' that he handed to me. I still got the card.

"I asked the cop, why did those guys beat the old guy down so bad? He said, 'Man, it's just cause he was wearing the wrong colors in the area he stumbled into.'

"What area are you talking about officer? I thought I knew the Crews over here. I didn't recognize any of those 'Bangers.' Now there seems to be two groups out there. What's up with that?"

"The Sergeant leaned back a little and a puzzled frown turned his rock-jawed face into a likeness of 'John Wayne's.' His lips puckered a little as he spoke sounding like a 'John Wayne' Character. 'Look friend. You got to be careful over here now. You got the Salvation Army's building on one side of you. You got the Tom Thumb Strip Mall next to that Tonsler's Park is on your other side. On your side of Cherry Avenue it is now ruled by a notorious gang that had its origin out of California. It is called The Bloods. Their Color is Red. The Westside Crew that used to be in charge from Cheny Avenue over to Prospect Avenue, Forest Hill, all the way to Willoughby Square, is now under the auspices of 'The Bloods.'" 'Another gang, originally from California, calling itself The Crips, now claims the rule over an area from Cherry Avenue up past Fifth and Dice, to West Main, and from Ridge Street up to Ninth Street Southwest. These two gangs are trying to seize each other's Turfs. All the different Crews have join one of these groups for control of the dope trafficking that seems to be growing all over The 'Ville.

"'Then there's a gang out of Columbia, South America calling itself The MS-13, that is the main supplier of the dope coming into the Charlottesville area. Its members hang out on Sixth Street Southeast It seems to be against another group, calling itself The Mexican Mafia. It hangs out on Rougemont Avenue and South First Street They are primarily gun-runners and ammunition suppliers.

"'MS-13 is tight with The Bloods. The Mexican Mafia is tight with the Crips.

"'The Crips now rule over Tenth and Page, Tenth-and-a-Half Street, Hardy Drive, Tenth Street Northwest:, Rose Hill Drive and the Washington Park area. Their Colors are Blue and Black.

"'MS–13's Colors are Gold and Yellow. The Mexican Mafia's Colors are Green and Grey. In terms of the Bloods and the Crips, they won't let you wear another gang's colors on their turfs; especially when they are on the Set.

"'You better ask Colonel Sanders to change your Colors. It may be dangerous for you all to come to work on certain days wearing the wrong colors. See, you live in one territory, but have to cross over to the other to go to work. You better get to know the Gang Leaders of both Gangs so their Bangers will know not to step-to-you and ask you that awful question: Who You With? You don't want to have to answer that question. Your life could depend on what you say. The old guy the Crips beat to death was wearing the Bloods' colors. He didn't know how to respond to their ridiculous question. They beat him to death to send a message: The Crips rule over here! that's all.'"

I didn't know what else to say, so I asked: "Captain, can I get you something to eat or drink?" He thought for a moment. Then I asked: "Well, Sir, what took you all so long to get over here, though?"

"The Cop smiled. 'Well, Mr. BENNY, I'll take a diet Coke. I'm a Sergeant of The Special Weapons and Tactical Team, better known as S.W.A.T. We have to come on our calls fully equipped to deal with anything that may be gang-related. We're paramilitary and we are called to the most dangerous areas, that local law enforcement may not have the fire-power to handle. That's what this area over here has become. Fifeville is rife with gangs, drugs, prostitution, and murders. Complaints come in all the time. People are selling drugs at all of the Bus Stops, School Yards, Vacant Lots, Private Homes, and even in the Parking Lot of Este's Supermarket. The Bloods have almost taken over The Tom Thumb Strip Mall. You got some ten-year old dope-dealers over at Forest Hill Elementary. You got some gun-toting hit-boys over at Buford Middle School.

> "'The Gangs love to use underage assailants. They know that the guys will be tried as Juveniles. That they will get out of the juvenile correctional system early on. That makes for a very bad, deadly, and dangerous situation for all of Fifeville, but not only so, it is affecting everyone in Charlottesville. Parents need to take more account of who their children are hanging around with at and after school.'"

"The Cop sipped the last of his diet Coke through the straw and set the cup on a nearby table. 'Thank you for calling us, and for the Coke. I am Sergeant Jeremiah Bosnia. Here is my personal card. ff you find out any names, or have any information you want to share with me, call the number on this card, and you will have a direct line to me,' Bosnia said. He handed the card to me. He placed it on the end of the counter that separated the dining room from the cash registers and kitchen area, after I didn't immediately take it.

"I am surely interested in finding out more about what you said about these out-of-town Gangs setting up business in the 'Ville. It's bad enough to have to deal with the Crews I know about But Gangbangers from California, Mexico, Columbia in South America, and whatever, is too much for me to cope with. I'm glad I had this little talk with you though, Sergeant. My name is Benjamin L. Slokum." I told him. Then I shook Bosnia's hand.

"Bosnia looked around at the inside of the KFC Store. He shook his head and gave me a ten-cent smile as he moseyed on out of the plate-glass doors to the broad sidewalk. at the front entrance of KFC onto Cherry Avenue. He stopped and paused for a moment to stare at a group of young men who were standing in the Este's Supermarket parking lot wearing Crips' attire. They were anxiously watching the Sergeant and the nine, or so, SWAT Team officers who had come with him. The Cops all climbed back into a black armored truck, except for the Sergeant. He rode in a large-black Police Van that more resembled an Army Tank. Both vehicles had 'S.W.A.T.' painted on the sides of them in very large 'White Letters.'

"I grimaced at all of those 'Ugly Guns,' those SWAT Law Enforcement Officers had brought with them. I felt like such armaments ought to be restricted to the battlefields in the Middle East, or somewhere like that; not in 'Hoods like Fifeville."

Ben was in distress. "Mo, I had no idea that we were in such deep shit over here in Fifeville. I need help with dealing with it all. Baby, we're in the middle of a Big O' Gang War, that I couldn't have imagined was going on. A lotta young people are gonna die, needlessly. I thought when we got rid of Jamie Charles, and the Posse, that all of that shit would die down. Dope is gonna happen as long as people want to kick-it with that But all that Sergeant Bosnia dropped on me! All that I saw happening with my own eyes: Baby, what do all that mean?" he bellowed.

Mo stepped to Ben and put her arms around him as best she could.

"Baby, it's gonna be alright You'll find a way. After I have our baby, I'll get back out there with you. We'll do it together. God will be with us. I got a feeling things will fall into place for US-just wait and see.

"Oh-h-h, Ben, my stomach hurts so bad! Oh!" Mo screamed.

Chapter Eleven

Ben paced the floor in the waiting room for expectant fathers on North One. In September he had rushed Mo to the Emergency Room for stomach cramps. But all the hospital did was put her on bed-rest But this morning in early November, her water burst shortly after Ben had gotten home from work.

Ben rushed her to the hospital in the VW Bug. The Emergency Room forwarded her up to The Delivery Room for birthing mothers on West One. Mo was crying out in pain. They could not immediately give her any anesthesia until she was examined by an OB Physician. One-on<all was paged.

"Doctor Foxx ... Dr. Matthews Foxx ... You are urgently needed in the OB Delivery Room ... Dr. Foxx . . . You are urgently needed in Room 1001 on West One in the Delivery Room."

A short man wearing green-physician-Scrub clothes came rushing onto West One with two Nurses wearing green Scrub-Gowns. These all ran past Ben who was standing at the wide doors at the entranceway of the OB Delivery room.

Dr. Foxx guessed right when he saw Ben. "Hi, are you the father?" he asked. "Yes sir, I am," Ben said, excitedly.

"Good," said Dr. Foxx. "I like to see the fathers present at these times. Would you like to be in the Delivery Room when your Child comes into the world? That will be a precious memory you will cherish for the rest of your life. If you would like that, I'll have the Nurses bring you a scrub gown so you can come in and observe-okay, Sir?"

Ben netv011sly answered, "Yes, yes sir."

Dr. Foxx went through the huge doors and came back with a manila folder in his hand. He smiled at Ben. *A* dark-skinned Nurse wearing all-white including a surgical mask, and a white full-hairnet, and a pair of rubber surgical gloves, told Ben, "Turn around." She opened a package and shook out a white gown.

Ben turned around and the Nurse wrapped the gown around him seemingly backwardly. "Mr. Slok.um you can tie up the strings to your gown in the front. Then put on this surgeon's mask. to protect your wife and newborn from bacteria. Understand?" she said.

"Yes Ma'am," Ben said.

The Nurse led Ben through the huge brown entrance door. He found himself in a hallway with several doors on either side of it, some open and some closed. There were wheel chairs and blood pressure machines, weighing scales, and stretchers along the walls. Doctors and nurses were busy traveling from room-to-room checking on various women who were all grunting and groaning in the throes of childbirth in the rooms. The lights were very bright all over the place. The tiles and wall coverings were all of very light colors that reflected and amplified the florescent lights to a great degree. Ben figured that they needed that to be able to see what was really going on.

The Nurse stopped at room number 1001. The door was partially open. A big blonde Nurse was sitting beside Mo. Dr. Foxx was standing observing Mo and encouraging her: "Push, Moisha. There you go. The head is crowning. Push! ..."

Ben thought Dr. Foxx resembled a version of a dwarf with a neatly-trimmed black mustache, and a long pointed nose. He had a bald pat.ch on the top of his head, and that made his head look like "Larry's" of the "Three Stogies," except that Larry had blond hair, and Dr. Foxx had black. He was very energetic and was speaking to Mo softly but demandingly. "That's it, Moisha, that's it. We're almost there. One more big push, you can do it girl."

When Ben took a good look at Mo, he saw she was covered across her breasts with some garment that had an opening so that her lower body was exposed. Her legs were up in stirrups that raised and spread them. All of her pubic hair had been shaved away. All that were left were her bared "Labia Majora" and "Labia Minora," spread open to a disgusting degree. Ben saw blood and other flurids coming out of Mo's Vagina. Her face was contorted as she breathed hard, panting, and straining as she pushed with all of her strength. Her fists were balled up as tight as she could get them. She pumped them as she grunted and groaned.

Ben's stomach became very queasy. His nerves rewed up. His breathing was like wind gushing out of his spread nostrils. Then he saw the bloody head of Mo's Baby inching out of her body. He heard Mo screams: "Oh, God! Help me Lord! Oh-h-h! Ah-h-h-h ..." Then Mo fainted.

The floor seemed to have come up and slapped Ben in the face. Everything went beige, then blue, then black. He thought he could hear Mo screaming in the back of his mind: "Oh God, not again. Oh God, Help me!"

Ben came-to sitting in a wheel chair. The dark-skinned Nurse and the big blonde-one were on either side of him. The dark-one used smelling salts to revive him.

The dark-one allowed: "You big-strong men, so brave, so tough, huh! But, look. at you, a little blood from childbirth and you can't stand to wat. ch for a minute." She laughed out loud, sounding like a hyena.

The big blonde-one said: "Now, we know who is the stronger of our species, don't we?" She laughed even louder than the other one.

Ben didn't think. they were very funny. But he had a greater concern. "How's my wife?" he asked.

"Oh, your wife and your Two Sons are doing fine. She is in recovery on North One. Your healthy Boys are in the Nursery on South One," the blonde Nurse said.

"Can I see them?" Ben asked. All of his energy returned like lightning.

The dark Nurse said: "Yes, you've been out for thirty minutes. You can see your family now."

The dark Nurse pointed to the left of the entranceway and gave Ben instructions: "She's in room 1013 over there on North One. Take your time, don't run, you might trip over one of those wheel chairs. She'll be there when you get"

Ben dashed up the hallway through the entranceway doors, turned left onto North One and sought out Mo's room, "1013." A tall, "But.ch-Looking" Nurse raised her hand. "\Who are you, and why are you running around on my Ward?• she asked.

Ben looked at her mannish face and blurted out., "My wife just had Twins. I wanna see how she's doing.

Can I see her?" he said.

"What's your name? I'll go to the Nurses' Station and see if your wife can have visitors right now.

What's her name?" The Nurse asked.

"I'm Benjamín Slokum. My wife is Mosiha. She just had Twin Boys. I want to see how she's doing. I didn't expect she was carrying Twins. Please, lemme see her, Miss Mars." Ben said in a moan.

The Nurse wore a pair of white pants, and a blouse that had a little black string-necktie tied in a looping bow with golden tips on the end of the strings. She did not have on a hairnet or Nurse's cap perched on top of her head like the rest of the Nurses had. Her shoes were not white, but beige with black strings. Her lips were red without lipstick. Her face was made-up with eyeliner and mascara. Her red hair was cut Pageboy style, and she did not speak like the other Nurses did, like a little girl talking to her father, but like a very confident individual. On her UVA nametag was the name: "Shawn Mars, RN." Ben figured that she must be one of the new Feminists, and her mode of dressing was indeed a symbolic protest

"I don't like being addressed in that Male Chauvinistic way. I'm not and will never be a 'Miss or Mrs.' When addressing me, call me 'Shawn, or Mars.' Is that clear, Benjamin?" Shawn said, as she bobbed her head in a semi-circle.

"Alright, Shawn. Now, will you lemme see Mrs. Moisha Slokum?" Ben replied. He rolled his eyes. Shawn looked at him unblinkingly with the temerity of an angry Loin. "Men!" she said in a huff. She marched down the hallway to the Nurses' Station, flipped open a Patient Registration Notebook.. She turned and spoke in a voice that was almost masculine, "Yes, Benjamin, you may visit with your wife at this time. Go down the hallway to room 13, she's in there-because of you!"

Ben snapped, "I beg your pardon!"

Shawn stood akimbo, patting her right foot not uttering another word, letting little gushes of air out of the side of her full lips. She eyed Ben as he made his way to his wife's room, thinking: "Man, I'm glad that I'm Gay and will never let a man make a 'Baby Machine' out of me!"

Ben noticed that a member of other normally-dressed Nurses on the floor were chuckling at him as he walked by them. He was glad that Mo wasn't like the Feminists. He wondered: "What in the Hell would I do if Mo got like those Feminists?"

Mo was in a room by herself. There was another empty bed over against the adjacent wall. She was fast asleep. Ben sat in an easy chair right next to her bed. He took her hand gently in his so as not to suddenly awake her. He wanted to apologize for not being conscious when she fought to bring their Twin Boys into the world. His touch-even though it was ever so gentle-awakened Mo immediately.

"Oh Ben*n*, she whispered. "Baby, I'm so glad that you're alright I saw you hit the floor pretty hard.

You didn't hurt yourself did you, Boo?"

· Ben had tears in the comers of his big eyes. "Don't worry about me, Baby. I'm fine. It's you that I'm worried about Mo, Baby, you just had Twin Boys. Whoa! Now how about that 'Two for the price of one.' I'm so grateful to THE GREAT CREATOR, for blessing you all with good health," Ben said.

Mo was still very tired and a little dazed. "Ben, a woman came in as soon as I got into this room, and left some brochures for me to read. She said with a twisted little smile: 'I'm with Planned Parenthood Federation of America.' I don't know much about it. I will read what the lady left. She was white, well dressed, and didn't say anything else after she left the package on my bed table. Do you know what this Planned Parenthood Organization is?

"Included with the Planned Parenthood literature is a Brochure from The National Organization of Women (NOW). Do you know anything about them?" she said.

Ben scratched his head. "No Mo, I don't I know much about them. All I know is they claimed they are fighting for Women's Rights. I know they do a lotta demonstrations in certain parts of the Country, and especially in Washington, DC. I think we better read-up on who they be, if they're leaving Brochures in New Mothers' rooms-don't you think?

"It's a wonder the UVA allowed them in to do that, it being so conservative about women's rights."

Mo picked up the four Brochures, and flipped through them. One was titled: “A Woman’s Right to Choose.” She allowed: “I got one Brochure here, and I think I will start with that. It’s about ‘Abortion Rights.’ People are discussing that right here in the ‘Ville. I think a woman’s Reproduction Decisions ought to be exclusively her own in consultation with a competent physician. It’s her body after all. But I know the men in-charge of our Government think that they have the right to dictate to us what we can do with our own bodies, including banning abortions against our will. I wanna see what NOW and PPFA say about it all. I’m not a Feminist. I feel that some of them are too extreme. But I like to read about the issues they present sometimes.”

Ben really didn’t want to go down that road at all. “Mo, I feel that NOW and PPFA can divide the Black Community against itself by pitting the young women against the young men in a political slug-fest. Baby, we don’t need to be any more divided. Women vs. Men, is a really bad scenario. It puts the basic foundation for the reproduction of the Human Race at stake.

“Sometimes, I think the so-called Feminists are just bored white-women who need a life. They get to sit around all day and envy the accomplishments of the men in the world. So some of them may wish they had a Dick like a man, so that they can Fuck over everyone like the men in their society do. So, they want an Equal Right to be bold, aggressive, Sons-of-Bitches, like the men in their Race.

“Don’t get me wrong. I believe in equal education for women; and the right to run for public office even the presidency. I believe in a woman’s right to get equal pay for any work she’s capable of doing. But an equal right to kill a baby before it comes into this world, I disagree with. Half of any baby belongs to its father. Not Planned Parenthood, or NOW will ever say anything that will change me on that. Maybe when a father has been raping his daughter; or a mother her son; or when sister-and-brother incest might be responsible for a pregnancy, then I feel abortion might be the right thing to do. But not just on the demand of a disgruntled woman or a man. That leaves out the Will of THE DMNE CREATOR.”

Mo replied: “Ben, what you are saying, I agree with to some extent. But the right to do with my body what I will or may, is a right I simply will not yield up to any man, as much as I love you, and Pops. One way or the other, I’m going to decide what is best. No one would be able to stop me if I wanted to terminate a pregnancy. That being true, I feel it would be best if all concerned would allow me to do that in a sterile environment, with a doctor, and medical staff, to guard against me permanently injuring my health.

"Now, since we already have two children, and limited means to raise them, I've decided that we should not have any more. So, would you object to me having a Tubal Ligation?"

Ben slowly stood up. "I'm glad you shared that with me, first. I agree with you, Baby," he said.

Mo blinked her eyes. Her face showed she was experiencing a little fatigue. She had to s1IUggle to stay completely awake, but managed to ask: "Ben . . . how did the woman get in here to leave Brochures?

There are no soliciting signs all over the Hospital. I wonder"

Bespoke loudly, "Baby, you got a fire-breathing Feminist in charge on this of all floors, the Maturity Ward. It doesn't seem to add up. But the times they are a-changing. Back in the day, Nurse Shawn Man would be fired for disseminating unwarranted material on the Hospital's grounds. But you know?

"By the way, which one of the Twins was born first?"

Mo slowly blinked her eyes. "The biggest one is the First Born. He came out with a head full of Red Hair, and is vecy light-skinned, with light-brown eyes. He screamed and cried even before the Doctor slapped his little behind. He probably took back off of Pops' side of the family.

"The other boy was smaller. He has a little trace of black hair. His skin is nut-brown, and he more resembles you. He's like a mini-you," she spoke in a near-whisper.

Ben anxiously replied: "Babe, I gotta go see my Boys. I can't wait ..." He left the room, went to the Nurses' Station and asked: "Can I see the Slokum Twins, I'm their Daddy?"

Ben was led down the hallway to South One. A couple of Nurses pushed two basinets to the observation window. Both Babies were on their stomachs with their legs balled up into a kneeling position, and were sucking on their knuckles. Ben took one look at the robust First Born and decided, "His name is Esau Luther."

He took a look at the other child that was an exact copy of him in infant form. He decided, "His name is Jacob."

Tears eased from Ben's eyes. He wanted to give these Boys everything that would make them a "Credit to My Race." He wanted to make an example of them that could be emulated throughout the 'Hood. He figured that Esau looked like the beginning of a real champion. He was strong-looking already. He was a healthy-looking baby. He would probably be an athlete: Maybe, a football or basketball player.

Jacob would probably be the wiser one, Ben thought He was blinking his little eyes already. His little brain was most likely wondering "what is going on, and where is my Brother who's been with me for nine months?"

The two of them could be as close as Ivy and he had been, Ben was thinking. He would teach them how to be loving, caring, men, who will be leaders in the 'Hood, respectful to women, and good fathers to their children.

An old gray-headed Nurse, with streaks of blond hair, patted Ben on his back. She wore thick homed rimmed glasses. Not only did her lips smile, but her voice smiled as well when she talked. "Mr. Slokum, don't cry. It's a Gift from God to be the Father of Twin-Boys. It means that your Boys have a special destiny. They're going to mark some very significant change in your community, and that will influence something very important in the whole scheme of things. That's how The Lord Works. God don't make no mistakes."

Ben watched her walk. on up the hallway. When he turned around, it seemed like both of his newborn sons had been turned on their sides and were looking directly at him. He waved at them. "Hi, little Baby Slokurns. Daddy's so proud of you. Daddy loves you. Oh, Daddy loves you so very much," he said.

Esau started to cry as loud as he could. Right away so did Jacob. It was like one was throwing out a wail and the other was catching it and throwing it back.

Two Nurses rushed over wearing protective gowns. Each one picked up one of the Twins. They held them close to each other. Jacob took hold of Esau's left heel. Both quieted down immediately.

One of the Nurses smiled and said: "Twins are like that. They don't want to be separated. See how they're clinging to one another? It's like the two of them have One Soul."

It was time for the little boys to be fed. The Nurses took them out of the Nursery to Mo's room. Ben followed them. Once they were in the room with Mo, The Nurses laid them on the bed with their Mother. One of the Nurses allowed: "You can feed whichever one you want to first, Mrs. Slokum. We'll be back in a little while to check on you all."

Mo put a bulging breast in Esau's mouth. The Infant nursed her vigorously. "Go ahead, Ben. Pick up little Jacob. Watch out for his head and neck. Be careful there," Mo said.

Ben nervously handled the swaddling-clad bundle carefully, holding Jacob's head so that it did not dangle. He placed the baby's smooth skin next to his face away from the stubble on his chin. He loved the smell of his Infant Son. Jacob touched his Father's face with his tiny hand and relaxed in his arms. Ben's heart beat like a drum with love and approval of the Gifts that THE GREAT CREATOR had blessed them with.

"Tell the people who will come to take these Boys' names, that I want my First Born to be 'Esau Luther,' and his Brother to be 'Jacob Luther,' "he told Mo, with pride and joy beaming out of his eyes like the rays of the Sun on an early spring morning.

Mo smiled, "Alright, Boo. That's what we agreed on. I'm sticking with that bargain. Guess I'll never get to name a daughter. I feel that two children nowadays are plenty. We wanna give 'em the best we can. Raising two Boys will take a lot nowadays.

"I still wanna go on to Nursing School this January. By then I'll wean the Twins and put them on Formulas. We can get Mrs. Aileen Walla to babysit them 'til they get old enough to be enrolled at Barrett Daycare over on Ridge Street. Mrs. Walla takes in infants. She's the only one around here that I've heard of that will babysit infants. What do you think about that, Ben?"

Ben shook his head in agreement. He exchanged Jacob for Esau. "Yeah, Mrs. Walla lives right up the Street from us. That would be alright by me. I hear she's pretty reasonable too on costs. I know her. She's a nice quiet old lady, and a good Church-Woman. She attends The True Holiness Apostolic House of God Church. She always wears all-white: white-dress, white-hat, white-stockings, and white-shoes. Her husband passed away some years ago. He was the Pastor at that Church down there on Seventh Street Southwest. Now I think a Reverend Cornelius McHale's the Pastor.

"I'd trust that Lady with my life, and I think she'll take good care of my Boys. She takes care of about fifteen or twenty kids at a time. She and a few attendants use the Church's Basement as a Nursery. It's nice down there. It will be good for Esau and Jacob. Yep, I'm with you on that, Mrs. Mo. Slokum," Ben said.

Mo smiled. "Then we'll all set now. In a couple of days we will all be home. The Pediatrician says that Esau and Jacob are healthy as little lambs. I'm doing fine too.

"I'm going to take all of us up to meet Pops as soon as we get back to the house. I bet he will be so glad to meet his beautiful Grandsons," Mo chimed.

It was discharge time and Mo was up walking around very well. She was a little sore from the Tubal Ligation. But all of that had gone well. The Twins were smiling at her already. When she placed her face on either one of the Twins, he placed his little hands on a side of her face and smiled.

Mo had her Twin-Infants in Pampers, and gray jumpsuits, and blue booties. Each one was wrapped in a matching blue blanket. Two Nurses came into Mo's room and placed the Infants in Mo's arms. She sat in a wheel chair wearing a midi-dress she would not have been able to wear a month ago.

Ben brought the car to the Main Front of the Hospital, parked it, and was up on North One when the final discharge papers were given to Mo. The Nurses placed one baby in Mo's arms, and Ben earned the other.

A transportation worker dressed in blue khaki pants and shirt, with the red UVA logo on the pockets of his shirt, was there to roll Mo and little Jacob down to the Main Front There, she and Ben had to make arrangements to satisfy the Hospital's Bill.

The Business Office was the first petitioned off area to the left of the automatic doors of UVA's Main Front There were several women and men dressed business style, sitting at five or six desks. When Mo was rolled up to the first desk, a plump, female asked: "Hello Ma'am, how may I help you?"

Mo handed the Betty Crocker-looking woman her discharged papers. The lady took those, looked them over and told Ben and Mo, "Wait here, I will go to the computer and show you a copy of all the charges that will be billed to your insurance, or you will have to make arrangements to satisfy our Bill."

Beads of sweat formed on Ben's brow. He didn't have any insurance that would cover childbirth. He didn't think that Mo had either. At KFC, only the Manager and First Assistant Manager had such coverage. All other employees had to pay a large portion of their check to get the kind of insurance coverage that would include their spouses. So all Ben had with KFC was accident and long-term illness, and he felt like that was costing him an arm-and-a-leg.

As soon as the lady went over to her bulky IBM Computer Terminal with the weird-looking keyboard, and started typing some infonnation into the noisy machine, Ben said to Mo: "Baby, I got a bad feeling about all of that" He pointed to the lady at the computer terminal.

"Don't sweat it, Boo," Mo said. "I got this covered. Yep. 'Home-girl be all over this one, yo,'" Mo chuckled.

Ben didn't think that anything was funny. "Come on, Girl. Don't play! We could be in deep do-do. I know we don't have the money this bill is gonna sock to us. For-real!"

The Computer started to buzz and hum. A line of paper was being printed out like a wide-paper ribbon coming out of the side of the machine. It went for several pages and those were folding neatly into a paper box right beside the printer. The lady tore off a portion of the paper-ribbon. She came back to before Ben and Mo with a sad smile on her fat, ruby-red lips and allowed: "The final charge is on the last page of this list of charges.

"I have another form for you all to fill out if you do not have insurance, or cannot pay the amount you owe in-full or in-part. Take a moment and look at the charges and the form and then tell me what you have decided to do."

Ben took the computer print-out and the three-paged form the lady gave them. He flipped over to the last page of the print-out and saw the final figure. It read: "$1, 250.00. You must make arrangements to satisfy this Bill or collection procedures will commence immediately."

Ben turned to Mo. She was holding both Babies. "Mo, we owe these people Twelve-Fifty. Where are we gonna get that kinda money? I'm . . . I don't know"

Mo smiled. "Boo, I saved every penny I got from working up at the

Hospital. I got it all in the Bank. I made Fifteen-Hundred and Seventy-Five Dollars. That will take care of this Bill with something left. So don't sweat it I'll transfer all of it to your Bank Account and you can make-out a check for the Bill."

Ben was so happy he almost cried. "Baby, I knew I was getting the best of the deal when we got together. Man you're always right-there for me. I love you, *Mo,"* he blurted out.

Ben beckoned for the lady in the business office to come over and talk with them. He was all smiles.

When Mo fed Esau, Jacob seemed to sense it. He screamed as loud as he could until his tum came to be fed. Jacob was always more demanding about diaper changes, being fed, and waking up at night to be cuddled. He screamed and cried louder to get his way than Esau his Twin. Mo hoped he would grow out of that

"Hello Pops." Mo was glad to hear from her Father. He had been very quiet and reserved since she had defied him and married Ben. But the time for them to get together and allow the family to meld was sure at hand. "It's so good of you to call, Pops. We have Twins. Ben named them Esau and Jacob. Esau looks like a carbon copy of you, and Jacob resembles Ben to-a-T. I want to bring them up to get your blessing ."

Mo heard her Father sobbing on the phone. He spoke between sobs. "Baby Mo, I've been a bastard about all of this. Forgive your old Dad.

"Bring everybody up for Thanksgiving Dinner. We will have a traditional meal that we all will always remember. I'll have a big surprise for you then. I love you all. I have to admire Ben's courage. He's a lot better man than I ..."

Mo interrupted: "No Pops. No man will ever take your place in my heart. I will be glad to bring everybody up for Thanksgiving. I'll make a Mincemeat Pie. I've gotten good at putting together recipes since Ben and I got together. He loves my cooking. I've forgiven and still love you, Pops. I just wish my Moms could at least be a part of all this. Do you know anything about where she is?"

Philip paused. He coughed. "Mo, I'm afraid that that news is not good. She left America and migrated to a place in Kingston, Jamaica. She settled in a 'Slum' in a 'Ghetto' called 'Trench Town.' She never remarried. I heard that she worked in a restaurant in Kingston. She passed away several years ago. Her remains are resting in 'Calvary Cemetery opposite Greenwich Park Road.' That's where all of the Catholic Dead from Trench Town are buried. 'Trench Town Ghetto is a Shantytown near Jamaica's Capital, Kingston.' That's all I've heard. Your Mother and I never communicated with each other after she left us.

"She must have converted to Christianity to be buried where she is. I still loved your Mother, Mo. But I could never accept her Rastafarianism. I could not accept 'Haile Selassie as God Almighty.' I could never accept their abuse of 'Marijuana as a Divinely Inspired Sacrament' I saw all of that as Pagan-and I did not want you to grow up under that kind of influence.

"I'm sorry for the pain that have caused you. As you observed, I've never followed 'Bob Marley,' or his 'Reggae' or 'Nazarite Hair Style.' I was more an Evangelical Christian until I decided that Religion was something to subvert the minds of its so-called 'Believers.'

"I still feel that way about Rastafarianism. Haile Selassie was just another demigod, like we have today in the so-called 'Moral Majority.' They're just men who have made some Man into a 'Divine Myth.' That's how they then can persuade the ignorant to accept their 'special form of dogma' and build an entire religiosity around misguided notions about spirituality. People are murdering each other all over the world because of 'that truly ridiculous act of mysticism.' All seem to be trying to: 'Kill their way to Peace-like in Islam; or Hate their way to Love-like in Christianity.' Why don't they all just Love one another and then we will all have Peace. There wouldn't be any more need for Wars, or Rumors of Wars.'

"Do you understand me, Mo, Darling?"

With big tears running down her cheeks, Mo said: "Yeah, Pops. I understand more than you know. It's what is going on in the whole world, in Asia and America, people want to be free. All over Africa and Latin America, people want to be free. But they are all going at it the wrong way. War is not the answer."

Both Mo and Philip paused. Mo allowed: "That's why, though I may not believe in worshipping Haile Selassie H.I.M. (His Imperial Majesty), as Bob Marley and the Wailers did, some of what they were saying in their music is true. Their song, 'Who The Cap Fits, Let Him Wear It,' is a true indictment of all my false friends. Their song, 'War And Rumors of War,' is another one. Until all people are free all over the world there will always be Wars. So, I will not 'Throw the baby out with the bath water,' on them. But I have the good sense to choose what is good about anything, and to reject what is not

"I believe in Christianity somewhat, but I have some qualms about that. I cannot accept that THE HEBREW MESSIAH that had Black Parents could've been a White Man. I do not believe that Yahweh (GOD) ever meant for The Hebrews, or any followers of theirs, to erect Racist Temples, Synagogues, or Churches anywhere. Yahweh does not have A CHOSEN PEOPLE. 11IE ELOAH'S Chosen People are any people who do what THE LAW given through Moses states that they should do. Therefore, THE JEWS, one of THE ORIGINAL Twelve Tribes of Ancient Israel, are not Yahweh's or GOD'S Chosen People, to the exclusion of all others. I believe that that whole idea is totally ludicrous. They were just one people to whom The Law was introduced. They took that to mean it was only meant for them, exclusively.

"Therefore, I think that when Bob Marley calls those killing the Palestinians today, 'BABYLON' I have to agree with that to some extent. And when he says that those people who are today calling themselves, 'JEWS' are not people descended from Abraham, Isaac, or Jacob, but are of Babylon, there is a lot of truth to that statement. Also, 'Ras Tafari,' (Haile Selassie, I. Emperor of Ethiopia in 1930), did trace his ancestry back to The Queen of Sheba, Sovereign Ruler of Ethiopia, and King Solomon of Israel. Therefore he is descended from the Ancient Hebrews, but not those people who are oppressing the people of Ancient Israel today. They have no blood-affinity to THE JEWS, or Ancient Hebrews. They are Racist Imposters, and purveyors of anti-Semitic Genocide. They came out of Europe, not Ancient Israel. They are murdering the Descendants of Abraham, Isaac, and Jacob. That's why Marley referred to them as Babylon. And Marley was on an 'EXODUS': and was 'Marching Out of Babylon to Ethiopia, the Promised Land.'

"So Pops, I may not groove to a lot of Reggae Music, but I have read about who Bob Marley, and the Wailers were, and why they sang the songs that they did. There was never any danger of me becoming one of those

'Pagans' as you would call them. However, one woman's pagan is another woman's saint."

Philip drew up a hushed breath. "Little Mo, I'm so proud of the fact that you have kept your head in a lot of books. You had to read a lot to know the 'His-Story' that you know. There are a lot of people who have killed a lot more people to keep that knowledge from being disseminated. There were times, that I must confess, I've clung to the European concept of history, and their many philosophical and religious notions found in the Bible, and the many books written by them to obscure the truth, I had to read to stay afloat But, I sometimes knew better than what was written because of all that I heard or saw going on all around me. It was easier to fall in-line than to raise any protest at all. That's how I have been able to provide such a good life so that you were able to have a better go of things.

"Mo, your children will not have to hide their real feelings about what they know to be real. This is what is so good about your generation. You all have your problems that you must solve, but you have a lot more avenues open to you that my generation did not have. Mo, I attended predominantly Black Schools. It made me question everything around me. I had to decide whether to be a 'True American,' or to be trapped in the World of African-American mediocrity. I thought I was making a wise choice when I backed away from my Racial Reality. I've made a lot of mistakes. I'm so proud of you and the way you are stubbornly forging ahead regardless of the obstacles standing in your way. I love you, Baby Girl."

Mo's only moist reply was: "See you at Thanksgiving, Pops-Love You!" She hung the phone up.

"Ben, we're be going to Pops' place for Thanksgiving. Is that alright with you?" Mo asked.

Ben laughed. "Yep, we're be closed all that Day. It is just one of the days we're not open for business.

The other one is Christmas." He laughed again. "What's so funny, Ben?" Mo asked.

"\Veil, I'm amazed at how well you have shaped back up after just having Twins. You still are a little potty in the gut, but not bad. You almost got your sexy curves back in place, Baby Girl. Mo, you're the prettiest girl in the 'Hood, the 'Ville, or the World to me. You're my 'Miss Universe!'"

"Ah-h-h Boo, flattery will get you everywhere," Mo said with a schoolgirl giggle.

Thanksgiving Day was dreary, drizzling, and very warm for November. Ben got dressed in a light-blue summer suit. Mo wore a white spring dress, no sweater, and no hat. She put blue matching jumpsuits on the Twins. They were not identical, in that Esau was "Red-Bone," (had red hair, light-brown eyes, light brown skin, and had freckles on his broad nose). Jacob was dark-brown-skinned with black hair and black beady eyes, with an aquiline nose. It was too warm to wrap the Boys in blankets. So Mo totted one and Ben the other. It was three in the evening. They all got into the VW Bug. Ben drove up to Main Street. He turned left onto West Main, and in about ten minutes they arrived at Mo's former address on Fourteenth Street Northwest.

Ben climbed out of the car first, ran around to take one of the Twins so that Mo could get out of the car.

She was holding onto Jacob, and on her back she carried a Diaper Bag with ample Pampers for changes.

Philip ran down the driveway to meet them. He laughed gaily. "Hi Mo. Hi Ben. Let me see my Grandbabies.

"Ah, they are so handsome. Take after their Grandpa." He said. He laughed even louder.

Philip kissed Jacob and then Esau. He did that before Mo got to say, "Pops, meet your Grandsons ..."

Ben stood by as Philip hugged and kissed Mo and extended his right hand to him. Ben took it and gingerly shook it. He knew the battle to win Philip's love and respect was not over yet. Ben figured that "Philip still feels like I stole Mo away-or something like that."

While still holding Esau, Philip beckoned for them to go on up the steps to the porch and on into the house. The aroma of roasting Turkey, Prime Rib, and Baked Ham, Candied Yams, and Pumpkin pie, filled the air and reminded Mo that she had a Mincemeat Pie in the trunk of their Car.

"Ben if you don't mind, go get the pie I baked. It's in the trunk area in the front of the Bug. Thank you, Baby," Mo said.

"Yo, got you covered," Ben said.

Mo walked into the house carrying Jacob on her hip. Philip carried Esau. Air hissed through Mo's lips just as she came through the front door. She saw a slender but shapely woman that seemed to be in her middle-twenties. She was cream-colored, with auburn hair, and blue eyes. Her Cupid Bow lips parted to show even-white teeth. She wore a dress with red-roses on a light-green background. She had on brown stockings but no shoes. She had made herself quite at home. She wore a white-cotton apron with lace edging around its borders. Mo's eyes were spread opened wide.

"Mo, I want you to meet Mademoiselle, Babette Lenoir, my fiancée," Philip said to his astonished Daughter.

"Babette, this is my only child, Madame Moisha Andrea Slokum," Philip said.

Babette extended her right hand to Mo. "Very pleased, Madame Slokum. You are 'beau-ti-ful.' Your 'ba-bies' are good 'co-pies' of you. They are mag-ni-fi-cent, like your Father," she said.

Ben walked through the door carrying the Mincemeat Pie.

Ben almost dropped the pie. Then, he thought: "In a way, this is not a SUIJ>rise. He's always been partial to White People."

"Ben, I want you to meet my fiancée, Babette Lenoir, from Paris, France," said Philip proudly.

Babette was gently shaking Mo's hand. Mo had laid the Twins on a Settee. Babette hugged Mo like she had known her for all of Mo's life. She kissed Mo on one cheek then the other.

Ben took the pie into the dining room and put it on the table among a number of desserts, a souffle and fruit-pastries. He did not mean to be disrespectful, but needed a moment to get down with the situation. He returned to the Front Room area with a sheepish smile on his lips.

"Nice to meet you, Miss Lenoir. You're French ..." gushed up out of Ben. He gave a little nervous chuckle. Mo's rolling eyes stopped that.

Babette laughed. "Ah, you Americans. You are so-how you say-inquisitive. Yes, I am from 'Gay Pair ree.' I am a French National Studying at the UVA, who have decided to remain here. I love this Country.

"I met your Father-in-law, and he loves me very much. I love him right back. There can be no other alternative but marriage. I am Catholic and we will have to marry so that our Love can be completed. We will marry by the end of this year. Do you agree, Monsieur, no?"

While shaking Babette's hand, Ben uttered all the French he knew: "Oui, Oui, Mademoiselle." Babette kissed his right cheek than his left. "I must return to the kitchen. Phil purchased a crib for the children. It is in the next room. We will bring you something to drink.

"Moisha, come help me, Darling. I have sparkling water and fruit juice. I understand you do not drink wine. It is the nectar of life. You are missing out. I have a bottle of Burgundy chilling in the pantry. In 'Pair-ree' we all have wine with every meal. It is good for our health, no. I will sip a glass or two while we serve dinner to our Monsieur, Oui?"

Ben was very fascinated with Babette. He loved the way she talked. He loved the graceful way she moved about. He didn't want Mo to get angry so he diverted his eyes away from the French Beauty. He went to check on the Twins. He took them to a side-room to a large crib and laid them there. They remained fast asleep.

Mo was thinking: "Pops might be doing all of this out of spite. He never showed that much interest in marrying anybody before now. All of a sudden he's getting ready to marry a French National who wants to 'remain in America.' That might be the only reason she's marrying Pops. I don't want to interfere with Pops having a little happiness if that's what is going on here. But, Pops could be in for a lot more pain than what he claims that my Moms caused him. I won't interfere. Pops is a Grown Man. He should know what he wants out of Life"

"Moisha, Darling, will you get the dishes that should be dry now on the drain-rack and help me set the table, plea?" Babette said.

"Yes, why not," Mo replied. "Merci," Babette said.

Chapter Twelve

Mo got started on her Nursing degree at the UVA in January, 1986. She finished her program in 1990. She was State-certified in 1991 as a Registered Nurse. She was assigned to the OB/GYN Ward at the UVA on North One. She worked the 7: 00 a.m. to 3: 00 p.m. shift, Mondays-through-Fridays.

Ben finished his Associate's degree in Small Business Administration in 1987 at PVCC. It had been a very exhausting two years. He was so tired most of the time that he didn't know whether he was going or coming. Ben worked the 4: 00 p.m. to 12: 00 a.m. shift, six-days-per-week, Salaried.

After the arrival of the Twins: Esau (nicknamed: "Saw,") and, Jacob (nicknamed: "Jay"), Ben had to help care for the needs of his Boys at night when they seemed to be crying just to get someone up to hold them. Or they were wet and needed changing. Or they were hungry and needed formu1a; etc. Saw had the loudest voice and cried the most Jay always laid-back and waited until Ben or Mo was finished with Saw and then he screamed and cried. Oh, they made getting a full-night's sleep *very* rare. But "They are the Joy of my life," thought Ben, and that was often stated by Moisha, whenever she felt like slapping them silly.

Sister Walla, and her "Prayer Warriors," at The True Holiness Apostolic House of God, took excellent care of the Twins while Ben worked at KFC and Mo studied at the UVA. The Twins turned Five years old in 1990. They had outgrown Sister Walla's babysitting facilities in 1989. They attended Barrett Day Care Cent.er on Ridge Street for pre-school until 1990. In 1990, they were enrolled at Forest Hill Elementary on Ninth Street Southwest and Prospect Avenue for Kindergarten.

Ben was promoted to First Assistant Manager at KFC. Mo was enrolled in courses in the UVA'S Employee Enrichment Program. She selected courses that would help her earn a Master's degree in Post Natal

Maternity Care. These courses were at half-cost. The UVA paid as long as the student made passing marks. Mo was an excellent student

Mo got up this morning and got a pot of oatmeal cooking on the stove, some coffee percolating in a pot on their GE Electric Range Stove, and bacon frying in one of her no-stick frying pans. She got a big mixing bowl out of the cupboard and cracked into it six eggs, beat those to scrambled, and put in six slices of bread in her Convention Toaster. She was getting ready to leave a breakfast on the stove before she got in her new Ford Mustang to go off to work.

Someone yelled: "Motherfucker! ... What 'sup, yo?" Then several shots rang out The news on the television said, "President Bush is facing stiff competition from the left from an Arkansas Democrat He is a strange social mixture, a political alloy of Southern sentiments and Northern liberalism. He has risen to the top of the Democratic Primary race, and will challenge incumbent President George H.W. Bush for the presidency. Political pundits on the right say he has little chance of defeating the GOP's most powerful and conservative, popular leader ..."

Mo turned the forty-eight inch SONY Television down low. She ran over to look out of her front-room windows. A Red SUV sped down Fifth Street like a "Bat Out Of Hell!" Mo's heart sank to her knees when she saw what looked like some science-fictional weapon out of the "Star Trek" series, dangling out of the front passenger's side of the vehicle.

A young man dressed in a black jumpsuit, with his face covered in a black and blue bandana, and he had a black. baseball cap on his head with the brim turned around backward, was yelling vile curses at the fleeing vehicle. He waved and pointed a Glock Nine firing off two shots as the SUV disappeared down the hill. The guy ran back up Fifth to his house. It had several bullet holes along its front exterior. Mo could see that from her front-room windows.

The news went on, "President Bush, speaking before Iowans yesterday said: 'I will get tougher on domestic criminal activities by cutting taxes so that companies will be able to invest in creating new jobs. That's the way to get rid of a lot of criminal activity. I would not do what the Democrats have done in the past, when they let a Murderer out of prison early so that he could kill again. William Clinton is the wrong choice to run the United

State's of America. He has no foreign policy experience. He manipulated his way out of serving in the military by getting furloughs to go study in colleges abroad when his country needed him to defend America's interests at home and abroad. And, he's soft on crime.

"'Governor Clinton has a foundation to help more convicts get early release from their just sentences. He is all wrong for America, domestically, economically, and in terms of his lack of foreign policy experience. Our country doesn't need to pivot to the left at this momentous time. We need to sally forward to more Conseivative values that will lead to prosperity for all. Clinton does not have that kind of a vision for America ...'"

Saw and Jay came into the kitchen in their pajamas and asked simultaneously: "What's for breakfast, Mommy?"

Mo's voice trembled as she spoke, "Boys, go wash your hands and face in the bathroom. You're having bacon, eggs, and oatmeal this morning. Then get your clothes on so I can see what you look like, alright?"

Sirens blared. Several police vehicles came suddenly from the Cherry Avenue side of Fifth and a SWAT vehicle came down the Main Street side. Ben came running into the kitchen. He was in his pajamas too. "Ah, Hell! That's getting to be too often around here. Who got shot this time?"

Saw allowed: "The Moo-Man said that the Bloods are out to get him! He says he capped one up at the 'Tokyo Rose,' and got away clean. But now they know who he is . . ."

"Who is this 'Moo-Man?' And what're you all doing talking to him. I told you all to stay away from gang members. That means, you don't talk to them either, is that clear?" Mo yelled.

Saw and Jay were nine years old and didn't understand why their Mom didn't want them to talk to one of the main homeys on the block. Moo-Man-Dushan Stinne-was the "Crips'" contact with the young prospects in the 'Hood. When a "Dude" reached the age of nine, it was time for him to be "Jumped-In," or "Beat-Up," by a group of nine-year-olds. That was one year before he would be used as a lookout for the Set. He would be issued a Walkie-Talkie and his function would be to warn the Homeys on the Set when Five-O (the Law), had made-the-scene. He would also be used as a "Carrier for the Set." He would be sent by the Drug-Dealer to the Stash, in an abandoned building, in a parked car, or to an individual hidden away, to get the amount of Dope a buyer wanted, bring that back to a third person, a hand-off man, or woman, who would hand the Dope off to the buyers on the streets, or other specified places.

The little homeys were issued a fast-bicycle. They were not allowed to be armed with a gun, but was allowed to carry a knife-usually a switchblade, or buck-knife. They ranged in ages ten-through-fourteen. At fifteen they were thought to be "Soldiers on the Set." Occasionally, the Crips would use one of the ten year-olds to actually gun-down someone. But that was very rare. They were more likely to be used as little "Tough Guys" to terrorize someone in the 'Hood who the Crips perceived to be a "Snitch."

One day, Moo-Man approached Saw and Jay walking home from Forest Hill Elementary. Saw was walking next to an Oriental Girl. Jay walked behind them. The trio was on the Comer of Grove and Ninth Street, Southwest. Moo-Man was standing in front of the Store on that Comer.

"Hi, Saw, what-up, my Nigga? How you be?" Moo-Man asked. He is very dark-skinned and his head is shaved clean. His face bears the scars of having been beat-up several times. He's wearing garb that makes him resemble "Mr. T." of the TV Series. He's sporting highly-polished Combat Boots, with white strings. He is wearing a pair of black trousers and a blue Dashiki. He has a golden medallion with an Egyptian Pharaoh imprinted on a large disk at the end of a long gold-chain that hung around his thick neck. He has gold rings on all four fingers of both his hands. A couple of the rings were diamond-studded.

"I'm just chilling with my Bro. and 'Leann Ming Chen Xing.' We're on our way walking home-girl to her door and whatnot What-up with you, Moo-Man?" Saw said.

Moo-Man got out a pre-rolled Reefer, and a book of matches out of his pants-pocket and lit-up. "You all wanna drag?" he asked, handing the joint in the direction of Saw.

"Naw," Jay said. "We don't blast like that, man. It's for the dumb. My Dad schooled us way back not to get down like that-so we don't; alright?"
"Yep, true-that, Moo-Man," Saw added.

"Suit yourself. I'm always getting down like that It's my way, yo. It's who I be." Moo-Man said. He took a big puff off the joint and blew the smoke out so it spread all over Saw, Jay and Leann.

"Saw, I got to go on home. My Mom will come looking for me very soon if I'm not over on Grove Street twenty minutes after school closes. Alright?" Leann said.

"Moo-Man we gotta bounce my-man. I'm gonna see my girl, Leann, over the way. She's late and whatnot," Saw said.

"I heard that, yo." Moo-Man said. "Later, Saw. Later Jay. But, it's time for you all to be putting in time on the Set, yo. Your Dad's got a 'Ghetto Pass,' but you're not 'Made' yet. You gotta show love for the 'Hood and the Homeys. You gotta help protect the 'Crips' Nation.' That's how it be. Either you're in or you're not. You down with that?" Moo-Man said.

"Later for you and all of that, Moo-Man. I gotta go. You keep on doing whatever it is that you're doing. I'll do the same," Saw said. He noticed Leann rolling her eyes at Moo-Mann, especially when Saw left too much room for Moo-Man to assume he might join the Crips.

While walking along, Leann allowed: "Saw, Mom, 'Mei Ming Chen Xing,' has to go to work up on the Corner of Fourteenth Street Northwest and West Main. She cooks at the 'Thai Wok Cafe.' She has to be there at exactly Four every evening. If she is ever late even once, they will fire her on the spot. I will walk with you as long as you make sure that you get me to my door on time, because my Mom will not go to work until I have arrived at home safely; okay?"

"I got you, Leann. Sorry, and whatever," is all that Saw said.

"No, that's not all, Saw," Leann said, her little eyes were moist. She trembled a little. "What then?" Saw asked. "What else did I do wrong?"

"My Mom was considered an outcast in Vietnam. She was the Daughter of a 'Hoa' parent and a Black Soldier. She was hated for being a 'Con Lai, (mixed-race), or as a Black, 'bui don' (The dust of the earth). She was refused an education. She was denied her basic civil rights. Her hold on humanity was the support she got from her Ebony Father. He gave her clothes, food, and a rudimentary grasp of American English. But the Americans withdrew in 1973.

"Mom was one of those refugees who was able to get on an evacuating helicopter in 1975, she was ten years-old at the 'Fall of Saigon.' She was paired with a group of Vietnam mothers with similar children called, 'Amerasians' ..."

Saw was puzzled. "What do you mean, 'A Mirror Raisin?' What's that?" Leann answered: "No silly, American and Asian-Amerasian."

"Oh, alright, then," Saw said. He was still puzzled.

Leann continued. "Mom, an orphan, grew up near an Army Base in Washington State, called Fort Lewis. She learned to read and write English and got her GED diploma at age sixteen. She worked as a cook in one of the cafeterias at Fort Lewis. Mom is a very pretty woman with a dark hue to her skin like I have and she was loved by the Black G.I's.

"In 1985, Mom met a Soldier she says his name was, 'Chad Eubanks.' He was an African-American who was very light-skinned and Mom says he was 'drop-dead' handsome. She fell madly in love with him. They shared a lot of secret moments together. Then I happened.

"Soon after I was born, my Father, 'Chad' was stationed in Germany. He had promised to marry Mom, but never did. He told her that he was from Virginia, and that his family lived near the University of Virginia, and that one day, he would come back and marry Mom and we would all be a Happy Family. He never came back.

"So, Mom wants to find him, or his family. Around Charlottesville and Albemarle County there are several different Eubanks' families. Some are Whites, and some are Blacks. But so far Mom has never been able to locate an ex-soldier named, 'Chad.' I wish I could meet my Father, Saw."

Leann cried silently. Saw grabbed her to him. "Don't you worry, Leann, I'll always be here for you. My Moms feels the same way about her Moms as you feel about your Father. You stick with me, and I'll stick with you, and we'll find out what's up together; alright?"

Leann said: "I just knew that there was something special about you. I'm glad I met you. She giggled.

Saw got his first real kiss from a girlfriend. When Jay tried to get one too, Saw shoved him back and allowed: "No Bro. go get your own."

Mo was very angry at Saw and Jay for breaking the rule of never talking to any of the Crips. She yelled, "You and Jay better come right to this house after school, you're grounded!" The Boys slipped on out the door and went down Fifth Street towards school. Mo turned her attention to Ben.

With a little heat in her voice Mo intimated: "Ben, our boys are starting to talk like the Boys on the Block, like the Crips, or the Bloods. They try to dress like them. They swagger along when they walk just like them. I don't want my Boys to be imitating the cut-throat, gangbangers around here.

"They're not having the kinda influence on their peers that you hoped for. This whole neighborhood is like a 'Dragon,' Man. It's devouring everything that it comes in contact with. We gotta do something, Ben. That's all to it, or we gotta move from over here."

Ben stood looking down at his feet as Mo spoke. "What else can I do? I'm meeting with a man I met last week. He came into the restaurant to get a twenty-one piece Meal. His name is Kermit Lyles. He says that he's running an 'At Risk' Program up at the Community Center on the Comer of East Main and Ridge Street. He and his 'Despised Few' have managed to get in touch with Dick Gregory's Outreach Program for Troubled Youth. Mr. Gregory has agreed to come lead a March in the Fifeville area soon.

"I took Kermit's card and an application to join his group. I've filled it out and I wanna be a part of the March. What about you? Do you wanna March too?" he said.

Mo now looked down at her feet. "Ben, we Nursing Students at the UVA had to sign a pledge that we do not belong to any 'left-wing' organization, and that we will not participate in any activity that may be associated with such organizations. The UVA has loosely defined any protest movement as one of those organizations, since the days of Dr. Martin Luther King, Jr.

"Ben, when the area that used to be called 'Gospel Hill'; behind the new Hospital on Lee Drive, including old West Eleventh Street, and the eastern edge of Jefferson Park Avenue and Ninth Street Southwest was condemned, we were told by our Nursing Director and Dean not to participate in any of the demonstrations that were going-on on grounds at the UVA in 1987-through-88, or we would be dropped from the rolls. Many of the students marched, and I wanted to, but I was a good Nursing Student, and I wanted to finish school, Ben. Many of them did get dropped from the rolls. Law Suits followed. Some were settled, and others were not.

"Gospel Hill was razed to the ground, all twenty or so homes on it.

'The area was rezoned from Residential to Development via Eminent Domain.' By 1988 the UVA expanded its New Hospital in that area. Ben, I work on Eight East of the New Hospital because I weaseled-out when I had a chance to stand up for what I really believed in. I'll support any effort you want to make. But I have to do so behind the scenes. They'll find some reason to get rid of me if I dare to do anything else. Do you feel me?" Mo said.

Ben said: "Yep, I do. I know where you're coming from. I was forced to sign a KFC Affidavit stipulating that: 'I am not, never have been, and never will become a Member of the Communist Party, on pains of Immediate Termination upon Discovery.' I should be able to join any political party that I want to. I didn't see anything about 'The American Nazi Party, The Ku Klux Klan, or the Mafia.' I guess it is alright to belong to those 'Un-American Organizations.' Just don't be a 'Commie.'"

Mo looked at her watch. "Baby, I gotta go to work. Talk with the Boys some more about the company they're keeping, alright," she said. She hugged Ben and they kissed a long-lingering kiss. "Ah, look at you, Ben. What you wanna do now?" Mo said.

"You know, Baby," Ben said.

Mo laughed, then giggled. "You're so crazy. You know I gotta get to work. Save all that for tonight," she said.

Ben was on the phone. "Hello, is this Kermit. I'm in my-man. Tell me when we're gonna meet and where. I'm fired up and can't take no more. We over here in Fifeville are afraid to walk the streets. We're afraid that our children are gonna end up in a gang or gonna end up killing for one," Ben said.

Kermit Lyles was working with Jacque Minders at the Community Center that was next to the Trailways Bus Terminal on the Comer of East Main and Ridge Street. Minders, an Ex-Con, had become an Anti-Drug Activist. He had gone to college while pulling fifteen years in Federal Prison for using and selling Cocaine. He had to fulfill hundreds of hours of public service after his release. He put in his time by forming an "At Risk Outreach Program," that was under-written by the Regional Rehabilitation Services for Youthful Offenders, that was partially funded by the Federal Government, the State of Virginia's Drug Enforcement Administration, and by the Mental Health Association of Charlottesville. Jacque was a City Hall Janitor.

Kermit and Jacque had about fifteen or so members secretly working with them who lived in and around Charlottesville who wanted to remain anonymous for fear of reprisals from local gangbangers. They invited Ben to come up to their office located in a brick building that was attached to the Trailways Bus Terminal. It was once used as office space for Trailways. Kermit was a senior at Charlottesville High.

The entranceway to their office was on the Ridge Street side and Ben rang the doorbell there on this morning in 1994. A chubby young man came to the door with a shaved head that he had covered with a black Yankee's Baseball cap with the rim turned around backward. Ben thought that he had come to the wrong place. Kermit wore black culottes, a bulky-white sweatshirt, with the Red Skins' Logo printed in front and in back of it, and he wore Red Air Jordan Tennis. He was soft spoken.

"Come in, Mr. Slokum, I'm Kermit," Kermit said, sticking out his hand for a shake. 'I'm very pleased to meet you. Come on down the hallway and meet Jacque."

Ben followed the plump youth to a large brown door with a door-pane that went from top to bottom. Most of the door was like a window. A short man with a slight mustache and tiny goatee under his bottom lip got up from behind a large brown desk. He was dressed to the nines. He had on a two-piece gray suit, a blue dress-shirt, and a red-and-blue striped tie. He wore brown wing-tipped shoes that had been "spit shined."

Kermit opened the door and Jacque came to shake Ben's hand. "How're you doing, Mr. Jacque Minders. I've heard a lot about you and the programs you are sponsoring," Ben said.

"I'm fine. I'm busy, and that's a good thing. Our people need all of us to be very busy. That's the only way that we're going to do anything to help heal our neighborhoods. None of us can do it alone.

"Come on in my office. We're just here to serve our people the best way we can. We have to make our youths aware of what they're up against. I learned a lot in prison. I went back to school in there. I got my G.E.D. and went on to earn my Master's in Sociology right behind bars. Today, I'm a Changed Man! Praise Be to Allah, God, Yahweh, and Whomever!" Jacque said.

The sound of Jacque's voice touched an emotional chord in Ben's heart. He could hear and feel the sincerity in what this older man was saying. Jacque had straight-black hair that was gray on his sideburns. There were wrinkles on his hands, his neck and his face. He was light-skinned, but had an aging tint to his complexion. His voice rattled when he pronounced his words at the end of his sentences.

Ben vigorously shook Jacque's hand, and took a seat in a green loveseat in the office. Jacque sat in a large fluffy office swivel chair behind the desk. Kermit sat in a green end chair. He got up went to a file cabinet and laid a stack of documents on Jacque's desk.

"Brother Ben, these are copies of some of the documents that I have collected over the years since I've been let out of prison. I want you to go through these and then we will get together to strategize on how to move forward. We've got the attention of a well-known activist, Dick Gregory, who wrote a Book that came out in 1978, with Mark Lane titled: 'Code Name Zorro.' We're organizing a 'March Against Fear' to take place around here in a couple of weeks or so. I hope you will join us," Jacque said.

Ben picked up the stack. of Xeroxed papers. He flipped through them. "I'll read these thoroughly," he said. "I feel you all the way on getting some direct action going around here, Brothers. It's a wonder that either one of you all is able to be as active as you seem to be. But I wanna be in this just like you. I feel that our future existence depends on our present actions. Dr. King, Dr. Lowery, Dr. Hosea Williams, Dr. Ralph Abernathy, Mr. John Lewis, Mr. Jesse Jackson, El Hajj El Malik. Shabaaz (Malcolm X); and Shirley Chisholm, Mrs. Coretta King, Betty Shabaaz and Fannie Lou Hammer, all gave up a lot more than a job so that we could be as far up the road as we are.

"Continuing the Marching and Protests, that's the least we can do. rm willing and able. I'm with you all one-hundred percent I got nine-year old Sons who'll be by my side. Just let me know the day and time," Ben said.

Kermit and Jacque came over and gave Ben a Black. Power Hug, and grand slapping of the hands. Ben took. up the stack of documents and went to the door.

"Have someone stay by the phone. Mr. Gregory says he is committed to coming to march with us. He has just got to make time. He's involved with such direct action all over America. His life has been threatened several times. He was swindled out of a multi-million-dollar Weight Reduction and Healthy Living Business. His Ranch and Home for several years were taken from him by the Federal Government for income-tax evasion. He lost all of that but kept going. Several assassination attempts have been thwarted by his bodyguards. Someone high-up wants him dead. Those documents you are holding in your hands will explain a lot of what is happening to the Brother and by whom-you may be very surprised.

"While talking to me over the phone, Mr. Gregory says that he is not a Comedian just for laughs or for entertainment He says that he has to maintain a very healthy sense of humor to remain sane. He says he tells some tenable truths in the form of jokes. The Brother is not stupid, ludicrous, or silly. He is no 'Jim Crow,' either. But, this man knows how to get the attention of an audience with his stand-up act, while imparting cold-hard, undeniable facts about American injustice to us and all other minorities. That's why he's hated by J. Edgar Hoover, Nixon, Bush, and Reagan. They can't buy him off. He doesn't fear them. He doesn't fear death. And, the 'Whores' who were sent out to circumscribe his integrity failed. He knew they were government-sponsored call-girls. Most importantly, he is very accessible to the common people like us. It does me wonders just to hear the Brother speak," Jacque said.

Just before Ben went out the door he allowed: "I have never paid that much attention to Mr. Gregory to tell you the truth-but I will when he comes to town. My Wife and Sons will no doubt be very eager to meet him. They pay more attention to personalities on the TV than I. But I'm feeling that Mr. Gregory is much more than just a TV Personality. He's a very 'Down-Brother.' He's down in the 'Civil-Rights Trenches' with us. I look forward to meeting with him. Thank you all for inviting me over and for these documents that I will read thoroughly and take to heart I'll see you all later."

Ben came out of the front door and a carload of white youths sped by. Two of them '.Flipped-the-Bird' at him. One of them yelled: "Love America, Nigger, or, Leave It!"

Ben knew what they meant They saw him as a threat to White Supremacy. Therefore he was, to them, "a threat to America." He was threatening to shake them out of their "Comfort Zone." He wanted to change the way that they were used to when it came to misusing, misguiding, and misjudging African Americans. No, they didn't love America any more than him. He just loved all of America and not just a Racial Corner of it They really didn't love America with all of its diversity, racial identities, and cultural entities. They just loved the way White-Americans thought everybody and everyone should bow down to the demands of a few rich White Guys who were in charge of the economic realm. He felt sorry for them.

Ben had parked the old VW Bug across the Street near the Comer of Garrett Street that led to South First and Water Streets. When some white person treated him like a non-person, it always made Ben feel terrible inside. He was born in America. He'd lived in Charlottesville all of his life. Yet, now even the young White Kids were entertaining notions that he was not really a "First-Class Citizen." Why didn't they think he "Loved America?" Why did they think that he being in a place where civil rights activism was known to originate that that negated his "Love for America?" His "Love for America," made him want to make It better for every American. Tears came to Ben's eyes. He felt as though those kids were just repeating what they had heard harangued at home and in their neighborhoods.

He took the stack of Xeroxed papers to the VW Bug, opened the door and threw those into the backseat He cranked the Bug's motor. He wanted Saw and Jay to grow up in a better situation than what was present at that moment in time. He wanted them to put their trust in "Hope," not "Dope." He wanted them to see themselves as "Equal to Anyone else in America-regardless of their Race, Color, Religion, or place of Origin." He wanted them to show no loyalty to any Gang or Gang-Member.

Ben zipped on home with a heavy heart because Saw and Jay were in schools with kids who may think just like those who had called out racial slurs at him that day. After all of the Civil Rights Gains Black People had fought for during the 1940s-through-to-the-1990s, and accomplished-at least on paper-Ben figured it was time that White and Black People at least should have learned to get along with one another. But that was not the case.

Saw and Jay rushed through the front door soon after Ben got home. Saw said: "Hi Dad. What's Up?" Jay said: "What's going down?"

Ben responded: "Hold it. Damn-it! I want you all to stop talking like you're some ten-cent 'Hood Rats!'

When you address your Mother or Father in this house, you will use Standard English. Is that dear? You all are not Bangers, and you're not going to be those as long as I'm raising you. I don't want to hear that you been on the same street as that horrible character 'The **Moo-Man.'** Is that clear?" Ben yelled at his astonished Sons.

"Yes, Dad," Saw said. "Yes Sir," Jay said.

Ben stood looking down at them with a harsh frown on his face. "Now, go on in your room and study your books for the rest of the evening. Got that?" Ben yelled.

The Boys hurried on quickly to what was once Ivy's Room. Ben had converted that into their bedroom. They screamed and cried so bad when Ben and Mo tried to give them separate rooms that their parents relented and allowed them to sleep in the same room.

Ben picked up the first Xeroxed pages of the stack. Several pages from one book had been stapled together. There were several of these bundles in the stack. Ben picked up the first bundle and began to read. . . .

Chapter Thirteen

"Hello ... Hello, Pops ..." whined Mo into one to the hospital's wall-phones' receiver. She chose one well around the comer on Eight East so no one would be able to hear her.

"Hello, Baby Girl," Philip said. "How is it going with you?"

Mo sobbed a little. "Pops, I'm in distress over what's happening over where we live. People are getting shot at all the time. Some just because they didn't know what 'Colors they ought to be wearing.' I'm afraid for my Boys. They try to hang out with one of the most notorious of the Gang Leaders, one calling himself the 'Moo-Man.' He's called that because of the way he drawls. He has a very 'Carolinian Accent/ and he drags the endings of some words so that people say that he Moos when he does that.

"He dresses very colorful and the youngsters in our Neighborhood see him as some kinda local hero. He's been shot several times by the 'Bloods,' but survived every time. He's been beat-up several times by whomever, and he survived that too.

"The young boys in our community all try to dress like him, talk. like him and I'm afraid Saw and Jay are among them. I want to move away from that house we live in Pops. I'm scared to death all the time that Ben, Me, or my Boys are going to become the next victims. But Ben doesn't want to move because of the memory of his Grandmother, Brother Ivy, and Cousin Roy. Pops ... someone's house right up the Street from our place got shot all up. SWAT came, but arrested no suspects, and nothing else was done," Mo whined.

Philip was saddened by what he heard. "I knew your move to that part of Town was downward," he said. "I have some friends up on Pantops Mountain. They're building houses in a new neighborhood they've named, 'The Key West Subdivision.' I can bid for one of the individual houses for you, and the Boys, or on a Duplex, if you want to get away from down where you live to a more civilized neighborhood."

Mo hated it when her Father spoke about African-Americans as being "Uncivilized." She blurted out: "Pops, I do not believe that the people over here in Fifeville are uncivilized, any more than the people in Atlantic City, New Jersey are. A lot more people are killed by White Gangsters up there than down here in Charlottesville, Virginia in Fifeville. But no one calls those 'Organized Gangsters,' uncivilized. Okay?"

Philip responded with, "Sorry. Mo, I meant that some people are . . . well . . . not ... not who you would want to live right next to. Is that right?"

Mo knew that that argument was going nowhere. "Oh, whatever, Pops. I would like for you to look around for me for some other place for us to go. If you find the right place, I might be able to convince Ben to move us away from Fifeville. But it has to seem like the whole thing was his idea. You understand, Pops?" Mo said.

He paused for a second and said: "Yes, I do. I'm a proud man too. I know Ben is. He is set in his ways. He has an agenda that is slated to fail because there are too many obstacles standing in his way no matt.er how stubborn he may be in pursuing his lofty goals.

"Might I suggest that you should go up on Pantops Mountain to the Key West Subdivision and take a look at an Open House to see if you'd like one. You don't have to choose one of those. There is a new neighborhood in Southwestern Albemarle with several Condos for sale called the 'Millcreek Village.' There's been a new Elementary and High School built near there in the Monticello School Complex. It's quiet and exclusive and only middle to upper-income people are able to live there. That would be excellent for the Boys; right?"

Mo came back with: "Pops, you will never understand where I'm coming from-I don't think. What I want for my Boys and what you think I want are miles apart. I'll go visit the Open Houses in both of those locations. That does not mean that I will choose either one."

Philip coughed. His voice lowered as he spoke: "Babette left for Paris, Mo. She finished her degree from the UVA. I found her note on the table the other day. She says she missed 'Gay Pa-ree.' She was afraid that I would never understand her so the note said. So, she wanted me to get on with my life and she would go back home to hers. That's that, Mo. I feel like such an old fool. I think she used me to a great extent to have a comfortable place to 'crash in' while she went through the work to earn her PhD. Once she got it, she wanted to go back to France. She used me like that

"Besides, Mo, Babette wanted an open-marriage. She wanted to be able to date other men. She said it was alright for me to date other women. I was very uncomfortable with that so I told her never to let me catch her out with another man. I think that was 'the straw that broke the camel's back.' She was fooling around and was afraid that I would find out She even brought one of her sultry French Classmates home to meet me. She almost stripped nude, down to her skimpy panties and no bra, in the front of me when Babette allegedly went out to the store to get another bottle of the fine wine they had been drinking. That girl was all over me, but I was not in the mood for that kinda shenanigans. The young blonde got dressed and ran out my front door in tears.

"Babette came back shortly and asked where 'Suzette Lorraine' had run off to? I said I didn't know. The next day Babette asked me sternly, 'Why couldn't you have been more hospitable toward my friend?' She said not another word to me for days after that. Then she got into bed with me shortly after that and made mad love to me! ..."

> Mo interrupted: "Pops, that's too much information."
>
> Philip continued: "Well, she's gone. I'm all alone again. All I got are you and my Grandsons." Mo sighed. "Pops, I'm glad that you are free from her. She meant you no good."

"I know that now, Baby Girl. I went down a one-way road to despair. I'm sorry"

Mo interrupted him: "Pops, you men seem to be weak to the charms of a beautiful woman. Don't beat yourself up too bad over Babette. She saw how vulnerable you were and she took advantage of all that.

"I love you Pops. I don't want you to think that I'm presumptuous enough to be able to criticize you for whatever choices you have made in life-except for your letting my Moms leave us. But Pops, you seem to be trying to travel down a road that does not want you to be one of the travelers allowed passage on that road.

"You want redemption from being what you are. You seem to be seeking absolution from the very source of your condemnation. You can never become one of the people you want to be. Nothing that you do will make them see you as their equal. After they use you for whatever intrinsic or extrinsic reasons, they will then disallow your real humanity and Constitutional Rights; like they do to Latino and Native American (Indian), Soldiers. They fought in foreign wars to come home to be treated like second-class miscreants; and the Native Americans and Mexicans are called 'Aliens,' in their own Ancient Homelands.

"It does not matter who you many, Pops. It does not matter who you internally wish you were. It matters more, what the people who you want to accept you, see you as. I learned that early on even in New York. Even in Harlem, when I was just a little girl. After we came to Charlottesville, my Race was always in question. Many White Mothers did not want their Daughters to bring me home to meet their families. In the homes where I was allowed, or tolerated, many times hard questions about 'Black people and why We are the way We seem to Whites,' were put to me, a little girl who didn't have a clue. It made me feel like I was not a little girl anymore. I felt like a 'Bad, Ugly, Thing' that had crawled up out of a crack in the floor and needed to be driven back to where I belonged. At one point, before I became an avid bookworm, I wished I could wash my 'Blackness' off. Many nights I cried myself to sleep.

"When I tried to tell you about my experiences, you shied away from hearing me. You wanted me to 'have a positive attitude.' My attitude had nothing to do with what I was going through. It was like being a 'Closeted-Gay Person.' Except my reason for being singled-out was very evident by my physical appearance; and a 'Closeted-Gay Person' may not be discovered unless he or she discloses to someone that secret and that person announces it

"So Pops, I had no one to confide in. Unfortunately, other Blacks didn't want to talk about what we all were experiencing. They were all trying to 'Fit-In,' somehow, into the 'White Majority.' I kept my feelings to myself. I suffered in silence. I became like 'Maya Angelou, said she became, an avid Reader.' I found solace in the myriad books I intellectually devoured, just like she had done.

"Pops, you're sighing, you seem bewildered. I didn't mean to hurt you . . . I'm sorry. I"

"No Mo, Baby Girl," Philip spoke choking a little on his words. "I didn't mean to subject you to all of that No, I wanted you to have a better life, that's all. I'm sorry for all of the pain I've caused you, and now myself. I have to take a good look 'at the man in the mirror.' I have to find a way to change, to move away from the pain, to become a better man. I love you, Mo. I'm so proud of how you've grown intellectually.

"Bring the Boys up next weekend to see me. I got a new Game they can hook up to their Color TV and play right along with it It's called Xbox, something of other. Tell Ben, I said, Hello."

Mo sighed. "I love you too, Pops. I'll see you real soon. Goodbye." Mo hung the phone up. She ran into an empty room and the tears came running down her cheeks. She sobbed deeply.

On this evening Ben picked up the Stack of Xeroxed Bundles Kermit and Jacque had given him. He selected one and put the rest back on his desk in his study. Even the title of this one was startling:

Robert Harris and Jeremy Paxman, *A Higher Form Of Killing; The Story of Chemical and Biological Wanare., 1982:* This bundle of pages was thick. Ben was very astonished at the contents of this accusatory list of horrendous practices the Federal Government was alleged to have carried out on innocent military personnel and people in various communities across America. Paxman and Harris alleged:

"That Federal Government Scientists went into immediate research directly after the 1954 Supreme Court's Ruling, outlawing Public School Segregation. Out of Labs in Maryland, Missouri, California, Virginia, and New York, a number of experiments were first done on Mice, Rats, Dogs, and then on Primates (Monkeys and Gorillas).

"By 1964, a number of newer more potent, and thus lethal, substances had been gleaned out of Cocaine, Heroin, and, a new Drug (LSD, Lysergic-acid-diethylamide), was created, that was very hallucinogenic, and addictive.

"From Cocaine, a very powerfully addictive form of the drug was synthesized, and baked into pebble-like pieces of highly purified cocaine to be smoked (on the streets of America these pebble-like pieces are called Crack-Rocks). 'Crack' was found to be the most addictive of all of the drugs tested on Mice, Rats, Dogs, and or Primates.

"The first Humans the above Drugs were tested on were American Soldiers. They were fed the drugs unknowingly. Many of those went mad and were confined in insane asylums. A group of Research Scientists were at a Resort in the Blue Ridge Mountains for a little Government-Sponsored R&R. Their Drinks were secretly laced with LSD, again unbeknownst to any of them.

"All of the men developed mental problems. In two cases, irreversible psychosis plagued those Researchers. They became very aggressively violent and had to be carted away to very secluded Government Asylums. Others became very paranoid and passive. One would not come near his wife. She appeared to be some kind of monster to him. All of the Researchers' careers were ended.

"Crack was tested on Jail Inmates in various Jails in California. It was found to be so addictive that Inmates would kill anyone close to them to get access to more of that Drug. Once Crack had been introduced to an Inmate, nothing else seemed to matter to him or her. They would do almost anything to get more of the Drug. Nothing was too disgusting, sordid, or immoral for them to gain even a little piece of 'Rock-Crack-Cocaine.'

"By 1964, Government Agents introduced LSD to College Students. They posed as Hippies. They gave 'Free Parties,' and told the attendees that they had a 'Far Out' new Drug, that 'Will Expand Your Mind.' Old Beatnik Gurus helped carry out this Debacle. They freely disseminated the Drug in the Haight-Ashbury area. They set up so-called 'Free Clothing Stores, Restaurants, and Flop-houses,' where students and the general public could come to and 'Dropout, Tune-In, and Tum-On.' LSD became a Trend on College Campuses all over California. Other Colleges and Universities soon followed the Trend.

"Because Powered Cocaine was too expensive for poor Ghetto-Dwellers to afford, Crack was introduced to these areas. It was much cheaper. It was more addictive. It was Tailor-Made for the Ghetto. Ten Dollars-a-pop, gave you a Fifteen minute, fantastic high, that some described as a massive, full-bodied multi orgasm they did not want to come down from. When that happened, they became very depressed and would do anything to get back up there again. Thus, Crack. was more addictive than all of the other 'Government-Created Designer Drugs.'

"In the l 920s, the Italian Mafias were the great disseminators of Heroin. That Dope was made available via Dance Halls, Ballrooms, Backstage in any Pop performance genre, and addicts of every walk of life accepted the reality that 'Horse' as the Drug was called, was an unfortunate, ongoing, reality.

"Heroin, called 'Stuff, Shit, That Monkey, A Shot, That Groove, Etc., ruined the lives of Billie Holiday, her Band Member, Lester Young, James Brown, Jirni Hendrix, Janis Joplin, Sha Na, John Belushi, Charley Bird, Kurt Cobain, John Coltrane, Wes Montgomery, Tupac Shakur, Easy E. Elvis Presley, Marilyn Monroe, and etc.

"The Mafias were Sicilian Families that were Gangbangers in Italy before they were mysteriously imported to America after the fall of Italy in the 1940s (WWII). Whole families with last names like, 'Luciano, Constellano, Gotti, and Capone,' called 'Godfathers,' were brought to New York. New Jersey, Illinois, California, Nevada, Florida, Texas, Columbia, South America, and Cuba. These families set up a criminal Network that spread across America with deep-roots in All Sports' Genres, The Garment Districts, The Jewelry Trade, All Trade Unions, The Hollywood Movie Industries, All Music Genres, Illegal and Legal Gambling, High-and-Low-Level Prostitution Rings, Drug-Dealing at every Level, and Avid Police and Judiciary Corruption.

"J. E, Hoover, The Director of the FBI either couldn't break the 'Code of Secrecy' of these families or he didn't try. Some have it that they held the scandal of 'Hoover's Homosexuality' over his head. So, he pretended that these mafias did not exist, even when they were very active all- around Washington D.C., New York, Pennsylvania, and New Jersey, right in Hoover's backyard. The Mafias had free reign in most of America's major cities, especially near university campuses.

"Heroin became multimillions of Americans 'Dope of choice' from the 1920s to the 1960s. The other such Drug was Marijuana, followed by Booze. The Mafias (or the Mob as they were euphemistically called), peddled all of the above with impunity all over America. 'Mob Guys' like Gotti, Capone, and The Ice Man' became cult heroes and were reverenced as 'Godfathers.' Soon a Mob Crowd emerged, called 'The Jewish Syndicate' that shared a huge portion of the Dope, Prostitution, and Corrupt Money-Laundering for the Mafias and other organized criminals. Money was spirited away to secret accounts in the Caiman Islands, and Cuba. An Irish Mob followed, and a Black One followed them, headed by S. Saint Claire, a Numbers Writer Mogul, and her Head-Hoodlum, 'Bumpy Ellsworth Johnson,' brought up the rear. Johnson became a notorious Heroin Peddler in Harlem, Chicago, Camden, New Jersey, and as far away as Los Angeles, California. Bumpy's confidence man was Frank Lucas, who formed 'The Council,' with Nicky Barnes that became the most horrible mob of killers up until 1976. Then Lucas and Barnes were arrested and convicted and sentenced to fifteen years to life but served very little of their sentences. They turned State's Evidence and were put on the 'Witness Protection Plan' and were given provisional Paroles.

"In the 1960s, CIA Agents posing as 'Mob Guys' concentrated on California because of the 'Crews' in Compton and Oakland. Each neighborhood had its own little clique. They were not well organized and were just a bunch of rowdy, noisy, violent teenage delinquents. So-called 'Mob Guys' moved into nearby neighborhoods to Watts, and from there secretly organized and armed two groups of the above delinquents. One called itself, 'The Bloods.' The other called itself, 'The Crips.'

The Bloods and Crips were armed with AK-47s, *45* Automatic Pistols, Sawed-off Twelve Gauge Shotguns, and a Hand Grenade or two. The Mafias and the leftover members of 'The Council,' supplied the newly organized 'Gangbangers' with cocaine and showed them how to cook it into 'Crack.' Makeshift Crack Factories sprung up all over Watts, Compton, and Oakland. Heroin was still pushed, but Crack became the most lucrative drug of choice, because of its tremendous High, in California and because it was cheap and had more kick than Heroin or Marijuana.

"By the 1970s, a terrific Gang War was going on in California between the Crips and the Bloods. Those Gangbangers fought each other to the death daily for control of drug Turfs, in the ghettoes of Watts, Compton and Oakland.

"Blood still runs in the streets of California like rainwater during a torrential thunderstorm.

Dope flowed through California like flood waters during a hurricane. The Police could no-longer control the streets. Neighborhoods fell apart. Those who could move moved as far away from troubled areas as possible. That left dilapidated and economically-blighted areas peopled by poor desperate low-to-no income welfare recipients. The young felt as though Gangs were the only way to survive the Ghettoes. So they became part of the Crips, Bloods, and a Salvadoran Gang, 'The MS-13,' The Mexican Mafia, and 'The 213Gang de Sur, and de Norte.'

"Among the Poor-Whites, the Hells Angeles dominated. But they were opposed by the 'Mongols, The Pagans, and The Confederate Angels.' These were all at War with each other.

"Korean Gangs were formed. Japanese Gangs sprung up. Vietnamese Gangs came into being. The Jamaican Posse expanded. These all peddled Dope, Guns, Ammunition, and Prostitution, but used legitimate businesses to laundry their dirty-ill-gotten gain. And, they were all at War with each other.

"Thus Paxman and Harris concluded that the Central Intelligence Agency (CIA), The Federal Bureau of Investigation (FBI), The Drug Enforcement Agency (DEA), and The Alcohol Tobacco and Firearms Agency (ATF), were derelict to totally corrupt in that they neglected to do their duties. Local Police, State Troopers, Sheriff Departments, and Federal Marshals were also guilty of 'Being on the Take,' and sometimes turned their backs to poor-white and or poor-black neighborhoods. It seemed to Paxman and Harris that no one seemed to care what happened to Blacks, Latinos, and or Poor-Whites in terms of Dope Addiction, Gun-Violence Victims, and Gang-War Murders. It seemed that as long as all of the above were kept far away from Upper-Middleclass-White Neighborhoods, like Semi-Valley, or the murders of Sharon Tate, et al, in 1969 by 'The Manson Family,' in Benedict Canyon, the rest could go to Hell!"

Ben put that Bundle down. He got up and made himself a Chocolate Milk. He came back to his Study shaking his head. He thought "Is what is going on in California going on right here in Fifeville?"

The next Bundle was from a Book titled: *The Big Uilute Lie,* By Michael Levine with Laura Kavanau Levine, 1993. Several pages had been Xeroxed and stapled together. Levine said:

"He was a High-Ranking Drug Enforcement Officer that had progressed up the ladder of success in the DEA. The problem was that he was seeing too much corruption among fellow agents who let thousands of felons go free instead of arresting them and charging them with the crimes that he had seen them commit.

"When Levine took his complaints to higher-ups, he was reprimanded for interfering with Agency Policies and Matters that were none of his Business.

"The Straw that Broke the Camel's back came at the end of the Vietnam Conflict. Levine saw tons of Cocaine and Heroin being shipped to Columbia in South America. Tons more were shipped to Mexico. Often US Military Planes and Personnel were engaged in the loading, transporting, and unloading of the Dope. When Levine and his office inquired as to what was going on, they were told that it was 'Top Secret' and they were to forget what they saw because the 'Operations' were 'Classified.'

"A little bit of nosing around revealed that the Dope was being turned over to Organized Criminals in Columbia, The Philippine Islands, Mexico, and Jamaica. These Criminals made their money from selling to dealers in America. These dealers were set up in Florida (Maimi), California (Los Angeles), Virginia (Norfolk, Virginia Beach, and Portsmouth), Washington State (Seattle), New York (Brooklyn), New Jersey (Camden), Las Vegas, Nevada, Arizona (Phoenix), Illinois (Chicago), and Texas (Huston).

"Levine found out that a notorious Hispanic Female 'Double-Agent,' he called 'The Snow Queen' had been imported from 'Columbia to America' to orchestrate the moving of large quantities of Dope from the original points of entry to the middlemen Dealers in the inner-cities.

"What angered Levine was that a Lieutenant Colonel **O.N.,** that had been appointed to The National Security Council Staff, was supplying Dope to 'The Snow Queen,' using American Military Planes to transport the Drugs to Colombia, Panama, and Jamaica, from Mexico (Marijuana), Thailand, Sargon, Bangkok, India, and Iran. He took the money the sale of Guns and Dope generated and gave it to so called, 'Freedom Fighters, The Contras in Nicaragua,' to help them topple the 'Leftist Sandinista Government.' This Debacle is called the 'Iran-Contra Affair,' that took place under 'The Reagan Administration in the 1980s.' Drugs and Guns poured into Mexico, Iraq, and Iran. Drug Cartels emerged in Mexico that overwhelmed that Nation's Police Forces. America turned its back on that government's pleas for intervention and or help. Guns were sold to Iranians, Iraqis, and Saudi Arabians.

"The guns that were sold to Saudi Arabia, Iran and Iraq fell into the hands of radical antigovernment forces that came to be called 'Insurgents,' that threatened America's overseas interests. Violent revolutions ensued. The weapons that were sold to Mexicans fell into the hands of radical criminal elements that increased the drug-flow that helped to inundate American inner-cities. Billions of dollars' worth of Marijuana, Cocaine, and Heroin crossed the Mexican border into Texas, Louisiana, Florida, South Carolina, North Carolina and Virginia. Thus we have the start of 'The Crack Epidemic,' of the 1990s.

"The above weapons were military-grade, and in 1989-1991, when Russia lost the 'Cold War,' to America and her European Allies, stockpiles of small aI1llS and ammunition stood in warehouses in Poland, Czechoslovakia, Chechnya, Hungary, Moscow, Crimea, and East Germany. Some of these weapons had been imported from Mainland China, and some from Israel.

"From 'The People's Republic of China' such weapons were among the stockpile as the *QBZ-95,* QBZ- 95-1, and the QBZ-97 Fully-Automatic Assault Rifles with 650-rounds-per-minute magazines. From Russia there were the AK-47 Assault Semi-Automatic Rifles. These had 1-30 rounds-per-minute capabilities. Among the stockpiles was The AR-15 Assault Rifle, manufactured in America by ARMALlTE Industries near Hollywood, California. Bringing up the rear were the Uzi, and RK-62 Yisrael Galil Assault Rifle with its Armor-Piercing Ammunition. These are the weapons and ammunition that ended up in Mexico, Iraq, Iran, Yemen, Libya, Egypt, Somalia, Mozambique, Uganda, and South American guerilla insurgents. Many of these Military Assault Rifles found their way into the hands of Gangbangers in America. By 1994, the streets of America had become very dangerous because all police forces were completely outgunned.

"The Russian Mafia put all of the guns in Russia's 'Cold War Stockpiles' on 'The Black Market.' They were sold to the highest bidders. Thousands of Russian Mafioso migrated to America in the 1990s. They got in got set-up, and got into the gun-running and drug-dealing rackets. Like the Sicilians, the Russian Mob seems to have somewhat of a 'Security Blanket' from the CIA, FBI, NSA, and local police forces.

"Levine confronted those DEA Officials over him. They told him to 'shut up.' He refused. He was told that he had to resign his post as an DEA agent. Bogus charges were brought against him. While fighting these, one of his children-with no history of drug abuse-died from a 'Heroin Overdose.' All of the rest of his family members blamed him for the death of his child. He found himself divorced. Alone. And finally, he had to flee for his life from the same people he had worked beside for over twenty years. He barely escaped from his 'Counter-Intelligence Pursuers,' on a number of occasions because there were still DEA officials who were loyal to him and knew of his innocence. They warned him when 'Hit Squads,' had been sent out to kill him on-sight. That was why he had written the Book."

That was the end of the Bundle. Ben felt a lump in his chest. It was not a pain, but like something he could not completely swallow. This thing that was going on in Fifeville was much bigger than he could have previously imagined. A terrible fear bordering on xenophobia engulfed him.

Chapter Fourteen

On this hot afternoon in July, Ben made his way to The Community Center on the Corner of Ridge and East Main Streets. He was driving his new 1994 GMC Jeep Cherokee. He had just been promoted to Manager of KFC on Cherry Avenue. He thought he could afford to "Live a little."

Kermit called him that past Sunday evening to announce: "Hey, Brother Man, Mr. Gregory is coming to Town this coming Thursday. We will hold a rally at the Center on Friday evening. He will speak along with some dignitaries he will bring with him. We will only allow invited guests to attend that rally. The March will start on that Saturday Morning at 10:00 a.m. from The Center. Mr. Gregory will lead the way and we of The Center will walk beside and behind him. The whole Town is invited.

"Can I count you in?"

Ben was very excited. "Man, you better believe it! Since I read his books, I'm dying to see this Icon in person and to shake his hand. There are so many famous Clowns out already, like 'Flip Wilson, Pig Meat Markham, Moms Mabley, Redd Foxx, Ben Vereen, and Richard P:ryor,' who're no better than modern-day 'Jim Crows.' People looking for a way to cast aspersions on us as a Cultural Group, seem to look no further than at the 'Jim Crows,' the dominant culture has made famous. 'These Clowns have made us the laughingstock of the Civilized World.' But Mr. Gregory is not a Clown or a Jim Crow.

"Yeah, Brother, count me in. I'll bring my Boys to the March too. They need to be exposed to the frontlines of the battle to gain our real Freedom from Hate, Racism and Fear. What time will the rally get cranked up? I'll be there early on."

Kermit paused. "Well ... I see that it's slated to begin at Eight. But ... we will get going as soon as Mr. Gregory's Security People check our place out thoroughly and clear him to appear. You know how that is? Well, it's best for you to be there at about Six or so."

Ben hung the phone up.

The traffic was thick as fleas on a stray dog's back that afternoon. It was bumper-to-bumper all the way down East Main to The Community Center. There was nowhere to park. The Water Street Parking Garage had a full-sign out front All of the two-hour parking spaces were full. The metered parking places were full. Ben had to drive all the way down Ridge to Maclntire Road to the County Building (old Lane High), to find a place to park. He had to walk several blocks uphill to get back to the Center.

He got half-way up the sidewalk on Ridge and he ran into a large crowd of people. They were pushing their way up Ridge toward the Center. Ben got out of the mob and went across the Street to the other sidewalk. adjacent to the Omni Hotel Parking Garage. The crowd over there was less dense. Ben thought to himself: "Kermit must not have told these people that the rally was for 'invites only.'"

Ben was glad that he had come much earlier than he had at first planned to come. It was only Five p.m. He knew that if he would've! waited until Six, he'd never get up to the door on time. When he finally made it to the door, he saw that the crowd was filling up the Bus Station area, and standing on the sidewalks on both sides of Ridge Street across from the Center. Some people were going into the Mt Zion Baptist Church that stood right beside The Cent.er.

Kermit and Jacque were standing on either side of the entrance to The Center. When someone came to the door, they said, "Come in," or "Sony, this is a private meeting. You'll be able to hear what is going on by close-circuit TV over at Mt Zion."

Ben shook Kermit's hand, and noticed that he was wearing a white-shirt and a pair of gray slacks. Ben had only seen him in very casual hip-hop attire. He looked like a very different person. He smiled and took Ben's hand in both of his and laughed. "Good afternoon Mr. Slokum," he said.

Jacque was wearing a Tuxedo, fluffy shirt, and all. He hugged Ben. "Good of you to come, Mr. Slokum," he said.

Inside of the Center, Jacque and Kermit had been busy. They had borrowed about one-hundred-fifty folding chairs from Baldwin Johnson

Funeral Home. Reverend Alonzo Johnson Pastor of The Pilgrim Baptist Church's Brother owned the Funeral Home. The Funeral Home was one block from the Church, but ten blocks from the Community Center. Good thing the Center had a Van on loan to it from "The Mental Health Organization."

A new, thick, fluffy, red-carpet had been installed on the floor. The large area that was once just a cafeteria and conference room was now a makeshift auditorium. Ben observed that pretty red-white-and blue draperies were hung at the windows with white valance, featuring fluffy red-white-and-blue balls that hung on the bottom edges of the valance by strings. "These were donated by the City of Charlottesville," Ben was told by Kermit when he saw Ben staring at the draperies. "So was the carpet," Kermit said. They both had a good laugh.

"They certainly want us to remember where we are and who is in charge, don't they?" Ben allowed. Kermit came over to where Ben sat on the edge of the fifth row. "Brother Man, you're one of us.

You're not a guest If you wouldn't mind, help us pass out some Programs. Man, as you can see, all of the chairs are jammed. The hallway is jammed, and the Fire Marshal has ordered us not to let any more people in here or in Mt Zion. You know, I never would've thought that Dick Gregory would've gotten this many people out to hear him speak on a Friday night It's Party Night, you know.

"Here's a stack of Programs. Pass them out It's around seven-thirty. It can't be long before Mr. Gregory will be coming along. He's bringing a Lady that was part of Mr. M. Berry's Administration when he was taken down from Mayor of D.C. for Drug Abuse. She helped authorities to take him down."

Ben heard sirens outside. Sounded like two or more police cruisers were passing by the Center. But the sirens stopped suddenly. That meant that they had arrived at the "Scene of the crime."

"Who called the cops, Kermit?" Ben asked. "I have no idea," Kermit replied.

Ben and Kermit made their way to the Center's entrance. A Police cruiser was parked in the Fire Station's Parking Lot. A Paddy Wagon was parked on the Street across from the Center's entrance. Two cops dressed in black combat outfits with silver helmets were sitting in the Paddy Wagon holding Twelve Gauge Shotguns.

Two more Cops, one with Sergeant's bars on his sleeves, and another with Corporal bars got out of the Cruiser and the Sergeant went along one side of Ridge Street, and the Corporal the other. They were ordering people to make a path so that pedestrians could easily walk by The Center. The Crowd did as they were ordered. The two in the Paddy Wagon were holding their guns at the ready as a black Limo approached the front of The Center.

A Black Man got out of the Limo. He wore green fatigues typical of a GI, except they were not pressed or squeaky clean like they would have to be in the military. He wore a black baseball cap with the Insignia: "FIGHT THE POWER!" in bold white lettering. He seemed to be about six-one, or so tall. His face was covered with a gray beard. His hair hung from under his cap and was salt-and-pepper in color. He wore a pair of black combat boots. He was sturdily built but was getting somewhat of a gut on him.

A Black Female got out of the car with the Black Man. She seemed to be about five-one tall. She wore a Kente Cloth Midi-Dress, with brown sandals. Her hair was in a large, fluffy, Afro. She wore a long necklace composed of maybe a hundred or so Cowrie Shells. She had no other makeup on her face or body. She appeared to be a beautifully shaped, graceful, African Princess. She walked slowly behind the Black **Man.**

The two cops holding the shotguns got out of their vehicle. They stood at attention. The Sergeant and Corporal stood on either side of the Center's entrance. The crowd did not surge forward. Some held up signs saying: "We Love You Dick Gregory."

Four Black men dressed in black suits and colorful bowties walked behind the Black Couple as they made their way into The Community Center. Then people started cheering and applauding. Once Mr. Gregory and his wife, Lillian, had gone inside, the crowd surged toward the entrance. All four Cops stood between the crowd and the entrance. The crowd backed up and some grumbled.

Carloads of Reporters suddenly appeared out of nowhere: TV Cameramen from Channel 6 WCHV, Channel 4 NBC 29, and Channel 3 WSVA. People carrying cameras with "The Tribune Weekly News," and "The Daily Progress," attached to the tops of those along with the

TV people were stopped at the entrance. Only a reporter and cameramen from the The Daily Progress, and The Tribune were allowed inside of The Community Center.

A portable stage and podium had been erected in the southern comer of the makeshift auditorium. They were seemingly made of hard plastic or some ceramic material. They were white in color and the lights reflected off of them very well.

There were eight folding chairs behind the podium. The four young men with insignia on their plastic ID Cards attached to their lapels with the black letters: "F.O.I." with a "Red Crescent Moon and Star," stood on the podium behind the chairs. They very thoroughly looked under and behind everything before Mr. Gregory climbed the two steps up onto the stage and went to stand behind the podium. Lillian followed him and sat directly behind Mr. Gregory. That left seven empty chairs.

The whole audience was composed of people from the Black Community. No Whites showed up.

Only the White Reporters and Cameraman from The Daily Progress were Caucasians.

There were only one-hundred-fifty chain available for guests. Those were filled to capacity. About that many more people stood in the aisles. Another two-hundred of so had jammed into Mt. Zion. Among those were the News People. They were eager to get what they could via close-circuit TV.

'When Ben heard the estimate from Jacque of how many people had showed up for a Peaceful Demonstration Rally, on a Friday Night, he was amazed. He heard that nearly half-a-thousand Black People had come out to hear Dick Gregory speak that evening.

The people in the aisles moved back to create a apace for the people who were heading towards the Stage. People cheered **as a** gray-headed gentleman walked slowly towards **the stage.** He wore a thin blue suit, white shirt with a red-white-and-blue tie, and brown wingtip shoes. He took a little bow. Mr. Gregory came down from the stage to shake the gentleman's hand. His wife did likewise. The gentleman took a seat to the right of Mn. Gregory's. Ben recognized him as Rev. Hosea Williams, a

Civil Rights Advocate who had marched with Dr. Martin Luther King, Jr. in Alabama in the 1960s.

A Local Peace Advocate came up the aisle next. Ben knew that he was Clive Da Silva, a retired Pastor of the Presbyterian Church on Preston Avenue. He and Rev. Bonn, then Pastor of First Baptist Church. had been instrumental in finding Dr. King lodging when he spoke at UVa's Newcomb Hall Ballroom in the 1960s. The Monticello Hotel, on East Jefferson Street, and The Albemarle, on West Main, did not "Serve Colored People." Neither did the Boars Head Inn, Farmington or Keswick Country Clubs serve Blacks back then. Dr. King was lodged at The Cavalier Inn on Preston Avenue, a Black. Motel. Mr. Gregory shook Rev. Da Silva's hand and he sat to the left of Mn. Gregory, wearing a blue white-collared clergy-suit.

After the entrance of Rev.'s Williams and Da Silva, Mr. Gregory raised both his hands. Ben felt like you could have heard a pin drop on cotton. Ben noticed that Mr. Gregory had never sat down. He had been standing for nearly an hour. He had continuously viewed the audience from side to side looking carefully as if to see something or someone . . . but Ben wondered for what or who he could have been looking for.

"Will those seated please rise," Mr. Gregory asked. He raised his outstretched hands toward the audience. Everyone stood up.

"I want you all to sing with me one Stanza of the 'Afro-American National Anthem,'" Mr. Gregory said. After the "Hymn," Rev. Williams, being a Senior Ex-Pastor, came to the podium to stand beside Mr. Gregory. He stood with his hands clasped together with his head bowed and his eyes closed.

"Almighty God, in the name of Jesus, we thank You for this opportunity to represent Your Love, Mercy and Forgiveness. Bless this **gathering** of Your People, and the cause for which they have come to dedicate themselves to do Your Will O' God. Anoint us for what will follow our course of action, our programs, our sacrifice O' Lord God, Our Redeemer. Go with us on tomorrow as we will endeavor to show Your Love toward those who have despitefully used us. Grant us the strength to continue on in the march to true racial equality and Freedom from Fear and Violence. Tonight we stand before You as Lambs seeking Your Divine Guidance. We pray for Your Protection and for all members of the Protest March to remain

Nonviolent no matter what may come their way. Bless our Leader, Dick Gregory, and the Members of The Community Center. Bless the leaden of the Charlottesville City Council, and even those who are opposed to this gathering and the March on tomorrow. We Thank You O' God of our Strength. These and all Blessings we ask in Jesus Name, Amen."

Rev. Williams shook hands with Rev. Da Silva, Mrs. Gregory, and Mr. Gregory. All of them sat down on the stage except Mr. Gregory. He intoned: "You all may be seated," to the audience.

Gregory looked the crowd over seemingly checking out parts of the audience slowly at first then quickly. "What's Up?" he said. "1 know that is an alleged 'Hip-Hop' greeting and, I am not a proponent of most 'Hip-Hop' recording artists. I am not a proponent of the Anglo -way of doing things either. When I have to make a choice, I will go the African-American Way

"I like one sound by 'Public Enemy Number One.' It is what I'm wearing on my hat: 'Fight The Power!' 'Cause Brothers and Sisters, we have got to 'Fight The Power That Be!' like Public Enemy **says.**

There's a true message in their Rap." The whole audience applauded. It quieted down immediately. "That's why our Dear Sisters, Mothers, and Grandmothers are naming their children 'Da' Shaun, Ma' Shaun, Lu' Sandra,' and whatnot. They're trying to take back their identity that was stolen from us during the Tram-Atlantic Slave Trade, and four-hundred years of slavery in America, and even longer in South America. Slavery didn't end in Brazil until 1888.

"I want to thank Brother, Jacque Minders, Kermit Lyles, and the members of The Community Center, and those good people on the City Council, as well as the Charlottesville/Albemarle Regional Mental Health Organization for making my visit here possible.

"Brothers a nd Sisters, as you can see, four chairs are empty up here. Up until the last minute, we were trying to convince the City Council to allow Mrs Fran Broader to appear with us tonight. She was an Administrator on D.C. Mayor, M. Berry's Staff when he was recently deposed. She was instrumental in turning State's Evidence. She testified against Mr. Berry, and helped to secure his conviction on 'Drug and Sexual Abuse Charges,' forcing him out of his Job.

"She is one of the most dynamic and outspoken leaders against teenage drug abuse in America. She is here in the Omni Hotel at her own expense, and a phone call can bring her over here; but, Mrs. 'Uursula Henry,' of Fifeville, and The New Drug Czar-newly elected the other day-Wilbur Wainwright,' conspired against us having Mrs. Fran Broader appear with us tonight, and from Marching with us on tomorrow. They claimed that The City Council is obligated to reject any person who may have been on Berry's Staff. That the State Funding it gets for Activist Activities will not be appropriated if drug criminals are glorified. Berry falsely accused Mn. Broader because he knew that she was a 'whistle-blower.' of being involved in 'Drug Dealing,' and fired her. That firing is on her 'Employment Record.' She is fighting to clear her Record, but ha1l not yet succeeded. So a majority of this City's Council-Members decided not to allow Mrs. Broader to participate in this Activity."

A loud groan came up from the audience.

Dick Gregory continued: "Mrs. Broader sends her regrets, She says she forgives Mrs. Henry, and The Drug Czar, Mr. Wainwright. They rneant well, but are very misguided. Mrs. Broader has three people with her. She did not give us their nsmel for security reasons. They are presently working for the D.C. City Government. If word got out on them, their Jobs would be on the line.

"You see, Brothers and Sisters, what we are up against? We have enemies at every level who will upend any bit of progress we try to make to end the Fear, Murder, and Drug Menace plaguing all of our Cities all over America.

"Here, in Mr. Tom Jefferson's Plantation,' that's what I see Charlottesville as, The UVA is the 'Big House.' The City of Charlottesville is just its 'Out Buildings.' You know the whole plantation have to agree with what the Master wants. That's what is going on here. This whole Town is still just like Mr. Tom Jeffenon wanted it to be. The people in charge here are mostly descendant from Slave Masters.

"They're still trying *to* protect Jeffenon's reputation. The UV A has, in conjunction with Hampton Inns, Inc., erected a Hotel on what is believed to be 'the final resting place' of Sally Hemings.

"University Hampton Inn is slated to open for business on about July,

1997. It is located on a lot off of 900 West Main Street. In the parking lot where that building is being erected was once a 'Colored Settlement' in back of the UVA. Some have it that Sally Hemings was freed after Jefferson's death in 1826, and that Sally went to Missouri to live with her Son, Eaton. But other biographers have it that Sally moved to a Settlement near the Comer of West Main Street and Ninth Street Southwest, and her bones may have been buried in an unmarked grave under where the Hampton Inn is now being built.

"Professor Amistad Robinson at the UVA, a Historian, found such a burial ground on what is now Jefferson Park Avenue across from Old Cabell Hall. A freed slave named Kitty Foster had a washhouse on the edge of the University, then, actually down the hill from the South End of the UVA. She and several of her family members were buried there and no grave markers were present to designate that place on her property as a graveyard.

"Some skeletal remains were unearthed when developers attempted to dig up a parking lot so that Cabell Hall could be expanded. The UVA had given the project to Dr. Robinson to study the area so that the UVA Historical Society could preserve the gravesites, So construction was halted in the late 1980s.

"But, when the same issue was raised concerning the Sally Hemings' 1Gravesite,' the construction of the Hampton Inn Project was hurried up. It would seem to me that Charlottesville has enough Hotels, Motels, and restaurant. I. So, why was there such a hurry?

"The Jefferson Historical Society is doing DNA Research on the remains of Eaton Hemings. It has come to believe that despite Denials by UVA Professors, Dumas Malone, *The Sage of MonticeUo, 1981;* Virginius Dabney, *Virginia: The New Dominion, 1956;* and, Douglas Adair, *Fame and the Founding Fathers, 1874,* Thomas Jefferson may be the Father of all of Sally Hemings' Children: Thomas, Harriet, Beverly, Madison, and Eaton. He fathered other children also; See: 'Clothel,' William Wells Brown, 1867.

"A Graduate Student at the UVA, Annette Gordon-Reed, has presented a Graduate Dissertation that convinced them that DNA results, so far, are conclusive that Jefferson was Eaton's Poppa. I hear that her Thesis is going to become a book that may be published any day now. It is tentatively titled: *Thomas Jefferson and Sally Hemings, An American Controversy, unpublished.* I've corresponded with her of late.

"The Historical Society is convinced. Members of Jefferson's family have launched their own research project. They are attempting to r epress, deny, and refute any notion that Uncle Tom Jefferson molested his beautiful, Slave-Chambermaid, Sally several times and fathered five or six children by her.

"Quite a lot of controversial noise is in certain News and Historical Journals making the UVA very nervous about their 'Saint Thomas Jefferson,' being found out to be just another 'Slave-Master Rapist.'

Slave women really did not have the option of saying NO! to their 'Massa's!'

So you can see Brothers and Sisters why The Board of Visitors at the UVA may have wanted to cover up Sally's Grave forever. That's what the UVA has always done. It hopes that we Blacks will not Read. That 'The Best Way to Hide Historical Facts From Blacks is to Put Them in a Book,' as our Brother Malik Shabaaz (Malcolm X) once postulated. They hope you will accept the lies White and pro-White Teachers peddle to you in Grade Schools and Institutions of Higher Learning and that you will go out believing that you are an Inferior, good-for-nothing, Race, with no History, except the one that Whites gave us. Just take a look at Carter G. Woodson's, *The Mis-Education of the Negro, 1938.*

"Tonight, I want to give you some important information that will help you find your way through the maze of confusion that will make you more understanding of what is going on in Fifeville, and the rest of the 'Hoods, in Virginia. Some of this information is easy to recognize. But some of it is very subtle and is hidden behind so-called 'White Liberalism.' We African-Americans must become very vigilant.

"From the days of Jefferson, even when he was a snotty-nose kid, as Kashif Malik Hassan-EL, in *The Willie Lynch Letter And The Making Of A Slave,* Unpublished, that will I believe be in book form, sometime soon, tells us in his 'Essays' that in 1712, A White Brazilian Slave Owner, William Lynch, came to America to address a meeting of Slave Masters in Virginia. Among them were Jefferson's future Father in-law, John Wayles. He was the father of Martha Wayles, Sally Hemings' half-sister. Thomas

Jefferson later married Martha, and after the death of her father, inherited all of John Wayles' slaves, including Sally, and her Brother and Sisters, all fathered by John.

"The Speech delivered to Slave Masters in 1712, in Williamsburg, in the Capitol, outlined how Africans were to be deprived of their humanity, by various methodologies, including sexual violation. Those with lighter-skins were to be pitted against those with darker hues. Those living in the Big House were to be pitted against those working in the fields. Those living in the cities were to be pitted against those living in rural areas. There were to be no kinship recognition. Slaves were to be bred like animals. They had to be forced to hate one another by giving one group a little more privilege than the others. Education was to be completely forbidden, especially about African History and Religion. All Slaves were to be forced to revere White People and White Culture. Thus God, Jesus, The Virgin Mary, and all Biblical Icons had to be presented as White even when History dictated otherwise.

"This was how Thomas Jefferson was indoctrinated. That's how he became the Racist, Rapacious, Vicious Slave Master he became. Just read his *Notes on the State of Virginia, Willaim Peden, Ed, 1982, first published by John Stockdale in 1787.*

"To make a long story short: if you look around you in Charlottesville, Virginia, that surrounds the University of Virginia, you will see clearly that, the people of this area-including Albemarle, Augusta, Louisa, Fluvanna, Greene, Nelson, and Madison Counties, intellectually, adhere to the basic philosophy that Jefferson put forth over two-hundred years ago.

"That's why in 1958, negotiations came into being concerning the 'urban renewal-Urban Removal renovation Project, that led to the Demolition of Black Vinegar Hill, by 1965. You see, Brothers and Sisters, the Supreme Court had 'let the Freedom Cat out of the Bag.' The basic white-racialists control methods that had kept African-Americans at bay since 1712 were scuttled. A new methodology was forged. "Directly after Vinegar Hill was razed to the ground in 1964, plans to devour Gospel Hill went into effect. By the 1980s, Gospel Hill was razed to the ground and became the home of The UVA's Urban Renovation Project Thus we have The New Hospital, even though the Old Hospital could have been expanded without destroying a Historically Black Community.

"Go down and look at the walls of City Hall, and you will see plans for the Gentrification of Fifeville, Rose Hill Drive, Upper Ridge Street, and the Gordon-Grady Avenues Corridor. Blacks are slated to be removed from the inner-city of Charlottesville. The City Council, and The Albemarle Board of Supervisors, as well as, The UVA Board of Visitors are all in cohorts to remove the descendants of ex-slaves out of the City of Charlottesville, and to scatter them in such a way, that they will never be allowed to become a voting block as has happen in Richmond.

"Brothers and Sisters, the Dope flowing up and down the Streets of Charlottesville and Albemarle County is no mistake. The exotic guns and ammunition, like Uzis and Automatic military-grade Carbines that have extended magazines and that shoot armor-piercing bullets, from Israel; the AK-47 with its thirty shot Magazines from Russia; the Glock semiautomatic pistol from Austria; and, various Beretta Automatic handguns from Italy, have no business being in the hands of 'The Bloods,' and 'The Crips,' in Charlottesville, Virginia.

"Brothers and Sisters, you have to ask yourself: 'How did all of the guns you see in the hands of our young boys, who do not have jobs, and who are not making enough money selling Dope to purchase the expensive guns they're terrorizing our 'Hoods with, get in their hands?'

"I don't want to play a morbid guessing game with you. So, I'll level with you from the onset

"The guns were stolen off of Anny Bases by crooked corrupt soldiers, who are in the top echelons of the Military Complex in America. A lot of the Top-Brass Officers are involved. They are using military planes, bucks, helicopters, tractor-trailers, and military transport bucks to bring guns to several and sundry private gun-show merchants all over America living near army bases. Several of these merchants are in Augusta County, working out of the Cities of Harrisonburg, Waynesboro and Staunton. They have for sale every kind of a gun from every kind of military base in the world. These Gunn Show Merchants do not have to worry about the existing Jaws banning the sale of military-grade weapons to private citizens.

"That's where the 'Crips' and 'Bloods' get their guns. These stolen guns are peddled to them at very discounted prices, along with tens-of-thousands of rounds of ammunition.

"Dope is being hauled from Guatemala, Brazil, Jamaica, Columbia, Nicaragua, Panama, El Salvador, and Chili, to Mexico. It is being transported by military and private transport planes to Texas, Florida, and Richmond, Virginia Beach, Portsmouth, and Norfolk, Virginia. Convoys of bucks are hauling millions of tons of Dope up 1-95- West to 64-West to 81-North. Other convoys are hauling tons and tons of Dope up route 6 to route 20 to 33-West. Charlottesville is like a sort of cross-roads in this whole process. Millions of dollars of Dope and or Guns pass through here every day. Hundreds of thousands stay here and are sold on the comers of Fifth and Dice in Fifeville; at Washington Park and the Rose Hill Drive area; on the comers of Prospect Avenue and Orangedale Drive; In Meade Park; and at some fraternities on Ruby Road, Chancellor Street, Culbert Road, Madison Lane, and, Gordon and Grady Avenues.

"Informed sources tell me that I can get as much Dope as I want any time of the day or night from Powered Cocaine to Heroin, to Methamphetamines, to Crack, in any quantity I want off of any of the comers I've just mentioned. In case you are wondering where that much Dope and guns can be stored, here's how:

"Huge storage facilities are in the Counties of Albemarle, Fluvanna, Louisa, Nelson, Goochland, Henrico, Caroline, Prince William, Powhatan, Buckingham, Madison, Prince George, and Chesterfield. The owners of these facilities are farmers, transport bucking company owners, small airport owners, car dealership owners, restaurateurs, and jewelry and clothing store owners; the very rich guys!

"A number of the above have made connections with the Italian Mafia. The Mafia owns Chain Grocery, Jewelry, and Clothing Stores; Shopping Malls, Hotel-Motel Complexes, and Liquor Bars; Hair Salons, Barbershops, and Exercise and Massage Parlors, and Cosmetic Dealerships. One of the main Motels in Charlottesville is Mafia owned. It has sprung up all over the place. It will eventually dominate the restaurant hotel-motel businesses in Charlottesville. Then the rest of that business ownership will have to pay this monster-chain to be allowed to stay in business. That is called 'Protection Money.' Or extortion!

"By the above, the dirty gun-dealing and Dope-Dealing Money is laundered.

"Brothers and Sisters, the way to stop the above from devouring us all is to 'nip it in the bud.' Don't let your children, young men or women, participate in a Gang. Don't let them wear gang paraphernalia. Young men should not be allowed to own military style assault rifles. When your youngster do not have a job, but is wearing all of the latest trendy, gaudy, hip-hop styles, you need to make them tell you where they are getting the money to buy those. Never buy a gun for your teenagers no matter what other parents are doing, unless it is for hunting. Never use Dope with your children or in front of them.

"It is not necessary for all the citizens in an area to move away to stop the problems from plaguing that area. It is necessary that all people in a troubled area become Activists. Join the NAACP. Join CORE. Join The Community Center. But do not set back and do nothing. You see, there is a Conspiracy that originated in the 1700s, that has changed but little over the last two-hundred years. Let me elaborate a little on this subject

"Jawanza Kunjufu, *Countering the Conspiracy To Destroy Black Boys, 1985; and, To Be Popular or SMART: The Black Peer Group, 1988,* are certainly Books you all should get copies of and share with all of your friends.

"Kunjufu, tells us that by the age of nine, little Black Boys become totally disillusioned about getting educated in so-called 'Integrated Schools,' because of their earlier educational experiences. In 'Countering the Conspiracy,' he brings to the surface what many Black parents know but try to ignore.

"There are no to very few Male Teachers in the early grades, K-6. Most of the Teachers are White Females. They tend to ignore most little Black Boys on a daily basis. When these children react to being ignored as children often will, they are classed as 'Retarded,' or 'Special,' and are separated from other classmates. They are housed in a 'Special Room,' or a 'Special Building,' and are stigmatized as incorrigibles. Their educational needs are forever ignored after that

"In 'To Be Popular or SMART,' Kunjufu, tells us that Black Boys react to being mistreated by 'white racist and or pro-white-racist Teachers' in so-called 'Integrated Schools,' with almost complete withdrawal from the will to get a good education. They come to see higher-education as a 'White Boy Thing.' They go to school and do nothing toward learning. They seek to become like those they see manifesting the 'Macho Image,' like Sportsmen, those with many different Girlfriends, Pimps, Dope Dealers, and Extortionists. By the time they are Nine, around the Fourth Grade, some will become little 'Hoodlums.' A lot of these will drop out of school and join Gangs. They lose faith in seeking a higher education to better themselves. This self-imposed genocide fits right into the hands of those wishing to destroy all of us.

"The Dope Dealers, Gun Runners, and Pimps they see up-close-and-personal every day, all around them, and those they see as 'Hip-Hop' and 'Gangsta Rapping,' Musical Icons, take precedence over their mental processes. They dream of becoming 'Hoodlums,' as a viable endeavor to strive towards.

"Nathan and Julia Hare, *The Endangered Black Family; Coping l½th The Unisexualization and Coming Extinction of the Black Race, 1986,* tells us that the disorientation of Black Boys away from the responsibility of becoming grounded family-men, due to the lack of a strong male presence in their early lives, too often cause them to become 'non-men.' Too many Black Boys are growing up in female-headed families. Mothers can feed, doth, and shelter a Boy. 'But it takes a Man to Tum A Boy into A Man.' Therefore many Boys are becoming like 'Prince' or 'Michael Jackson.' They are pursuing the 'Androgynous Lifestyle,' in the way that they dress, express themselves, and relate to each other. The Disco Mystique featuring 'The Police Group,' and 'Boy George,' is the example that these Boys follow.

"By-and-large, the above Boys will most likely not make good Fathers, good Role-Models, and or good providers to Black Women seeking husbands and or Men to help them raise their Boys into Men in the Black Communities.

"Therefore, the destruction of the African-American community has gotten started from within and from without. In 1968, Brother Eldridge Cleaver, A Black Panther Minister of Information, *SOUL ON ICE, 1968,* tells us that The White Dominant Culture was presided over by 'The White Male, Superordinate, Boss in the Front Office.' He had classed

Black Men as 'The Super-Masculine Menials,' he would allow to develop along Brawn, Muscular, Athletic Lines, but not as intellectuals, or as his social Equals.'

"The Omnipotent White Administrator forced White Women into a subservient role of being 'Dumb Blondes.' They were 'alleged Sexpots,' and were thought to be 'Weak-Minded, Weak-Bodied, Delicate Freaks.' Then he 'Placed them on Pedestals.' They came to represent '\White-Female-Repressed Sensuality.' He forced Black Women into 'Aunt Jemima Bandana-Covered-Head,' denizens of female inferiority. They were thought of as 'Reliant Amazons, deposited in the Omnipotent Administrators' Kitchens.' But they could be Molested, Raped, and Sexually Abused with impunity at the Bosses' Whims. They came to represent to the Bosses, an opportunity to express White-Male Unbridled Sexuality.

"The Black-Male Menials were forbidden to look upon the Dumb Blondes with lustful desire. He had to repress his lusts for her, while he was forced to watch the white Bosses have Aunt Jemima at their will.

"All the Brains were thought to be in the White Boss in the front office. All of the brawn, Muscle Mass, was allegedly in the Super masculine Menial Black Men. The White Bosses thus kicked him out into the Field. White men never wanted White of Black Women, or Black Men to get educated and be competitive with 'the Brains of the White-Male Administrators.' That's where the White Man's logic broke down. 'You cannot separate a Body's Brain, from the rest of its Members, and the Body's other members from its Sensuality and Sexuality.' American Society, regardless of what racists think, is just one Body made up of many Members.

"The above so-called minority groups did get educated. They were actually the Majority Population in America, and eventually became a voting majority of the electorate. That culminated in the 1950s-1960s Legislation outlawing Public School Segregation; gave Black People Equal Rights, Voting Rights, and Matrimonial Desegregation across America. By the 1970s, White Men were murderously angry with Black Men, White Women, and the Supreme Court for 'Freeing' the most hated groups the alleged White Superordinate, Omnipotent Administrator Boss in the Front Office, wanted to stay subordinated, socially, politically, and economically.

"Therefore, the Tenets of the 'Wille Lynch Letter,' were the foundation that 'The Slave Codes,' were built on. When Slavery ended in 1865, those same Tenets were revamped into 'States Rights and Introspection' and became 'The Black Codes,' restricting Blacks' ability to enjoin few Constitutional Protections-especially in the South-across most of America. 'Separate-But-Equal'-that was very 'Unequal for Blacks'-put African Americans in a state of *defacto Slavery,* after Plessey vs. Ferguson, in 1896.

"After the 1960s Legislation allegedly 'freed Blacks,' the Tenets of 'The Lynch Letter', morphed into subtle racial discrimination, through the 'Unequal Application of Legal Justice,' across the boards in America. Blacks were charged with crimes they did not commit and were convicted and sentenced to prison. Their Civil, Voting, and Human Rights were henceforth suspended. In a real sense of the word, they became no better off than the ex-Slaves were directly after the Civil War.

"The Corporate Structures here are moving jobs overseas along with their counterparts in every State in America. There are a couple of Documents I acquired from the National Security Council, that I feel that all of you should write to Washington D.C. and get a copy of these.

"The Guns and Dope flowing up and down the streets of Charlottesville are no accident. Within the documents I found, is 'The National Security Decision Memorandum **[NSDM]** 314 (26 November, 1975)'; and, 'The National Security Study Memorandum [NSSM] 200 (24 April, 1974).'

"The above Documents were addressed to: 'The Secretaries of Defense and Agriculture; The Director of the CIA; the Deputy Secretary of State; and the Administrator for International Defense.

"American Foreign Policy (National Security) Officials were to withhold food and medical supplies, and by the aid of Multinational Corporations, break the backs of so-called 'Third World Countries.'

"Holly Sklar edited, *TRILATERALISM: The Trilateral Commission and Elite Planning for World Management 1980,* and she reveals the following: There is an Organization that cuts across the Sovereign Boundaries of all Nation States, and Border Restrictions. It is headed by Big Oil Moguls (Standard Oil: The Fords, The Bushes, The Reagans, The Nixons, The Johnsons, The Kissingers, and their Underlings), The World Bank and The Federal Reserve (The Rothschild Family), and the CEO's of the Military Industrial Complex (General Dynamics, and Lockheed-Martin). A number of IT&T CEO's were recruited to be functioning members.

This Clandestine Organization has amongst its membership almost anyone in America, Britain, France, Italy, Germany, Israel, The Arabic Emirates, Egypt, Libya, Iran, South Africa, Somalia, Nigeria, Panama, Brazil, Mexico, Columbia, Japan and South Korea, who is in control of substantial long-term wealth, and or, natural resources.

"It got started directly at the end of WWI. During the War, a wealthy family controlled the majority of the world's money and resources industrialized nations needed to expand and grow into the 'Metropolitans' that America, Britain, France and Russia became. One of the wealthy families were Bankers who Adolf Hitler borrowed from. He used the money to manufacture the Planes, Bombs, Ammunition and Guns used in W\VII. But all who participated in that War, including Japan, used the same Bank. Once it had created 'The Trilateral Commission,' directly after VVWI, it decided who would go to War with whom; who would divide up the spoils; and who would be allowed to grow, to become industrialized; and who would be a permanent member of the 'Third World.' It directed everything through NATO, and the World Bank. Big Oil and the American Industrial Complex were some of its most powerful and Allegiant Adherents.

"Today, 'Trilateralism,' is a by-word. We say today: 'Multinational Corporations.' These are in every developed and developing Nation on earth. Our New President, Bill Clinton, has just signed into Law NAFTA (The North American Free Trade Agreement), on January 1. It makes it easier for goods and services to move between Canadian, Mexican, and American Borders. It makes it easier for planes to come and go from here to there, and from them to us.

"Let me make a long story short: Many commercial transport planes have secret compartments that are filled with Cocaine from Mexico to America and Canada. Once unloaded in America and or Canada, these planes are filled with Guns and Money. Heroin comes in from China, Burma, Thailand, Sargon, Hong Kong, India, Afghanistan, Pakistan, Iran, and Korea, on planes that land in Los Angele11, and Texas. These plane11 are filled with money and returned to the senders. Millions of dollars are paid under the table to the Chinele, etc. NAFI'A makes this very easy.

"Millions of Guns are smuggled into America, Mexico, Brazil, Jamaica, Columbia, El Salvador, Panama, and all over South America.

Such trafficking has all but put Remington, Springfield, and Winche1lt. er Gun Manufacturers out of business. The Ghetto's choice is the Glock-9's, from Germany, AK-47's from Russia, and Automatic Field Rifles, and Uzis, from Israel. All of **these** are imported to North and South America by the Tractor-Trailer Loads, along with millions of tons of all kinds of Dope.

"Millions of tons of Cocaine are smuggled into Florida, Texas, Virginia, New York, Illinois, California, Pennsylvania. Washington State, and North and South Carolina on plane1 in secret compartments. These planes are filled with money and Guns and returned to Mexico, Columbia, El Salvador, Jamaica, Panama, and many other South American Countries.

"The Dope you see here, everywhere, by the tons-per-day comes from a long way off. So do the Guns. We can march tomorrow, but it will take more than that. Get registered. VOTE! Stay in the face of your elected officials. That will only be a start. You have to give an account of yourself and your family.

"I say that to mean, you have to watch out for all of the ways 'The Dominant Culture' is attacking you and the ones you love. Like: Do not believe the 'Hype' that has appeared in *The Discover Monthly.* It said, recently, that 'the HIV/AIDS disease came out of Africa'! That it was originally a 1lymbiotic viru1 that existed in the veins of Vervet Monkeys that live in the tops of trees in Africa's Tropical Rainforests,' That White Gay Men somehow contracted the disease from Africans. Then they brought it back to America and spread it all over California, New York, Denver, Colorado, and then we have 'The AIDS Epidemic.'

"Frances Cress Welsing, *THE ISIS PAPERS, 1991,* an acquaintance of mine, a profound Psychologist and Pyschoanalyst, tells us that the White Collective would not hesitate to commit an act of Genocide against Black Americans if it concluded that White People were somehow threatened by Black&. Black&' Civil Right! pins in the 19601 and 19701 were seen by the White Collective as threatening to White Supremacy, and had to be remedied,

"She asserts that 'The 900 Black Americans killed by The Rev. Jim Jones on November 18, 1978, was 'A Dre11-Reheanal and forerunner for the launching of the HIV/AIDS Invasion,'

11Another correspondent of mine was Michael Meiers, *Was Jonestowwn*

A CIA Medical Experiment? A Review of the Evidence, Volume 35, 1988, asserts that the murder of the above people was a US Government Sponsored Experiment. He says that government scientists were testing the resolve of the American People to see how they would react to the mass murder of large numbers of Blacks because that was what was on the Drawing Boards from the 19601-on.

"Dr. Frances Cre111 Welsing referred me to, John Cookaon and Judith Nottingham, *A Survey of Clmnical And Biological Warfare, 1969.* Cookson and Nottingham tells us that ex-Nazis were smuggled into America directly at the end of WWII. Hundreds of them were Scientists, Prior to the fall of Nazi Germany these Scientists were working on isolating a Virus that lived in the veins of Green Monkeys they had studied. By 1948, the Virus had been isolated.

The virus, though innocuous to the monkeys, was a deadly immune suppressant in Humans, Many of the Jewish Inmates used to carry out the Monkey Experiments became fatally ill, They developed a Blood Disease that made them very susceptible to opportunistic infections, and blood-born Cancers. The Monkey Virus was excreted in the victims' Urine, and was found to be Sexually Transmittable. The final analysis was that the Virus was highly suppressive to the Victims' Immune Systems,

"In 1968, the ex-Nazi Scientists had perfected the isolation of the particular Virus that Nazi Scentists had discovered. They were working in Laboratories in America. In the 19701, their experimentation moved up into another level. They went to work on 'Germ Warfare.'

"Cookson and Nottingham referred me to Dr. Robert B. Strecker, a Virologist, and Infectious Disease Scientist, He sent me a copy of his, *'Is AIDS Manmade?' THE STRECKER MEMORANDUM (1988), And, '2000 AD. No One Left: The Cause, The Effects, And The Possible Cure For The Pandemic A.I.D.S., A VIDEO, 1988.* Dr. Strecker and his Brother, Theodore, another Virologist, believed that HIV/AIDS could not have become an infectious disease in and of itself. They asserted that the way the pandemic got 1wted was unprecedented in the hi1tory of infectious diseases that were transmitted from animals to humans, Therefore they concluded that HIV/AIDS was created by Humans, It had to be trained to recognize Human Tis1ue11 and be taught how to infect Human T-Cells. 'Therefore no monkey bit an African on the ass, and you have AIDS all over America.'

AIDS could be cured with ultraviolet Rays, "In 1990, I discovered a Book by Dr. Alan Cantwell, MD., *AIDS, AND THE DOCTORS OF DEATH: An Inquiry Into The Origin Of The AIDS Epidemic.* He states that HIV/ AIDS was not 'A Gay

Disease.' That gays had gotten a 'Bad Rap,' from the American Scientific Community.

"He asserts that HIV/AIDS was created in a Lab in Bethesda, Maryland called 'Litton Industries.' This company was operating under the auspices of the OA and NSA on behest of the Nixon Administration to find ways to combat the Disease and Germ Warfare Weapons being developed in Russia and Communist backed Countries.

"After the Blacks would not quiet down and accept America's 'Pacification Programs,' and the Gays and Feminists joined them to 'struggle for Racial, Sexual, and Feminist Equality, the push to find a way to stop them all was put on the table in 1969. Then, Conservative Congressmen called for the HIV/AIDS Viral Killer 'On Page 1239 of the Congressional Record, Tuesday, July 1, 1969.' They asked Congress for Ten Million dollars to create a new Virus that would be detrimental to the Human Immune System. They wanted to find ways to deploy the 'New Weapon' without the target's knowledge until the Disease ran its course. Congress appropriated the requested funding.

"A Lab was chosen and by 1970, Litton Industries stated that their Scientists had perfected a Virus through 'Gene-Splicing and Genetic Engineering Technologies.' The new Virus was named: 'THE HUMAN IMMUNE DEFICIENCY SYNDROME.' It caused the depletion of the T-Cells in Humans and made them highly susceptible to Opportunistic Infections.

"In 1973, A Smallpox vaccination program in Africa resulted in all of those vaccinated becoming sick with Carinii Pneumonia, Kaposi Sarcoma, and Death by 1978. A thousand had succumbed. Shortly after that in America, in 1970 1000 Gay men were allegedly vaccinated against Hepatitis B. They all became sick shortly after their vaccinations. In 1983, a Dr. W. Szmunes, a Russian Emigre, inoculated another four thousand Bisexuals Men in Several Northern and Midwestern Cities, and California. He was working in conjunction with the World Health Organization (WHO),

The Center for Disease (CDC), and the New York Blood Bank. By 1989, all of the Gay Men developed Life-Ending diseases caused by HIV/AIDS. The scientific community blamed the Gays for the incubation and spread of the Disease. But the Disease was a Federal Government Experiment aimed at the three most hated groups in America by Conservative White Men in charge: 'Gays, Blacks, and Feminists.'

"The Bisexuals were the 'Trojan Horses,' the 'Doctors of Death' used to launch an HIV/AIDS Pandemic to rid America of Blacks, liberal 'whites and Gays. Intravenous Drug Abusers and Bisexual Men having sex with Women spread the Disease for and wide. That is how it got into the Heterosexual Community.

"Finally, Dr. Welsing warns us that 'During a period 1979-80, 15 Black Children were reported missing in Atlanta, Georgia. Eleven were found murdered and the rest were presumed to be dead. I believe that the CDC was involved with their deaths. I believe that they were used to extract Interferon from their Genitalia. A little Black Girl was included in the murders as a possible cover-up tactic.

"So, Brothers and Sisters, watch out for your Children from outward and inward threats to their health, well-being, and survival that may be in the works. We know that a lot of people in power want us to accept that there is no conspiracy against Black Americans, never had been one, and never will be one. We all know that this is an unmitigated Lie.

"So I invite all of you to come March with us on tomorrow and show that we are not afraid to confront the forces working against us. Thank. you all for coming tonight."

So Ben watched everyone applaud for nearly six minutes. All on the stage stood as Dr. Da Silva gave the Benediction, and dismissed them.

Mr. Gregory did not linger. He was whisked away down the aisle and was out the door right after he finished his speech.

Chapter Fifteen

The sun rose that morning with a magnificent brilliance. It shone like Ben had seen it do once when his Dad had taken him and Ivy to Virginia Beach, and they stood on the boardwalks at the Chesapeake Bay and watched the rays of the sun sparkle as it blessed the Bay's Waves. He was just six years old then. But that glorious experience filled him with a longing to know, "What or Who," was responsible for such Majestic, Natural Beauty as the Bay, the Sun, and all that those presented. Now, he had that same feeling about what may lay ahead for him, his sons, and his people.

It was seven in the morning, and no one but Ben was up. Mo was fast asleep. She could barely stay awake that last evening to hear what had happened at the rally. She fell asleep in a fluffy end chair hugging a big, black, stuffed animal that she liked to caress at idle times. She had listened as carefully as she could, Ben knew that, because she asked questions about what he told her and what that all meant to them going forward. Ben let her go to bed and he watched TV until the early morning hours, because it was hard for him to go to sleep.

He turned the TV on that morning to hear the Early Morning Local News: He heard a news anchor reporting a News Break: "Members of the Charlottesville City Council, and The Albemarle Board of Supervisors were alarmed at the Controversial Speech presented by Noted Comedian Dick Gregory last night. City Councilman, Morpheus Commons, newly elected, a graduate of the University of Virginia, the University of Milan, Italy, and The University of Manchester England, with degrees in Urban Planning, Architecture, and Ancient European Political Systems, stated: 'I am an African American. My father was born and raised in Shadwell, Virginia. He married my Mom who happens to be a British Woman he met when he was stationed in England as a CIA Attaché Officer to the

British-American Intelligence Force. What I read about **Mr.** Gregory that was stated in this morning's papers was, I feel, almost treason.'

"'We have to come together to solve the Drug and Gun problems plaguing our Fair City. We must not throw around conspiracy theories. Such thinking is counter-productive. I blame you, you blame me, we all blame somebody else. This will not work. I will consult with Mr. Wainwright, the Drug Czar for Charlottesville. I'm the newly appointed Mayor. The City Manager, **Mr.** Nassar Hindi, and I will meet today with Mr. Wainwright to discuss the future of the City's funding of The Community Center. The Center is moving too far to the Left. We will not support that move!'

"Mr. Chandler Woodstock, Chairman of the Albemarle Board of Supervisors, had this to say: 'We feel that our County Government can no longer support The Community Center. We feel that it has gone too far to the Left for us to continue to invest in its future.'

"Our Reporter got to speak to a concerned citizen, Mrs. Ursula Henry, a resident of Fifeville, and the Mother of two teenage Sons. She is very outspoken and is very active as an independent force in the community. She had this to say: 'Any Organization that would stoop to bringing in a convicted criminal to participate in a stupid Rally and March up and down the streets with an out-0f-touch comedian is the wrong way to do anything around here. I'm opposed to everything that that Community Center stands for. I know Jacque Minders. He's nothing but a convict himself. How can he lead anybody anywhere? I will work with Mr. Wainwright to shut that Center down. We don't need it!'

"Mr. Gregory has refused comment. So have Mr. Kermit Lyles, and Mr. Minders, who run the Community Center. That's it for Our Early Morning Newsbreak. Get your Local News at Noonday and at Six P.M. on Channel 29 at NBC. Now back to Katie and Bryant."

Ben wondered why people were so negative toward Activists who were trying to help bring about positive change in the Community. He didn't hear Mr. Gregory say anything that he didn't back up with a number of written sources. The City and County Governments should be very willing to aid and help anyone who was fighting to end what the drug-dealers and gun-runners were doing to the youths of Charlottesville and Albemarle.

Yet, a citizen with two teenage boys living right in the 'Hood was opposed to The Community Center and its main avenues to political and social activism in Charlottesville. None of the African American Activist Groups: the N.A.A.C.P., S.N.C.C., or *C.O.R.E.,* was directly confronting Drug-Dealers or the violence perpetrated by local Gangs. Somebody had to make a move, to get the ball rolling. At first, a lot of people were opposed to Dr. King. So, "Here We Go Again."

Ben walked down the hallway to Saw's and Jay's room. He knocked gently on the door. "Get up sleepy heads. It's time to get cracking. It's going on to be eight o'clock. We want to be there at the start of the March. We're going to walk up to the Center. No use in trying to drive. Most of the streets leading up there are going to be blocked. You all get on up," he yelled at the door to his Sons' room.

"Yo, I'm down, Dad," Saw yelled back. "Yo, Dad. I'ma get right with that," Jay said.

Ben thought: I wish those boys would not use that old "Hip-Hop, Gang-Thing" way of speaking to me. "Y'all hurry up. It's getting close to the time we're going to have to leave. Your Mother left some Com Beef Hash Patties and Cheese Omelets for us to Microwave in our new Little Oven."

Ben had on Green Cargo Pants, a Black Pullover Nikki Shirt with short sleeves. He wore Red-and Black Air-Jordan Tennis. He asked his Sons: "What're you guys gonna wear?"

Saw and Jay came out of the room dressed in Matching, Black, Baggy Cargo Pants, Black-and-Gray Plaid Shirts with the sleeves removed and with Large Black Spiders on their backs. They were wearing Tan Timberland Boots. Each sported black baseball caps with the brims turned around backwards.

Ben's eyes flew open wide. "What the . . . What in the What're you all thinking you're trying to do?" he yelled. "You're not going to wear that 'Gangland Shit!' anywhere with me. Go get something else on Saw, Jay, right now."

The Twins scratched their heads. Saw walked towards his Dad. He had a puzzled look on his young face. Of late he'd started to closely resemble

Ben. Jay was a masculine-copy of his Mother. "Dad, can I rap ah, talk to you a little about this, okay?" Saw asked.

"Yeah, Saw. You can talk to me about anything. But if you wanna dress like a Gangster, we're going to have a lotta problems while you're living in my house," Ben replied. He frowned with his mouth resembling an angry snarl. "Go ahead, shoot"

Jay stood right beside Saw with a dead-serious facial demeanor with his arms folded over his chest like he'd seen Moo-Man doing when he was confronted by someone in the 'Hood.

"Dad," Saw carefully began to speak, "we live over here in Fifeville. Whether you want to accept that or not, we're part of this 'Hood. I'm growing up over here. All Our Homeys are 'Crips.' I know you say it's all bad, Dad. But I don't have nobody but you and Mom to look up to, except for the Homeys on the Block. They're in this War with the 'Bloods.' They're trying to confront the 'Man,' too, Dad, who's doing us all in every day. You and Mom I see all the time working your fingers to the bone. But you don't seem to be getting anywhere. That makes schooling and all that look like nothing I want to become. I'm getting tired of going to school and hearing 'how inferior Blacks are.' Nothing but tired-ass White-Women teaching us to be 'Good Niggers,' that's what I'm getting at school. 'Makes me want to holler and throw up both my hands,' Dad."

Ben's frown turned to a more understanding grimace. He turned to Jay. "What are you feeling, Jay?" he asked. "And, y'all watch your language, now."

"Dad," Jay stammered a little, "I'm feeling what Saw is saying." He put his arm around Saw's left shoulder. "Dad, we got to be Soldiers over here. It's all that we have to do. We're fighting for our lives every time we hit the Streets. It's like the Bangers know we're from Fifeville because of the way we walk or something. I hear all the time: 'Them's Crips, Man! Get your Piece!' then we gotta run or be gunned down. It's like that, Dad. So, no matter what, we gotta represent. It's not even up to us. I haven't been jumped-in to the Set yet But Dad, I gotta level with you and Mom, I've been thinking about it If for no other reason, I feel we need the protection of the Homeys. When the 'Bloods' or the 'MS-13' or the 'Barrios-IS' or 'El Mexico Familia,' roll up on us, they don't care whether you are jumped-in or not, they will open-fire, Dad. When you were on the Set, you only had to worry about 'The Posse.' But right now there're a lot more Bangers to worry about They know the Moo-Man. They see us talking to him, and figure we're 'Crips' or might become them. So, they may gun us down to nip-it-in-the-bud. So, for want of finding a better way to say it, Dad, that's how it be, yo!"

Ben's facial expression became very somber. "Boys, I know what you're saying. I'd almost forgotten how it was back in the day. That's why I'm insisting on you all going with me today. I want you to get a sense of what your decision to go with the flow will lead to. You're talking about becoming crazed killers. You're talking about becoming a Dope-Dealer that is nothing short of dealing slow-death to your own people. You're talking about dying or killing other Black Folk in the prime of their youth. You're talking about Pimping-or making whores out of-our beautiful young women. How would you like it if I had your Mom out on the Block like your Second Cousin Roy's Mom was? She probably would have ended up in an early grave like Roy's Mom did.

"You all got a great chance to be different and to show that that difference can be homegrown."

"But Dad ... "Jay tried to interrupt his Father. "You don't understand ..." he stammered.

Ben was adamant He knew what he was talking about "Boys, I've been through what you all are talking about and I know what can happen. You're both headed to an early grave. Or, you're going to send some other young person ahead of you to an early grave. You're gonna compromise the lives of thousands of other people with your dope. Look around you, at all of the boarded-up buildings. The whole community is headed south. All of us who are not fighting to save our space are contributors to its downfall. Can't you see that?" he preached.

Saw got stiff-legged as he spoke. "Dad, I gotta join the Set to keep you, Mom, me and Jay alive. It's not up to me. It's like it was when you say you grew up over here. You had to represent. Only those who were down with you, really understood what it was that you were going through. Unlike Ivy and Roy, you tried to maintain a certain distance from the gangbanging extremes. But you had to be down with the Homeys to some extent They had to see you as 'One of Them.' It's like that with Jay and me. So, it's really not up to us. It's this 'Hood! It's this life! We're stuck in it! It's where we are, Dad. Either we have to get-with-the program, or we gotta bounce, yo. That's all to it, Dad!" he responded to Ben.

Jay lightened up a little. "Dad, I will change clothes. I will go with you to the March. I feel you there. I'm down with what you're trying to do. It's good. It's what's up. We all need peoples like you. But, what if your life depended on you being down with the Set? What then? You gave in Dad. You are alive. So you are our Father. As you have said: 'I almost bought-it that day Jamie 'Nern rolled up in here.' It's like this, Dad. Our Cousin Roy and Uncle Ivy 'bought-it,' but you are here today. Cold as that sounds, it's what's up Dad. For-Real!" he rapped. "So Saw and I will go along with you for now."

Mo heard all of the noise. She got up and put on a heavy flannel robe. She moseyed down the steps. "What're you all yelling at each other about? You are about to go to a Peace-March. You have to at least start out in a peaceful mind. I've already cooked breakfast for you all. All you gotta do is microwave it. What're you all quarreling about this time?" she asked.

"How long have Saw and Jay been allowed to leave this house wearing this gangland crap they have on this morning, Mo?" Ben angrily snapped. "They never have that on before I go to work."

"Ben," Mo tightened up the belt of her robe. "Look . . . I understand where you're coming from. With most of what you are saying I agree. But, Ben," she walked over to stand directly in front of her tall husband. "I never drank, smoked dope, or slept around the whole time I was growing up in Harlem as a little girl, and down here in Virginia from then on. But I wore hot, tight, titillating clothing, and some sheer blouses and sometimes shorts. But I was not loose or high on anything.

"It was what my Peer Group wore. I hung out with popular kids. They were all around me, so I found out early on that I had to at least look like I was one of them in order to hang with them. The alternative was staying home, or hanging with the most boring kids around. I was like that up until I met you. You became my Peer Group and my new reference point. I could relate to you. We got on the same page right away. But I felt lost before you came into my life, even though I was allegedly surrounded by so-called 'good friends,' like Carolyn and Cynthia. I was nothing like them. But I hung out with them like they were my 'Sisters.' I lived next to them. My Dad was professional like theirs, and we shared a lot of the same ideas and social reference points. But that's where the similarity ended; as you well know.

"To remedy the situation, we have to change the scenery. We have to change the relative social reference points by supplying another potential pathway in life. I mean, our Twins are going to grow into what they 'Covet.' And, 'They Covet what they see every day.' And, what is that? They want to be the meanest, badass, Gangbangers on the Block. That's what they see around them every day."

"But, Mo, that's not the image that you and I are presenting to them. What they see us doing, that's what I want them to emulate. Why can't they see the value in that?" Ben alleged.

"Ben, what you're saying is almost 'Divine.' But I studied some child psychology and learned that children when developing an Ego, that starts at about nine for boys, are usually going to resist whatever they have seen their parents doing. It does not matter what that is. They are going to seek answers in the wrong places from their friends and associates-their Peer Group. That's what is going on here.

"Like you did when you were growing up, and knew that what your Grandma Mildred said was right, you followed Ivy and Roy, and the Fifeville Crew, who are now Dead or in Prison. You're one of the Lucky Ones. But you 'Threw Caution to the Winds,' and did what the Crew wanted you to do-to some extent.

"Now, you go to work before the Boys get ready for school. I have to deal with the problems that they bring to me. I try to keep an open-mind about the realities that they are expressing to me: like how they are under a lot of pressure to join the Gang. They are threatened at school by 'The Bloods Gangbangers.' The 'Crips' are more notorious on the Block, they are saying. They believe that if they look like they are 'Junior Crips,' the other Bangers will not 'Step to Them!' So, I guess I'm at fault for allowing them to wear some 'Crips' 'Attire, even though they are not 'Strapped,' and do not function as 'Drug Carriers,' or 'Lookouts,' for the Gang. So, you have to direct some of your anger at me. I'm sorry, Baby. Short of having them get 'Jumped-In' to the Gang, I didn't know what else to do."

Ben went slowly over to Mo and took her in his arms. He was angry, but did not want to have it out with her that morning. The comers of his eyes were moist. He felt as though the very thing that Mr. Gregory had spoken about was completely- "all up in"-his family. Mo's eyes eased some cold tears down either side of her nose. She laid her head on Ben's strong chest. "We'll talk more about this later, Mo. Okay?"

"Okay," Mo said.

Ben watched Mo go back up the steps. He called out to the Boys. "Come on, we gotta eat and get on up to the Center. You all are old enough to get your own Hash Patty, and Omelet. Put that on a plate and put it in the microwave oven, push cook, and it's ready. Come on out here so that I can see what you're wearing, Saw, Jay," Ben called to his Sons.

The Twins came into Ben's presence wearing blue Gucci Pants, and beige Nikki Pullovers. Both wore Black Reebok Tennis. Neither one of them had on their Sassy Baseball Caps.

"Dad . . . Is this alright?" Saw said. He spun around a little and chuckled.

"Okay, Dad, we're decent, right?" Jay said. He imitated his older Brother.

"Yall go on eat so we can get going," Ben said.

Ben came out on the sidewalk in front of their house. The sun was shining brightly and getting hot already. Saw and Jay walked behind their Father. Moo-Man yelled, "Yo, Saw. Yo, Jay. Put in a good word for the 'Hood, yo. 'Member, who you gotta represent, yo!"

Ben answered Moo-Man: "They're gonna represent Good Sense, like you ought to be doing. You ought to be ashamed of yourself. You're a grown man. You ain't doing nothing but helping those who hate us destroy what little we have accumulated up to now in this 'Hood."

"ff it weren't for the memory of Ivy and Roy! ..." Moo-Man shot back at Ben. He shook his balled up right fist at him.

"Go head-on Moo-Man," Saw shouted at him.

"Don't threaten my Dad, Moo-Man. We know where you live, yo!" Jay snapped.

"Come on, Boys, we'll be late if we don't get on up the way," Ben said. "Forget that Fool."

A tall, stout, but shapely woman, wearing a white dress, with a white turban wrapped around her Natural, and with large golden-earrings dangling from her earlobes, stepped in front of Ben and his Sons. She had diamond rings on each of her fingers. She carried a large-beige leather lady's bag. She walked up close to Ben and stopped. Her lady's bag hung from a strap that was looped around her left shoulder. She had her right hand partially down in her carryall bag. She shouted at Ben:

"I don't know what in the Hell is up with you, Blue. You ain' been right since Ivy got capped. He and Roy were in the 'Crew.' They were Soldiers. When you're in battle, somebody's gonna die. That's why it's called war.

"Fore long ago, we didn't have nothing at all. We worked for them 'Whitties' and brought home just enough so that we had to keep-on keeping-on for them Whites. They didn't get what they got by 'Non• Violent Protests!' Those racist bastards violently robbed my peoples, the Indian Peoples, and all the Peoples of the world to get what they got. We been enslaved by them Assholes, Blue! Do you wanna keep on being treated like that?

"We gotta take from them what we can't get by the Law. We gotta break their Laws. We gotta fight them to the death. No, but you're playing their game, marching up and down the streets begging them sons of bitches to give you what is rightfully yours by the Constitution of The United States of America. The White man wrote those Laws though. Shit!

"Iain' gonna beg them no more. I and my two Sons, Waddell and Radcliff, we're gonna use everything possible to bring these White Mens down to they knees.

"So, you carry your sorry ass on up to that March. Go on! But we see you as a traitor to the 'Hood!

You're cashing in on your 'Ghetto Pass!' It's just 'Later for you all, and Shit!'"

The saddest look Ben ever had came across his face. He looked like he might cry. "Mrs. Ursula, I know your Husband, Armando, was worked to death on the Rail Road. I know how hard it's been raising two boys on your own. But if you keep doing what you say you're doing, you're just gonna lead your grown boys to an early grave like Roy's and Ivy's. I don't want that for my Boys. They can't change the past. But I want something better for their future. I'm hoping to help change our situation peacefully.

"I thought that you were working with the Drug Czar to help do that How can that be?"

Ursula Henry snapped: "My work with that stupid Cracker ain' nothing but a Smokescreen. I'll undermine him every way that I can. I don't want the Drugs to stop." She pulled out a wad of Dollar Bills and held them up so that Ben could see them. "I got more money in my hand right now than you're gonna make in two years at your 'Nigga-Baiting Chicken Joint' So you go on with your program, and I'll go on with mine. We'll see who will end up the better for it. You got that, Blue?"

"Please don't call me by that name. My name is Benjamin," Ben pleaded.

"Well ... You're always gonna be Big Blue Slokum to me and my Boys. And you can take that Shit on to the Bank. Now get to stepping," Ursula yelled. She put her hand back into her carryall bag.

Ben could see the print of a Glock in the bottom of her Bag. That made him nervous. Saw turned toward Ursula, but Ben shushed him up. "Come on, Boys, so that we won't be late. Mrs. Ursula got her two--cents worth in. Just remember what she said. But don't even think about becoming like her. She's like a Female Version of the 'Grim Reaper.'

"Dad, why are there tears in the corners of your eyes?" Saw asked. They were on the outer edge of the huge crowd of people heading to the Community Center. Ben wiped his eyes and spoke softly:

"I feel so sad about what we just witnessed in what Moo-Man said. And that was followed by Mrs.

Ursula. This March will only be the beginning of the struggle. That makes me very sad, Boys."

Chapter Sixteen

To Saw's and Jay's surprise, a medium-height caramel-colored woman with an oriental-slant to her eyes, that appeared to be like dark-brown almonds in her forehead, with lips like 'Connie Chong's' stood beside a smaller version of herself. Both wore Japanese Kimonos that had all of the primary colors of light like a rainbow surrounding them. Both sported a pair of sandals that seemed to be made of bamboo slats and red cord. Each one had her hair rolled up in a red scarf. Saw wondered what they were doing at this March.

Saw was glad that they were over near the outer-edge of the huge crowd of people up near the Community Center. He went right over to the older lady and bowed his head slightly as she had told him to do before speaking to her when he had walked Leanne home in the evenings.

"Hi Miss Xing, I want you to meet my 'Poppa-Son,' Benjamin," Saw said to the lady.

"Hi, Mr. Benjamin, *very* good to meet you. You have *very* good boys. Oh, yes, I see them a lot. Very good, yes sir. You may call me Mei. I am Mei Ming Chen Xing, and this is my Daughter, 'Lian'. She and Saw, *very* good friends. I work at a Thai Wok Restaurant on Main Street. You come, bring family. We fix you *very* good meal. Love to have you and family," said Mei, as she slightly bowed before Ben.

Ben noticed that when she smiled, her mouth was full of very white teeth. He didn't know what else to do, so he bowed a little to her. "I heard that Saw and Leanne were good friends. Nice to meet you. I will take you up on that invitation real soon."

Mei asked: "Mr. Benjamin, I wonder do you know of a Mr. Chad Eubanks?"

Leanne blurted out: "'Mama-Son,' don't! ..." The rest was in Chinese or something, Ben didn't understand. The lady adamantly repeated her question.

"Ma'am, I can't say I do. But up in Schuyler, there're hundreds of people with that last name. I'd start my search there," Ben said. He looked at Leanne. She seemed like she was ready to *cry*.

"'Mama-Son," Leanne exclaimed. "You're ...Don't ask everyone that question-it's too embarrassing-please!" She stepped over closer to Saw. He hugged her briefly. She sighed.

Mei replied: "'How I gonna find Chad? How . . . if I don't ask his people where to look? Come on

'Lian,' get a good sign. We're here to March. Maybe we see Chad somewhere today. His cold heart will melt when he sees the beautiful daughter I had for him! ..."

Saw watched Leanne walking away with her mother. Mei carried a Red Sign with the Words in Blue: "'More Cops on the Beat!" written in bold letters. Leanne did not carry a Sign.

Ben watched Leanne too, thinking that she resembled a miniature version of 'Connie Chung.' She more resembled an American Indian than a Chinese. She had smooth-brown skin. Her hair was long and was straight and shiny black. Her eyes only had a slight slant to them, unlike her Mother's. Her body was budding womanhood, and that was evident even on her nine-year-old frame. He imagined that she would be a lovely lady one day·. Maybe . . . she and Saw might become . . . ah, that was too far in the future to even think about-they were just little kids. "'Puppy-Love," that's what I see in Saw's eyes, right now.

"'Saw, Jay, go over to the stack in front of the Community Center's entrance and get three different signs for us to carry. Make sure they're not the same; alright?" Ben said.

Saw and Jay pushed and shoved their way through the Crowd to the front entrance of the Center. Saw picked up a Blue Sign with the Red Words: "'Give Us Hope Not Dope," written on it in very bold letters. He gave that to Jay. He picked up another one that said: "'Give Us A Career Not Fear!" He told Jay, "Hold that." He picked up a third one, it read: "Jobs Not Mobs!" "I'll give this one to Dad," Saw said.

A black Limo pulled up and stopped near the front of the Center. Kermit and Jacque came rushing out of the doors of the Center. The Crowd parted to let them through. Mr. Gregory got out of the Limo. Two of his bodyguards got out ahead of him and two behind him. They were the same "Fruit of Islam, 'Soldiers' dressed in all Black with red bowties," who had guarded him the night before. Ben was amazed at how the people in the crowd responded to the Guards. Nobody would rush-in too close to Mr. Gregory. He stood on the steps in front of the Center. He lifted his voice using the aid of a bullhorn:

"'Brothers and Sisters, it is good to see you all out here this morning. As we get ready to embark on this March into our future destiny, we must reflect on our African Ancestors. THE GREAT CREATOR put us here to do just what we are doing. Nothing happens in this world just so. We all are meant to be here this morning for a Specific and Divine Reason, that we do not yet fully understand, but it is mandated by A Higher Power, that we do particular things at various times and places. Unfortunately, Slavery and Jim Crow were some of those.

"So, we will march and chant using our Ancient Ancestors' 'Call-Response Aesthetics,' to convey the message that we are demanding change and we want it now!

"Are you all with me?"

The Crowd shouted in unison: "We Are With You, YEAH!"

A Group of young people wearing red T-Shirts with all of the messages that were written on the Signs came down front and center. All held bullhorns. One chanted: "What do we want?"

The Group chanted: "Hope Not Dope!"

The first One Chanted: "When Do we Want It?" The Group Chanted: "Now!"

The Group went through all of the messages on the Signs. The Crowd got Fired Up! They joined in on the Call-Response Chanting. Mr. Gregory came down to stand in front of the Group. The Bodyguards fell in behind him. Kermit stood on his left and Jacque on his right. Mr. Gregory yelled through his Bullhorn: "We're going down Ridge to Preston, up to Washington Park, then down Tenth to West Main.

"We will travel down West Main to Seventh Street, Southwest; then down Seventh to Dice, up Dice to Fifth Street Southwest, down Fifth to Tonsler's Park." He stepped off and a huge Crowd flanked him and his core troops. Ben did not see his wife. He figured that she would hold down the fort-so to speak.

Ben noticed that all of the local news people were present. There were WVIR NBC, WSV ABC, and WRVA CBS. Their news trucks were parked along Ridge Street in places where normally no parking was allowed. Several technicians carried hand-held camcorders. Others carried large cameras and voice recorders. Reporters were sticking microphones in the faces of people in the Crowd and asking them questions. Some responded gleefully, and others looked very annoyed.

All of the local newspapers were there too. The Daily Progress; The Tribune; The Charlottesville Observer; and, The C-ville Weekly. Their reporters were sticking mikes and phones in everyone's face and asking them a lot of questions.

As the Marchers made their way down Ridge to Preston Avenue, the Crowd was thick and lively. A mixture of everybody under the sun marched along chanting in unison. The cops had blocked all the streets along the way of the marching route. No traffic was allowed. Ben felt like that was mostly all the protection he'd ever seen cops providing to large numbers of Black People in his life.

From Ridge Street to Washington Park there were mostly businesses. The owners stood in front of their stores looking worried. Some waved at the marchers and others "Flipped the Bird."

Once they arrived at Washington Park, Mr. Gregory made a speech reiterating what he had said that morning and the night before the rally. People cheered. The news networks had portable units at the Park to record what Mr. Gregory exhorted. He yelled over-and over again: "Get Registered! Go Vote! Join Some Activist Organization! Fight the Power!" He wore a Black Baseball Cap with a White X on its crown to honor Malcolm X. When he yelled, "Fight the Power!" Young people gave a loud cheer followed by loud clapping and applause.

Once the Marchers started down Tenth Street Northwest, the Crowd started to thin out, so did the Network People and the Newspaper Reporters. Only NBC Channel *29* stayed with the troops. Only the Tribune Reporters stayed with the Marchers down Tenth to West Main. The Black People who lived along that Street came out onto their porches cheering the Marchers on.

About a hundred people wearing *tN* A Sweat Shirts had started out with the Marchers from the Community Center. But, like so many other "White Participants, they were very reluctant to march through the Black areas. Ben looked around for them and they were few and far between. He noticed that Mr. Gregory never broke his stride.

As the Troops came down West **Main** to Seventh Street Southwest, the entire group had dwindled to just about one-third of what it had started out as. There were only about nine or ten "White People remaining with the Marchers. All the News People were absent. **Mr.** Gregory led the Troops on into the heart of Fifeville.

Some people in the 'Hood came out to stand in front of their homes. They were mostly elderly people yelling: "Thank you **Mr.** Gregory. Thank God for You! Thank you for thinking of us!"

Ben noticed **Mr.** Gregory had tears in the comers of his eyes. He chanted a little louder as he led the troops to Dice and up Dice to Fifth and on down Fifth. Several Crips stood on the sidewalks on the Comer of Fifth and Dice Streets. Mr. Gregory stopped the group. They went through all of their chants before moving on down Fifth to Tonsler's Park.

When they arrived at the Park, Ben was surprised to see all of the News People lined up around it. Someone had delivered a portable Podium to the middle of the Park.

A crowd of people were standing all around the park cheering like they would at a Rock Concert. Ben had not seen that many people marching along with the Troops as were now at the Park.

Ben thought that if the people that he saw along the sidewalks as they marched were part of the troops, the number of marchers would have tripled. Some chanted with those leading the chants and others "Flipped the Bird." He wondered why more Black People were not among those marching that day.

Mr. Gregory stood on the podium and the cameras flashed all over the place as reporters roamed throughout the crowd sticking microphones in the faces of the "Despised Few," who had endured the March from start to finish. Some backed away from the horde of News People, but others quickly volunteered to answer any questions asked of them.

What made Ben a little nervous was that there were probably more than a hundred young people on the southwest hill next to the Park all wearing Red Jerseys. They were sitting around and angrily eyeing what was going on in the Park.

Across the street in &te's Grocery Store Parking Lot there were probably just as many young people wearing blue-and-black Plaid Jerseys. He knew that the "Crips," and the "Bloods" were present to assert their hegemony. Ben hoped the March did not end in a massacre or anything like that.

Mr. Gregory seemed to be paying no attention to the presence of the Gangbangers. He raised up his voice:

"You all must not let Gangbangers scare you away from doing what you know is right. Don't let this march be the only time you protest. March often! Keep on stoking the flames. You must get the City and County Governments' attention, and once you have that, you can make your demands in such a way that they will not be able to ignore you.

"Register and Vote for those who will listen to you; and against those who continue business as usual. Demand that they get all the corrupt cops off the Police Force, and the corrupt Sheriffs, and the Judges who give Black People lengthen sentences and let White People go with a 'Pat on the Wrist,' for the same crimes. Government Officials will have to listen to you if you vote in large enough numbers.

"Make sure all of your school-age children are in school every day. Make sure you know where your children are going every time they leave your presence. Do not allow them to just loiter around street comers or spend too much time hanging around Parks unchaperoned. Put more Books in their hands about who they are, and those books that will tell them about their great ancestry

"I'm going to be on a plane in a couple of hours on my way to New York. The people up there are having a lot of trouble with 'Cops stopping and Frisking them for no apparent reason.' I can't solve your problems for you down here. I've done all that I can do. The rest is up to you. You have to keep the Faith; and, Fight the Good Fight; and may THE GREAT CREATOR save us all!"

Camera flashes lit-up the early evening air as the Activist Icon stepped down from the podium to shake Jacque's and Kermit's hands.

Ben, Saw, and Jay shook Mr. Gregory's hand when he walked past them making his way to a waiting Black Limo parked in the driveway area of Tonsler's Park. Four F.O.1. Bodyguards came over to Mr. Gregory and escorted him over to the Limo. He hurriedly got into the vehicle.

Ben, Kermit, and Jacque waved vigorously as the Limo took off, heading West up Cherry Avenue. Saw and Jay waved too. The crowd quickly melted away. The Camera and News People did a fantastic disappearing act. Then Kermit and Jacque walked off. Jacque said: "Brother Ben, we're meeting at the Center next week to discuss strategy for future activism. Hope you will join us next Tuesday. Hope to see you then. Thank you for coming out today; and God Bless you and yours."

There were tears in the comers of the eyes of Saw and Jay. They walked behind their Father as they entered the Este's Grocery Store's Parking Lot.

About ten "Jr. Crips," came within a few feet of Ben and his sons. They were anxiously prancing around.

They stared menacingly at Saw and Jay. They followed Ben and sons at about two feet behind them.

A chubby youth crossed his chest with his bulging rums and yelled: "Yo ... JaySaw, you got to be in the Game or out-you got that?"

Another taller one yelled: "We're Bloods' Killers. Are you gonna be on the Set or will the Set have to be on top of you, yo?"

One other of them yelled: "We gonna jump you in or weed you out, Dog!" "Up you all!" Saw yelled. He "Flipped the Bird!" using both his hands.

Ben shushed his Boys. "Don't respond to that nonsense. I don't want you all out to kill no one. Not everyone in Fifeville is a Gangbanger. Not all of the Young Men and Women over here are in the 'Crips,' or any other Gang.

"Families with the last names, Brown, Stuart, Gault, Murray, Sampson, Tonsler, Carter, Frye, Scott, Keys, Lowsey, and many more, raised children that have gone on to college and are nurses, college professors, professional star athletes, military officers, medical doctors, business owners, and government administrative employees. So that proves to me that if you want to become someone better you can do that. That's what I want for you all. You and your Mother are all that I have in this world. I won't let a Gang-or anything else-come between us. Do you all hear what I'm saying?"

"Yes Sir," Saw said. "Yes Dad," Jay said.

That night when Mo came through the doors, Ben set the table with Glazed Duck a La Orange, with Rice Pilaf and Snow Peas. He had put the Twins to bed even though it was a Saturday night and they were usually allowed to stay up a little later. He wanted to talk to Mo alone.

He poured two tumblers of Martinelli's Sparkling Cider over miniature ice cubes and said: "Baby, go get relaxed and come back to dinner. I'll tell you what we witnessed today. I know you watched some of it on the evening News, but it was something else to be there."

Mo took a brief shower and dressed in a relaxing evening gown that was good for hanging around the Crib. She wore no shoes. After standing on her feet all day in nursing shoes, she wanted her feet to be free. "I have a vegetable and fruit salad to get us started." Ben served peach halves, whole strawberries, diced tomato cubes, and Julianne cheddar slices on a red lettuce bed, with an oil and vinaigrette dressing.

Mo got into the salad right away. "What's going on?" she asked. Between mouthfuls of salad that he washed down with Cider, Ben related:

"Baby, the problems we're going to face over here are much greater than I could have imagined. I have been thinking about taking you up on us finding some other place for us to live. We might be better off, I'm starting to think."

Mo finished her salad. Ben soon followed her. "Baby, it seems that Saw and Jay are leaning toward becoming one of the Homeys on the Block. I observed that today up close and personal. I didn't think I'd ever agree with you on that. So much of my life has been lived on this Street in this House, and the Memories of my Dead Relatives are like Living Ghosts all over this place. Leaving here, I thought would be like abandoning them. So, I'm clinging to a Macabre Dream, or something, Mo." He carved the Duck and served it with the rice and Snow Peas. He poured more sparkling Cider in each of their glasses. Mo dug in. Ben got seated. He ate his Duck heartily.

"Ben, Darling, I had hoped you'd come to that conclusion. I have felt for a long time that if you stayed over here much longer, you would, no matter what you tried to do-good or bad-this situation would pull you down into the Abyss with it. Honey, Fifeville is going there, and it's not your fault," Mo said.

Ben reflected for just a moment. **"Mo,** the journey to anywhere starts with one step by one person to any direction. If everyone confronted with what seems to be an insurmountable problem were to walk away, we would not be flying through the air in airplanes; or lighting our homes with electric lights; because we would not be able to conduct electricity through wires. Maybe, we are put here to begin one of those journeys," Ben said.

Mo reflected for a couple of seconds. She allowed: "The question is, how much are you willing to-or who or what are you willing to-sacrifice to get to the top of that philosophical hill? Are you willing to let go of yourself, your Sons, or even your Wife?"

Ben breathed deeply. "Mo, I don't feel as though I need to do either one of those. All I want either one of us to do is be the example that we would want others to become. I think that would be quite enough. But the way to that high mountain is troublesome, I know. Many Spiritual Leaders have been stopped on their way there; like, Dr. King, Malcohn X, Medgar Evers, Ghandi, and all of the Civil Rights Martyrs. But this is another day. I hope we Americans have gotten past violent dissent through murder to 'Come Let Us Reason Together.'"

"That would be marvelous if it were true," Mo said. "But today, in the mean Streets of Gangland, violence is the only way those youngsters know to show dissent or disagreement, and to seek a resolution to what bothers them. It is the way of the world they see all around them. Just look at America and our participation in the Vietnam Conflict. Look at how long we fought the Cold War. Just think about how neglectful our State and Federal Governments have been in depriving our own Citizens of their basic needs so to be able to fund those 'useless wars.' Violence is a primary choice we all seem to cherish over peaceful negotiations. That's what we are witnessing being played out in the Streets. They feel as though they are in a 'Kill or be Killed World.' So, ironically enough, that is how they act and react to any disagreeable situation confronting them.

"So, I feel as though the problem is bigger than any one person can solve. No one group of people will be able to solve it either. No more than the 'Godly Sacrifice of Jesus Christ did not immediately save the World.' Therefore, 'many of His Followers have become totally disillusioned.'

"America shot Peace Down, when it gunned-down Dr. Martin Luther King, Jr. in 1968. So we have No Justice. And that is why we have no Peace. Can't you see what I'm saying?"

Ben replied: "But Mo, that's a long stretch from one group of people of the same racial community taking up guns and killing each other because some of them are wearing different colors; and they are willing to sell dangerous drugs to anyone of any age to members of their own group; and, that they will kill anybody that their Crew Boss designates. It is as though Satan Himself has come upon the earth and is the Commanding Officer of the Gangbangers; and He lives right around the Comer from our Home."

"That's mostly how I see it," Mo said. "We have a number of options. One is to stay here until the 'Grim Reaper' comes knocking on our door. Or, we need to quit while we are ahead. We need to move out of 'Hell's Half Acre."

Ben cleared the dishes off the table. He got out a couple of serving saucers. "I've got some Blackberry Pie, Mo. Want some?" he said.

"Yes, Honey. And get the Ready Whip out too. I'd like a heap of that on top," Mo said. Both Mo and Ben ate dessert quietly. They were meditating on what both had said.

Mo got up from the table and stretched. "I'm going up to bed, Baby," she said.

"I'll wash up the dishes, and dean up the kitchen, and then I'll be on up too," Ben said. "Love the meal. Love you too," Mo said. She went on up the stairs to bed.

Chapter Seventeen

When Ben arrived at work the Monday after the March, he saw a Black Cadillac Escalade parked in the back of the KFC parking lot. He got out of his car carefully looking this way and that He could see that two young men were seated in the front of the vehicle. Both wore red pullover shirts.

He did not fear the Bloods Gang, per se, because he knew many of its older O'G's. They respected him because they had rolled with Roy and Ivy before they became Bloods. He'd been jumped-in by them.

The two men got out of the Escalade and slammed its doors loudly. One seemed to be seven foot tall.

The other was short and stocky. They wore black Levi Slacks and red Air Jordan Tennis.

The tall one yelled: "Blue. Ben . . . or whatever you're calling yourself right now. My Main Dog here got a Beef with you, Dog." The words shot out of his mouth like a bullet out of a pistol. He pointed his finger at Ben as though it were a gun.

The second one stood against the Escalade with his arms folded over his chest, very gangster style. "Come on over here, Blue," he beckoned with his left hand. His voice was thick and coarse.

Fear engulfed Ben, but he knew that to make this thing go away he had to show fortitude. He had to stand up. He tried to sound a little gangster for the moment. "Oh yeah, what's up with y'all?" he snapped. He walked slowly toward the menace. He did not see any weapons. He reasoned that this was good. It was too early for the first people to come in to work. He knew that he could be gunned down and nobody would claim they knew who or what Gang had done the deed.

Both of the Bloods stood next to the Escalade with their arms folded over their chests. The short one walked to within a food of Ben. He pointed his finger at Ben's chest as he spoke in a high-gangster threatening way:

"You don't remember me now, but I was part of your jumping-in Cats. What's up with you, now?" Ben backed up three, then four steps. He had trouble controlling his fear, his lips started trembling.

Ben nervously answered: "I'm trying to do everything I can to save us, my man. That's what I'm about the question is: what's up with you all? Drop the Guns! Register and Vote!"

The short one came over a little closer to Ben. He pointed his finger almost in Ben's face as he yelled:

"Yo Dog. It's me, Shorty Williams, from up on Ridge. Ev' body know me. I got much references. You know me, and you know I could step to you and snap your neck like I would a paper plate. That's what I be about. My Main Dog tell-me go get 'em and I go do that! Now, we got to first get you told and drop the word down on you hard, so you'll know how it be from now on, yo.

"It's like this-here, Homey, you brought Five-O down on the 'Hood. You and your Marching with Gregory 'n'nem. Five-O busted fifteen people already. Five of them is Crips. They be from off your turf. Got 'em all out of bed and shit. My People had an ounce or two of Jays and a couple of Rocks of Cocaine in they belongings and Cribs and whatnot. You know all of them is going down the road for a long time, 'cause Bill Clinton signed that 'Get Tough On Crime Bill.' That's the first thing he did.

"Is that what you wanna be about now, Nigga?" Shorty shouted.

"No-no-no, you don't understand," Ben stammered. "I'm not a part of that so-called 'War On Drugs.' I know that's just another way for Racists to hassle Black People. But, your drug-dealing to our youth is no better than them being sent to prison for life. Some of them are strung out on drugs for life. You take the money you get from selling them 'powered death,' because that's what Cocaine is, and you take it back to them who are directing you to peddle that Shit in the first place. You buy expensive liquor, jewelry, clothes, cars, guns and whatever, and all that money get returned to those at the top. We on the bottom get shoved down lower-and-lower each and every year. I don't like what Clinton is doing. But we can't keep doing what we're doing either. The Jails and Prisons are full of Black People. Can't you see where that's at? ..."

The tall guy cut in: "Look. Ben, the Homeys all say you's one-a the smart ones of them Slokums. But it's like this, yo: Your life and the lives of your family is like up for grabs, G. Big Mamma Ursula and her Sons got a contract out on you. It ain't but about five-hundred dollars right now. But they will up that if nobody takes that in.

"I be about my knife. I'm Arty Tyree, from down on Rougemount. I'll take-a dude out so fast he won't feel the stabs he'll be dead so quick. But I ain' go do that to you, Blue. The Bloods got a thousand dollar hit on your head too, though. So, look-here, watch your back. I can see that you be about some righteous Shit. So, I'll do what I do, but I ain' go stop you from doing what you do. We gonna be on up outta here, Blue, later and shit."

Ben's stomach was knotted in fear. He fumbled with the ring of keys to KFC doors until he got the right key in the door lock. He was so happy to hear the lock click. He quickly turned on all of the lights to the place and turned off the night lights. He had watched the Escalade speed out of the parking lot scratching wheels loudly as it hit Cherry Avenue. He knew that Shorty and Arty did not know that the Car they drove was a main part of the problem. They probably thought they were getting over on "The Man," when the truth was, "The Man was already over on us all."

The thought of what the 'Hood had become literally made Ben sick to his stomach. It was like he had swallowed a mouthful of blood. He vomited profusely into the commode in the Men's room. The first employee came through the front door. In walked Star Henderson.

Ben washed his face and came out of the Men's room. "Good morning, Star. How're you doing?" "I'm doing fine, but the Homeys on the Block say I need to get on up outta here 'cause they gonna

Bum-Rush this place one-a these days with AK-47's and shit. But I'ma stay with you Mr. Slokum."

Ben looked at the five-one caramel-colored woman in her KFC uniform and said: "Thank you, Star."

Right away, Ben sent a Fax to Johan Haggle, the Regional Manager for KFC in Virginia. "Mr. Haggle it has become entirely necessary for a Security Guard to be posted on the premises at KFC. My life and the lives of our customers and employees have been threaten by local Thugs. I know you will agree that we must keep our customers and employees as safe as possible. Yours Truly: Benjamin L Slokum, Store Manager."

In about fifteen minutes Haggle replied: "'Got message. Will contact S&PI Security Services immediately. They hire local police officers part-time. Should come to you right away. Today. Or next. Stay Safe: J. Haggle, Regional Manager KFC Virginia Division."

That evening, a short, stocky, well-built uniformed police officer came into the front of KFC. He approached one of the four cash registers on the counter in the back of the dining area.

"Hey there. I'm Officer Palmer Smithson. I work part-time for S&PI Security Services. I'd like to speak with Mr. Slokum. Tell 'im I 'am out here, would you please?" said the light-brown-skinned man. He stood with his cop hat tucked under his left arm. He was dean-shaven accept for a thin-line mustache across his top lip. He had very broad features. His voice was coarse and thick like the "TV Series Columbo."

A heavyset, Peg Best, stood behind the cashier stand and she got nervous at the sight of a cop on the premises. "I'll see if Mr. Slokum is in," she blurted out. She was a Jehovah's Witness, and the only one of the cashiers allowed to wear a dress at work. The others were forced to wear tan khaki slacks, a blue and white blouse, and a blue and white striped tam cap.

She ran back through the swinging doors and allowed: "Mr. Slokum, a cop's out in the dining room wants to talk to you. Are you here?"

"Yes, Peg, tell 'im I'll be right out," Ben said.

When Ben walked out to the front of the store, he beckoned to Officer Palmer Smithson, toward the three booths and five table and chair sets in the small dining area. Palmer took a seat on the edge of a booth. Ben sat in a chair he pulled up from one of the tables and positioned it directly across from Palmer. "I get it that Mr. Haggle sent you over for the Security Job. Please to meet you. We need someone to guard this store from about five until dose on weekdays. That's when most of the trouble gets going around here. Can you do that?" Ben said.

"I work the morning shift at headquarters. I'm there at six. I get off most days by four-thirty. I think we can swing that for you. I'll get another guard to sub for me on my days off and when I can't be available. Is that alright with you?" Smithson said.

Both stood and shook hands. "See you tomorrow evening Mr. Smithson," Ben said.

"No, call me, Palmer. You don't have to 'Mr. or Officer' me, unless we're at headquarters. I'll be right over here tomorrow-see you all then," Palmer said. Ben noticed that he had sergeant's stripes on his sleeves. He went out to a black-and-white police cruiser. A young-white-female policewoman was his driver. Ben thought: "'Oh how far we have come since the 1960s."

Ben got home that evening tired as usual. His cook hadn't showed up that day and he had to fire up all the pressure cookers to cook the chicken, as well as do all of his managerial tasks. Old Lady Peg had a number of over rings to make matters more difficult. Star had to get off early because her babysitter had to leave early. So Ben had to cook the chicken, help serve it, and then take the cash at one of the registers when it was time for the customers to pay. By the time he finished the paperwork, he felt like taking a nap right there at his desk. He was glad the evening shift came in on time. He told the Assistant about the cop.

When he got home, he saw Saw watching TV with his left eye swollen shut. His face was bruised badly.

"Saw, what in the Hell happen to you?" gushed out of Ben's mouth. He stood in the hallway holding a copy of the Daily Progress that the boys had neglected to bring into the house again.

"Dad, I begged Mom not to call you and tell you about this. I knew you would get too mad. See, you're all worked up. I ... I got into a little fight after school today, that's all," Saw said.

"You should-a seen the face of the other guy, Dad," Jay interjected. "Two black. eyes!" Ben thought for a moment: "They're coming at us from all angles. What to say"

Ben came completely into the living room closer to Saw. He sat beside him on a fluffy sofa. "Son, little scrapes and toils are gonna come into everyone's life. We have to learn from what led to them, and make a plan to not go there again. We have to seek the silver-lining in every dark-cloud that comes into our lives. Remember: 'What don't kill you, will make you stronger.' That's an Old Proverb. You understand?"

Saw shook his head enthusiastically. "Yes sir!" he said loudly.

"Y'all go on in and help me put supper on the table. I can smell the Pork Chops and Gravy. Ain't it good that your Mom can cook so good?" Ben said.

Saw said: "Sure you're right, Dad."

Jay said: "Her cooking's Dope! I mean, Great!"

Later in bed that night, Jay allowed: "Saw, you lied like a skunk to Dad. What you think Dad will do when he finds out the truth? It's gonna hurt him to his heart. I don't see how you're gonna square this with either Mom or Dad"

Saw got a little angry with Jay. "Man, you're acting like a weak sissy. Look, man, Moo-Man dropped the word on me. Said: 'Saw, the Homeys gonna come down on your family big-time. Big Momma Ursula got a thousand-dollar hit out for not just your Dad, but your Mom, and you and Jay, man.' The only way I got that turned around was to let them 'Jump-Me-In!' The Homeys will give us protection from the Crips. None of the Bloods will roll up in this 'Hood to put a hit on anyone over here right now. We got the Juice! We Rule!

"That's what it's all about Its love for the Homeys, the Family and the Crips' Nation, Jay!"

Jay asked: "How can you trust that? Man, Big Momma's in the Crips Nation now. Her Sons are Big Dogs over here. I heard that she was very righteous when our Homeys were just the Fifeville Crew. Some of the old G's who're now Bloods still got love for her. Word. But all of them got it in for Dad 'cause he took part in that March, and we were with him too. They hate that we brought Five-0 down on the Bangers. Aren't you playing right in their hands, man? What will Leanne say when she finds out that you went against your word and joined the Crips?"

Saw allowed: "Jay ... I gotta keep all that on the 'Down-Low,' till I figure it all out. You got to promise me that you won't let your 'loose lips sink my ship,' yo, Jay. Don't snitch!"

A sad facade came over Jay's face. "Saw, we came into this world together. You and me, against the world, yo. That's how we started out and that's how it is. I will never betray you, unlike the Jacob in the Bible. We will never become enemies. I'll go down swinging by your side. We're

Rocking this Shit together. What does Moo-Man have you pegged to do on the Set? I'm not gonna get Jumped-In, though."

"I got to be a Saturday and Sunday Lookout for the Fifth Street Homeys. I got a Walky-Talky in the dresser drawers. That's all I'll be doing right now. I'm doing it to save our skins, man," Saw said.

Saw coughed. "Let's get some sleep. I'm sore all over man. They beat me for fifteen minutes. I thought some of them Junior Crips were trying to beat me to death. **Moo-Man** stood by, he could've stopped them from hitting me so hard. Sometimes, he ain't about nothing, yo. Goodnight, Jay," he said.

"Goodnight, Saw," Jay said.

Ben got ready to head out the door that morning and the paperboy almost hit him in the face with The Daily Progress. Then, the headlines hit him harder.

"THE MAYOR AND CITY COUNCIL WILL MEET TO DISCUSS PIANS FOR FIFEVILLE TODAY," was one. "DOPE HAS TAKEN OVER FIFEVILLE NEIGHBORHOOD," was another one. "THE CITY COUNCIL CONSIDERING INVOKING EMINENT DOMAIN FOR THE REDEVELOPMENT OF FIFEVILL," shook Ben completely awake.

Ben didn't have time to read the articles right then because he had to get over to the Community Center to see what was going to be Kermit's and Jacque's next move. He felt like it was time for some radical new direct action, seeing as how Fifeville was under attack by the same forces that took Vinegar Hill down, and saw it razed to the ground.

Ben decided to jog up to the Center because he was getting plump in the middle. He could not get into some of his newer sportswear he'd just purchased. Within twenty minutes he arrived in front of the Community Center. He saw a big-white poster with black writing on it, stating: "The Fire Marshal Has Issued A Ruling That This Building Is No Longer Suitable For Mass Meetings, Effective Immediately. For More Information Call The Community Center Leaders At Their Previous Phone Numbers."

It was going on to be eight in the morning. Nobody was present He jogged back home hoping to be able to call either Kermit of Jacque. He felt like he had to know what was going on right away. He had planned to meet with them briefly then he would go on to work. He had the previous evening given the store keys to Starr so she could initially open up that morning. Now that he was home he knew that he had to get washed up, get dressed, and make it on down to the KFC Restaurant He got into his uniform and zipped on down Fifth Street Southwest to the Store on Cheny Avenue. He passed a couple of Bloods who were stationed over in Tonsler's **Park.** One drew his finger figuratively across his windpipe at Ben. The other one shook his right fist at him.

Ben wished that Palmer Smithson could be there in the mornings when he had to come open that restaurant The Bangers were becoming more and more threatening every day.

He burst through the front doors of the restaurant and greeted Starr: "Good morning, Starr."

"Good morning, Mrs. Slokum," she said. "The phone's been ringing off the hook, Sir. I answered one, and a Mr. Minders was calling for you."

"Thank You, Starr," Ben said.

"Mr. Slokum, I told him you'd be coming in late. He told me to tell you to call him as soon as you got, m.

"Thank you again, Starr."

After three rings, Jacque picked up the phone. He said: "Hello. Ben. I got caller ID. It lets me see the number of the caller. How are you doing this morning? Well, they closed the Center."

"I'm confused. Where are we gonna meet now? Ben asked.

"Ben, we may have to scrape the whole project. The Fire Marshal has condemned Mount Zion too. He says the Church members have to do hundreds-of-thousands of dollars of renovations in order for it to meet the new building standards to be allowed to accommodate masses of people during services. We were going to use it, but that's off the table now too. Rev. will have to find another site to rebuild Mount Zion. I heard that the City is going to help him relocate by matching the funds he raises toward building another Church Home. Meantime, they'll have to find another place to worship, temporarily, until the new Church gets erected. Right now, the old Church doors are closed.

"Man, they are shutting down a place that have a lot of good memories for our whole community."

Ben thought for a moment, then he said: "That Sounds a lot like what happened to Vinegar Hill. My Grandma used to tell me about that. The City got rid of Zion Union Baptist Church just before it got ready to demolish that whole neighborhood. I wonder is that what they're gearing up to in Fifeville? Mt. Zion stands right on the edge of Fifeville. It's one of our three Churches."

"Brother Ben, First Baptist has been inspected by the Fire Marshal and cleared. The Pentecostal Church down on Seventh Street Southwest has not been inspected as far as I know. But these Churches were not involved with the March.

"Brother let me be clear. What is going on right now is retaliation against us Activists for daring to bring the problems we're trying to address to the forefront of the public's consciousness. The City Government wants to shut that up as much as possible. Make no mistake about that.

"I've been in conversation with the City Manager and the Director of The Charlottesville Regional Mental Health Organization. They are not going to fund the Community Center any longer. We would have to find another building to rent. We are out of luck. The Drug Czar says he will not give us any help. So, we got to keep fighting as individuals until we can get a coalition together, and then we will have to find a funding scheme to meet the needs that will arise along the way.

"Thank you for your concern and participation so far. You have Kermit's number and mine, and you can call us at any time. I'll work with you anyway that you see fit, and I'm sure Kermit will too," Jacque said. "I hope we can work together again soon. Until then, I wish you and yours the very best. Goodbye Ben."

"Goodbye, Jacque. I will be in touch with you as soon as I can," Ben said.

The phone went "Click," in Ben's ear. He wondered what he could do next The Crips were dealing drugs right out in the open on the Comer of Cherry Avenue and Six-and-a-half Street, and the Bloods were doing that in the Tom Thumb Strip Mall on Ninth Street Southwest and Cherry Avenue. Both Gangs had prostitutes as young as seven years old, but as old as sixty, plying their trade in that area. Tonsler's Park was full of them. All of that was right in sight of KFC.

The cops rolled up one evening and arrested Waddell and Radcliff

Henry in the Este's Grocery Parking Lot. In The Daily Progress that next day Ben read: "Two Drug-Dealers were arrested in the Fifeville area. Each had one to two grams of cocaine and an ounce of Marijuana."

Ben thought that was a joke. He knew that tons of dope were coming through the Cherry Avenue area from the Comer of Ridge Street to the Strip Mall on Ninth Street. He knew that anyone with the money could purchase all of the dope he wanted any time of the day or night. So, why were The Daily Progress publishing an arrest on its front page about a drug-bust that was less than a drop in the bucket? It was so minimalist in terms of truthful reporting on Dope-Trafficking in Fifeville, or anywhere else in Charlottesville. Ben knew that those arrested were Ursula's "Boys." He wondered how she was taking that? A week after their arrests, it was reported in The Daily Progress, that Waddell and Radcliff were convicted of Narcotics Trafficking and Racketeering. They were sentenced to twenty years in prison without the chance of parole for their first offense.

What was ironic, was that Ben saw several other Bangers dealing drugs in that same Parking Lot the very same evening after the Henrys' arrests. The new dealers seemed to have no fear of being arrested. The dealing got worse and worse it seems the more Bangers got arrested. That meant that more dope tonnage was coming through Fifeville. When the arrests were announced, that told the buyers where to go to look to make a dope purchase. It alerted all where the "Open-Air Drug Market was."

Ben saw rich-looking upper-class people frequently driving through Fifeville, stopping and buying dope like they were going through a drive-through at McDonald's. The vast majority of those doing the buying, Ben noticed that they were predominantly white.

Ben was perplexed about all that he was seeing on a daily basis. He asked Palmer Smithson about it

"Hi Palmer, how're you doing this evening?" Ben asked. "I stayed over to ask you about something that's been bothering me for a while."

Palmer had to wear his Cop's Uniform even though he was not on duty for the City. He stopped just inside of the entrance of KFC. "Go ahead shoot, Brother Man. I'm all ears," he said with his broad lips, making him resemble a brown version of "Detective Columbo."

"Let's go over to the booth over near the right side so we can rap in peace," Ben said.

"What's bothering you my man?" Palmer asked. A look of some concern dispelled his smile. He took a seat in the booth.

Ben sat down across from Palmer. He had a dead-serious look on his face. "Palmer, you're on the Police Force. How is it that tons of Dope keep coming in to this area, and getting distributed on the streets over here, but when there is a bust, it's only a 'Nickel-'n'-Dime' Bust? The very next day the Bangers will put a Dealer right back on the same block where the bust just took place. Sometimes more Dealers will be in place where the bust just happened. It's like this Shit is being orchestrated from somewhere up top, man. What's up with that?"

Palmer cleared his throat by coughing and swallowing. "First of all, let me drop this on you. I was slated to be the first Black Investigative Detective on the Police Force. I'd moved up the ranks from a Private to a Corporal to Sergeant. I was going to be a Captain, or maybe a Lieutenant. I knew the rules and I played by them. I did what was asked of me. Never failed in making an arrest, and never failed in supplying the evidence to secure a conviction after an arrest. What took me down was . . . well"

He stopped talking for a moment and asked Ben: "Secondly, I gotta have your absolute confidence that you will never breathe a word about what I'm going to tell you. Can I trust you on that?" Palmer pled to Ben.

"Man, you got my word on that. What you tell me will stay in my head, only. Word!" Ren said.

A tall light-skinned woman in her mid-twenties, who was very shapely in her uniform, came over to the booth and asked: "Mr. Slokum, Mr. Smithson, can I get y'all anything to eat or drink?"

"Yes, Mere, bring me a large Coca Cola," Ben said. "I'll have a large cup of coffee," Palmer said.

On the woman's nametag was "Meredith Van Howe Assistant Manager." She served the drinks ordered and went back through a backdoor to the kitchen.

Palmer took a sip of his black coffee and cleared his throat again. **"Man,** I've been demoted. I was rolling with the Plain-Clothed Detectives for about a year. I'd just been promoted to the rank of Sergeant. I was sent out to get Black Suspects. A lot of those were the 'Nickel-'n'-Dime' busts you mentioned. I always got a conviction on those.

"A couple of months ago, I got a tip from one of my snitches that a couple of rough-looking White Guys were held up in the 'Red Carpet Inn' on Twenty-Nine North. My snitch said he had one of the maids 'turning tricks,' on the side for him. She was in a room with both the dudes and knocked both of them out. They slept like lambs for an hour or so. The maid got to nose around while they slept.

"The tough guys had left their footlocker unlocked. The maid saw four blocks of a white substance along with scales and plastic packets. From what my snitch said the maid saw, I figured that they had four kilos of Cocaine or Heroin up there. I went to the City Magistrate to get a warrant so that the Narcotics Squad and I could go make an arrest. That's when the 'Shit hit the fan!'

"I was told by the Magistrate that the Judge would not sign off on the warrant to do that bust. I was told to stand down. That the people I wanted to arrest were already under surveillance."

"What do you mean by them being under surveillance?" Ben asked.

"Well, Ben, I mean, that we had cops watching them to see who they were working with. To see where and from whom they were getting their Dope from. The hitch was, that they wanted to make a big bust one day in the future that would end the drug trafficking once and for all," Palmer offered.

Ben shook his head in disagreement and disbelief. He opined: "In the meantime, the Dope is coming to our Streets in huge amounts, while the Police do nothing but watch those doing the dealing, and that Sucks!" **He** spoke very slowly and passionately. "What that has to mean is that the cops know who is responsible from up top to the bottom of the Dope-Dealing Chain. So, they are as guilty as the Bangers on the Streets; especially, if they do not do anything to stop the Flow of Dope. People are killing each other over that Shit. The Dope is killing others who are addicted. Our whole community is being gutted from within and from without."

Palmer shook his head in agreement with Ben. "My Man, I agree with you one-hundred percent. That's why I tried to go over the head of the Magistrate to get a warrant. I secretly formed a Sting Operation with some officers who were as concerned as me. We got my Snitch to go and buy a kilo of Cocaine from the Pert's. We used traceable money in the transaction. He copped the Dope from the Guys at Red Carpet Inn. My Snitch wore a wire. I got the goods on those Dealers.

"Before you interrupt me, let me tell you what happened next: I took a report of the Sting and the Evidence I had collected to a meeting with a Liaison Officer of the District Attorney; the Director of the Internal Affairs Division of the Police Department; and a Police Commissioner's Representative. I had gone over a few heads, but I expected to be rewarded for making a Big Bust.

"What happened next, you will not believe. My Snitch got picked up by the Police and was brought up on Drug-Trafficking Charges. He's now in Prison in the Powhatan Correctional Center. He's lucky.

"I was brought before Internal Affairs for a Review. I was told that I was insubordinate and out of order. They suggested that I was delusional and needed time to repose myself. I was told that I had to see a Psychologist and be cleared by that person before I could resume my work on the Police Force. I was given sixty days of unpaid leave to get my thinking in line with proper Police Procedures.

"When I finished with the Shrink, I was demoted to a Patrol Car. I could no longer do Detective Work or be involved with investigations at that level any longer. My salary was readjusted. I'm not permitted to tell you or anyone what I make as a Cop because of the Confidentiality Agreement I signed-into when I was first hired. But my salary was reduced by one-third, a big let-down.

"I have a Daughter at Duke University in Political Science. She wants to become a Lawyer. My Son is a senior at Nelson County High. He will graduate this fall. That's why I work for S&PI Security. I'm negotiating with the City to let me back up to my old Job. I feel that I didn't do anything wrong. I feel like I did my job right, and that I'm being punished for doing that. I got a Lawyer and the Police Union is looking into how my case was handled. That's been about two months ago. I haven't heard a word from anyone. I'm still hopeful everyone will see reason."

Ben frowned, and it covered his face. "I'm sorry to hear that. What you're saying is that those who are supposed to be there to protect and serve us are really our main enemies. Looks to me like the Drug Dealers are getting more protection from our Police Force than we are. That makes them equally as criminal as the Dope-Pushers, Gun-Runners, and The Pimps."

Palmer coughed and cleared his throat and swallowed again. "I'm a

Cop. I know that there are a lot of good Cops out there. But there are some who are just as rotten as any criminal. The Rot goes all the way to the top. You're right about that My Man. Nice talking to you. Let me check around the premises."

Mo was off that evening when Ben got home. As soon as he walked through the door, Mo stood in the kitchen with a white apron on top of her blue-gingham dress. She spoke as though she had to keep what she was about to say, "on the down-low."

"Ben, you will not believe what was in the papers today," Mo said.

'What's got you so fired-up, Baby?" Ben responded. "'Where're the Boys?"

"The Boys are out hanging out with their 'Homeys,' I reckon," Mo said. "That's what they now call their friends."

"Well, what's in the papers that got you so hot 'n' bothered?" Ben said.

"'Detective Victor Splendera, Chief of Narcotics and his Assistant, Detective Marcus Thorn were suspended after their urine tests turned up positive for Cocaine Abuse. They were both asked to resign from their jobs. They have been put into a compulsory rehabilitation program. They had been promoted up from Cops walking the beat to Detectives in four years. They were trained in Anti-Drug Enforcement Policies and were elevated to the Narcotics Division of the Charlottesville Police Department. An unexpected request for a Urine Sample proved to be their undoing. Internal Affairs conducted the tests. The Detectives will be suspended without pay for the time of their rehabilitation until they have been cleared by an independent psychiatric evaluation. Then they will have to start at the bottom again as Privates on the Police Force.'

"Ben, how do Cops get away with using Drugs and get just a slap on the wrist, compared to People over here who are sent to Jail and 'they throw away the key.' What is up with that?" Mo said.

"Mo, I'm not surprised at all. I talked to Palmer today. He opened my eyes about the Cops and Dope in a big way. Sounds like to me that the Cops are in the Drug-Trafficking Problem up to their necks. It's only reasonable to assume that they would be using too.

"I do not believe that Splendera and Thorn are the only culprits. They all know the 'Shit' on each other, so nobody will blow the whistle. But the corruption goes right up to the top.

"The worst of the problem is that when law enforcement deals with the problem, they do so by busting from the bottom up. My understanding thus far is that the problem starts at the top with greedy middleclass businessmen who become backers of drug trafficking, by making available legitimate facilities to store and disseminate huge quantities of illicit controlled substances. That's how legitimate businesses become sure covers for the illegal drug traffic, as well as gun-trafficking, and the smuggling of 'The Blood Diamonds,' that help to finance bloody wars in Africa, Asia and Latin America. The busting for Drugs needs to start from the top-down"

Mo interrupted: "What are 'Blood Diamonds?'" she asked.

'Well, Mo, what was in the papers Kermit and Jacque gave me made me hip. The recent massive diamond trading in Angola, the Ivory Coast, and Sierra Leon in Africa was on the backdrop of civil wars. Combatants needed guns and ammunition to fight and kill each other. To gain the guns they had to force the combatants they captured, and often, their own citizens, into underground mines to dig for diamonds, that American and European Merchants gobbled up to satisfy their Jewelry Industries' demands.

"Even little ten and twelve-year old were used as soldiers to terrorize large areas in Africa to force victims to work in underground diamond mines to the death. Thus, we have the term 'The Blood Diamonds,' because of that. Though laws have been passed in Europe and America outlawing the trade in such diamonds, the underground trafficking has never been abated. The markets are saturated with 'Blood Diamonds,' even until today. It is likewise with Gold and Silver mining over in Africa. That 'Bling' Bangers like to sport came from a very bloody origin to a Jewelry Store on every corner around here."

Chapter Eighteen

Ben got up this morning to the noise of unfamiliar voices in the Streets. He sat on the side of his bed and stretched, got into his housecoat, and went over to the window to gaze outside. He saw several men wearing white smocks and white construction helmets. They were looking at the houses all along Fifth and Dice Streets, carrying clipboards, they wrote on as they went along.

Ben heard a thump at his front door. He knew that was the paperboy delivering the Daily Progress. He got on his house-slippers and ambled down the stairs to the front door, opened it and got the paper. The main headline told the story: "City Council Officials, Mayor Morpheus Commons, and City Manager, Nassar Hindi, Declared Fifeville Neighborhood Condemned."

The lead article went on to say that, "Building Inspectors after examining the buildings and structures on Oak, Dice, Fifth Street Southwest, Seventh, Sixth, and Sixth-and-a-Half Streets, Nelle, Ninth, and King and Grove Streets, have decided that Fifeville is an economically-blighted area. Fifeville's buildings exist on the visible edge of the University of Virginia and must be upgraded to meet the standards characteristically acceptable to insure the architectural integrity that such a neighborhood should have in that geographical location. Many existing buildings and structures will have to be removed. Others will be upgraded to meet the New Standards set forth by the Director of The Housing and Urban Development (HUD) Department, Mr. Lam Brighten. HUD Inspectors will do further inspections to decide which buildings will be spared and those that will have to be demolished"

Ben ran back up the stairs and almost yelled at Mo. "Baby, wake up!"

Mo got up quickly and sat on the side of the bed. She wiped her eyes and blinked them completely open. "Ben ... What's ... What's the matter? Why are you so excited?" she asked.

"That noise you hear outside are Building Inspectors condemning the whole place," Ben shouted.

"How do you know . . . I heard that might happen . . . Are they up to that already?" Mo said with a gasp.

"It's right here in The Daily Progress this morning. They aren't wasting any time at all!" Ben said.

Mo got out of bed, put on a housecoat and went over to gaze through the pink venetian blinds. She could hear the men talking and laughing, but could not see them. They had gone around the comer down Dice Street. She could see that a lot of people were coming outside to watch the Inspectors do what they were sent to do. "Ben, Baby, we better get ready. The worst is probably getting ready to happen over here," Mo said in a little whine.

"I'll get ready to go to work. Get the Boys up, make sure they go on to school. We have to just keep on keeping on. That's all we can do right now. Just keep on ..." Ben said in a slow groan. "It's that 'Eminent Domain' that we been hearing so much about.

"In 'The Letters to the Editor Section of the Progress,' a lotta students have complained about 'The Planned Gentrification of Fifeville.' They decried the fact that 'the UVA and the City of Charlottesville want to put all of the poor Blacks out of sight to make this area look richer, so Rich-White UVA people won't feel uncomfortable when they have to look at low-income Blacks.' That 'Mixed-Up' City Manager, and his 'Third World Cohort,' have gone along with what will lead to the end of Fifeville as we know it. What they are planning is: 'The **Ruin** of Fifeville!'"

Mo, cleared her throat. She got into her bedroom slippers. "I will look into where we might have to move to when this is all over with. Don't you think that would be a good idea, Ben?" Mo said.

"I guess so, **Mo,"** Ben responded with a little bit of sarcasm vibrating in his husky voice. "I hoped that we would never have to ever do that."

Ben showered, got into his KFC Uniform, and ate only two leftover doughnuts he got out of a comer of the refrigerator. He gulped down a couple swigs of coffee. He kissed Mo. "See you this evening, Babe," he said.

Mo noticed that there seemed to be a tear or two in the comers of Ben's eyes. Mo had done a little research on Fifeville. She learned: That back in the 1840-50s, a White Farmer named "Coville Fife" owned a Farm on what came to be called Fifeville. But a portion of the area was developed by a man named "Allen Hawkins," and was called "Castle **Hill."** Castle Hill was home to prominent Blacks and Whites until the Twentieth Century. In 1912, the City of Charlottesville decreed that it was illegal for Blacks and Whites to live in close proximity to one another. All of the Whites moved out. The area has been predominantly Black ever since. People associated the Fifth and Dice area with the "heart of Fifeville," because that was where the old Farmer's house once stood, the name: "The Fifeville Neighborhood" stuck from 1930 on.

Mo reasoned: "A place that has stood for all of these years is now going to be razed to the ground to please some more Racist people who want to get rid of some more Black People. That was what they have been trying to do since slavery ended in the South in 1865."

The weeks following Ben's rude awakening, he noticed that the fifty-six-acre area of Fifeville was becoming empty of many of its 2,400 residents. U-Haul Trucks were pulling up to house-after-house and people were loading up all of their belongings and getting in them and driving away. It seemed like all of the prominent Black families were gone, like the Browns, Lowseys, Gualts, Sampsons, Murrays, and Stuarts. **A Man** Ben knew as "Judas Millwright," had grown up in Fifeville. He became a building contractor and was buying up many of the homes people were moving out of in conjunction with Real Estate IV. Some homes he redeveloped and others he boarded up. "For Sale" signs were posted everywhere. One of the boarded-up homes really surprised Ben.

Ursula Henry's house was boarded up. She'd moved away so fast that Ben never saw her packing up or saw the truck hauling her away. The so-called opened-mouth militant supporter of "Gangsterism" had abandoned ship early on. He saw her as a "Betrayer of Black People in Fifeville," in every way he could think of. She was a Mother, a Grandmother-because both of her sons had gotten more than one young woman pregnant and abandoned them-and she was an "Elder," that should have made her someone all could respect. But she had led her sons to be cheap-hoodlums. They had sold Narcotic-Death to hundreds of Addicts; and had caused the addiction of hundreds more. Now that the Cops were putting on a farce of "Getting Tough On Crime," she was fleeing with all of her ill-gotten gain.

That next morning, Ben stumbled out of bed when he heard the Paper hit the front door. He was being shocked everyday by some News Headline. Wearing his pajamas covered by a housecoat he snatched the front door open and picked up The Daily Progress. A Headline Read:

"A BODY FOUND OUT AT RIVIANNA RIVER DAM WAS THAT OF A LOCAL TEENAGER." Ben went back to the kitchen table and put on a quick pot of coffee. While it percolated, he got the paper and read the article. It said: "State Forensic Scientists have concluded that the young woman's body found at the Charlottesville Reservoir was that of nineteen-year old 'Jolie Wainwright' the Daughter of Drug Czar, 'Wilbur Wainwright.' A preliminary investigation of the corpse showed that the victim's body had not been brutalized by blunt-force trauma and did not show any outer signs of bruises or lacerations. Doctors examining the body believe that Miss Wainwright died from an overdose of barbiturates in combination with Heroin and other Depressants. Miss Jolie's body has been released to her family. Police have ruled her death a Suicide. Miss Jolie was a student at Piedmont Virginia Community College in Business Management Courses. She still lived at home with her parents.

"Her Mother, Paula, said, 'I never saw my Daughter use Drugs of any kind. I'm so disturbed by all of this I can't think straight We have got to get rid of the Drug Dealers and Narcotics Kings in this City. I raised my Baby to be liberal and non-racist. She once dated a Boy who lived in Fifeville. They're the real Culprits, if you ask me. And, a lot of Doping is happening over there in that Fifeville Slum!'

"The Police are asking that if anyone has any information about Miss Jolie to come forward at once. Mr. Wilbur Wainwright had this to say: 'I'm disillusioned about being able to help at-risk people in Fifeville and areas in Charlottesville being affected by Narcotics-Trafficking. I have tended my resignation as the Drug Czar effective immediately. Obviously, I've failed. I couldn't keep that Drug-Dealing Monster away from my only Baby. She's gone and was a sacrifice to the Demon of Narcotics. I only wish I had left here before this happened. I'm from Up-State New York. Up there, our young ladies don't get mowed down by Drug-Dealing Pimps. So, if any of you all know anything that may help in this investigation, please come forward.'"

Ben took a sip out of a big-white coffee cup. He could not understand how the Wainwrights could blame their Daughter's suicide on anybody over here in Fifeville. They had failed their Daughter in a number of ways that had nothing to do with drug-dealers over here or anywhere else. Ben was not going to believe that Jolie was doing Narcotics and that there was never any tell-tale sign. That was where they had failed her. The lines of communication were too blurred in that household. Jolie never got a chance to tell her parents where her emotional pains were, and why she felt like she had to blunt that pain with dangerous Drugs. Who gave her the money to buy those drugs? She lived at home. She was a student at PVCC. Ben felt like the Wainwrights were the main cause of their only child's suicide; Jolie had died from Neglect.

Saw got up a little early that morning. "What's sup, Dad?" he asked Ben.

"Boy, I thought I told you to not speak to me like that. I'm not a 'gangsta' nor are you," Ben snapped.

"Dad . . . Dad . . . I didn't mean it like that It's just that all of the Homeys talk like that nowadays. We're rocking Ice Cube of NWA, Snoop Dogg, Iced Tea, Tupac, Dr. Dre, Biggy, and whatnot I'm not trying to be 'gangsta,' with you. I'm not tripping like that Word. But I'm just used to rapping like my Peeps on the Block-like you did when you were coming up," Saw said.

Ben bellowed: "Yeah, but that's why I don't want you all talking like I did back in the day. It was stupid and ridiculous. I wish I had not made any of the mistakes I made back then. You will be better off if you stay clear of all of that bad Shit Believe me!"

"Yeah Dad," was all that Saw replied.

"Aren't you coming down on us too hard though Dad?" Jay asked. He got a couple of slices of bread out of the bread box on the kitchen sink counter. He put them in a stainless-steel toaster. He turned to face his Father.

"Yes, I am, Jay. I want what is best for both of you all. I want you all to stay as far away from that Gangbanging Shit as you possibly can. I want you to become like another Andy Young, Julian Bonds, Jesse Jackson, John Lewis, or somebody like them. Be a good example to everyone looking for someone special to emulate. That's what you ought to be doing. That's what our West Coast Advocate, 'Dr. Maulana Karenga,' said to us in his books about 'KWANZAA.' Get as many books by him as you can and read about how we people of African descent ought to be patterning ourselves after our Great Ancestors who once ruled Africa," Ben said. "We're been a lot more than White-Masters' Slaves and generational Victims of Jim Crow. Go and learn about who we were before we were piled in the holds of Slave Ships and brought to America to make 'America rich, racist, and killers of the dream!' I'm talking about the Dream Dr. King related during the March on Washington. Where we will all he Free! Truly Free!"

Jay walked over to Saw with a couple of tears in the comers of his eyes. He pat Saw on his left shoulder. Jay went back by the steps to his and Saw's bedroom. He closed the door. He got down on his young knees and prayed: "God Almighty. Save us. Save Saw. Help him see how wrong he is. I'm so worried that something really bad is going to happen to my older Brother. He's trying to act like a man even though he's only nine going on ten. He's even begging Leanne 'to Do The Nasty,' with him. I'm so glad that she's a really nice girl. Forgive him Lord. Forgive me for lying to Dad. Forgive Saw for betraying Dad and Mom. Forgive me for not telling Mom and Dad on Saw. Thank You Lord, In Jesus Name, Amen."

Jay let the tears come down his cheeks. He wiped them away. He came back past the steps in the hallway and back into the kitchen. He got his toast out of the toaster. He got a dish of butter out of the 'Frigidaire' and set that on the kitchen counter. He got a jar of Strawberry Preserves out of the overhead cabinets over the refrigerator. He buttered both pieces of toast and spread the preserves on both slices. He picked up one piece and Saw picked up the other. They seemed to bite into the slices the same way and were chewing that up in their mouths the same way. Both of the Twins were thinking: *I don't know what I'd do without him by my side.*

"Saw, Jay, why are you all up so early this morning?" Ben asked.

Saw answered: "Dad, Mr. 'Mikil Polamo,' a Coach is giving the football tryouts for the 'Fifeville Red Skins,' over at Buford this morning. I might try out for Defensive End. Jay wants to be a Running Back. If he likes us I'll bring you the paperwork. It *costs* twenty-five dollars to sign up and that will be fifty in all. I don't want you to pay unless we are qualified. If that's alright with you, Dad?"

Jay had nodded his head in agreement with Saw. He and Saw got into Red Skin Jerseys, white football trousers, with white-athletes' socks with red stripes on the tops of those. They carried cleats on their shoulders. They went out the door. Jay said: "It's a damn shame how bad you lie to Dad and Mom, Saw."

Saw stopped on the sidewalk to face Jay. "My Brother, my Nigga, my main yard dog, yo-you be all of that. But I'm getting tired of you bitching about what I've got to do on The Set They haven't been on your ass about getting jumped-In 'cause I'm doing all that So chill out. Lemme get on with that-aw-ight?" he· yelled practically down Jay's throat "I'm looking out for Mom and Dad too-you know that"

"Aw-ight, Brother," Jay gulped. "Butwhat'cha gonna tell Dad when he checks with coach Mikil and you know he's gonna say he never saw us?"

"Jay, I've thought of that I'll just tell 'im that you chickened-out I'll tell 'im that I tried to get you to go on with the plan and that took me all day long, but I couldn't get you to man-up. So, I finally gave up and that's why we took so long to come back home," Saw said, gesturing with his hands, waving them in a circle, and then snapping his fingers to illustrate that he had just laid down an air-tight plan.

Saw and Jaywalked down Fifth Street to the Este's Grocery Store Lot **Moo-Man** and some of the Crew were there to get to work on the Set Moo-Man said: "Saw you got your Walkie-Talkie. You get on the Comer of Fifth and Cheny. Jay, you have his back. Let us know if you see any of them Five-O on the Beat Or if you see any of the MS-13 Bangers coming through here. They be with the Bloods lately. They wanna shut the Crips down off this Block. I got some Homeys strapped with Uzis and whatnot. They're here to represent now, yo!

"Saw, put your Bandana on your head. Jay-never-mind. Y'all just stay alert now. It's getting tough out here these days. Don't be afraid to get on up out of here if the shit gets too thick for you to come out on top. Y'all got that?"

"Yeah Man," Saw said.

"Uh huh," Jay uttered. He wished he could go home right then. He didn't want to be anywhere that violence might erupt. He'd only been around when one of the Homeys stuck a knife in one of the Bloods in the Este's Grocery Parking Lot. It made Jay sick to his stomach. For days after that he felt like vomiting whenever he remembered that stabbing victim puking up blood and trying to scream out in pain from that knife in his guts. He saw that Dude scrambling around on the Asphalt calling out: "Momma! Momma! Momma...." Then he balled up in a knot like a little baby. His body jerked and trembled all over. Jay didn't ever want to see anything like that again. He was scared and nervous. He decided he'd hang-tight with his brave older Brother. He had enough courage for the both of them.

It was Saturday, and Ben was off. It was nearing four in the afternoon and Mo had gone off to work. Ben got ready to pick up the phone to call Coach Mik.il when he heard a loud knock on the door. He put the phone down and went to answer the front door. A rounded Dude stood at the door. His head was shaved clean. He wore bulky Denim Jean Pants and Jacket. He had on a white T-Shirt under the unbuttoned Jacket He wore a pair of Tan Timberland Boots. His face looked sort of familiar, but Ben could not completely make out who he was.

"Hello, may I help you?" Ben said.

"Yep, you can help me. You can by to remember who I am, Negro!" the fat Dude said in a chortle. "I pull some time 'cause I didn't rat you out, Dog."

It hit Ben. This Dude was Harry. "Damn, Man, come on in. How you be?" Ben reached out to Harry. They Bear-Hugged each other. Then pulled apart

"I see you're still living in this Crib. I don't see how you could do that. The memories and all. I'd freak out every time a car backfired if it was me, man," Harry said.

Ben allowed: "Catch me up on things, like what happened to Brute and Poochie, man?"

Harry's fat face, with cheeks almost puffy, with a flattened-nose from it having been broken more than twice, squinched-up his broad facial features before answering Ben. "Man, doing time is hard; especially when you're too young to be in a prison's general population. Man, me and Poochie were teenagers. We got tried and sentenced as adults.

"We were put in the Joint Security Complex over on Avon Street I was in a Six-by-Nine Cell with two bunk beds. The Cell was designed to house two cellmates. With two bunk beds jammed in that Cell you had to walk sideways to get in and out of it. Four cellmates were piled-up together like cattle in a ham.

"The Jail was built to house three-hundred Inmates. But because of Bill Clinton's Maximum Sentencing Policies, the Jail had nearly a-thousand Inmates. I was in a Cell with a known Killer and two other Cons who had been convicted of violent assaults.

"Men were housed in the laundry room, the conference rooms, and in empty beds in the Infirmary.

There were no spare spaces. We were packed-in like a can of sardines.

"We got to shower once-a-week. In the shower I was approached by a big bull of an Inmate with jagged scars on his face and neck. He dropped his soap and yelled: 'Mo'fucker, pick up that damn soap, you got that!'

"I yelled just as loudly, 'Pick up your own damn soap King Kong!'

"He picked up his bar of soap and began to lather himself. Then he said: 'You got some nice hams on you, Fish'-(that's what they called new inmates). 'I'm looking to get me some-a that. I wish you's in my Cell. I'd make you scream out my name. I'll see if I can arrange something for us, Honey-Pants.'

"I got madder than a pit-bull. I yelled: 'You ain't go do nothing to me Mo'fucker. I'm in here for killing a mo'fucker, and I'll be in here longer for killing your ass if you don't back-down-you got that! I ain' go be nobody's punk-pussy!' (I lied about what I was in there for. All of us did that.)

"He laughed and said: 'I guess I better go get O'lady Palm and her five daughters, then.' He grabbed his huge prick and jerked-off without any shame at all. He had a twisted smile on his thin-wet lips. Then he came and squirted it at me, but it hit the shower floor in front of me. The Con laughed and lathered up again with a sinister smile on his ugly face. Then he allowed: 'You better watch out 'cause somebody might get-a-slice-a your Hams, and that might be me!'

"There were other Inmates standing around in the Shower Room that had ten shower-heads. They were all long-timers, I could tell by the way they looked. They were all holding their pricks waiting to see what the first one did to me. I guess they were planning on joining in on the rape if one took place. Man, I wanted to get the hell out of Dodge City right then, Shit!

"I knew better than to take cigarettes, candy, fruit, or anything any of them offered me. I knew that they were trying to find an excuse to screw me over. But Poochie and Brute were taking their gifts, man. Poochie was even trying to become friends with an older Inmate. I guess he thought he was handles.

"We were all sent to Jarratt Virginia Correctional Center on the East Coast. It was jammed too. Man, I heard that Poochie was raped by a bunch of Inmates and had to be put in the Infirmary. He had to be in protective custody after that. The inmates would do anything to get near him, man. One even grabbed him and threw him to the floor in the laundry-room and was trying to rip-off his clothes. He was saved from that time, but several guys got hold of him later that night somehow-favor from the guards or something-and he was put in the Infirmary again. Then he tested positive for HIV, man, a life sentence.

"Big Brute became a 'Prison Who'e.' He turned upside down, man. Started to wearing his hair long and curled like a girl's, and he even wore women's underwear. I had to cut both of them loose. I didn't want anybody associating me with them. I was sent to a new Prison in West Virginia, 'a Private Institution.'

"I didn't want to"

Ben interrupted Harry: "Man, how can all of that shit go on without the Guards and Warden knowing about it?"

"Well," Hany intimated, "The Guards and Warden were just as sick as the inmates, man. Check this out: how do you think Dope got into the Prison? Lemme answer that right quick. The Guards. I could get all the Dope I wanted, man. All I had to do was ask the right Prisoner. He knew which Guard to go to get as much Dope as I was able to afford. As long as I kept my mouth shut, man, it was cool. The problems happened when I no longer wanted to get high. I became a risk then. I had to be sent away. I knew too much.

"I had learned that the Warden was sharing in on the profits made from inner-prison dope-dealing. It was 'Dead-Money.' That's money that no tax is paid on. Prisoners have been beaten to death; put in constant Solitary Confinement; put in cells with crazed homosexual rapists; and, taken to the infirmary and castrated for not cooperating with the 'Action' that go on behind the prison's walls, man. It's more than you could imagine.

"Ben, Prostitutes-and some of these were Inmates from nearby Women's Prisons-were sneaked into the Prison by Guards. The Warden knew about them. Some Inmates were like Pimps. We made Fifty Cents an hour. We got paid in script we could use in the PX for whatever: candy bars, shaving cream, deodorant, cigarettes, extra fruit, like oranges, grapefruit, and grapes. So, Guards dealt in script with the Inmates. With enough script you could get all the dope you wanted, or get a Guard to hire a Who'e, slip her into the Prison and you could have a night with her in a special place in a secluded Cell. That turned some of the Inmates into ravenous predators, man. The Guards could tum the script into real money. So, the vicious preyed upon the timid. The Warden turned his back on that criminal activity. He was on the take. There was nothing going on that could be classed as rehabilitative, though, man.

"Ben, man, think about what men who have gone through that kind of experience and then let loose right back on the Streets of Charlottesville in Fifeville will be like once they have no prison bars to keep them at bay, and no guarded routine to keep them in line. I worked in the kitchen three times-a-day. After clean-up I got to go to the library. I started to read. I got to go back to school and I earned my GED by taking correspondence courses. I earned an ASS degree. I went on to earn my BA in English from Virginia State University. Then I stopped Doping and Drinking 'Hooch,' (bathroom gin). I was turned-in to the Warden as a 'Threat to the General Population.' I was put in Solitary Confinement for a whole year. Then I got transferred to Angola Correctional Corporation up in West Virginia, a Private Prison."

Ben was puzzled. "Harry, you didn't do anything at all to get that? They did that to you just like that, man?" he asked.

Harry's eyes got a little teary as he spoke: "Yes! Man, coming into Angola tucked away up in the Mountains, all you see are trees and cow pastures for miles and miles, until you come to this place that resembles college dorms with razor-wire fencing all around it. There were Eight Guard Lookout Posts all around the buildings. The Guards seemed to all be armed with AK-47's man. They were dressed in Jungle Camouflage with black helmets with white death heads on the crowns. Then I learned my new names from the all-white Guards at Angola: 'Nigger! Boy! Punk Pussy! Shit-Colored! Black Cocksucker!'

"Upon arrival I was strip searched. Only that Guard took some kind of sick pleasure at ramming four fingers of his left hand all the way up my Butt. Man, that hurt. I groaned, he laughed like a Demon from Hell! The hallways were narrow and when walking from cell-to-cell we knew Inmates got our Butts felt as we walked by. Some of those Cons yelled: 'I'm go do something nasty to you, Honey Pants!'"

"Man, I know that had to make you feel bad-right?" Ben said.

Harry allowed: "Yeah, man, I got a lotta respect for women now. I know how they must feel when we stand on the Block and leer at them passing by. I know now how that makes them feel. I felt like a piece of raw meat in a Lion's Den. It's a disgusting feeling. We should never do that to our women.

"Man, we were jammed into about twenty two-story buildings in Angola in a Complex that was surrounded by thirty-foot fencing, topped with razor-edged-barbed-wire. Each building housed about one hundred Inmates. There were a kitchen, dining area, and Infirmary in a separate building.

"The food sucked. It consisted of a lot of cornbread and gravy in the morning, and an occasional serving of scrambled eggs and fatback on weekends. Most nights, some kind of Pinto Beans were served with rough biscuits. On weekends sometimes, we got fried chicken. We got to drink warm water all the time. Now and then on a very cold morning we got oatmeal and coffee, a piece of fatback and some cornbread. We never got any sugar, cream or milk to go with that. Our food was sparse-never enough to satisfy my hunger, or the other two-thousand Inmates.

"We were given rough-thick striped coveralls to wear. I was issued two pair of those when I entered Angola. I was there for two years until my release. That was all of the clothing we got. No underwear, unless someone from home sent those, and the Guards allowed the Inmates to keep them-which was very seldom.

"We were issued one washcloth and a towel when we entered the Complex. We got one bar of Octagon Soap. When those wore out, we were out of luck. We could not have a regular razor to shave with. We could have a little comb and some hair grease, but no toothbrush or toothpaste.

Eight men were assigned to four bunk beds in a Cell. There was one sink. and one stool. We were issued one roll of toilet tissue per month for each Cell. That was very unhealthy, if you can imagine.

"We were paid one-dollar-an-hour for our semi-slavery. We were worked supposedly forty hours per week, but we worked from can-see to can't-see six days per-week. We were paid in script. We had to take that to the PX to buy what we needed, like toilet tissue, at five dollars a-roll. Disposable razors were two dollars a-piece. A small bar of Ivory Soap was five-dollars. Small candy bars were two dollars a-piece. Out of our Forty-Dollars for a week's work, twenty dollars were withheld for 'Room 'n' Board.' A small bag of pop com or potato chips costs two dollars. We could charge up to twenty dollars a-week from the PX. So, most weeks I had nothing left from my pay. A towel costs five dollars. A washcloth cost three. A tiny can of hair grease costs six dollars. A thin-flexible comb costs three dollars.

"Man, we had no sheet on our rough mattress. One thick blanket was all of the bedcovering we got.

One pair of heavy steel-tipped boots was all the shoes we were issued and no socks.

"I was assigned to work in a meat packing facility near Angola called the Morning Star Corn Beef Corp. I worked in an area where slabs of frozen meat came into an unloading area and I had to load the slabs into huge pressure-cookers. It was backbreaking work. The cookers were on an assembly-line that proceeded on and came out at the other end as cans of unlabeled Corn Beef. Those were shipped to various com beef manufacturers to be labeled and sold as their product.

"That was the problem, man. Angola, like one-hundred-fifty other Private Prisons, is a Private Corporation. It is allowed to use 'Slave Labor' in the name of a Prison. It does not have to comply with State or Federal Laws governing how such places are to be run. Angola is there to make money. That's all. Man, I saw Guards wearing **KKK** robes. They had miniature nooses on their belts and KKK tattoos on their arms. I felt like I was a Slave. My rights as a Felon made me a nobody, politically, and as an inmate at Angola, I was made to feel that I didn't matter as a Human Being. I'm glad I survived, man."

Ben asked: "How how the Hell did you do that, man?"

"I kept my mouth shut and didn't complain, even when Body Lice and Shingles broke out in my Cell and I had to scratch myself until welts came up all over my body. I bathed when I could and at other times, I stunk like a skunk. But my condition was relative, Ben. So, I guess there's strength in numbers," Harry said, like in a sad groan.

Ben shook his head and said: "What will that all mean for the 'Hood, Harry?"

Harry shook his head as he answered: "Man, what it means is that there are a lot of Homeys who'll be coming back to Charlottesville, to Fifeville, who'll be messed up for life.

"Look, I got a **BA** degree now. But the minute I put down that I'm an Ex-Con, on an application I won't get hired, or I know I'll be fired the minute my employer finds out I've served time in prison. I got a job as a Janitor at the UVA. I didn't tell them that I'm an Ex-Con. Hope they never find out.

"I applied for courses at the UVA. I need Financial Aid. My Financial Aid Application was rejected because I had served time on a Felony Charge. So, I can't afford to go further in college right now. The fact that I've paid my debt to society doesn't matter. I'm branded for life. I can't vote!

"I've noticed too, that a lotta homes over here are boarded up now. "Whole Blocks are empty. All of my people have moved away. "'7hatever support my family might could give me is gone, man. I see too, that IX, GE, Comm Dial, Bell Telephone, Sprint, Dupont, and Morton Frozen Foods, have moved their factories or have closed down. Thousands of jobs have vanished. The UVA is getting ready to go Serni Private, and that means a lotta State Jobs will end for people in the 'Hood. Since it's hard for an Ex-Con to get a job anyway, what else is left for him except returning to a life of crime? I won't do that, but I know a lotta guys will. They're gonna prey upon the 'Hood even more, man: More Drug-Dealing, More Gun Running, and More Murders!

"They have spent years behind bars getting abused and hardened by the Criminal Justice Industry, and they have no sympathy for anyone. You gonna see a lot more horrible homicides. Single-Parenting will be the Norm. Generation-after-generation will remain stagnant in terms of relative progress. Those who will get displaced by convention will experience 'Culture Shock.' Our youths will seek a job with their local

Gangs. That will be all that they see going on around them, and that's what they will aspire to become: Crazed Criminals. You see where I'm coming from?"

"Yes, I do, Home-Slice, and I'm trying to remedy some of that by staying in the 'Hood and showing everybody that there's a better side of life, and all they have to do is just live it," Ben said.

Harry stood up and said: "Look, my-main man, it's been good talking to you, but I got to run. I work the night shift up at the UVA. I gotta go punch-in, man. I met this 'Girlie.' She's this little Blonde Chick who works in the Business Office, man. Her name is 'Ramona.' We went out to dinner at The Omni the other night. She knows that I'm an Ex-Con. She's not holding that against me. She says she sees me as being reformed. None of the 'Sisters,' would have anything to do with me. I don't wanna be a Monk, so I went to where the hunting was better. You can't blame a dude for that; right?"

Ben just slapped hands with Harry. They briefly hugged each other. "Stay strong my-man. Don't let the Bad Shit get you down. That's all that matters," Ben said. He watched Harry head on out of the door.

Ben noticed that it was four-thirty-five. He wondered where Saw and Jay could be. Tryouts were no longer than two to three hours. They've been gone all day long. Ben got in one of his red and black jogging suits and jogged down to Tonsler Park. He found his Boys talking to Moo-Man again.

The boys ran toward Ben the minute they spied him coming down Fifth Street. "You're grounded for two weeks!" Ben yelled at his crestfallen Sons.

Chapter Nineteen

Ben watched his Sons like a hawk after they seemed to be tied to **Moo-Man** like a horse to a hooking post. He was trying to keep them totally away from that Hooligan. They were ten now. It was September 1995.

Saw's muscles were expanding like he was a potential athlete. Jay was thickening but was more refined in his musculature. Saw could have passed for twelve or thirteen in appearance. He had an arrogant air about himself typical of young Gangbangers. Jay was cool, laid-back, and paid more attention to the books than his slightly older Sibling. Both of the Twins had quite a few local girls coming on to them. Saw told Jay: "Man, I done been all the way. I'm a man, already!" He pumped the air with both fists.

"I'm too young for all of that, Saw. I got plenty of time. I'll wait for the right girl to come along before I go that far, man," Jay answered him. He brushed off his left shoulder with his right hand to diss the idea.

"I just wish I could get Leanne to give-it-up, man. She's my main-squeeze. I want to stay with Home Girl forever, yo," Saw said. "I'd make sure she'd love me forever." He flicked his tongue at the air.

"Leanne is not that kind of girl. You ought to be proud of that. A lotta girlies around here got it on at age six or seven. Some of them didn't even know what they were doing. Some of them are somebody's who'es already. You know, Connie, up the Block, she's just eleven and she's got a baby, man. She's one of Moo-Man's Hookers. That's messed-up, G," Jay said. "I don't wanna be responsible for none-a-that."

"Yeah, but I don't mess in Moo-Man's business. I got a stack of Bills hid away 'cause of the Moo-Man. It's in a little place I found in back of the closet in our bedroom. Don't tell Dad, now. I'ma be on top of the world one day. You got to have a lot of paper for that. You hit ym.n- books. I'm gonna hit the Streets," Saw said. They strode on up Nelle Street to King, then to Grove. Saw's eyes spread open wide.

"Hi, Leanne, what's up with you this morning?" Saw asked. Leanne pranced out onto Grove Street wearing a skin-tight red spandex outfit topped with a thin beige jacket. "You look so nice, Shorty-Girl."

Jay allowed: "You got those leg-warmers, they're Dope! Home-Girl's in style, yo! GUCCI-down!" "Ah, these old thing-s," Leanne spoke in a very superficially modest way.

"You're the best, Babe. You're like 'A Bright Morning Star.' I'm so glad that you like me. You're my Girl now. One day soon I hope to make you my woman. We can make it together. I know my Dad likes you. My Mom does too. Your Mom likes me. So that's all good; right?" Saw bragged.

Sadness pervaded Leanne's eyes instead of her usual Oriental Smile showing her two pronounced front teeth. Her little eyes were open wide as she spoke. "My Mom and me found out about my Dad," she groaned like the words hurt her throat coming out as she uttered them.

Saw stood on one side of her and Jay the other. "Go head on, let it all out, Baby, we got your back," Saw said. "I know you've been hurting inside a long time about this one. What'd you find out?" he asked frowning.

Leanne got closer to Saw so that she was looking up at him. She pressed her body closer to him. Teardrops came out of the comers of her eyes. "We heard that my Dad's real name was Chadwick Moor Eubanks. He lived up in North Garden, you know, up Twenty-Nine South. I got two Sisters. They seemed to be White Girls. One's Named Miami Slater Eubanks, she's Twelve, and Jada Britain Eubanks, she's fourteen. Their Mother's name is Rosetta Velvet Eubanks. Her maiden name was Darden. I did not get who her parents were. I don't want to know. (I feel mixed-up enough!) We viewed them from afar.

"Mom found out about them from a Veteran, named Conroy McHale, who had served with my Dad at Fort Lewis. Sergeant McHale came into 'The Thai Wok' for lunch one day. When Mom found out that he had served in the Army, and that he was a Black Man from Albemarle County, she started asking him the same question she'd been asking people for years: 'Do you know Chad Eubanks? Where can I find him?' 'It all came out in conversation,' Mom says.

"Sergeant McHale told her, 'Yeah, Chad once lived up in North

Garden with his Wife and Daughters. He'd been married to Rosetta for over fourteen years. I think he's dead now. He's buried in the North Garden Baptist Church Cemetery. He's got a Military Headstone. He's been dead for about four years now ...'

"That means that I'm, like Diana Ross says in her Big **Hit** Record, 'A Love Child.' Mom and I went up to North Garden Baptist Church to my Father's Gravesite. We both just stood there and wept for a couple hours. It was like I had lost 'a Father,' and she 'a Husband.' I was crying out of regret that I will never get to meet my Dad and have him know me. Saw, he was married when he got my Mom pregnant. He lied to her. He rejected me. He never tried to find me or see me. He used my Mom. His whole life was a lie!

"Mom decided that we will not interfere with his 'White Family.' Mom says that my Father was Nut Brown-Skinned with black, silky-straight, hair. He had bluish eyes, though. Maybe he was just light enough to, pass-or it didn't matter, even up in Racist North Garden. No matter, he's buried in a Black Baptist Church's Cemetery. 'I see him as my Black Father, and I'm his Black Daughter.' That's enough for me.

"Mom sees him as her 'dead husband.' She says we will 'Visit and Bless' his grave at the beginning of each year. I'm thinking about adding Eubanks to my last name. But I do not ever want to meet my 'older half-sisters.' I don't want them to know my Mom slept with their Father and conceived a Daughter with her out of Wedlock. If we fall deeply in love, Saw, promise me you will never deceive me like my Father did to my Mother. If I can trust you to never do that, I will be your Girl in every way you want. Right now, I feel that you are very special to me. I Love You." She pressed her body very tight to Saw. She dug to him and wept.

When she pulled away Saw said: "I promise to always be there for you one-hundred percent."

One day Saw went up to the Moo-Man's Crib to play XBOX War Games. Moo brought Connie into the game room that was also a bedroom. The 1V was set up in a comer of that bedroom. Moo turned off the XBOX Game. Connie walked close behind the Moo-Man. Saw could see that she was just wearing a black Bra and matching Panties only.

She whispered sultrily to Saw, "You're still a little boy. Moo says it's about time for you to become a man. All Crips gotta be Real Men. A Real Man knows what to do with a Real Woman. I want you to take off your clothes so that I can make a real man outta you, Saw."

Moo-Man backed out of the room. Connie with her fluffy-brown Afro, with its outer-edges tinted light brown looked like an immature version of "Foxy Brown," the movie Star. She pulled off her bra and panties like a striptease act in front of Saw. She moseyed over to Saw. She pulled him up off the floor. She took one of his hands and crooned, "Touch me Saw, right there."

Once Saw had touched her, he got very excited. He had never been that close to a nude girl before. He saw them only in his dreams. He had read one of the books in Moo-Man's collection by Richard Pryor, about how he was seduced by a prostitute at the age of nine. Reading about that had really excited him to the max. Connie had never paid him any attention before. Now he was getting his chance do what Pryor had said happen to him.

Connie helped Saw out of his pants and sweat shirt. He removed the rest of his clothes. She pulled him to the Queen-size bed in the bedroom. "Saw, come let me show you had to make love. You will never be the same little boy after that. You will know what it feels like to really be a **Man!"**

Saw let her guide him to the well of lusts where he drowns his innocence in the waters of sin and careless abandonment He heard Connie moan and he had never experienced anything in life like that before. That was how Saw had been seduced into the adult passions of unbridled lust and immorality.

While he stood close the Leanne with her tender young developing body, he wanted to experience her the way he had Connie, but Leanne was no prostitute. He could only imagine what that would be like as he stood very close to her with her body pressed tight to him. He got very excited again and Leanne perceived his urgency.

"Saw, Honey, you're gonna have to wait a little while before I'll be ready to do all that If You can wait for me I promise you I will make it worth your waiting. Will you do that for me-for us?"

Saw replied: "If I have to wait, I'll wait. I can't hardly wait for the waiting to be over, though."

"Saw, I got one more thing to tell you," Leanne said. She stood very close to Saw again. "Mom and I we're gonna have to move. All the people up on Grove, King, Ninth, Nelle, Delevan Road, all the way to Fifth Street, will have to move. Some newly formed Company has taken over and is going to build a large complex of buildings all along that area Right now most of the houses are empty and boarded up.

"Mom got a loan from Virginia National Bank, and she is part-owner of the Thai Wok. She's buying a new house up on Pantops Boulevard up on the Pantops Mountain area. I'll be going to Monticello Middle School in a couple of weeks. We'll have to keep in touch by phone. You can have your Dad bring you up to see us sometimes. We can go to the Movies at the Jefferson on weekends. Mom says your Dad or Mom will have to come along to chaperone. But we will be able to be together. I love you, Saw. I think I will keep on loving you no matter where I live. Do you feel the same way about me?" Leanne said.

"I love you too, Baby Girl," Saw said. "Yeah, I want to always keep in touch with you. I'll make sure we get together every weekend. Word! I don't think my Mom or Dad will mind me keeping time with you, they love you too. It doesn't hurt that they know that you are a Math Whiz and a Rich Girl, now!"

The trio headed up Ninth Street Southwest to Forest Hill Road. Both Saw, and Jay were kind of sad. Once they arrived at school, Saw planted a sweet kiss on Leanne's lips. But she would not French Kiss him. He stood watching the love of his life and maybe future wife stroll on up the hallway.

All that day it dawned on Saw that he was not going to be as dose to his Main-Squeeze as he wanted to be. He decided that he would go hook-up with Connie until Leanne was ready to go all the way. But to his surprise, Connie would not have anything more to do with him. She was very negative toward him. She even yelled at him: "Little Boy, go get a bag of marbles to play with. I ain't got no more time for you! I did Moo-Man a favor. That's all!" She shouted, snapping her fingers around in a circle for emphasis.

"Go Away!" she screamed.

Saw had discovered that once he had been introduced to the level of lust that Connie had dropped on him, it was "like a dose of Heroin." He was addicted to Sex. He felt like he had to go find another "Fix," somewhere, right away. Jay just shook his head in wonderment as he watched Saw go after all the Ten Year-Olds in the 'Hood attempting to satisfy his new addiction. Sometimes Saw had his way, and at other times, not so much. Saw became very angry in general when he failed. He sometimes took that all out on Jay.

Ben woke up suddenly on this morning to a frightening Image sitting in a chair in the comer of his bedroom. Ivy was sitting there frowning at him and suddenly faded into a ghostly fog. It happened in a split-second. A Song he had heard all over the radio in the 1980s started to play in his head and he couldn't get it to stop. It was by Phil Collins. It was about him, "Getting This Feeling In The Air Tonight. ..." It was like a Song he would hear sung at a Funeral Dirge, and Ben remembered he didn't particularly like the Song at the time it used to play on the radio day-after-day several times each day. It was too sad, melancholic, and lonely.

But here the lyrics of that Song were inserting themselves in his brain and would not stop playing. It put Ben in a Dreadful Fog, even though he did not know why he felt so strongly under the weather. He went into the kitchen and got on a pot of coffee. It percolated. He poured himself a cup and stood at the kitchen counter sipping out of it, waiting for the paperboy to deliver The Daily Progress. He heard the paper hit the front door. He went up the highway to get to the front door. A sweet familiar voice asked: "Blue, what do you want for breakfast this morning?" It came from the kitchen area. Ben could 've sworn that it was the voice of his Dead Grandma Mildred. He jetted back into the kitchen. There was no one there. But there was a strange chill in the air.

Ben went back up the hallway to the front door, opened it, picked up the paper and to his shock, he saw Roy standing on the Comer of Fifth and Dice holding a Pistol in his left hand. The Ghostly apparition disappeared immediately. Ben closed the front door abruptly and stood against the wall near the front door scared as Hell about what hearing and seeing the Ghosts of his Dead Relatives could mean.

He got himself together, took a shower and got dressed. That Phil Collins' Song got to playing in his head louder, and absurdly, and became very intrusive until it was blotting out his rational thoughts. He did not read the Paper. He laid it aside. He felt like the News could be too bad, so that would have to wait. He had all of the intrigue he felt he could handle all at once.

Ben got down to KFC in a hurry. No one had arrived at work yet. He went back to his office in back of the Restaurant and heard the FAX Machine whizzing strongly. A long message was hanging down all the way to the floor. It finally stopped. Ben tore off the message sheet and folded it into pages. It read:

"Due to the decrease in business revenue, this KFC Store will close in forty days. All Employees in good standings will be given the chance to relocate to wherever a comparable position exists. Those who cannot relocate will be given a Comprehensive Severance Package in accordance with our stated policies in the Company's Handbook. We appreciate your service with us and wish you all the best: Johan Haggle, Mgr."

That Phil Collins' Hit exploded in Ben's mind. He was nervous and apprehensive. He had to tell Mere, Star, Peg, and Palmer that they no longer will have a job. He had to dismiss a whole night shift. Those people had families to support, bills to pay, and jobs were getting scarcer than Hen's Teeth. Since everyone losing their jobs couldn't be worse, what was that Song trying to tell his psyche?

He decided that he would work over that evening to talk to Palmer man-to-man. Palmer got out of a Police Cruiser as usual, moseyed on over to KFC's front door and strolled on in. He had a worse frown on his face than Ben had. He allowed: "Brother Ben. Man you must not have read the newspaper this morning. It said that they're going to shut your whole neighborhood down, man. Some new corporation was recently formed, called the 'Albemarle-Charlottesville Redevelopment Corp, (ACRC).' It's made of local construction companies, Charlottesville and Albemarle Bankers, members of the Albemarle Board of Supervisors and Charlottesville City Councilmen. Local Contractors have been given exclusive contracts due to low-interest loans made available to ACRC to build a complex that will start on Ninth Street Southwest and travel all the way down Main to Ridge Street; over from Ridge to Cherry Avenue; Down Cherry to Ninth and Cherry. All of the buildings in that area will have to be demolished. That would include Dice, Short Fourth, Oak, Seventh, Seventh-and-a-Half, Nelle, Delevan, Grove, and King Streets; as well as Sixth-and-a-Half, Sixth, and Fifth Streets. That's nearly almost all of Fifeville. It's gonna affect all 2,300 current residents. That will make what they did to Vinegar Hill seem like a Field Day outing. They're talking about destroying a **Fifty-Six** Acre Tract, man!"

Ben was sitting at a table in the deserted dining room. He jumped to his feet at hearing what Palmer had said. "No man, I didn't have time to read the papers, man," Ben nearly shouted. "All Hell seems to be breaking out all over us over here. Like *it* says in a Song I heard in the Eighties, 'I've been feeling this· coming for a long time ... 'I knew it was gonna happen. I just hoped that it would somehow go away."

Palmer sat down at a table in the dining room. "They say that they're gonna tum the Fifeville corridor into a 'Mixed-Use Area.' But get this: the lowest proposed costs of one of the new condominiums will be one-hundred-and-thirty-seven thousand dollars, and up. Most displaced people will be out of luck. Only rich people will be able to live in Fifeville, now, man. Reckon they'll be rid of the Gangs and everybody else over here right early, Brother Man," Palmer said.

"That's' The Ruin of Fifeville! 'I guess I finally got to get ready to get on up outer here, man, bad as I hate leaving where I grew up," Ben said. "We're gonna be gentrified-to-death over here. That was what I was trying to tell my people, man. I knew that they would come at us with all of their racist-guns blazing if we gave them any kinda chance. Gangbanging was all the reason to do us in that they needed. You know, Palmer, they had to Clean up the Slum,' 'they created in the first place. That's how that works, man.

"They brought in 'The Posse' to get us to organize into Crews to defend against the Jamaicans. Once we were organized, they brought in more Dope and more Guns. The Bloods and Crips came along to divide up our 'Hoods into armed camps. We started to kill one another to protect our Turfs. Then the MS-13 and the Mexican Mafia came along to supply us with tons of Dope and Exotic Guns and Ammunition. All the time we were becoming more demoralized and slummy as all of the best families moved away and Fifeville became an economically-blighted area. Now those at the top get to do what they have been wanting to do all the time: 'Get Rid of all of the Niggers! 'That's really what is behind all of this Shit, man.

"Palmer, the pain starts right here, man. KFC is closing down *this* Store in about forty days. All of you all who can't relocate will be laid off.

I'm sorry as I can be about that. I've had to tell all of the people here that shitty song 'n' dance. Hope you can find something better, Palmer. It's been good working with you."

Both men stood up and shook hands and briefly embraced. Then Palmer allowed: "Brother Ben, I have something I want to tell you."

'What's that, Brother?" Ben asked.

"Well, I don't like to get into other people's personal business unless it's when I'm doing police work. By the way, I'm gonna resign from the force. I can make a better living driving truck for Dettor, Edwards, and Morris, and working for S & PI Security. But . . . lemme start by saying: You know that child molester they call **Moo-Man,** who lives right up the street from you? He's pimping a little girl that seems to be twenty-one, but she's just turned thirteen. Her name is Connie Ann Lewis. I've tried to turn him in on a Juvenile and Domestic Charge, but nothing ever came of that They just weren't interested in busting Moo Man for that They picked the little girl up one day and took her to the hospital to be checked out She came up HN Positive, I later found out. They let her back out onto the streets. She doesn't seem to have any family around here. She says that she came from Fluvanna out of a place called West Bottom. There are a lotta people with the last name Lewis in West Bottom, none of them will claim to be kin to Connie. So, she and Moo-Man are really bad news. Guess he's acting as her 'guardian' or something. It's a shame!

"Well, some days, I've seen your Boys hanging around Moo-Man and Connie in the Este's Parking Lot Your Son, they call, Saw, I've seen him carrying a Walkie Talkie. He was wearing a black bandanna on his head, like the Crips. I didn't want to mess in your business. I didn't know ..."

"I wish you hadn't" Ben raised his voice up a decibel or two. "I told them to stay away from that Moo Man bastard. He's nothing but North Carolina trash. I've never hit one of my Boys, but I'm going to tonight. They deserve it," Ben grumbled.

Palmer warned: "You got to be careful with that one these days. You can get into a lotta trouble for doing what my old man did to me often. It never hurt me that bad. I think it made a better person out of me.

"Well, I'm gonna check outside, a crowd is gathering across the Street over at Este's. They'll liable to be scattering to over here any moment now. By the way, how much Severance will we all get?"

Ben scratched his head for a moment "Well Palmer," he said. "If you been here a year you get one extra week's pay after taxes. *H* you been here for two years or more you get two week's pay after taxes. Managers get one month pay after taxes. Those with less than one year's service get nothing. That's KFC's policy." He waved at Palmer going on out the door. Some people of the crowd were moseying over toward the sidewalk in front of KFC. It seemed like to Ben, they were Crips. Two of them seemed to have tears in the comers of their eyes. He wondered why they were staring at the building so intently.

A Black and White Police Cruiser pulled into the KFC Parking Lot. Out jumped Two Policemen. One wore a Blue Private's uniform the other wore plain clothes, (a black suit, red tie, over a white shirt with brown shoes). They sprinted around the building and into the front door.

The Phil Collins' Song became overwhelming in Ben's mind. It was like a drum booming at a parade. The plain clothed Officer presented his Badge. "Hi," he said. "I'm Lieutenant Claiborne Christian with the Homicide Division of the Juvenile and Domestic Department. Are you Mr. Benjamin L. Slokum?"

Ben stammered: "Yes, yes, yes sir, I am. What do you Officers want with me?" he asked. He was almost out of breath.

Lieutenant Christian said: "Your folk are down at the Station. We need for you to come with us Mr.

Slokum. It is a very important matter that only you can attend to right now, sir."

Mere was already at work, so Ben went out the door with the cops. He got in his car and drove behind them downtown to the Police Station. His heart was in his throat all the way to the station.

Lieutenant Christian led Ben to the side doors of the Station in the alley between the downtown parking garage and City Hall. They went up a long hallway in the basement of City Hall. The high beams of the Florescent Lights bounced off the white floor tiles and walls and hit Ben squarely in his big eyes. He shut his eyes tightly for a moment to adjust them to the light.

He opened his eyes to see Mo sitting in a wooden chair clutching Jay tightly. She whimpered like a child that had been whipped. A White Police Woman speaking in soft terms encouraged Mo: "Let go, he's safe now. You can trust us. We won't hurt him, Ma'am"

Mo held Jay so tightly it was uncomfortable to him. She shook her head in disagreement with the kind urgings of the Police Woman, who gave up the minute Ben walked into the interrogation room.

The room reminded Ben of the one he had been placed in after the murder of his people a few years ago. "Mo, what's going on, Baby?" Ben asked.

Mo did not utter a word. She looked at Ben with a horrible frown on her face. She placed her head against Jay's back. She wept in loud sobs.

"Jay, what's going on here?" Ben yelled at his whimpering Son. "What're you all doing down here?

And, Where's Saw?"

Jay pointed at Lieutenant Christian. "Dad ... They got Saw. They got 'im, Dad. We lost Saw, Dad. He's gone! They got 'im, Dad. They killed **Moo-Man** and Connie too. They tried to get me, but I saw them and ducked. Oh Dad, I want my Brother back, Dad!"

"Who did that, Jay? Who killed Saw? What're you talking about, Son?" Ben yelled. Jay screamed: "Arty and Shorty, Dad! ..." Jay's voice broke up into uncontrollable sobs.

"I'll kill 'em! I swear I'll kill 'em both!" Ben yelled. He walked around in the room like a caged Tiger. "Those sons-of-bitches told me they'd not touch me or my family. Then they busted a cap in my Son! Tried to kill both my Boys! I'll go to Jail this time for I got to have their blood on my hands now!"

Lieutenant Christian walked over and stood in front of Ben. "Mr. Slokum, we have the two suspects in custody. After the killings they gave themselves up right away without incident. The one called Arty was the shooter. He says he meant to kill Moo-Man, only. He confessed. He says that he didn't see who was with Moo-Man until the shooting had ended. He thought the people with Moo-Man were just some more Crips. Esau Luther Slokum, a juvenile, was hit four times, once in the head, once in the neck, and twice in the chest. He bled out very rapidly near the Comer of Fifth and Dice. Moo-Man was hit several times in his head, as was Connie Ann Lewis. They all died on the scene. I'm sorry for your loss. We have booked Arty Tyree with Capital Murder and Racketeering. He'll be eligible for The Death Penalty. His sidekick, Shorty, the one who drove the car during the drive-by, will probably spend the rest of his life in prison.

"I don't know if this will mean anything to you, but Arty has been crying almost nonstop in his Jail Cell.

He says, 'I want to go to the Gas Chambers. I ain't never wanted to kill no child. Man, I wish I could get that blood off my hands. Go ahead kill me! "Shorty wants to go to the Gas Chambers too. He has not uttered another word after saying just that. He just stares off in the distance like a crazy goon. So, neither one of them will get away with what they've done, Mr. Slokum. You don't have to try to take the Law into your own hands. Go try to comfort your family. Oh ... I need you to go with me to the Morgue to properly identify your Son's Body."

Ben went over to where Mo sat in an interrogation chair clutching Jay, and he knelt down on the floor and cried. "Mo, I'm sorry. Baby there are no words that I can say that will actually convey how I truly feel now. I've identified Saw 's remains. We got to go home now. We got to get ready to bury our First Born." Ben knew what Phil Collins' Song meant now. It was the Gateway into the Valley of Ultimate Sorrows.

Lieutenant Christian came into the investigation room. "You all can go home now until the Court date for the Swine that killed your Loved One. We will notify you when that is. I wish you all the best, and if there's anything else that I can do, please let me know. God Bless You All." He left them in the room.

Mo stood up holding onto Jay's arm, then his hand. "You stay close to Momma! "she whispered in very hushed, hysterical terms. She did not look directly at Ben. "I drove my own car down here. Jay let's go on back out to the garage and get in it!"

"Baby, I'm so sorry all of this has come down on us. I know you think that it is all my fault. Maybe some of it is. But I was trying to help ..." Ben groaned.

Mo turned away from Ben with a frown of disgust across her face turning her beauty to absolute scorn. "Let's go Jay," she said. She snatched Jay on out of the room and back down the hallway out to the Street leaving Ben in the room. Ben ran behind her but said nothing. He knew she needed some time to gain her composure.

When they both had arrived at their home, Mo got out of her car and grabbed hold of Jay's hand again.

She pulled him along toward the house. Jay did not protest. He got tears in the corners of his eyes.

Jay knew that his Dad was being blamed for what was Saw's fault He did not want to sully the memory of his Older Twin, but he didn't want his Dad to be the Scapegoat either.

"Mom ... Mom, I got to say something! ..." Jay said. Then, he fell silent

Mo ignored her little Son's plea. Ben came into the house. He spoke plaintively:

"Mo, darling, I love you and both my babies. I'm sorry we lost Saw. He's my First Born. I didn't want that to happen to him, Jay, or you. Please, do you have it in your heart to forgive me for whatever you think I'm guilty of. I accept that whatever it is. But we have to keep going. Honey, we have to keep on ..."

"No we don't!" Mo snapped. "I'm going to leave this house tonight and take my last child with me. I'm not necessarily leaving you, Ben. But I'm damn sure going to leave this house, this neighborhood, and this shitty situation that's devouring everybody and everything. I want out and I'm taking Jay with me. That's all to it, Ben. I'll be at Pops' place for a few days. If you still want to be with me, come on leave with me right now. Yeah, I still love you," she said in a little calmer voice, "but, I won't stay here and let you sacrifice our only child for this Godforsaken Neighborhood. It's not worth it, Ben."

Ben fell to his knees and moaned. He spoke in a growl: "Mo, don't leave, yet. Let's talk about this some more without all the anger. We can work this out. Can we do that?"

"No," Mo snapped. She got together a suitcase for herself and another for Jay. Jay dragged his suitcase and Mo pulled hers along. Ben stayed on his knees as one would in prayer as Mo and Jay went out the door. He thought about running after them but felt compelled to stay put as well. So he did.

It was like the door to reality had been slammed shut in Ben's life. He had been trying to do what he promised his Granny he would do to save himself and the 'Hood. All that seemed to have gotten him was sorrow, hate, and the murder of his First Born.

Now the woman he loved, the most important person in his life had walked out on him and taken his last remaining Son. His other Son had been sacrificed on the altar of corruption in Fifeville. Ben went to the kitchen and got out a sharp carving knife. It was stainless steel and guaranteed to remain sharp for five years. It could cut through brick. Ben was thinking that he would have no trouble using it to cut through the pain, the heartache, and the veins of his arms, to end a life that had become too unbearable to continue. He couldn't pull it across his wrists. He ran out of the kitchen up the stairs and fell across the fluffy goose down comforter on his bed. He wished he could just die and tum life off and be done with it.

Ben fell into a deep sleep, a trance, a crossover into the Neither world. He lay upon his bed. The thunder rolled. The wind picked up. He found himself, bodily, back to when he was a boy of fourteen or so. Granma Slokum stood at the foot of his bed. She was dressed in a flowing white gown. Her hair was crystal white. Her brown face glowed like polished gold. Her voice echoed as she spoke:

"Ben . . . Ben ... Ben, you must not live just for yourself, or your Sons, or your Wife. But your life means more than that to all who will come after you. You are one of our people's generational links.

"You must not cling to the past too tightly, Grandson. You should not wrap your life around a Memory no matter how dear it was to you, for Life must go on. The past has satisfied the terms of its existence. The present will make that relevant. The future is determined by how you interpret the other two. Do not compromise your Future by clinging too ardently to the Past. Let your present actions use what the past has taught you to help guide you to a better future. That is what you must do in the present. It is the true meaning of Life.

"Our Great Ancestors could all have lay down and died in the holds of slave ships. They could have all committed suicide. They did whatever they had to do to endure, suffering to stay alive so that one day you could come into being. Many died during the Middle-Passage. Many more succumbed to diseases communicated to them by their captors. Those who survived were subject to the rigors of American Chattel Slavery. Some ran away and were recaptured. They were severely punished and degraded for wanting to be treated like Human Beings. They survived. They lived. They were your Great-Great-Great Grandparents. Had they given up and succumbed to suicide, you would not exist. Your Twin Sons would not have been born. Your Ancestors survived so that you might have life.

"You must leave this house, Son. You can take the Memories of the life we once had here with you. But your plight in life now is that you must be there for your Wife and Remaining Son. Remember, you are Our People's Link to the next generation. No matter what has happened to you, you must strive to 'Keep On Keeping On,' till you have overcome every obstacle put in your way; or you must lay the foundation for the future generation so that they may overcome. That's why THE GREAT CREATOR caused you to come into the world. Now, get up off this bed of sorrows. Get up and live. Live to keep on living. Defy the odds. It is Our Destiny."

Ben awoke out of his Dream. A loud knock on his front door meant someone was trying to get his attention. He felt faint, weak, thirsty, and very hungry. His underarms were very pronounced. He felt like he hadn't bathed for two or three days. He moseyed down the stairs to the front door. Harry and Mere were there.

"Mr. Slokum. Mr. Slokum, you in there?" Mere yelled.

"Ben. Blue. My Main Dog. You in there, G? "Harry called out.

Ben said: "Wait a moment, I gotta get dressed." He ran back up the steps, splashed some water on his face, and dried on a towel, got into a pair of denim slacks and a T-shirt, and came down to open the front door. In walked Mere followed by Harry.

They followed Ben into the living room. Harry sat in one end chair and Mere the other. Ben's eyes were swollen from crying. His hair was uncombed. His body odor was rich. He was not the slick-looking, laid-back guy Harry or Mere was used to seeing.

"Mr. Slokum, Mr. Haggle gave your last pay and severance checks to me to deliver to you. I have those here for you. They closed the restaurant yesterday. Mr. Haggle said he was not going into this neighborhood. So he sent me. How're you doing Mr. Slokum. I told Mr. Haggle that you were not feeling too good. I hope you're alright," Mere said.

Mere gave Ben two envelopes. She embraced Ben and said: "It's been a pleasure working with you Mr. Slokum. I have a job now with Boars

Head Inn on *250* west. I'm going to be a Banquet Waitress. I'll be working with Barney Wilcox an Assistant Banquet Manager. I wish you all the best. If there is nothing I can help you with further, I've got to get back home to my family." Mere turned and went down the hallway and on out the door. "Why don't you come apply at Boars Head Inn?" she said over her shoulders.

Ben said to Harry, "Man, she's a single mother. She got three children to support. She seems to be a nice person. I hope the job at Boars Head Inn pays her enough to do all that."

"I don't think that lady's stupid. She seems to be very intelligent. I think she'll do fine. But what about you? You've been up in here by yourself for days. Ben, if you don't mind me saying so, man, you look bad, Bro. You got to get cleaned up and get back in the groove. That's how we gotta roll in the 'Hood. I know you just lost your Son. But . . . that kinda loss is part of being a 'Hood-Rat. See, only the fattest, baddest, rats get to survive. The weaker ones all get eaten up by the stronger. That's the unwritten Law of the Ghetto, Ben. You grew up over here. You know what I'm saying? If you live in this place you got to become one who will do the most harm to others. You gotta become the 'Illest Criminal on the Block.' Otherwise, you gotta move out-Y'know, bounce on up outta here. You know it's like that, Bro." Harry said.

Ben stood up out of the end chair he had been sitting in. "Yeah, man. I just wish I had come to that before this Jungle over here consumed up my Esau. My Wife's gone. My other Son's gone. All I've got over here is horrible memories: of Granny's murder; Ivy's murder; Roy's murder; and now Saw's murder.

"Mo said she still loves me though. That's a start man. I'm gonna get on up out of here and start over, Harry. I had a dream about my Granny. She told me in that dream to 'tum the Past loose.' I'm gonna take Her up on that. Mo and Jay are up at her Father's Crib. I'm gonna close this scene down over here right away. I 'ma get in gear, Harry. I've clung to the past long enough," he said.

Harry said: "That's it!" He laughed. "You can start by chasing that skunk out of here." "What skunk?" Ben asked.

"The one that got glued to your underarms," Harry said. Ironically, Ben found that joke a welcome break from his psychosis. He smiled. "Stay still my-man, I'll get on upstairs and rock my waterfall. Be right back. Hold tight." He felt the pain inside ease a little bit.

A loud knock came from the front door. Ben went up the hallway to the door. A Sheriff was standing on the deck. Ben opened the door. "Hi Officer. How may I help you?" He asked.

The White Man spoke in a slow Southern Drawl: "I have here an Eviction Notice. You have forty days to yield up the property. The Albemarle-Charlottesville Redevelopment Corporation now owns this House and its Environs. You can get in touch with ACRC through Real Estate IV. The number to call them is in the Warrant." He handed Ben a brown Manila Envelope. "You have a nice day now," he said. He turned away from Ben and headed on to his County Car.

Ben watched the car turn the comer down Dice Street. Even though he knew this was coming he hated the way it finally came. Big tears came streaming down his cheeks. Harry came over to where he stood in the hallway.

"Ben, this can't be any surprise to you. Think of it as a good thing. It's what's gonna push you forward,

G. It's like the 'Hard Knocks and Experiences' that our people be always talking about. Now let nothing stand in your way. Go find Mo and get back to where you belong, Dog," Harry said. "By the way, I'm gonna marry that girl Ramona. She's gonna be a Momma soon. I don't want her to be just my Baby's Momma. I'm gonna be there for my children, man, unlike my Dad, who abandoned us from day one."

"Yeah, man, my Dad died when I was real young. I've never stopped missing him. You're on the right track there. I'm so proud of the way you have overcome. That is what I wished for all of us who got shucked into that 'Gang Thang,' man," Ben said.

Harry walked toward the door as he said: "Ben, now that we've got you up on your feet and back among the living, I think it's time for me to go. I can see by the flashing light on your ID Answering Service that your Answering Machine is maxed out. You must not have answered the callers in days. But before I go, lemme ask you something," he said.

"What's that, Harry?" Ben replied. "We can talk about anything, you and me."

"Well, Ben, I'm been wondering since I was a little guy. Who was that Cat everybody used to call?

'MASTER D, THE GRAND MACK DADDEE?' "Harry had a very serious look on his face.

Ben had a little chuckle. He walked over to stand in front of Harry. "Harry, here's what I think about that The reason no one ever got to see the Dude was because no one like that ever really existed. 'MASTER D. was just a Symbol,' man."

"You mean the Dude was never real?" Harry asked. He had a puzzled frown on his face.

"Yeah, man, I think' THE GRAND MACK DADDEE,' represented those at the top who are in charge of everything coming into and out of the 'Hood, especially the Crime. We conjured that up in our own minds as being a 'Great Pimp' of sorts. So, this 'Imaginary Pimp' was like 'the Very people conjured up Santa Claus at Christmas Time,' but really, he only exists in people's minds. It is just a way to excuse our guilty consciences when we have done something unspeakable to hustle some money or whatnot. We could always say that 'MASTER D' made me do it. The person we'd be talking to will just say 'Oh, okay.' That's how that came to be."

'Well, I'm gonna take that at face value until a better explanation comes along. Nice to see you Ben. I gotta run, man. Keep on keeping on now," **Harry** said. He went out of the front door. Ben watched him walk on up Fifth Street. He knew that Harry had not moved back to the 'Hood. He had moved to a house over on Berkmar Drive in a very "Mixed" Neighborhood. Ben wondered was that where all the people being forced out of Fifeville might end up, in neighborhoods like that?

Ben shot upstairs got into the showers and took a good scrubbing. The hot water and suds revived him even more. His right mind came slamming back to him. He'd been mentally absent for a couple of weeks. Oh, Damn! He thought. He had to go see about Saw's burial arrangements. He knew that Mo had the Universal Life Policy that paid five thousand for college if the insured survived until eighteen. Or it paid three thousand if the insured died before his eighteenth birthday. Mo could handle arrangements if she wanted to. But he knew she may be angry at him, but she still loved and respected him.

Ben dried off got dressed in a Joseph O Banks Black Suit, black wingtip shoes, and a blue shirt and red tie. He was thinking that Mo must be thinking that I've gone crazy. I'm twenty-eight, we been married since we were eighteen. I've never been away from her for two weeks. I gotta get to see Mo right quick!

Ben went over to the phone to playback all of the messages recorded on it.

The first message was: "Ben, come over to Pops' house. We got to talk about a lotta things!" it said.

Then, "I'm not going to let Saw stay over after. Bell Funeral Home much longer."

Then, "Ben, Jay, Pops and I put Saw in the ground at Oakwood Cemetery today. Wish you had come. I'm not coming back to that neighborhood ever again. I will never see you unless you come out of there."

And Finally: "Ben, I've moved into a three-bedroom apartment, with a bath and-a-half, a den, a living room, a full kitchen and dining room. It's on Millcreek Road in the Millcreek Subdivision at 2020, Apt 1. Come and talk to me when you feel better. Jay talked to me and told me some things you need to hear."

Ben called Mo at her new number: "Baby . . . I'm sorry . . . I love you and Jay. You're all I've really got in this world. Please forgive me for being blinded by the memory of my dead. I'll make it up to you. Let me come see you and we'll talk ..." Ben spoke in sobbing terms. Mo cut in:

"I've always loved you from the first day we met. I still love you. It will take some time for me to get over losing Saw like we did. But now that I have the whole story, you are not totally to blame.

jay told me that Saw had joined the Crips. He'd slept with Connie, who was sick with HIV. His whole life would have been ruined if he had lived. I can't hold everything against you. I didn't take the influence of Fifeville and what it had become seriously enough either. I should've left with my Boys a lot sooner even though I love you dearly. So I'm partially to blame.

"Get a U-Haul truck and pack up the Tudor Dining Room Set, and the Steinway Furniture, and our pots and pans. Leave everything else at

Goodwill. Come over here and we will work things out just fine. People who love each other can endure anything for 'Love Covers the Multitude of Sins.' We'll visit Saw's Grave together and weep as a family after you come over. And, I know I will forgive you Ben. You are the only Man I've ever loved," Mo said.

Ben cried out: "It's so good to hear you say that, Mo. Darling! It's so good! ..."

Ben rented a U-Haul truck and got a couple of winos to help him load all of the furniture and things Mo had requested. He stood out front of the House he'd finished growing up in and cried like a spanked child. Fifth and Dice would never be what it had been. All of the houses on upper Fifth Street Southwest were boarded up. As he drove down Dice to Seventh Street, he saw the Wrecking Cranes, Backhoes, and Caterpillars busy tearing the residential guts out of Fifeville. The place looked like a Ghost Town. There were no Gang Crews standing around. There were no Crips there to defend the 'Hood. They 'd been killing each other for over ten years. But now the forces of convention had chased them all away.

As the hired hands unloaded the truck and carried *in* the contents to the apartment, Mo and Jay ran out to hug Ben.

"Dad, I miss you so much. I'm so glad you're back. Forgive me for not coming to you sooner. I love you Dad. Saw was wrong, but he was trying to protect all of us. He didn't mean you and Morn no harm. Oh, Dad, I feel like half of me is gone. But I can still hear Saw's voice inside of me. That will stay with me forever!"

Ben said: "I know Son. Sometimes, I feel like I can hear Granny as plain as day. I guess that will stay with me forever too."

Mo didn't utter a word. She just seized Ben *in* her strong hands and rocked the both of them from side to side. She wept.

Ben shut his eyes and let her rock him. Then he said: "Saw's Murder on Fifth and Dice represented

The **Ruin** of Fifeville."

(Ben was hired at Boars Head Inn as a Chef Apprentice. In two years he became a Banquet Chef.)

-Finis-

Epilogue

I lived in Charlottesville during the 1990s. I witnessed the efforts of "Judas Millwright," and the crackdown of the police against gangbangers, the push against ending prostitution in Fifeville, and the roundup of over a hundred Gangsters in the area. The above may on the surface seem good law enforcement But what followed those activities was not good at all. Over 2000 law abiding Citizens lost their residential properties. The low-interest loans made readily available by the **"ACRC,"** drew an avid number of investors and speculators. Most rich families in Charlottesville, Albemarle, Greene, and Augusta Counties focused on capitalizing on the opportunities that Fifeville presented. The immediate effect ·was that Twenty-Four houses were gutted within a year. They were renovated along Fifth and Dice Streets. This project was started in 1995. It ended in 2003. On Nelle, Seventh, and Seventh-and-a-Half Streets several homes were demolished. New modem dwellings seemed to have sprung up overnight to replace those.

225 apartments that became condos called "Walker Square," a large development that went from Ninth Street Southwest (now Roosevelt Avenue), down Main to Seventh Street Southwest, down Seventh across Dice to Cherry Avenue, was completed in 2005. In 2006, six cottages were completed on Fifth, and were joined by "The Fifth Street Flats Buildings," consisting of twelve condos and an Architect's Office.

Several boarded-up buildings are still being renovated on Grove Street under the auspices of a so-called "Green Development Initiative." On the Comer of Ridge and Cherry Avenue, owned by upper middle class Blacks and some "White Absentee Landlords, who formed a strong Neighborhood Association, was slated for renovation in the 1990s. The neighborhood association withstood that effort up until 2014. In 2016, the above Comer is under construction. The entire Fifeville Neighborhood has become almost entirely White-Owned, except for a few Blacks who are married to or cohabitating with White People. Most of the previous residents cannot afford to live there.

One consequence of the crackdown on Crime in Fifeville was that a number of petty drug-addicts and prostitutes filled up the Jail on Avon Street. A Complex built to house 300 units became overcrowded to the level of over a thousand constantly.

The State Board of Prisons sought a solution to the problem of overcrowding of prison facilities around the State, after President Bill Clinton's "Get Tough on Crime Laws." It was simply nowhere to house such a huge number of nonviolent prisoners that kept filling up Jails and Prisons daily. So in 1998, Virginia allowed the first Private Prison to be erected in Lawrenceville. It consisted of a 1,500-bed medium-security facility.

The Private Prison phenomenon is spreading and is in twenty-six States and in DC, where there are 154 of them. In these prisons, inmates are predominantly Black, and are re-enslaved. These Prisons sprung up in most of the Southern States after the 1990s, like Florida, Texas, Arizona, Washington DC., and Virginia. It is slavery, only it is just not called that

Hundreds of Inmates who go through these prisons come back to Charlottesville ruined for life. They go in petty criminals. They come back hardened miscreants who will kill at a drop of a hat. I feel that the high murder rate in Charlottesville may be due in part to these types of recidivists, who have become animalistic and bestial in a prison environment that shaped their psyches into the likeness of brute beasts.

More private prisons are vying to relocate to Virginia. WE DO NOT NEED THEM!!!!!!!!!

Appendix

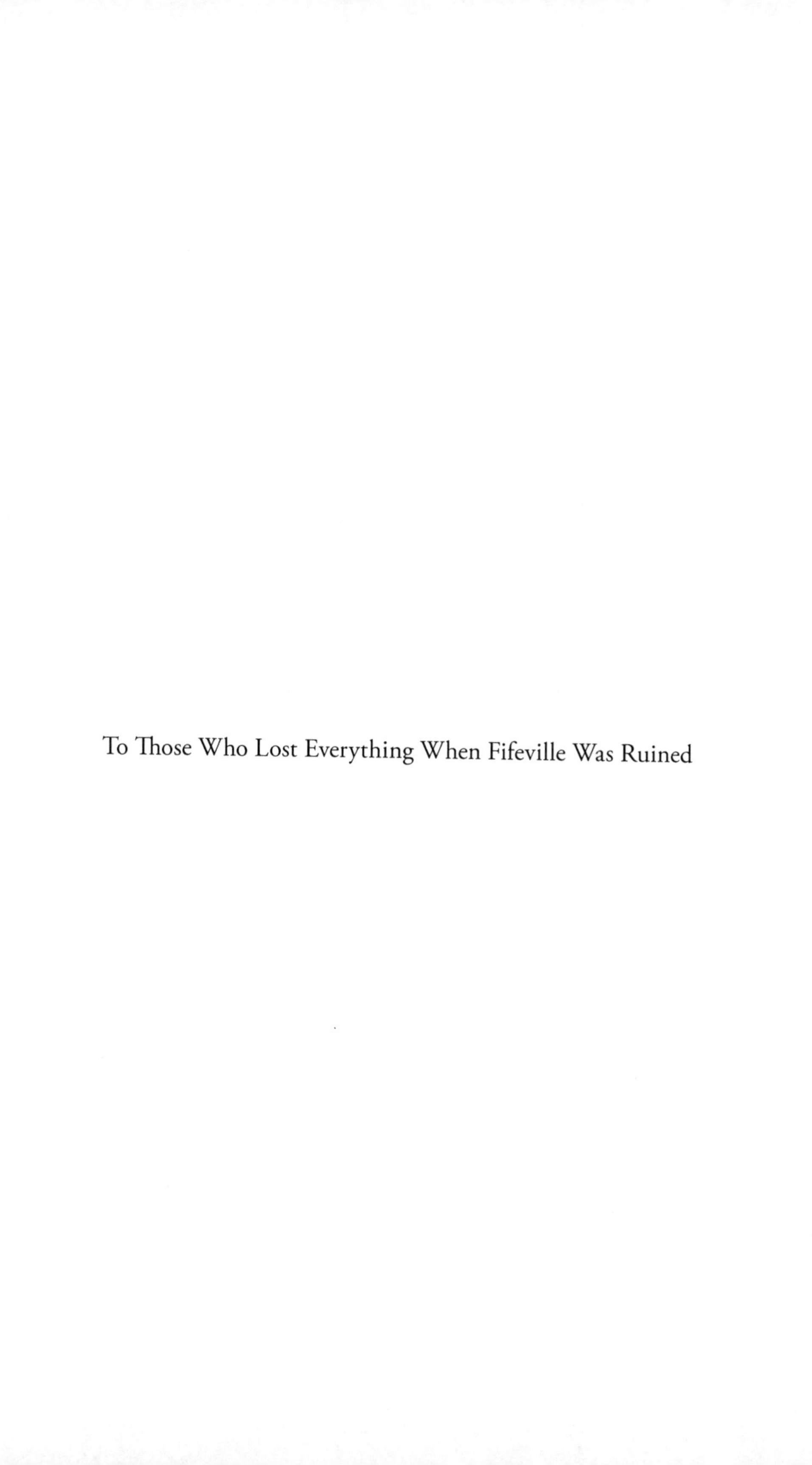

To Those Who Lost Everything When Fifeville Was Ruined

A Synopsis

This story is woven around actual occurrences that took place in Charlottesville Virginia from the 1960s- 1990s. I used a fictional family the Slokums to depict the reality of the devastation of a once thriving African-American Community that was demolished starting in *1995.* 2,300 people lost their homes to Eminent Domain and the fears of the Predominantly-White City Government in Charlottesville.

Though illicit controlled substances were part of the problem in Charlottesville, and Gangs had sprung up to deal the drugs, the main problem was not really related to the Drugs and or the other Crimes used as an excuse to rid the City of a concentrated Black Voting Block. That was the real problem.

The Drugs were trucked in to Charlottesville, as were guns, and even some of the Gangs were imported to the area. No one in Fifeville grew poppy flowers and could not refine Heroin from them. The Cocoa Leaf did not grow in Fifeville, so Cocaine could not be refined from them in that Neighborhood. There were no gun or ammunition factories in Fifeville. All of the above guns and dope were imported to Charlottesville from as far away as China, Russia, Israel, Guatemala, Mexico, Jamaica, Panama, Bolivia, Iran, Iraq, Afghanistan, India, Thailand, Vietnam, and the Mid-Western Industrial Complex within the borders of the USA.

Therefore Fifeville was so-called ruined from the trafficking of guns, dope, and the organization of the "Bloods" and the "Crips." These two notorious Gangst.er Transplants came in to help Local Cliques form Gangs to resist the Jamaican Posse. Once guns and dope-dealing were introduced from the top-down, and money flowed-up to the rich from those, a turf war ensued. Over a hundred young people filled up the prison rolls and returned to Charlottesville from penitentiaries as hardened

Killers. Hundreds of the Fifeville population suffered thereafter. All of the prominent citizens who could do so moved away from the Neighborhood leaving behind a completely economically blighted area.

Then the Charlottesville City Government labeled Fifeville a **"Slum,"** that had to be removed from being too close to the University of Virginia's out.er-boundaries. You know: "It was very unsightly."

Thus, we have families like the Slokum Family suffering through the Gangbanger-murders, drug-dealing, prostitution, and mayhem on a daily basis. Like Ben Slokum there was nothing they could do to change their dire situation, though they used *very* noble efforts in an attempt to do so. They were consumed by circumstances not entirely their own. They lost loved ones, self-esteem, pride, and eventually all of their residential properties. Finally, they were told that they had to leave and vacate their homes. They stood afar off and watched their Neighborhood, their Pride, their Church, and their Culture get razed to the ground. They witnessed "A Murder On fifth And Dice And The Ruin of Fifeville."

Suggested Reading

Since Slavery ended in America, the American Prison system has been used by the dominant culture to replace Chattel Slavery. To understand this quagmire, see the following:

Blackmon, Douglas A. Slavery By Another Name: The Re-Enslavement of Black. Americans From the Civil War to World War II. New York: Anchor Books, 2008.

Robinson, Randall. The Debt: What America Owes to Blacks. New York: Dutton Books, 2000.

-------. Quitting America: The Departure of A Black Man From His Native Land. New York: Dutton Books, 2004.

------. Reckoning: 'What Blacks Owe to Each Other. New York: Plume of the Penguin Group, 2002.

Since the 1950s, the dominant culture in Charlottesville, Danville, Lynchburg, Roanoke, and Richmond have been getting rid of Blacks' residential enclaves to prevent the presence of Black Voting Blocks. To understand this America-wide phenomenon better see:

Fullilove, **M.D.** Mindy Thompson. Root Shock: How Tearing Up City Neighborhoods Hurts America; And What We Can Do About It New York: One World/Ballantine Books, 200S.

James, William A. Sr. In The Streets of Vinegar **Hill.** New York: iUniverse, Inc. 2007.

Saunders, James Robert Shackelford, Renae Nadine. Urban Renewal and the End of Black Culture in Charlottesville, Virginia. North Carolina: McFarland & Company, Inc. 1998.

To get a better understanding of the "Gang Thang," in Charlottesville and other places see:

Dogg, Snoop. Ws. David E. Talbert. Love Don't Llve Here No More. New York: Atria Books, 2006.

Hopkins, Evans D. Life After Life: A Story of Rage and Redemption. New York: Free Press, 200S.

Jackson, Curtis James. From Pieces to Weight: Once Upon A Time In Southside Queens. New York: Pocket Books, 200S. See:James, Marlon. A Brief History of Seven Killings. NY: Riverhead Books, 2014.

McCall, Nathan. Makes Me Wanna Holler. A Young Black Man In America. New York: Random House Publishers, 1994.

Shakur, Tupac. The Rose That Grew From Concrete. New York: Pocket books, 1999. Simpson, Colton. Ws. Ann Perlman. Inside The Crips. New York: St Martin Press, 200S.

Acknowledgements

I am grateful to THE ALMIGHTY CREATOR, YAWEH, in the name Yahushua, MESSIAH, for the time to write. I thank my wife Sarah and my daughter Barbara for their patience with me during the time I worked on this manuscript, and for them reading each page with me, and giving useful criticism on how to create Moisha a major character in the narrative. And, special thanks to the ladies at The Jefferson Madison Regional Library at its Central, Northside and Greene County Branches for their timely help.

They were very instrumental in showing me where to look for helpful relevant pieces. And last but not least, I am grateful for the good people at The Albemarle-Charlottesville Historical Society for finding useful pieces on local history.

About the Author

William A. James, Sr., is the Author of IN THE STREETS OF VINEGAR Hill, 2007, and six other Books. He lives in Ruckersville, Virginia with his Wife of Fifty years, and his youngest Daughter.

Other Books by William A. James, Sr.

A Case of Religiosity, 1988; The Skin Color Syndrome Among African-Americans, 2003; A.1.D.S., 2004; Living Under The Weight of the Rainbow, *2005;* Ace Blackman and the Blues He Sings, 2007; and, The Witch of Gravel Hill, 2009.

A Murder On Fifth and Dice And the Ruin of Fifeville, is written to be read by Adults or with Parental Guidance. It contains graphic violence, explicit sexual content, and language that may not be appropriate for underage children.

To Contact the Author

Wjpublications@aol.com

Printed in the United States
By Bookmasters